A LICK OF FROST

a novel

LAURELL K. HAMILTON

BALLANTINE BOOKS • NEW YORK

A Lick of Frost is a work of fiction. Names, characters, places, and incidents are the products of the author's imagination or are used fictitiously. Any resemblance to actual events, locales, or persons, living or dead, is entirely coincidental.

2008 Ballantine Books Mass Market Edition

Copyright © 2007 Laurell K. Hamilton
Excerpt from *Swallowing Darkness* copyright © 2008 by Laurell K. Hamilton

Published in the United States by Ballantine Books, an imprint of The Random House Publishing Group, a division of Random House, Inc., New York.

BALLANTINE and colophon are registered trademarks of Random House, Inc.

Originally published in hardcover in the United States by Ballantine Books, an imprint of The Random House Publishing Group, a division of Random House, Inc., in 2007.

This book contains an excerpt from the forthcoming book *Swallowing Darkness* by Laurell K. Hamilton. This excerpt has been set for this edition only and may not reflect the final content of the forthcoming edition.

ISBN 978-0-345-49591-4

Cover design and illustration: David Stevenson, based on a photograph © Jim Erickson / Jupiterimages

Printed in the United States of America

www.ballantinebooks.com

OPM   9   8   7   6   5   4   3   2   1

Praise for Laurell K. Hamilton

A Lick of Frost

"For fans of Hamilton's imaginative . . . series, *A Lick of Frost* is evocative and satisfying."
—*Omaha World-Herald*

"Secret plots, dangerous adventure and sizzling romance pave the way in Ms. Hamilton's well-drawn and faerie-filled world. The many twists and turns will entertain . . . and leave fans eagerly awaiting more in this extraordinary series."

—*Darque Reviews*

A Kiss of Shadows

"I've never read a writer with a more fertile imagination."
—Diana Gabaldon

A Caress of Twilight

"Sensual, without a doubt . . . This book moves like a whirlwind."

—*St. Louis Post-Dispatch*

Seduced by Moonlight

"This [faerie] society is one of the most detailed, imaginative, and lovingly drawn in all fantastic fiction, and the Meredith Gentry series has become something special."
—*San Jose Mercury News*

A Stroke of Midnight

"Nonstop action . . . This book will leave you breathless."
—*St. Louis Post-Dispatch*

Mistral's Kiss

"Steamy . . . will have Hamilton's fans panting for more."
—*Publishers Weekly*

By Laurell K. Hamilton
Published by The Random House Publishing Group

Books published by The Random House Publishing Group
are available at quantity discounts on bulk purchases for
premium, educational, fund-raising, and special sales use.
For details, please call 1-800-733-3000.

I SUMMON TO THE WINDING ANCIENT STAIR;
SET ALL YOUR MIND UPON THE STEEP ASCENT,
UPON THE BROKEN, CRUMBLING BATTLEMENT,
UPON THE BREATHLESS STARLIT AIR,
'UPON THE STAR THAT MARKS THE HIDDEN POLE;
FIX EVERY WANDERING THOUGHT UPON
THAT QUARTER WHERE ALL THOUGHT IS DONE:
WHO CAN DISTINGUISH DARKNESS FROM THE SOUL

From "A Dialogue of Self and Soul"
by W. B. Yeats
(*The Winding Stair*, 1933)

TO JONATHON, WHO WALKS THE STAIR WITH ME.

Acknowledgments

The staff: Darla, Mary, and Sherry. Chaos would ensue without them.

Charles, who requested not to be Chief Security Officer as I put in the last acknowledgment, but to be Head Grunt. I should have remembered that his highest official rank had been sergeant. Sergeants work for a living; they are not officers.

My writing group, The Alternate Historians: Tom Drennan, Rett MacPhearson, Deborah Millitello, Marella Sands, and Mark Sumner. Insanity ensues with or without them, but with them, it's much more fun.

Chapter 1

I WAS SITTING IN AN ELEGANT CONFERENCE ROOM AT the top of one of the gleaming towers that make up part of downtown Los Angeles. The room's far wall was almost entirely of glass, so that the view was nearly agoraphobic. They're predicting that if the big one—the big earthquake that is—hits, this section of L.A. will be eight to fifteen feet deep in glass. Anything on the streets below will be cut to pieces, crushed, or trapped underneath an avalanche of glass. Not a pretty thought, but it was a day for ugly thoughts.

My uncle Taranis, King of Light and Illusion, had pressed charges against three of my royal bodyguards. He had gone to the human authorities with charges that Rhys, Galen, and Abe had raped one of his court's women.

In all the long history of his reign in the Seelie Court he had never gone outside to the humans for justice. Faerie rule; faerie law. Or truthfully, sidhe rule; sidhe law. The sidhe had ruled faerie for longer than anyone could remember. Since some of those memories stretched back thousands of years, maybe the sidhe had always been in charge, but it tasted like a lie. The sidhe do not lie, for to truly lie is to be cast out of faerie, exiled. Since I knew that the three bodyguards in question were innocent, that raised interesting problems with Lady Caitrin's testimony.

But today we were just giving statements, and, depending on how that went, King Taranis was standing by for a group call. Which was why Simon Biggs and Thomas Farmer, both of Biggs, Biggs, Farmer, and Farmer, were sitting beside me.

"Thank you for agreeing to this meeting today, Princess Meredith," one of the suits across the table said. There were seven suits across the wide, gleaming table, with their backs to the lovely view.

Ambassador Stevens, official ambassador to the courts of faerie, was sitting on our side of the table, but he was on the far side of Biggs and Farmer. Stevens said, "A word on faerie etiquette: You don't say thank you to the people of faerie, Mr. Shelby. Princess Meredith, as one of the younger royals, will probably not be offended, but you will be dealing with some nobility who are much older. Not all of them will allow a thank-you to pass without grave insult." Stevens smiled when he said it, his blandly handsome face sincere from his brown eyes to his perfectly cut brown hair. He was supposed to be our voice to the world, but, truthfully, he spent all his time at the Seelie Court sucking up to my uncle. The Unseelie Court where my aunt Andais, Queen of Air and Darkness, ruled, and where I might rule someday, was too scary for Stevens. No, I didn't like him.

Michael Shelby, a U.S. Attorney for L.A., said, "I am sorry, Princess Meredith. I didn't realize."

I smiled, and said, "It's fine. The ambassador is correct, a thank-you won't bother me."

"But it will bother your men?" Shelby asked.

"Some of them, yes," I said. I looked behind me to Doyle and Frost. They stood behind me like darkness and snow made real, and that wasn't far from the truth. Doyle had black hair, black skin, a black designer suit; even his tie was black. Only the shirt was a rich royal blue, and that had been a sop to our lawyer. He thought black gave the wrong impression, made him seem threatening. Doyle, whose nickname was Darkness, had said, "I am the captain of the princess's guard. I am supposed to be threatening." The lawyers hadn't known what to say to that, but Doyle had worn the blue shirt. The color almost glowed against the rich, perfect black of his skin, which was so black there were purple and blue highlights to his body in the right light. His black eyes were hidden behind wraparound black-on-black sunglasses.

Frost's skin was as white as Doyle's was black. As white as my own. But his hair was uniquely his own, silver, like metal beaten into hair. It gleamed in the tasteful lighting of the conference room. Gleamed like something you could have melted down and made into jewelry. He had tied the top layer of it back with a barrette that was silver, and older than the city of Los Angeles itself. The dove-gray suit was Ferragamo, and the white of his shirt was less white than his own skin. The tie was darker than the suit, but not by much. The soft gray of his eyes was bare to the room as he scanned the far windows. Doyle was doing it, too, behind his glasses. I had bodyguards for a reason, and some who wanted me dead could fly. We didn't think Taranis was one of the people who wanted me dead, but why had he gone to the police?

Why had he persisted in these false charges? He would never have done all this without an agenda. We just didn't know what that agenda was, so just in case, they watched the windows for things that the human lawyers couldn't even begin to imagine.

Shelby's gaze flicked behind me to the guards. He wasn't the only one who kept fighting not to glance nervously at my men, but it was Assistant District Attorney Pamela Nelson who was having the most trouble keeping her eyes, and her mind, on business. The men across the table gave the guards the glances men give when they see another man whom they are almost certain could take them physically without breaking a sweat.

U.S. Attorney Michael Shelby was tall, athletic, and handsome, with a gleam of white teeth, and the look of someone who had plans to rise above being the U.S. attorney for the Los Angeles area. He was over six feet, and his suit couldn't hide the fact that he worked out pretty seriously. He probably didn't meet many men who made him feel physically weak. His assistant Ernesto Bertram was a slender man who looked too young for his job, and far too serious with his short dark hair and glasses. It wasn't the glasses that made him look too serious; it was the look on his face, as if he'd tasted something sour. The U.S. attorney for the St. Louis area, Albert Veducci, was here, too. He didn't have Shelby's tan. In fact, he was a little overweight, and he looked tired. His assistant was Grover. He'd actually introduced himself only as Grover, so I didn't know if it was his first, last, or only name. He smiled more than the rest of them and was attractive in that friendly, walk-you-home-on-campus way. He reminded me of guys in college who were either as nice as they seemed or absolute bastards who only wanted sex, for you to help them pass a class, or, for me, to be close to a real live faerie princess. I wouldn't know which kind of "nice guy" Grover was for a while. If things went well, I'd never figure it out, because I'd probably never see him again. If they went badly, we might see a lot of Grover.

Nelson was the assistant district attorney to *the* district attorney for Los Angeles County. Her boss, Miguel Cortez, was short, dark, and handsome. He looked great on camera. I'd seen him on the news often enough here. The trouble was that he, like Shelby, was ambitious. He liked being on the news, and wanted to be on the news more. This accusation of rape against my men had all the earmarks of a case that could make your career or break it. Cortez and Shelby were ambitious; it meant that they would either be very cautious, or very incautious. I wasn't sure which mood would help us the most, yet.

Nelson was taller than her boss, close to six feet in her not-too-high heels. Her hair was a vibrant red that fell in waves around her shoulders. It was that rare shade that is deep, rich, and as close to true red as human hair can get. Her suit was well cut, but conservative and black, her button-up shirt white, her makeup tasteful. Only that flame of hair to ruin the almost mannish exterior she portrayed. It was as if she were hiding her beauty and drawing attention to it at the same time. Because she was beautiful. A sprinkling of freckles underneath the pale makeup didn't detract from the flawless skin; it added. Her eyes were green and blue at once, depending on how the light caught them. Those undecided eyes couldn't stop looking at Frost and Doyle. She tried to concentrate on the legal pad she was supposed to be making notes on, but her gaze kept rising, and finding them, as if she couldn't help herself.

That made me wonder if there was more going on than just handsome men and a distracted woman.

Shelby cleared his throat sharply.

I jumped and looked at him. "I'm terribly sorry, Mr. Shelby, were you speaking to me?"

"No, I was not, and I should have been." He looked down the table on his side. "I was brought into this as a more neutral voice, but let me ask my fellow members of the bar if they are having trouble forming questions for the princess."

Several of the lawyers spoke at the same time. Veducci just raised his pencil in the air. Veducci got the nod. "My office has dealt more closely with the princess and her people than the rest of you, which is why I'm carrying certain remedies against glamour."

"What sort of remedies?" Shelby asked.

"I won't tell you what I'm carrying, but cold steel, iron, four-leaf clover, Saint-John's-wort, rowan, and ash—either the wood or the berries—have been known to work. Some say bells will break glamour, but I think high-court sidhe won't be bothered much by bells."

"Are you saying that the princess is using glamour against us?" Shelby asked, his handsome face no longer pleasant.

"I am saying that sometimes when dealing with King Taranis or Queen Andais, their presence overwhelms humans," Veducci responded. "Princess Meredith, being part human, though beautiful—" He nodded in my direction.

I nodded at the compliment.

"—has never affected anyone so strongly, but a lot has been happening in the Unseelie Court in the last few days. Ambassador Stevens has filled me in, as have other sources. Princess Meredith and some of her guard have moved up the power grid, so to speak." Veducci still looked tired, but now his eyes showed the mind inside that overweight, overworked camouflage. I realized with a start that there were other dangers besides ambition. Veducci was smart, and hinted that he knew something about what had happened inside the Unseelie Court. Did he know, or was he fishing? Did he think we'd give something away?

"It is illegal to use glamour on us," Shelby said, angry. He looked at me now, and his look was no longer in the least friendly. I looked back. I gave him the full force of my tricolored eyes: molten gold at the outer edge, then a circle of jade green, and last, emerald to chase around my pupil. He looked away first, dropping his gaze to his own legal pad. His voice was tight with controlled rage. "We could have you arrested, or deported back to faerie for trying to use magic to sway these proceedings, Princess."

"I'm not doing anything to you, Mr. Shelby, not on purpose." I looked at Veducci. "Mr. Veducci, you say that simply seeing my aunt and uncle was difficult; am I difficult now?"

"From my colleagues' reactions, I believe you are."

"So this is the reaction that King Taranis and Queen Andais have on humans?"

"Similar," Veducci said.

I had to smile.

"This is not funny, Princess," Cortez said, his words full of anger, but when I met his brown eyes, they dropped from me.

I looked at Nelson, but it wasn't me distracting her; her problem was behind me.

"Which one are you staring at the most?" I asked. "Frost or Doyle; light or dark?"

She blushed in that pretty way human redheads have. "I'm not . . ."

"Come, Ms. Nelson, confess, which one?"

She swallowed hard enough that I heard it. "Both," she whispered.

"We will charge you and these two guards with undue magical influence in a legal proceeding, Princess Meredith," Cortez said.

"I agree," Shelby said.

"Neither I, nor Frost and Doyle, are doing this on purpose."

"We are not stupid," Shelby said. "Glamour is an active magic, not a passive one."

"Most glamour, yes, but not all," I said. I looked down the table at Veducci. They'd put him farthest from the center of the table, as if being from St. Louis made him less. Or maybe I was just overly sensitive for my hometown.

"Did you know," Veducci said, "that when you see the Queen of England, they call it being in the presence? I've never met Queen Elizabeth, and I'm not likely to, so I don't know how it works for her. I've never spoken to a human queen. But the phrase 'in the presence,' to be in the presence of the queen, means more when it's the queen of the Unseelie Court. To be in the presence of the king of the Seelie Court is also a treat."

"What does that mean?" Cortez asked. "A treat?"

"It means, gentleman and ladies, that being king or queen in faerie gives you an unconscious aura of power, of attractiveness. You live in L.A. You see that it works in lesser ways for major stars or politicians. Power seems to breed power. Dealing with the faerie courts has made me believe that even us poor humans do it. To be around the powerful, rich, beautiful, talented, whatever, it isn't just human nature to suck up. I think it's glamour. I think that success of a certain level has a glamour to it, and you attract people to you. They want to be around you. They listen to you more. They do what you say more. Humans have a shadow of real glamour; now think about someone who is the most powerful figure in faerie. Think about the level of power surrounding them."

"Ambassador Stevens," Shelby said, "shouldn't you have been the one who warned us about this effect?"

Stevens smoothed his tie, played with the Rolex watch Taranis had given him as a present. "King Taranis is a powerful figure with centuries of rulership. He does have a certain nobility that is impressive. I have not found Queen Andais as impressive."

"Because you only talk to her from a distance, over the mirrors, with King Taranis by your side," Veducci said.

I was impressed that Veducci knew that, because it was absolutely true.

"You're the ambassador to faerie," Shelby said, "not just to the Seelie Court."

"I am the United States Ambassador to the courts of faerie, yes."

"But you never step foot into the Unseelie Court?" Shelby asked.

"Uh," Stevens said, running his fingers over and over the watchband, "I find Queen Andais a little less than cooperative."

"What does that mean?" Shelby said.

I watched Stevens play with the watch, and a tiny bit of concentration showed that there was magic on it, or in it. I answered for him, "It means he thinks the Unseelie Court is full of perversion and monsters."

They were all looking at him now. If it had been purposeful glamour on our part, they wouldn't have. "Is that true, Ambassador?" Shelby asked.

"I would never say such a thing."

"But he believes it," I said, softly.

"We'll all make a note of this, and make sure the proper authorities know of your gross dereliction of your duties," Shelby said.

"I am loyal to King Taranis and his court. It is not my fault that Queen Andais is a sexual sadist, and quite mad. She and her people are dangerous. I have said so, for years, and no one has listened to me. Now we have these charges, proving what I have been saying."

"So you told your superiors that you feared the queen's guard would rape someone?" Veducci asked.

"Well, I, no, not exactly."

"What did you tell them?" Shelby asked.

"I told them the truth, that I feared for my safety at

the Unseelie Court, and that I would not be comfortable there without an armed escort." Stevens stood up, very tall, very certain of himself. He pointed at Frost and Doyle. "Look at them, they are frightening. The potential in them to do carnage, why, it just radiates off of them."

"You keep touching your watch," I said.

"What?" He blinked at me.

"Your watch. King Taranis gave it to you, didn't he?" I asked.

"You accepted a Rolex watch from the king?" Cortez made it a question. He sounded outraged, but not at us.

Stevens swallowed, and shook his head. "Of course not. That would be totally inappropriate."

"I saw him give it to you, Ambassador," I said.

He ran his fingers over the metal. "That's simply not true. She's lying."

"The sidhe don't lie, Ambassador, you know that. That's a human habit."

Stevens's fingers were practically rubbing a hole through the watchband. "The Unseelie are capable of every evil. Their very faces show them for what they are."

It was Nelson who said, "Their faces are beautiful."

"You are fooled by their magic," Stevens said. "The king gave me the power to see through their deceptions." His voice was rising with each word.

"The watch," I said.

"So this," Shelby gestured at me, "beauty is illusion?"

"Yes," Stevens said.

"No," I said.

"Liar," he screamed, shoving his chair back so that it rolled on its wheels. He started walking past Biggs and Farmer, toward me.

Doyle and Frost moved like two halves of a whole. They simply stood in front of him, blocking his way. There was no magic to it, except the force of their physicality. Stevens stumbled back from them as if he'd been struck. His face contorted in terror, and he cried out, "No, no!"

Some of the lawyers were standing now. Cortez said, "What are they doing to him?"

Veducci managed to yell above Stevens's screams. "I can't see anything."

"We are doing nothing to him," Doyle said, his deep voice cutting under the higher-pitched voices like water undercutting a cliff face.

"The hell you aren't," Shelby yelled, adding to the noise of Stevens's screams and those of the others.

I tried yelling above the noise, "Turn your jackets inside out!" No one seemed to hear me.

Veducci bellowed, "Shut up!" in a voice that smashed through the noise like a bull through a fence. The room was stunned into silence. Even Stevens stopped screaming and stared at Veducci. Veducci continued in a calmer voice, "Turn your jackets inside out. It's a way to break glamour." He moved his head toward me, almost a bow. "I forgot that one."

The others hesitated for a second. Veducci took off his own jacket and turned it inside out, then put it back on. It seemed to galvanize the rest. Most of them began taking off their jackets.

Nelson said, as she folded her jacket so the seams

showed, "I'm wearing a cross. I thought that protected me from glamour."

I answered her. "Crosses and bible verses would only work if we were of the devil. We have no connection to the Christian religion, either for good or ill."

She looked down, as if embarrassed to meet my eyes. "I didn't mean to imply anything."

"Of course not," I said. My voice was empty as I said it. I'd heard the insult too often to take it to heart. "One of the things the early church did was to paint anything they could not control as evil. Faerie was something they could not control. As the Seelie Court became more and more human-friendly, the parts of faerie that could not, or would not, play human, became part of the Unseelie Court. Since the things that humans perceive as frightening are mostly at the Unseelie Court, we got painted as evil over the centuries."

"You *are* evil!" Stevens screamed. His eyes bulged, his pulse was racing, and his face was pale and beaded with sweat.

"Is he sick?" Nelson asked.

"In a way," I said, softly enough that I wasn't sure any of the other humans in the room heard me. Whoever had done the spell on the watch had done too good a job, or a bad one. The spell was forcing Stevens to see nightmares when he looked at us. His mind wasn't coping well with what he was seeing and feeling.

I turned to Veducci. "The ambassador seems ill. Perhaps he should be taken to see a doctor?"

"No," Stevens yelled. "No. Without me here they

will take over your minds!" He grabbed Biggs, who was closer. "Without the king's gift you will all believe their lies."

"I think the princess is right, Ambassador Stevens," Biggs said. "I think you *are* ill."

Stevens's hands dug into the inside-out designer jacket that Biggs was now wearing. "Surely you see them for what they are now?"

"They look like all the sidhe to me. Except for the color of Captain Doyle's skin, and the princess being petite, they look like nobles of the sidhe court."

Stevens shook the bigger man. "The Darkness has fangs. The Killing Frost has skulls hanging from his neck. And she, she is withered, dying. Her mortal blood contaminates her."

"Ambassador . . ." Biggs began.

"No, you must see it, as I do!"

"They didn't change at all when we turned our jackets inside out," Nelson said. She sounded a little disappointed.

"I told you, we are not doing active glamour on any of you," I said.

"Lies! I see the horror of you." Stevens hid his face against Biggs's broad shoulders, as if he could not bear the sight of us, and perhaps he could not.

"It is easier not to look at them, though," Shelby said.

Cortez nodded. "I can focus better now, but they look the same."

"Beautiful," Bertram said.

Shelby gave him a sharp look, and the assistant apologized, as if that one word was totally out of line.

Stevens had begun to sob into Biggs's designer suit. "You must get him away from us," Doyle said.

"Why?" one of the others asked.

"The spell on the watch makes him see monsters when he looks at us. I fear his mind will break under the strain of it without King Taranis nearby to ease the effects."

"Can't you just undo the spell?" Veducci asked.

"It is not our spell," Doyle said simply.

"Can't you help him?" Nelson asked.

"I think the less contact with us, the better for the ambassador."

Stevens had seemed to be trying to bury his face into Biggs's shoulder. The ambassador's hands twisted in the seams and lining of the coat.

"Being near us is hurting him," Frost said, speaking for the first time since the introductions. His voice did not have the depth of Doyle's, but the width of his chest gave it weight.

"Get some security up here," Biggs said to Farmer. And though Farmer was a very powerful man in his own right, and a full partner, he moved for the door. I guess when your daddy is one of the founders of a firm and you are the leading active partner, you still have clout, even over other partners.

We stood in silence, the humans' awkward body language and facial expressions saying that they were terribly uncomfortable with the display of mad emotion. It was a type of madness, but the three of us sidhe had seen worse. We'd seen madness that had magic to it. The kind of magic that could steal the breath from your body on a laughing whim.

Uniformed security came. I recognized one of the

guards from the entrance desk. They had a doctor with them. I remembered reading several doctors' names on the board beside the elevator. Apparently, Farmer had exceeded his orders, but Biggs seemed very pleased to hand the sobbing man over to the doctor. No wonder Farmer had made partner. He followed orders to the letter, but built on them, made them better.

No one said anything else until they led the ambassador from the room and the door closed quietly behind him. Biggs straightened his tie and tugged at the wrinkled suit jacket. Inside out, or right side out, the suit was ruined until a dry cleaner got hold of it. He started to take the jacket off, then glanced at us and stopped.

I caught his eye, and he looked away, embarrassed. "It's all right, Mr. Biggs, if you're afraid to take your jacket off."

"Ambassador Stevens's mind seems quite broken."

"I would advise the doctor to have a licensed practitioner of the arts look at the watch before you simply remove it."

"Why?"

"He's worn that watch for years. It may have become a part of his psyche, his mind. To simply remove it could do more harm."

Biggs reached for a phone.

"Why didn't you say something before he was led away?" Shelby asked.

"I only now thought of it," I said.

"I thought of it before they left," Doyle said.

"Why didn't you speak up?" Cortez asked.

"It is not my job to protect the ambassador."

"It's everyone's job to help another human in such a state," Shelby said, then he looked surprised, as if he'd just heard what he'd said.

Doyle gave the smallest curl of lips. "But I am not human, and I think the ambassador is weak and without honor. Queen Andais has lodged several complaints with your government about the ambassador. She has been ignored. But even she could not have foreseen such treachery as this."

"Treachery of our government against yours?" Veducci asked.

"No, King Taranis's treachery against someone who trusted him. The ambassador saw that watch as a mark of high favor, when in fact it was a trap and a lie."

"You disapprove," Nelson said.

"Do you not also disapprove?" Doyle asked.

She started to nod and then looked away, blushing. Apparently, even with her jacket turned, she couldn't help reacting to him. He was worth reacting to, but I didn't like that she was having this much trouble. The charges would be hard enough without us making the prosecutors blush.

"What would the king have gained from poisoning the ambassador against your court?" Cortez asked.

"What have the Seelie always gained from blackening the name of the Unseelie?" I asked.

"I'll bite," Shelby said. "What *have* they gained?"

"Fear," I said. "They have made their people fear us."

"What did that gain them?" Shelby asked.

Frost spoke. "The greatest punishment of all is to be cast out of the Seelie Court, the golden court. But it is punishment because Taranis and his nobles have convinced themselves that once you join the Unseelie Court you become a monster. Not just in actions, but in body. They tell their people that they will become deformed if they join with the Unseelie."

"You talk like you know," Nelson said.

"I was once part of the golden throng, long, long ago," Frost said.

"What did you do to earn exile?" Shelby asked.

"Lieutenant Frost doesn't have to answer that," Biggs said. He had stopped fussing with his suit and was back to being one of the best lawyers on the West Coast.

"Is the answer prejudicial to the charges brought against the other guards?" Shelby asked.

"No," Biggs said, "but since the lieutenant is not included in the charges filed, the question is outside the scope of this investigation."

Biggs had lied, smoothly, effortlessly; lied as if it were the truth. He actually didn't know if Frost's answer would have been prejudicial, because he had no idea why anyone but the three guards in question had been exiled from the Seelie Court. (Though in Galen's case, he hadn't been exiled because he'd been born and raised in the Unseelie Court; you can't be exiled from what you've never been a part of.) Biggs had carefully not allowed any questions that might interfere with a linear defense of his clients.

"This is a very informal proceeding," Veducci said with a smile. He radiated harmless good-ol'-boy charm. It was a trick, bordering on a lie. He'd researched us. He'd dealt with the courts more than any of the other lawyers. He was either going to be our greatest ally or our most difficult opponent.

He continued, still smiling and letting us see those tired eyes. "We are all here today to see if the charges that King Taranis filed on behalf of the Lady Caitrin should be followed up with more formal proceedings. Cooperation would give strength to the princess's guards' denials."

"Since all of the guards have diplomatic immunity, we are here out of courtesy," Biggs said.

"We do appreciate that," Veducci said.

"Do bear in mind," Shelby said, "that King Taranis has stated that all of the queen's guard, and now the princess's guard, are a danger to everyone around them, most especially women. He stated that this rape did not surprise him. He seemed to think it was the inevitable outcome of allowing the queen's Raven Guard unlimited access even inside faerie. One of the reasons he brought these charges to the human authorities, an unprecedented action in all the history of the Seelie Court, is that he feared for us. If a sidhe noble of Lady Caitrin's magical powers could be so easily taken, then what hope did mere humans have against their . . . lusts?"

"Unnatural lusts," I said.

Shelby shifted his gray eyes to me. "I did not say that."

"No, you didn't, but I'm betting my uncle Taranis did."

Shelby gave a little shrug. "He doesn't seem to like your men much, that is true."

"Or me," I said.

Shelby's face showed surprise, and I wished I could

have told if it was genuine, or if he were lying with his face. "The king had only good things to say about you, Princess. He seems to feel that you have been"— he seemed to change what he was about to say at the last moment—"led astray by your aunt, the queen, and her guards."

"Led astray?" I made it a question.

He nodded.

"That's not what he said, is it?"

"Not in so many words, no."

"It must have been truly insulting for you to pretty it up like this," I said.

Shelby actually looked uncomfortable. "Before I saw Ambassador Stevens and his reaction to you, and the possible spell on his watch, I might have simply stated what the king said." Shelby gave me a very straightforward look. "Let's say that Stevens has made me wonder at the vehemence of King Taranis's dislike of all your guard."

"All my guard?" Again I made it a question with the upward lilt of my voice.

"Yes."

I looked at Veducci. "He charges all my men with crimes?"

"No, only the three mentioned, but Mr. Shelby is correct. King Taranis stated that your Raven Guard is a danger to all women. He thinks that having been made celibate for so long has driven them insane." Veducci's face never changed as he let out one of the biggest secrets of the faerie courts.

I opened my mouth to say, "Taranis wouldn't have told you that," but Doyle's hand on my shoulder stopped me. I looked up at his dark figure. Even through his black glasses, I knew the look. That look said "Careful." He was right. Veducci had stated earlier that he had sources at the Unseelie Court. Taranis might not have said it at all.

"This is the first we've heard that the king is accusing the Raven Guard of being celibate," Biggs said. He had glanced at Doyle, but now put his attention back on Shelby and Veducci.

"The king felt that the long-enforced celibacy was the reason for the attack."

Biggs leaned in to me, and whispered, "Is this true? Were they forced to be celibate?"

I whispered against his white collar, "Yes."

"Why?" he asked.

"My queen willed it so." That was true, as far as it went, but it kept me from sharing secrets that Queen Andais wouldn't want shared. Taranis might survive her wrath; I wouldn't.

Biggs turned back to the opposing side. "We are not conceding that this alleged celibacy took place, but if it did, the men in question are no longer celibate. They are with the princess now, and not the queen. The princess has stated that the three of them are her lovers. There would be no alleged celibacy-induced"—Biggs seemed to search for the right word—"madness." He made light of it with his voice, his face, and a hand gesture. It was a glimpse of what he'd be like in court. He just might be worth all the money my aunt was paying.

Shelby said, "The king's statement, the charges filed, are enough to allow the United States government to confine all of the princess's guard to the lands of faerie."

"I know the law you're referring to," Biggs said. "Many in Jefferson's government didn't agree with him allowing the fey to settle here after they were exiled from Europe. They insisted on a law that would allow them to permanently confine to faerie any citizen of faerie deemed too dangerous to be allowed among the human citizenry. It is a very broad law, and has never been invoked."

"It's never been needed before," Cortez said.

Doyle had stayed at my back, his hand resting on my shoulder. Either he knew I needed comforting, or he needed it. I laid my hand on top of his, so we could touch bare skin to bare skin. He was so warm, so solid. Just the touch made me feel more certain that it would be all right. We would be all right.

"It's not needed now, and you all know it," Biggs said. He *tsked* at them. "Trying to scare the princess by threatening to send all her guards back to faerie. Shame on you."

"The princess doesn't look scared," Nelson said.

I gave her the full weight of my tricolored eyes, and she couldn't hold my gaze. "You are threatening to take the men I love away from me," I said. "Shouldn't that frighten me?"

"It should," she said, "but it doesn't seem to."

Farmer touched my arm, a clear let-me-talk gesture. I leaned back into the weight of Doyle at my back and let the lawyers talk. "Which brings us to the law in question," Farmer said. "The royals of any court are exempt from the law Mr. Shelby has mentioned."

"We are not proposing to exile Princess Meredith to faerie," Shelby said.

"You know that the threat to put all her guards under some sort of legal confinement to faerie is outrageous," Farmer said.

Shelby nodded. "Fine, then just the three who are charged with rape. Mr. Cortez and I are both duly appointed officers of the United States attorneys' office. We are within our duty and rights to simply put the three guards back into the land of faerie until these charges are settled."

"I repeat, the law, as written, cannot be applied to the royals of any court of faerie," Farmer said.

"And I repeat that we aren't threatening to do anything to Princess Meredith," Shelby said.

"But we aren't referring to that royal," Farmer said.

Shelby looked down the line of lawyers on his side. "I'm not sure we're following your argument."

"Princess Meredith's guard are royal, for now."

"What does that mean, for 'now'?" Cortez asked.

"It means that when inside the Unseelie Court, they have a throne on the royal dais in which they take turns sitting beside the princess," Farmer said. "They are her royal consorts."

"Being her lover doesn't make them royal," Cortez said.

"Prince Phillip is technically still Queen Elizabeth's royal consort," Farmer said.

"But they're married," Cortez said.

"But in faerie, at any court, you aren't allowed to marry until you are with child," Farmer said.

"Mr. Farmer," I said, touching his arm, "since this is informal, perhaps it would go more quickly if I explained."

Farmer and Biggs whispered back and forth, but finally I got the nod. I was going to be allowed to talk. Oh, goody. I smiled at the other side of the table, leaning a little forward, hands nicely folded on the table. "My guards are my lovers. Which makes them royal consorts until one of them makes me pregnant. Then that one will be king to my queen. Until the choice is made, they are all royalty in the Unseelie Court."

"The three guards who have been charged by the king should be sent back to faerie," Shelby said.

"King Taranis was so afraid that Ambassador Stevens would see that the Unseelie Court was beautiful that he put a spell on the man. A spell that forced him to see us as monstrous. A man who would do such a desperate thing would do many other desperate things."

"What do you mean, Princess?"

"To lie is to be cast out of faerie, but to be king is sometimes to be above the law."

"Are you saying these charges are falsified?" Cortez asked.

"Of course they are false."

"You would say anything to save your lovers," Shelby said.

"I am sidhe, and I am not above the law. I cannot lie."

"Is that true?" Shelby leaned down and asked Veducci.

He nodded. "It's supposed to be true, but either the princess is lying, or Lady Caitrin is lying."

Shelby looked back at me. "You cannot lie."

"I have the ability, but to do so is to run the risk of

being cast out from faerie." I squeezed Doyle's hand tightly. "I just got back. I don't want to lose it all again."

"Why did you leave faerie the first time, Princess?" Shelby asked.

Biggs answered that. "That question is off-limits, and outside the charges in question." The queen had probably given him a list of questions I couldn't answer.

Shelby smiled. "Very well. Is it true that the Raven Guard were forced into centuries of celibacy?"

"May I ask a question before I answer that?"

"You can ask anything you like, Princess, but I may not answer."

I smiled at him, and he smiled back. Doyle's hand tightened on my shoulder. He was right—mustn't flirt, until we knew exactly how it would be perceived. I toned the smile down, and asked my question. "Did King Taranis himself say that the Ravens were forced into centuries of celibacy?"

"I've so stated," Shelby said.

"No, I mean as truth, Mr. Shelby. Please bear in mind that even a princess may be tortured for going against her queen's orders."

"You admit that they torture people at the Unseelie Court," Cortez said.

"They torture people at both courts, Mr. Cortez. Queen Andais just doesn't hide what she does, because she's not ashamed of it."

"Are you stating for the record . . . ?" Cortez said.

"This will be a sealed record," Biggs said, "unless it goes to court."

"Yes, yes," Cortez said, "but are you stating for the

record that King Taranis allows torture to be used as a punishment in the Seelie Court?"

"Answer my question truthfully, and I will answer yours."

Cortez looked at Shelby. They exchanged a longer-than-normal look, then both of them turned back to me. "Yes," they said at the same time. The two men looked at each other, and finally Cortez nodded at Shelby, who said, "Yes, King Taranis stated that the fact that the Raven Guard had been forced into centuries of celibacy was the reason they were a danger to women. He further stated that to then have the forced celibacy lifted for only one little girl, referring to you, Princess, was monstrous. For no one woman could satisfy the lusts of centuries."

"So the celibacy was the motive for the rape," I said.

"That seems to be the king's reasoning," Shelby said. "We haven't looked for a motive beyond the usual for rape."

The usual, I thought.

"I've answered your question, Princess. Now, are you stating for the record that the Seelie Court tortures its prisoners?"

Frost came to stand beside Doyle. "Meredith, think upon this before you answer."

I looked behind me, met his worried eyes, the soft gray of winter skies. I held my other hand out to him, and he took it. "Taranis let our cat out of the bag, Frost. It's only fair we let one of his out."

Frost frowned at me. "I do not understand this talk of cats, but I fear his anger."

I had to smile at him even as I agreed with him. "He began this, Frost. I will only finish it."

He squeezed my hand, and Doyle squeezed the other, so that my hands were crisscrossed over my chest, holding them. I held their hands while I said, "Mr. Shelby, Mr. Cortez, you asked me, am I stating for the record that King Taranis's golden court tortures as a punishment? I am so stating."

The record was supposed to be sealed, but if either of these secrets got into the press. . . . This little family feud was going to get very ugly, very fast.

Chapter 2

THE LAWYERS DECIDED THAT DOYLE AND FROST could answer some general questions about what it was like being part of my personal guard to give some background to the atmosphere that Rhys, Galen, and Abe had been living in. I wasn't sure it was going to be helpful, but I wasn't a lawyer, so who was I to argue?

Doyle sat on my right, Frost on my left. My lawyers Farmer and Biggs moved a few seats down to give them room.

Shelby got the first question. "And there are now sixteen of you with access only to Princess Meredith for your, um, needs?"

"If you mean for sex, then yes," Doyle said.

Shelby coughed and nodded. "Yes, I do mean sex."

"Then say what you mean," Doyle said.

"I will do that." Shelby sat up a little straighter. "I imagine it must be difficult to share the princess."

"I'm not certain I understand the question."

"Well, not to be indelicate, but waiting for your turn must be hard after so many years of denial."

"No, it is not hard to wait."

"But of course it is," Shelby said.

"You're putting words in the witnesses' mouths," Biggs said.

"Sorry. What I mean, Captain Doyle, is that, after so many years of needs unmet, it must be difficult to only have sex about every two weeks or so."

Frost laughed, then caught himself and tried to turn it into a cough. Doyle smiled. It was the first truly broad smile that he'd had since the questions had started. The white flash of his teeth in all that dark, dark face was startling if you weren't used to it. It was like having a statue suddenly smile at you.

"I fail to see the humor in being forced to wait weeks for sex, Captain Doyle, Lieutenant Frost."

"I would see no humor in that either," Doyle said, "but when the number of men grew larger, Princess Meredith changed some of the parameters for us all."

"I'm not following," Nelson said, "Parameters?"

Doyle looked at me. "Perhaps you better explain, Princess."

"When I had only five lovers, it seemed fair to make them wait for their turns, but as you point out, waiting two weeks, or more, after centuries of celibacy seems like another form of torture. So when the number of men went up to double digits, I upped the number of times I make love during a given day."

You don't get to see powerful, high-priced lawyers look that embarrassed often, but I got to see it then. They all looked at each other; Nelson actually raised her hand. "I'll ask, if no one else will."

The men let her ask. "How many times a day do you make love?"

"It varies, but usually at least three times."

"Three times a day," she repeated.

"Yes," I said, and gave her a blank, pleasant face. She blushed to the roots of her red hair. I was sidhe enough that I didn't understand this American trait of being totally fascinated with sex and totally uncomfortable with it.

Veducci recovered first, as I had figured he would. "Even at three times a day, Princess Meredith, that leaves an average of five days between lovemaking sessions for the men. Five days is a long time when you've been denied for centuries. Couldn't your three guards have tried to find something to occupy their time in between waiting?"

"A five-day wait implies that I'm only sleeping with one man at a time, Mr. Veducci, and most of the time I'm not."

Veducci smiled at me. It was a nice smile. It went all the way to his eyes, and folded the bags into smile lines that said here was a man who knew how to enjoy life, or had once. It was like a glimpse into a younger, less tired version.

I smiled back at him, responding to that joy.

"You are totally comfortable with this line of questioning, aren't you, Princess Meredith?" he asked.

"I am not ashamed of anything I've done, Mr. Veducci. The fey, outside of some of the Seelie Court, see no shame in sex, as long as it is consensual."

"All right," he said. "I'll ask the next one. How many men at a time do you routinely sleep with?" He shook his head when he asked as if he couldn't believe he was asking it.

"I don't think that's appropriate," Biggs said.

"I'll answer it," I said.

"Are you sure . . . ?"

"It's sex. There's nothing wrong with sex." I held Biggs's gaze until he looked away. I turned back to Veducci. "Average is probably two at a time. I think the max that I've ever done at once is four." I looked at Doyle and Frost. "Four?" I made it a question.

"I believe so," Doyle said.

Frost nodded. "Yes."

I turned back to the lawyers. "Four, but two is average."

Biggs recovered a little. "So, you see, gentlemen, ladies, a two-day wait between sex, or less. There are married men who have to wait longer than that for their needs to be met."

"Princess Meredith," Cortez said.

"Yes, Mr. Cortez." I looked into his dark brown eyes.

He cleared his throat and said, "Are you telling us the truth? You have sex three times a day with an average of two men at a time, and sometimes up to four. Is this what you want in the record?"

"It is sealed," Farmer said.

"But if this does go to court, then it may not be. Is this really what the princess wants the public to know about her?"

I frowned at him. "It's the truth, Mr. Cortez. Why should the truth bother me?"

"Do you honestly not understand what this information could do to your reputation in the media?"

"I don't understand the question."

He looked at Biggs and Farmer. "I don't say this

often, but is your client aware of what this record, even sealed, can be used for?"

"I did discuss it with her, but . . . Mr. Cortez, the Unseelie Court does not view sex in the same way as most of the world. They certainly don't view it as mainstream America views it. My colleague and I learned that when we prepped the princess and her guard for these talks. If you are hinting that the princess might be more careful about what she admits to having done with her men, then save your breath. She is absolutely not bothered by anything she has done with any of her men."

"Not to bring up a painful subject, but the princess didn't seem very happy in the media when her ex-fiancé, Griffin, sold those Polaroids to the tabloids a few months back," Cortez said.

I nodded. "That did hurt me," I said, "but because Griffin broke my trust, not because I was ashamed of what we'd done. I thought we were in love when those pictures were taken. There is no shame in love, Mr. Cortez."

"You are either very brave, Princess, or very naive. If you can use the word naive to a woman who is having sex with nearly twenty men on a regular basis."

"I am not naive, Mr. Cortez. I simply don't think like a human woman."

Farmer said, "King Taranis's allegation that the three guards he accused of this crime did so out of unmet sexual needs is a false assumption. It is based on the king's own lack of understanding of his sister court."

"Is the Unseelie Court so different from the Seelie

Court when it comes to matters of sex?" Nelson asked.

"May I take this one, Mr. Farmer?" I asked.

"You may."

"The Seelie try to ape human behavior. They're stuck somewhere between the centuries of fifteen hundred to eighteen hundred, but they try to play human more than the Unseelie. Many of those exiled to our court have been exiled because of simply wanting to remain true to their original natures, and not let themselves be civilized in a human manner."

"You sound like you're lecturing," Nelson said.

I smiled. "I did a paper in college on the differences between the two courts. I thought it might help the teacher and the other students understand that the Unseelie Court wasn't the bad guy."

"You were the first of the fey to attend human college in this country," Cortez said. He shifted through some papers in front of him. "But not the last. Some of the so-called lesser fey have actually gotten degrees since then."

"My father, Prince Essus, thought if one of the royals went, then our people might follow. He thought that learning, and understanding the country we lived in, was a necessary part of the fey adapting to modern life here."

"Your father never saw you attend college, though, did he?" Cortez asked.

"No," I said. The one word was clipped.

Doyle and Frost reached for me at the same time. Their hands found each other at the back of my shoulders. Doyle's arm stayed there. Frost's hand moved to cover one of my hands where I kept them still upon the tabletop. They were reacting to the tension in me, but it let everyone in the room know how concerned they were with me dealing with this topic. They hadn't reacted to talk of my ex-fiancé, Griffin. I think all my men thought they had washed his memory clean from me with their own bodies. I felt the same, so they'd read me right. Doyle was usually a good judge of my moods. Frost, who had his own moods, was learning mine.

"I think this topic is closed," Biggs said.

"I am sorry if I caused the princess distress," Cortez said, but he didn't sound sorry. I wondered why he'd brought up my father's assassination. Cortez, like Shelby and Veducci, struck me as a man who didn't do things without a reason. I wasn't sure about Nelson and the rest. I was counting on Biggs and Farmer being calculating men. But what did Cortez hope to gain from mentioning my father's death?

"I am sorry to cause distress, but I do have a reason for bringing the topic up," Cortez said.

"I don't see what relevance it could possibly have on these proceedings," Biggs said.

"The murderer of Prince Essus was never apprehended," Cortez said. "In fact, no one was even seriously suspected, is that correct?"

"We failed the prince and the princess in every way," Doyle said.

"But you weren't a guard for either of them, were you?"

"Not at that time."

"Lieutenant Frost, you were also part of the queen's Ravens when Prince Essus died. None of the current bodyguards of the princess were members of Prince Essus's Crane Guards, is that correct?"

"That is not true," Frost said.

Cortez looked at him. "Excuse me?"

Frost looked at Doyle, who gave a small nod. Frost's hand tightened over mine. He didn't like to speak in public; it was a phobia. "We have half a dozen guards with us here in Los Angeles who were once part of Prince Essus's Cranes."

"The king seems very certain that none of the prince's guards are guarding the princess," Cortez said.

"It is a recent change," Frost said. His hand tightened on mine until I used my free hand to play my fingers across the back of his. One, it would comfort him; two, it would keep him from forgetting how strong he was and hurting my hand. I played my fingers on the smooth white skin of his hand, and realized it didn't comfort just him.

Doyle moved closer to me so that he was more obviously hugging me. I leaned into the curve of his arm, letting my body settle into the line of his, while I continued to stroke the back of Frost's hand.

"I still see no reason for this line of questioning," Biggs said.

"I agree," Farmer said. "If you have any more questions that are relevant to the actual charges, we might entertain them."

Cortez looked at me. He gave me every ounce of those dark brown eyes. "The king thinks that the reason your father's murderer was never caught is that the men investigating it were the murderers."

Doyle, Frost, and I went very still. He had our attention now, indeed he did. "Speak plainly, Mr. Cortez," I said.

"King Taranis accuses the Raven Guard of Prince Essus's murder."

"You saw what the king did to the ambassador. I think that level of fear and manipulation speaks for my uncle's state of mind right now."

"We will follow up on Ambassador Stevens's . . . condition," Shelby said, "but doesn't it make sense that the reason no clues were found is that the men looking for the clues were hiding them?"

"Our oath to the queen would forbid us to do harm to her family," Doyle said.

"Your oath is to protect the queen, correct?" Cortez asked.

"We now belong to the princess, but the oath remains the same, yes."

"King Taranis alleges that you killed Prince Essus to keep him from killing Queen Andais and putting himself on the throne of the Unseelie Court."

The three of us stared at Cortez and Shelby. This was laundry so dirty that the queen had tortured people who had merely hinted at such things. I didn't ask if Taranis had actually said it, because I knew no one else at his court would have dared Queen Andais's anger. Anyone less than the king himself, and she would have called them out to a personal duel for such rumors.

Andais had a lot of faults, I knew that, but she had loved her brother. He had loved her, too. It's why he hadn't killed her and taken the throne, even though he felt that he would have been a better ruler. If he had lived, and my cousin, Prince Cel, had tried to take the throne, my father might have killed Cel to keep him off the throne.

Cel was insane, I think literally, and a sexual sadist who made Andais look mild. My father had feared the Unseelie Court at the hands of Cel. I feared it now. To save my life and the lives of those I loved, and to keep Cel off the throne, were the reasons I was still trying to be queen.

But I wasn't pregnant, and whoever got me pregnant would be king to my queen. I had realized only a day or so ago that I'd have given up everything to be with Frost and Doyle—including being queen—but for one thing: To keep these two men with me might require me to give up my birthright. And I was too much my father's daughter to let Cel have our people. But the regret in me was growing.

"Do you have a reply to the accusation, Princess Meredith?"

"My aunt is not perfect, but she loved her brother. I believe that with all my heart. If she discovered who killed him, her wrath would be the stuff of nightmares. None of her guard would have dared such a thing."

"Are you sure of that, Princess?"

"I think you might want to ask yourself, Mr. Cortez, Mr. Shelby, what King Taranis hopes to gain by this accusation. In fact, you might wonder what he might have gained from my father's death."

"Are you accusing the king of your father's murder?" Shelby asked.

"No, I am simply saying that the Seelie Court has never been a friend of my father's family. Whereas one of the queen's guard killing my father would have earned them a death by torture. I think if King Taranis could have plausible deniability of the deed, he would reward his own guard for it."

"Why would he kill Prince Essus?"

"I don't know."

"Do you believe he was behind the assassination?" Veducci asked. That fine mind was all there in those eyes.

"I didn't until now."

"What do you mean by that, Princess?" he asked.

"I mean I can't see what the king hopes to gain by the accusation against my guard. It makes no sense, and it makes me wonder what his true motives are here."

"He seeks to divide you from us," Frost said.

I looked at him, studying that handsome, arrogant face. I knew now that the cold arrogance was his mask when he was nervous. "Divide me from you how?"

"If he could plant such an ugly doubt in your mind, would you ever trust us again?"

I looked down at the table, at his pale hand on mine, my fingers against his skin. "No, I wouldn't."

"If you think about it," Frost continued, "the rape accusation is also meant to make you doubt us."

I nodded. "Maybe, but to what purpose?"

"I don't know."

"Unless he has taken leave of his senses at last," Doyle said, "he has a purpose to all of this. But I confess that I do not see what it could gain him. I do not like that we seem to be deep in a game and I do not know what we are playing."

Doyle stopped talking, and looked across the table at the lawyers. "Forgive us, please. We forgot where we were for a moment."

"Do you believe that this is all some sort of inter-court politics?" Veducci asked.

"Yes," Doyle said.

Veducci looked at Frost. "Lieutenant Frost?"

"I agree with my captain."

Last he looked at me. "Princess Meredith?"

"Oh, yes, Mr. Veducci, whatever else we are doing, it is most certainly intercourt politics."

"His treatment of Ambassador Stevens makes me begin to wonder if we are being used here," Veducci said.

"Are you saying, Mr. Veducci," Biggs said, "that you are beginning to doubt the validity of the charges made against my clients?"

"If I find out that your clients did what they are accused of, I will do my best to punish them to the greatest extent that the law allows, but if these charges turn out to be false, and the king has tried to use the law to harm the innocent, I'll do my best to remind the king that in this country no one is supposed to be above the law." Veducci smiled again, but this time it wasn't a happy smile. It was more predatory. That smile was enough; I knew who I feared the most on the other side of the table. Veducci wasn't as ambitious as Shelby and Cortez, but he was better. He actually still believed in the law. He actually still believed that the innocent should be spared, and the guilty punished. You didn't often see such pure faith in lawyers who had spent more than twenty years on the bar. They had to give up their belief in the law to survive as a lawyer. But somehow, Veducci had held on. He believed, and maybe, just maybe, he was beginning to believe us.

Chapter 3

WE HAD ADJOURNED TO A DIFFERENT ROOM. THE room was smaller than the conference room, but then so were some single-family homes. There was a huge mirror on one wall, the glass of which held small imperfections, bubbles near one corner. The mirror had an almost smoky quality in a few spots. Its frame was gilt edged, and worn with age. It had belonged to the original Mr. Biggs's great-grandmother. We were here, in Mr. Biggs's inner sanctum, to make a phone call of sorts, though no phones would be involved.

Galen, Rhys, and Abeloec had had their turn at the questioning in the conference room. They hadn't been able to do much but deny the charges. Abe had stood there with his perfectly striped hair: black, shades of gray, white, all perfectly even and artificial like some artful modern Goth, but it wasn't a good dye job; it was real. His pale skin and gray eyes matched the look. He looked odd in his charcoal-gray suit. No amount of tailoring could make it look like the clothes he would have chosen himself. He had been a party guy for centuries, and his clothes usually reflected that. Abe had no alibi because he'd been trying to crawl into a bottle with a drug chaser at the time of the accused attack. He'd been clean and sober only about two days. But the sidhe can't truly be addicted to anything, just as they can't truly drink or drug themselves into oblivion. It was an upside downside. The fey couldn't get addicted, but they couldn't use liquor, or drugs, to hide from their problems either. You could get us drunk, but only up to a point.

Galen looked cool and boyishly elegant in his brown suit. They wouldn't let him wear his signature green because it brought out the green undertones in his white skin. What they hadn't seemed to understand was that brown made the green undertone darker still, and much more noticeable. His green curls were cut short, with only one thin braid to remind me that his hair had once fallen in a glorious sheet to his ankles. He had the best alibi of the three, because he'd been having sex with me when the alleged attack took place.

Once I would have described Rhys as boyishly handsome, but not today. Today he seemed every inch the grown-up, all 5'6" of him. He was the only one of the guards with me today who was less than six feet. Rhys was still handsome, but he'd lost some boyish quality, or gained something else. A man who was more than a thousand years old, and had once been the god Cromm Cruach, couldn't grow up, could he? If he'd been human, I would have said that the events of the last few days had helped him grow up at last. But it seemed arrogant to think that my little adventures could affect a being who had once been worshipped as a god.

His white hair curled over his shoulders and down the broad plane of his back. He was the shortest of my sidhe guards, but I knew that the body under the suit was the most muscled. He took his workouts very seriously. He wore an eye patch to cover the main scars from an injury he'd received centuries ago. The one eye he had left was lovely, three circles of blue-like lines of sky from different days of the year. His mouth was soft and rich, and one of the most pouting of the men, as if his lips begged to be kissed. I didn't know what had wrought this new seriousness in him, but it gave him a new depth, as if there was more to him than there had been only a few days ago.

He was the only one of the three who had been outside the faerie mound, our sithen, when the attack was supposed to have happened. He had actually been attacked by Seelie warriors, and accused to his face of the crime. They had come out into the winter snow hunting my men with steel and cold iron, two of the only things that can truly injure a sidhe warrior. Most of the time even duels between the courts are fought with weapons that can't bring true injury, true death, to us. It's like one of those action movies where the men beat the hell out of each other but keep coming back for more. Steel and cold iron were killing weapons. That alone had been a breach of the peace between the two courts.

The lawyers were arguing. "Lady Caitrin alleges that the attack took place on a day that my clients were actually in Los Angeles," Biggs said. "My clients can't have done something in Illinois when they were in California all day. On the day in question, one of the accused was working for the Gray Detective Agency and was in view of witnesses all day."

That would have been Rhys. He loved being detective for real. He loved undercover work, and had enough glamour to be even better at it than a human detective. Galen had enough glamour to do it, too, but he couldn't play the part. Undercover, or decoy, work was only partly looking right. You also had to "feel" right to the person you were trying to catch. I'd done my share of decoy work in years past. Now, no one would allow me near the dangerous stuff.

So how had Lady Caitrin's attack taken place before we got to faerie? Time had started running differently in faerie again. Time had started running very differently in the Unseelie sithen around me. Doyle had said, "Time is running oddly in all of faerie for the first time in centuries, but it was running even more oddly around you, Meredith. Now that you have left, faerie time is running oddly, but no more oddly for one court than another."

It was both interesting and disturbing that time had run not exactly backward for me, but it had stretched out. It was January for us and the courts, but the date still wasn't the same. The post-Yule ball that my uncle Taranis had been so insistent on me attending was finally safely past. We'd all decided it was too dangerous for me to attend. The accusation against my guards confirmed that Taranis was up to something, but what? Taranis had a plan, and whatever it was, it would be dangerous to everyone but him.

"King Taranis has explained that time runs differently in faerie than it does in the real world," Shelby said.

I knew that Taranis hadn't said "the real world," because to him the Seelie Court *was* the real world.

"May I ask your clients a question?" Veducci asked. He'd stayed out of the squabbling. In fact, this was one of the first times he'd spoken since we had changed rooms. It made me nervous.

"You can ask it," Biggs said, "but I'll decide if they answer it."

Veducci gave a nod, and pushed away from the wall where he'd been leaning. He smiled at us all. Only a hardness to his eyes let me know that the smile was a lie. "Sergeant Rhys, were you in the lands of faerie on the date that Lady Caitrin accuses you of attacking her?"

"Of allegedly attacking her," Biggs said.

Veducci nodded at him. "Were you in the lands of faerie on the date that Lady Caitrin alleges this attack took place?"

It was nicely worded. Worded so that it was hard to dance around the truth without actually lying.

Rhys smiled at him, and I got a glimpse of that less serious side he'd shown me most of my life. "I was in the lands of faerie when the alleged attack took place."

Veducci asked the same question of Galen. Galen looked more uncomfortable than Rhys had, but he answered, "Yes, I was."

Abeloec's answer was simply "Yes."

Farmer whispered to Biggs, and asked the next round of questions. "Sergeant Rhys, were you here in Los Angeles on the date of the alleged attack?"

The question proved that our lawyers still didn't quite understand the quandary of time in faerie.

"No, I was not."

Biggs frowned. "But you were, all day. We have many witnesses."

Rhys smiled at him. "But the day in Los Angeles

was not the identical day as the day that Lady Caitrin accused us of this alleged attack."

"It is the same date," Biggs insisted.

"Yes," Rhys said patiently, "but just because it's the same date doesn't mean it's the same day."

Veducci was the only one smiling. Everyone else looked like they were thinking too hard, or were wondering if Rhys was crazy.

"Can you clarify that?" Veducci asked, still looking pleased.

"This isn't like a science-fiction story, where we have traveled back in time to redo the same day," Rhys said. "We aren't truly in two places at once. For us, Mr. Veducci, this day is truly a new day. Our dopplegangers are not in faerie reliving this day. That day in faerie is past. This day here in Los Angeles is a new day. It happens to have the same date, so outside of faerie it appears to be the same day, repeated."

"So you could have been in faerie on the day she was attacked?" Veducci asked.

Rhys smiled at him, almost *tsking*. "On the day she was allegedly attacked, yes."

"This will be a nightmare for a jury," Nelson said.

"Wait until we get done demanding a jury of their peers," Farmer said, smiling almost happily.

Nelson paled under her tasteful makeup. "A jury of their peers?" she repeated softly.

"Could a human juror truly understand being in two places on the same date?" Farmer asked.

The lawyers looked at each other. Only Veducci didn't share in the confusion. I think he'd already thought of all of this. Technically, his job description made him less powerful than Shelby or Cortez, but he could help them hurt us. Of everyone on the opposing side, Veducci was the one I wanted to win over the most.

"We're here today to try to avoid this going to a jury," Biggs said.

"If they attacked this woman, then at the very least," Shelby said, "they must be confined to faerie."

"You would have to prove their guilt before you could get a judge to mete out a punishment," Farmer said.

"Which leads us back to the fact that none of us really want this to go to court." Veducci's quiet voice fell into the room like a stone thrown into a flock of birds. The other lawyers' thoughts seemed to scatter like those birds, flying up in confusion.

"Don't be giving our case away before we've even begun," Cortez said, not sounding happy with his colleague.

"This isn't a case, Cortez, this is a disaster we're trying to avert," Veducci said.

"A disaster for whom, them?" Cortez said, pointing at us.

"For all of faerie, potentially," Veducci said. "Have you read your history about the last great human faerie war in Europe?"

"Not recently," Cortez said.

Veducci looked around at the other lawyers. "Am I the only one here who read up on this?"

Grover raised his hand. "I did."

Veducci smiled at him as if he were his favorite person in the world. "Tell these intelligent people how the last great war started."

"It began as a dispute between the Seelie and Unseelie Courts."

"Exactly," Veducci said. "And then spilled over all the British Isles and part of the continent of Europe."

"Are you saying that if we don't mediate these charges, the courts will go to war?" Nelson said.

"There are only two things that Thomas Jefferson and his cabinet made unforgivable offenses for the fey on American soil," Veducci said. "They are never again to allow themselves to be worshipped as deities, and they are never to have a war between the two courts. If either of those things happen, they will be kicked out of this, the last country on earth that would have them."

"We know all this," Shelby said.

"But have you considered why Jefferson made those two rules, especially the one about war?"

"Because it would be damaging to our country," Shelby said.

Veducci shook his head. "There is still a crater on the European continent almost as wide as the widest part of the Grand Canyon. That hole is what is left of where the last battle of the war was fought. Think about if that happened in the center of this country, in the middle of our most productive farming country."

They looked at each other. They hadn't thought about it. To Shelby and Cortez it had been a high-profile case. A chance to make new law involving the fey. Everyone had taken the short view, except Veducci, and maybe Grover.

"What do you propose we do?" Shelby asked. "Just let them get away with it?"

"No, not if they are guilty, but I want everyone in

this room to understand what might be at stake, that's all," Veducci said.

"You sound like you're on the side of the princess," Cortez said.

"The princess didn't give a United States ambassador a bespelled watch so he would favor her."

"How do we know the princess didn't do it, to trick us?" Shelby said. He sounded like he even believed it.

Veducci turned to me. "Princess Meredith, did you give Ambassador Stevens any object, magical or mundane, that would sway his opinion of you and your court in your favor?"

I smiled. "No, I did not."

"They really can't lie, if you ask the questions right," Veducci said.

"Then how did Lady Caitrin accuse these men by name and description? She seemed genuinely traumatized."

"That is a problem," Veducci admitted. "The lady in question would have to be lying, an outright lie, because I asked the questions right, and she was unshakable." He looked at us, at me. "Do you understand what that means, Princess?"

I took a deep breath and let it out, slowly. "I think so. It means that Lady Caitrin has everything to lose here. If she is caught in an actual lie, she could be cast out of faerie. Exile is considered worse than death to the Seelie nobility."

"Not just the nobility," Rhys said.

The other guards nodded. "He is right," Doyle said. "Even the lesser fey would do much to avoid exile."

"So how is the lady lying?" Veducci asked us.

Galen spoke, voice low, a little uncertain. "Could it be an illusion? Could someone have used glamour so strong that it fooled her?"

"You mean made her think she was being attacked when she wasn't?" Nelson asked.

"I'm not sure that would be possible on a member of the sidhe," Veducci said. He looked at us.

"What if it wasn't completely an illusion," Rhys said.

"What do you mean?" I asked.

"You make a tree by planting a stick in the ground. You create a castle from the ruin of one," he said.

"It would be easier to do such a thing if you had something physical to build upon," Doyle said.

"What could you build on for an attack?" Galen asked.

Doyle looked at him. The look was eloquent, but Galen didn't understand it. I got it first. "You mean the stories of our people appearing as dead warriors coming into the widows' beds, that kind of thing."

"Yes," Doyle said, "illusion used as a disguise."

"Very few in faerie have such power of illusion now," Frost said.

"There might only be one in all of faerie who could pull it off," Galen said. His green eyes were suddenly very serious.

"You can't mean . . ." Frost started to say, then stopped. We all thought it.

Abe said, "That son of a bitch."

Veducci spoke as if he'd read our minds. It made me wonder if without his protections from faerie magic I'd have read him as a psychic, or more. "The

King of Light and Illusion, how good are his powers of illusion?"

"Fuck," Shelby said. "You did not just say that. You did not just give them reasonable doubt."

Veducci smiled at us. "The princess and her men had reasonable doubt when they stepped into the room, but they would never have accused the king out loud in front of us. They'd have kept their secrets even from their lawyers."

I had an awful idea. I moved toward Veducci, only Doyle's hand on my arm stopping me from touching the man. He was right, they might see that as magical interference. "Mr. Veducci, are you planning on accusing my uncle of this plot on the mirror call today?"

"I thought I'd leave that to your lawyers."

My skin was suddenly cold. I felt the blood drain from my face. Veducci looked uncertain, and almost reached out to me. "Are you feeling all right, Princess?"

"I'm frightened for you, for all of you, and for us," I said. "You do not understand Taranis. He has been absolute ruler of the Seelie Court for more than a thousand years. That has led to an arrogance you can't even begin to imagine. He pretends to be the jolly, handsome king for you humans, but he shows quite a different face to those of us in the Unseelie Court. If you accuse him bluntly of this, I do not know what he will do."

"Would he hurt us?" Nelson asked.

"No, but he might use magic on you," I replied. "He is the King of Light and Illusion. I have stood in his presence, just over a mirror call, and he has almost bespelled me. I almost fell to his power, and I am a princess of the Unseelie Court. You are human. If he truly wanted to bespell you, he could."

"That would be illegal," Shelby said.

"He is a king with the power of life and death in his hands," I said. "He doesn't think like a modern man, no matter how much he apes it for the press." I felt dizzy, and someone brought me a chair.

Doyle knelt beside me. "Are you unwell, Meredith?" he whispered.

Nelson asked, "Are you all right, Princess Meredith?"

"I'm tired, and scared," I said. "You have no idea what the last few days have been like, and I daren't tell you."

"Does it have anything to do with this case?" Cortez asked.

I looked up at him. "You mean the reason that I'm tired and scared?"

"Yes."

"No, it has nothing to do with these false accusations." I reached for Doyle's hand. "Make them understand that they must tread carefully with Taranis."

Doyle took my hand in his and said, "I will do my best, my princess."

I smiled up at him. "I know you will."

Frost came to the other side of me and touched my cheek. "You are pale. Even for one of us with moonlight skin, you are pale."

Abeloec came closer to me. "I had heard that the princess was human enough to catch colds. I thought it was a nasty rumor."

"You can't catch colds?" Nelson asked.

"They can't," I said, pressing my cheek against Frost's hand, and still holding on to Doyle. "But I can. I don't get them often, but I can get them." In my head I added, "The very first mortal faerie princess." It was one of the reasons for all the assassination attempts on the Unseelie Court. There were factions that believed that if I sat the throne I would contaminate all the immortals with the disease of mortality. I would bring death to them all. How do you argue against a rumor like that, when they can't even catch a cold? And I was about to talk to the most bright and shiny of them all, King Taranis, Lord of Light and Illusion. Goddess help me if he realized that I was coming down with some petty human illness. It would just confirm for him how weak I was, how human I was.

"It's almost time for the king to contact us," Veducci said, looking at his watch.

"If his time is running on schedule with ours," Cortez said.

Veducci nodded. "True, but may I suggest that we get some cold metal for the rest of you to carry?"

"Cold metal?" Nelson made it a question.

"I think some of the office supplies of this fine law firm might just help the rest of you have clear vision when we deal with King Taranis."

"Office supplies," Cortez said. "You mean like paper clips?"

"Maybe," Veducci said. He turned to me. "What do you think, Princess, would a paper clip be helpful?"

"It depends on what it's made out of, but a handful of them might help."

"We can test it for you," Rhys said.

"How?" Veducci said.

"If it bothers us to touch it, it'll help you."

"I thought it was only lesser fey that couldn't touch metal," Cortez said.

"Some of them can actually be burned by the touch of some metals, but even the sidhe don't truly enjoy most man-forged metal," Rhys said, still with that smile.

"Burned just by touching metal," Nelson said.

"We don't have time to discuss the wonders of the fey if we're going to get those office supplies," Veducci said.

Farmer hit the intercom and spoke to one of the many secretaries and personal assistants who were in the offices outside. He requested metal paper clips and staples. I suggested, "Box cutters, pocket knives."

Shelby, Grover, and the other male assistant all had pocket knives. "You were pretty fascinated with the princess," Veducci said. "I'd add a handful of something else, just in case."

I watched Veducci hand out the office supplies. He'd taken charge, and no one had questioned it. He was supposed to be our enemy, but he was helping us. Had he told the truth? Was he here for justice, or was it a lie? Until I found out what Taranis wanted, I couldn't afford to trust anyone.

Veducci came to stand in front of where I sat. He nodded at Doyle and Frost, who were still pressed to me, one on each side. "May I offer the princess some extra metal to hold?"

"She is carrying metal, as are we all."

"The guns and swords, we see them." Then Veducci's eyes flicked to me. "Are you saying the princess is armed?"

I was, actually. I had a knife strapped to my thigh in a holder I'd worn before. I had a gun at the small of my back in one of those new sideways holsters that were designed to be worn there. We didn't actually expect me to use the gun for shooting, but it was a way to carry a lot of metal—steel and lead—on me and not make it obvious to Taranis. He'd see me wearing metal as an insult. The guards could get away with it, because they were guards; they were supposed to be armed.

"The princess is carrying what she needs to protect herself," Doyle said.

Veducci did a little bow from the neck. "Then I'll put the office supplies back in the box."

Trumpets sounded, sweet and clear, as if they rained music down upon us from some great height. It was the sound of King Taranis calling on the mirror. He was being polite, and waiting for someone to touch the mirror on our side. The trumpets sounded again as we all stared at the blank mirror.

Doyle and Frost got me to my feet. Rhys came in at my side, as if they'd discussed it beforehand. Doyle moved forward, letting Rhys take his place at my side. Rhys gave me a one-armed hug, and whispered, "Sorry to move your favorite out of his spot."

I turned and looked at him, because jealousy was supposed to be a human emotion. Rhys let me see in his face that he knew that my heart had chosen even if my body hadn't. He let me know that he knew how

I felt about Doyle, and that it hurt him. One look, full of so much.

Doyle touched the mirror, and Rhys whispered, "Smile for the king."

I let the smile I'd practiced for years slide over my face. The smile that was pleasant, but not too happy. It was a court smile, a smile to hide behind, and think thoughts that had nothing to do with smiles at all.

Chapter 4

THE MIRROR FILLED WITH LIGHT, SHINING, GOLDEN sunlight, until we all had to turn our eyes away or be blinded by the brilliance, the brilliance of Taranis, King of Light and Illusion. A man's voice, I think it was Shelby's, spoke from the dimness of my closed eyelids, "What the hell is this?"

"The king, boasting," I said. I shouldn't have said it, but I wasn't feeling well, and I was angry. Angry at having to be here at all. Angry and scared, because I knew Taranis well enough to be certain that the other shoe had not even begun to drop.

"Boasting," a joyous male voice said. "This is not boasting, Meredith, this is what I am." He'd used only my name, and none of my titles. It was an insult, and we were going to let him get away with it. But more surprising, he hadn't announced himself formally. He was being as informal as if we were talking privately. It was almost, as if to him, the human lawyers didn't really count.

Veducci's voice spoke out of the blinding light that had become the room. "King Taranis, I've spoken to you several times and never been so blinded by your light. If you could have pity on us mere humans and dim your glory just a bit?"

"What think you of my glory, Meredith?" the joyous voice asked, and the sound alone made me smile even as I squinted to save my eyes.

Frost squeezed my hand, and that touch of skin on skin helped me think. Taranis was not a power of flesh and sex. To combat what he was so good at, you had to use the magic you were good at, just to be able to think in Taranis's presence. I reached for Rhys, until my hand found the bare skin of his neck and cheek. The touch of both of them helped me think. "I think your glory is wondrous, Uncle Taranis." He'd been familiar first, using only my first name, so I figured I'd try to remind him that I was his niece. That I wasn't just some Unseelie noblewoman to impress.

I wasn't too insulted; except for his use of my first name, he did the same kind of crap to Queen Andais. The two of them had been trying to outmagic each other for centuries. I had simply been dropped into the middle of a game that I had no hope of winning. If Andais herself could not shut down Taranis's magic in a mirror call, then my own much more humble abilities were outclassed. My men and I had known that coming into this call. I had hoped that with the lawyers present, Taranis might tone things down a bit. Apparently not.

"Uncle makes me sound old, Meredith. Taranis, you must call me Taranis." His voice made it sound like we were old friends, and he was so very happy to see me. The voice alone made me want to say yes to anything and everything. Any other sidhe being caught using his voice and magic on another sidhe like this would lead to a duel, or to being punished by their queen or king. But he was the king, and that meant that people didn't call him on it. But I'd been forced to call him on something similar the last time I'd spoken with him like this; could I afford to start out as rude as I'd ended the last time?

"Taranis, then, Uncle. Could you please tone down your wonder so that we may all look upon you?"

"Is the light hurting your eyes?"

"Yes," I said, and there were other affirmatives from behind me. The full-blooded humans must have been in real discomfort by now.

"Then I will dim my light for you, Meredith." He made my name sound like a piece of candy on his tongue. Something sweet, and thick, and suckable.

Frost drew my hand to his mouth, and kissed my knuckles. It helped me shake off the effect that Taranis was trying hard to get from me. He'd done this last time, a magical seduction so powerful it damn near hurt.

Rhys snuggled closer to my side, nuzzling along my neck. He whispered, "He's not just trying to impress us all, Merry, he's aiming straight at you."

I turned into his face, even with my eyes still closed against the light. "He did this last time."

Rhys's hand found the back of my hair, turning my face toward his. "Not exactly this, Merry. He's trying harder to win you over."

Rhys kissed me. It was a gentle kiss, I think more conscious of the red lipstick I was wearing than of any sense of decorum. Frost rubbed his thumb over my hand. Their touches kept me from sinking into Taranis's voice, and the pull of the light.

I felt Doyle standing in front of me before I actually opened my eyes. He kissed me on the forehead, adding his touch to the others as if he already knew what Taranis was doing. He moved to my left, and at first I didn't realize what he was doing, then Taranis's voice came, not nearly as happy as he'd sounded before. "Meredith, how dare you come before me with the monsters that attacked my lady, standing there as if they had done no wrong? Why are they not in shackles?" His voice was still a good, rich voice, but it was just a voice. Even Taranis couldn't make those words, that outrage, work with the warm, seductive tone.

The light had dimmed some. Doyle was blocking some of my view, and partially blocking Rhys from the king's view, but I'd seen this show before. Taranis was dimming the light so that it looked as if he were forming from the brilliance. Forming a face, a body, his clothes, out of light itself.

Biggs said, "My clients are innocent until proven guilty, King Taranis."

"Do you doubt the word of the nobles of the Seelie Court?" I didn't think the outrage was feigned this time.

"I'm a lawyer, your highness. I doubt everything."

I think Biggs meant it as humor, but if he had, he didn't know his audience. Taranis had no sense of humor that I was aware of. Oh, he thought he was funny, but no one else was allowed to be funnier than the king. The last rumor from the Seelie Court was that even Taranis's court jester had been imprisoned for impertinence.

I'd have complained more if Andais hadn't slain her last court jester some four or five hundred years before.

"Was that meant to be humor?" The king's voice reverberated through the room, like a roll of quiet thunder. It was one of his names, Taranis Thunderer. Once he'd been a sky and storm god. The Romans had equated him with their own Jupiter, though his powers had never been as far-reaching as Jupiter's.

"Apparently not," Biggs said, trying to put a pleasant face on it.

Taranis was finally revealed in the mirror. He was edged with glow, as if the colors of everything about him wavered. His hair and beard were at least his true color, the reds and oranges of a spectacular sunset. The locks of his curling hair were painted with the glory of the sky when the sun sinks to the west. His eyes were truly multi-petals of green: jade, grass, shades of leaves. It was as if a green flower had been substituted for the iris of his eyes. As a small child, before I knew that he disdained me, I'd truly thought him handsome.

"Oh, my God," Nelson said in a breathy voice.

I looked behind myself at her, the wide eyes, the almost slack face. "You've only seen the pictures of him pretending to be human, haven't you?"

"He had red hair and green eyes, not this, not this," she said. Cortez, her boss, took her elbow and got her to a chair. Cortez was angry and was having trouble hiding it. Interesting reaction on his part.

Taranis turned those green-petaled eyes toward the woman. "Few human women have seen me in all my glory in many years. What do you think of me in my true form, pretty girl?"

I was pretty sure that you didn't get to be assistant district attorney in Los Angeles by letting men call you pretty girl. But if Nelson had a problem with it, she didn't say so. She looked besotted with him, drunk with his attention.

Abe came to join us in our huddled group. Galen trailed behind him, looking puzzled. It was Abe who leaned in and whispered, "There is some magic here that is not merely light and illusion. If it were almost anyone else, I would say that he has added love magic to his bag of tricks."

Doyle drew Abe closer to us all, and whispered, "A spell powerful enough that it is affecting Ms. Nelson."

They all agreed.

We hadn't meant to ignore Taranis, but he was so terribly busy flirting with Nelson that it was easy to forget that just because a king is ignoring you doesn't mean that you are allowed to ignore the king.

"I did not come here to be insulted," he said in that thundery voice. Once it would have impressed me, but I'd been intimate with Mistral. He was a storm god, too, but one who could make lightning pour down a hallway inside the faerie mound. Taranis's rumbly voice just couldn't compare to Mistral's. In fact, as the men parted so that I could see my uncle more clearly, he looked a little overdone, like a man who's overdressed for a date.

I looked at the men clustered around me, and realized that all of them had touched me, Rhys wrapped around my waist and side; Frost on the other side, arm a little higher; Doyle with his strong dark hands on my face; Abe with his hand on my shoulder so he could lean in and not fall (even sober his balance seemed shaky sometimes). Galen had touched me because he always touched me when he could. It was as if I'd reached a critical mass of touch. I could think. I was no longer besotted like the good Miss Nelson. Once I'd thought that Andais appearing on the mirror calls draped in men had been a way to taunt and shock Taranis and his court. In only two mirror calls of my very own, I'd learned that there was a method to her madness. For me, either five was the magic number or the mix of these five men's powers was what worked. Either way, it was going to be a different phone call than it would have been if Taranis's spell had worked on me. Interesting.

"Meredith," Taranis called. "Meredith, look upon me."

I knew that there was power to that voice. I felt it as one would sense the ocean. Whispering and close. But I was no longer standing in the water. I was no longer in danger of drowning in that voice.

"I see you, Uncle Taranis. I see you very well," I said, and my voice was strong and firm, and caused the arch of a perfect sunset-colored eyebrow to raise.

"I can barely see you through the crowd of your men," he said. There was a tone to his voice that I couldn't discern. Anxiety, anger; something unpleasant.

Doyle, Galen, and Abe began to move away from me. Even Frost started to pull away. Only Rhys stayed wedded to my side. The moment their hands fell away, Taranis was edged with light.

"Stay where you are, my men," I said. "I am your princess. He is not your king."

The men hesitated. Doyle moved back to me first, and the rest followed his lead. I put his hand to my face, and tried to tell him with my eyes what was happening. The spell was aimed so surely at me, like an arrow for my mind alone. How could I explain to them without words, what was happening?

Rhys settled himself more firmly around my waist, tucking me close, leaving just enough room for Frost's arm to slide back across my shoulders. Abe went to stand behind me, placing a hand on my shoulder closest to Rhys. Galen joined him, and though clearly puzzled, added his hand to my other shoulder closer to Frost. I gave the hand that wasn't wrapped around Rhys's waist to Doyle. The moment they were all touching me, even through clothing, the light around the king was gone. Taranis was handsome, but that was all.

"Meredith," Taranis said, "how can you insult me like this? These men attacked a lady of my court, savaged her. Yet you stand there with them . . . touching you, as if they are your court favorites."

"But, Uncle, they *are* some of my favorites."

"Meredith," he said, and he sounded shocked, like an elderly relative who just heard you say "fuck" for the first time.

Biggs and Shelby both tried to move in and smooth things over. I think the reason the lawyers hadn't interfered more before was that even the men were getting a sideswipe of the spell that Taranis had brought to this meeting. Either he had brought this magic for some specific purpose or he always held this magic when dealing with Queen Andais, and now me. I had not been able to sense it when we last spoke to Taranis. But then, neither had Doyle, or any of the other men. It wasn't just me who had grown in power from our few days in faerie. The Goddess had been a very busy deity. We had all been changed by her touch, and by the touch of her consort, the God.

"I will not speak of this matter in front of the monsters that savaged a woman of my court." Taranis's voice rolled through the room like the whisper of a storm. The humans all reacted as if it were more than a whisper. I was safe behind the hands of my men from whatever Taranis was trying to do.

Shelby turned to us. "I think it's a reasonable request to have the three accused wait outside while we talk to the king."

"No," I said.

"Princess Meredith," Shelby said, "you're being unreasonable."

"Mr. Shelby, you're being magically manipulated," I said, smiling at him.

He frowned at me. "I don't understand what you mean by that."

"I know you don't," I said. I turned to Taranis. "What you are doing to them is illegal by human law. The very law you have appealed to for aid."

"I have not asked for human aid," he said.

"You accused my men under human law."

"I petitioned Queen Andais for justice, but she refused to acknowledge my right to judge her Unseelie sidhe."

"You rule the Seelie Court," I said, "not the Unseelie."

"So your queen made clear to me."

"So when Queen Andais denied your request at her court, you turned to the humans."

"I appealed to you, Meredith, but you would not even answer my calls."

"Queen Andais advised me against it, and she is my queen and my father's sister. I heeded her advice." It had actually been more of an order. She'd said that whatever evil Taranis had planned I should avoid him. When someone as powerful as Andais says to avoid someone for fear of what they will do, I listen. I had not been so arrogant as to believe that Taranis's entire purpose was to simply have me talk to him on a mirror call. Andais had not believed that that was his purpose either, but now, today, I was beginning to wonder. I could think of nothing I could offer him that would make this much effort worthwhile.

"But now, because of human law, you must speak to me," he said.

Biggs said, "The princess agreed to this meeting out of courtesy. She was not compelled to be here."

Taranis's eyes never even moved to look at the lawyer. "But you are here, now, and you are more beautiful than I remember. I was very lax in my attentions to you, Meredith."

I laughed, and it was a harsh sound. "Oh, no, Uncle Taranis, I think you were quite thorough in your attentions to me. Almost more thorough than my mortal body could endure."

Doyle, Rhys, and Frost all tensed against me. I knew what they meant by it: Have a care, don't give away court secrets in front of the humans. But Taranis had begun it, dragging us out before the humans. I was only following his lead.

"Will you never forget that one moment in your childhood?"

"You nearly beat me to death, Uncle. I am not likely to forget it."

"I did not understand how fragile your body was, Meredith, or I would never have touched you so."

Veducci recovered first, saying, "Is King Taranis admitting that he beat you as a child, Princess?"

I looked at my uncle, so large, so imposing, so regal in his gold and white court clothes. "He is not denying it, are you, Uncle Taranis?"

"Please, Meredith, uncle seems so formal." His voice was wheedling. From the way Nelson began to walk closer to the mirror, I think the tone was meant to be seductive.

"He is not denying it," Doyle said.

"I am not speaking to you, Darkness," Taranis said, and his voice tried to thunder again. But as the seduction had not worked, so now the threat fell flat as well.

"King Taranis," Biggs said, "are you admitting that you beat my client as a child?"

Taranis finally turned to him, frowning. Biggs reacted as if the sun itself had smiled at him. He actually stumbled in his speech and looked uncertain.

Taranis said, "What I did years ago has no bearing on the crime that these monsters committed."

Veducci turned to me. "How badly did he beat you, Princess Meredith?"

"I remember how red my blood was on the white marble," I said. I looked at Veducci as I spoke, though I could feel Taranis's magic pushing at me, calling me to look at him. I looked at Veducci because I could, and because I knew that it would unnerve the

king. "If my Gran, my grandmother, had not interfered I believe he would have beaten me to death."

"You hold a grudge, Meredith. I have apologized
for my actions that day."

"Yes," I said, turning back to the mirror. "You
have recently apologized for that beating."

"Why did he beat you?" Veducci asked.

Taranis roared, "That is not the business of humans."

He'd beat me when I'd asked why Maeve Reed,
once the goddess Conchenn, had been exiled from his
court. She was the golden goddess of Hollywood
now, and had been for fifty years. We were all still living on her estate in Holmby Hills, though the recent
addition of so many men was beginning to tax even
her space. Maeve had given us some new room by
going to Europe. It was far enough away to stay out
of Taranis's way—or that was the hope.

Maeve had told us Taranis's deep dark secret. He
had wanted to marry her after putting away a third
wife for barrenness. Maeve had refused, pointing out
that the last wife he'd put away had gone on to have
children with someone else. She dared to tell the king
that it was he who was barren, not the women. A
hundred years ago Maeve had told him this, but he
had exiled her and forbidden anyone to speak to her.
Because if his court found out that a century ago he
had known that he might be barren, and said nothing, did nothing. . . . If the king is barren, the people
and land are barren. He had condemned them to a
slow death as a people. They lived almost forever, but
no children meant that when they died, there would
be no more Seelie sidhe. If his court found out what

he had done, they were within our laws to demand a living sacrifice, with Taranis in the starring role.

He had twice tried to kill Maeve with magic, horrible spells that no Seelie would admit to doing. He had tried to kill her, and not us, even though he had to wonder if we knew his secret. He feared our queen, or perhaps he didn't think his court would believe anyone who was part of the Unseelie Court. Perhaps that was why Maeve was the threat and not us.

"If you abused the princess when she was a child, that may affect this case," Veducci said.

"I now regret my temper in that moment with this woman," Taranis said. "But my one thoughtless moment decades ago does not change the fact that the three Unseelie sidhe before me did worse to the Lady Caitrin."

"If there is a pattern of abuse between the princess and the king," Biggs said, "then his accusations against her lovers may have a motive behind them."

"Are you implying a romantic motive for the king?" Cortez put a great deal of disdain in his voice, as if it were laughable.

"He wouldn't be the first man to beat a girl as a child, then turn to sexual abuse as she grew older," Biggs said.

"What did he accuse me of?" Taranis asked.

"Mr. Biggs is trying to prove that you have romantic intentions toward the princess," Cortez said, "and I am telling him that this is not so."

"Romantic intentions," Taranis repeated slowly. "What does he mean by that?"

"Do you have sexual or marital intentions toward Princess Meredith?" Biggs asked.

"I do not see what such a question has to do with the savage attack by those Unseelie monsters on the beautiful Lady Caitrin."

All the men touching me tensed again or went very still, even Galen. They had all realized that the king had not answered the question. The sidhe only avoided answering a question for two reasons. One, sheer perversity and a love of word games. Taranis had no love of word games, and was one of the least perverse of the sidhe. Two, that the answer was something that they didn't want to admit to. But the only answer Taranis could possibly want to avoid was "yes." It couldn't be "yes." He couldn't have romantic designs on me. He couldn't.

I looked up at Doyle and Frost. I looked for a clue as to what to do. Did I ignore it, or pursue it? Which was better? Which was worse?

Cortez said, "Though we have sympathy with the princess's childhood tragedies, we are here to investigate a new tragedy, the attack by these three men on Lady Caitrin."

I looked at Cortez. He actually looked away from my gaze, as if his statement sounded harsh even to his own ears.

"You do understand that you are all being magically influenced by him?" I asked.

"I think I would know if I were being influenced, Princess Meredith," Cortez said.

"The nature of magical manipulation," Veducci said, coming forward, "is that you don't know it's happening. It's why it's so very illegal."

Biggs faced the mirror. "Are you using magic to manipulate the people in this room, King Taranis?"

"I am not trying to manipulate the entire room, Mr. Biggs," Taranis said.

"May we ask a question?" Doyle asked.

"I will not speak to the monsters of the Unseelie Court," Taranis said.

"Captain Doyle is not accused of any crime," Biggs said. I realized that the lawyers on our side were having less trouble with Taranis's magical presence than those on the other side, except for Veducci, who seemed to be doing just fine. The lawyers had entered into an agreement with Taranis, just a verbal one, but that would be enough for someone of his power to have more of a hold over all of them. It was the subtle magic of kingship. If you agreed to be a true king's man, there was power to that agreement. Taranis had once been chosen by faerie to be king, and even now there was power to that old bargain.

"They are all monsters," Taranis said. He looked at me, gave me all the longing those green-petaled eyes could hold. "Meredith, Meredith, come to us before the power of the Unseelie makes of you something horrible."

If I hadn't broken his spell on me earlier, that appeal might have drawn me to him. But I stood safe among my men, and our power.

"I have seen both courts, Uncle. I found them both equally beautiful and horrible in their own ways."

"How can you compare the light and joy of the Golden Court to the darkness and terror of the Darkling Throne?"

"I am probably the only sidhe noble in recent history who can compare them, Uncle."

"Taranis, Meredith. Please, Taranis."

I didn't like his insistence that I call him by name and not title. In front of the Unseelie, he was always very aware of his title. In fact, he hadn't asked for all his appellations to be read. It wasn't like him to forgo anything that built him up in the eyes of others.

"Very well, Uncle . . . Taranis." The moment I said it, there was more weight in the air. It was harder to breathe. He'd joined his name to the spell of attraction so that every time I said his name, it would bind me more tightly. That was against the rules. Duels had been fought over less between the sidhe in any court. But you did not challenge the king to a duel. One, he was king, and two, he'd once been among the greatest warriors the sidhe could boast. He might be diminished, but I was mortal, and I'd swallow any insult he tossed our way. Maybe he'd counted on that?

Doyle said, "We need a chair for our princess."

The lawyers brought a chair, apologizing for not thinking of it sooner. Magic can do that, make you forget what you're about. Make you forget the mundane things like chairs and that your legs get tired, until you realize that your body hurts and that you've been ignoring it. I sat down gratefully. I'd have worn lower heels if I'd known I'd be standing this much.

There was some confusion as I sat so that for a moment not all my men were touching me. Taranis was edged with golden light. Then the men settled into their places and he was ordinary again. All right, Taranis was as ordinary as he would ever be.

Frost stayed standing at my back with his hand on my shoulder. I'd expected Doyle to take his place at my back as well, but it was Rhys who stood at my other shoulder. Doyle knelt on the floor beside me, with one hand on my arm. Galen moved in front of me so that he sat tailor-fashion at my feet, leaning his back against my hose-covered legs. One of his hands moved up and down my calf, an idle gesture that would have been possessive in a human but might have simply been nerves in one of the fey. Abe knelt at my other side, mirroring Doyle. Well, not exactly mirroring. Doyle had one hand on the pommel of his short sword, his other hand quietly on mine. Abe's hand gripped my other hand, squeezing. If he'd been human, I'd have said he was afraid. Then I realized that this might have been the first time since Taranis cast him out that he had seen his ex-king. Abe had never been one of Queen Andais's favorites, so he wouldn't have been included on the mirror calls between courts.

I leaned over enough so I could lay my cheek against his hair. Abe looked up, startled, as if he hadn't expected me to return his gestures. The queen was more for receiving than giving, in everything but pain. I gave his surprise a smile, and tried to tell him with my eyes that I was sorry I hadn't thought what seeing the king might mean for him this day.

"I must take part of the blame that you sit among them so happily, Meredith," Taranis said. "If you had only known the pleasure of a Seelie sidhe, you would never let them touch you again."

"Most of the sidhe around me now were once part of the Seelie Court," I said, simply leaving off his name. I wanted to know whether if I ceased to say "Uncle," he would try to get his name to pass my lips for some other made-up reason. I'd felt the pull of magic when I said his name.

"They have been nobles of the Unseelie Court for centuries, Meredith," Taranis said. "They have become twisted things, but you have nothing to compare them to, and that was a grave oversight on the part of the Seelie. I am most heartily sorry that we neglected you so. I would make it up to you."

"What do you mean, they are twisted things?" I asked. I thought I knew, but I'd learned not to jump to conclusions when I dealt with either court.

"Lady Caitrin has told of the horrors of their bodies. None of the three of them are powerful enough in glamour to hide their true selves during intimacies."

Biggs came to my side as if I'd asked. "The lady's statement is quite graphic, and reads more like a horror movie than anything else."

I looked at Doyle. "You read it?"

"I did," he said. He looked up at me, his eyes still lost behind the dark glasses.

"Did the lady in question accuse them of being deformed?" I asked.

"Yes," he said.

I had a thought. "The same way the ambassador saw you all."

Doyle gave the smallest movement of the corner of his mouth, hidden from the mirror. I knew what that almost-smile meant. I was right, and he thought I was on the right track. Okay, if I was on the right track, where was this little train going?

"How deformed did the lady say they were in her statement?" I asked.

"So much so that no human woman would survive an attack," Biggs said.

I frowned at him. "I don't understand."

"It is the old wives' tale," Doyle said, "that the Unseelie have bone and spikes on their lower members."

"Oh," I said, but strangely, that rumor had a basis. The sluagh, Sholto's kingdom within our court, had had nightflyers. They looked like manta rays with tentacles that dangled, but they could fly like bats. They were the flying hounds of the sluagh's wild hunt. A royal nightflyer carried a bony spine inside his member that stimulated ovulation in female nightflyers. It also proved that you were of royal nightflyer heritage, because only they could make the females give up their eggs so that they could be fertilized. Rape by a royal nightflyer might have given rise to the old faerie horror story. Sholto's father had been one of the nonroyals, because his sidhe mother hadn't needed the spine to make her ovulate. He'd been a surprise baby in many ways. He was gorgeously, wonderfully sidhe, except for some extra bits here and there. Mostly there.

"King Taranis," I said, and again his name pulled at me, like a hand tugging for attention. I took a deep breath and relaxed into the weight of Rhys and Frost at my back, my hands on Doyle and Abe. Galen seemed to sense what was needed because he slid his arm between my calves, so that he wrapped himself around one of my legs, and forced both my legs apart a little wider so he could cuddle more tightly. There were very few of my guards who would have been willing to look so submissive in front of Taranis. I valued the few who were more willing to be close to me than to keep up appearances.

I tried again. "King of Light and Illusion, are you

saying that my three guards are so monstrous that to lie with them is painful and horrible?"

"Lady Caitrin says that it is so," he said. He had settled back into his throne. It was huge and golden, and was the only thing that had not changed when his illusions were stripped away. He sat on what would cost, even today, a king's ransom.

"You said that my men could not maintain their illusion of beauty during intimacies, is that correct?"

"The Unseelie have not the power of illusion that the Seelie possess." He sat more comfortably on his throne, legs spread as some men do, as if to draw attention to their masculinity.

"So when I make love to them, I see them as they truly are?"

"You are part human, Meredith. You do not have the power of a true sidhe. I am sorry to say that, but it is well known that your magic is weak. They have fooled you, Meredith."

Each time he said my name, the air was a little thicker. Galen's hand slid up my leg until he found the top of my thigh-high hose, and could finally touch bare skin. The touch made me close my eyes for a moment, but it cleared my head. Once, what Taranis had said might have been true, but my magic had grown. I was no longer what I had been. Had no one told Taranis? It was not always wise to tell a king something he would not like. Taranis had treated me as lesser, or worse, all my life. To discover that I might be the heir to his rival court would mean that his treatment of me had been worse than politically incorrect. He had made me his enemy, or so he might think. He was far from the only noble in both courts to find themselves scrambling to make amends for a lifetime of ill treatment.

"I know what I hold in my hand, and in my body, Uncle."

"You do not know the pleasures of the Seelie Court, Meredith. Much awaits you, if only you could know it." His voice was like the ringing of bells. It was almost music on the very air.

Nelson started walking toward the mirror again. Her face was full of wonder. Whatever she saw was not real. I knew that now.

"I have told the lawyers twice that you are bespelling them, Uncle, but whatever you are doing to them makes them forget that. You make them forget the truth, Uncle."

The men in the room seemed to take a deep collective breath. "I have missed something," Biggs said.

"We all have," Veducci said. He went to Nelson, who was standing in front of the mirror, staring up as if the wonders of the universe were in that glass. He touched her shoulder, but she didn't react. She just kept gazing up at the king.

Veducci called back, "Cortez, help me with her."

Cortez looked like he'd been asleep, and had woken up somewhere else. "What the hell is going on?" he asked.

"King Taranis is using magic against us all."

"I thought the metal would protect us," Shelby said.

"He is the king of the Seelie Court," Veducci said. "Even the things I'm carrying aren't enough protection. I don't think a few office supplies are going to cut it today." He put a hand on each of the woman's shoulders and started pulling her back from the mirror. He called back over his shoulder, "Cortez, concentrate, help me with your assistant." He yelled it, and the shouting seemed to startle Cortez. He started forward, still looking startled, but he moved. He did what Veducci asked.

The two of them drew Nelson back from the mirror. She didn't fight them, but her face stayed upturned to Taranis's form as he sat above us all. That was interesting. I hadn't realized before that something about the mirror's perspective put him slightly higher than us. Of course, he was on his throne in the actual throne room. He was on a dais. He was, literally, looking down on us. The fact that I had only now realized that told me clearly that whatever spell he was throwing at me was having some effect. I was at the very least not noticing the obvious.

"You are breaking human law," Doyle said, "by using magic against them."

"I will not speak to the monsters of the queen's guard."

"Then speak to me, Uncle," I said. "You are breaking the law by the magic you are casting. You must stop it, or this interview is over."

"I swear by any oath you choose," Taranis said, "that I am not deliberately using magic on any full-blooded human in this room."

It was a pretty bit of lying, so close to the truth that it wasn't a lie at all. I laughed. Frost and Abe started, as if the sound hadn't been what they had expected. "Oh, Uncle, will you also take any oath of my choosing that you are not trying to bespell *me*?"

He gave me every ounce of that handsome, manly

face, but the beard sort of ruined it for me. I wasn't a fan of facial hair, but that could be because I grew up at Andais's court. For whatever reason, the queen's wish that her men not have beards and such had become a reality. Most of them couldn't have grown a good beard if they'd wanted to. Sometimes the queen's wish becomes reality in faerie. I'd seen the truth of that old saying in faerie for myself. I could police my words aloud, but when my very thoughts could become real, that had been terrifying. I was glad to be out of faerie and back to a more solid reality, where I could think what I liked and not have to worry about it becoming real.

I thought my own thoughts while Taranis pushed at me with his face, his eyes, the fantastic color of his hair. He pushed the spell he'd conjured at me. It was like a weight on the air, a thickness on my tongue, as if the very air was trying to become what he willed it. He was in faerie, and perhaps there, at his court, it would have worked exactly like that. Whatever he wanted from me, I might have been forced to give him. But I was in Los Angeles, not in faerie, and I was very glad to be here. Glad to be surrounded by man-made steel, concrete, and glass. There were fey who would have suffered illness simply by stepping into such a building. My human blood let me be unaffected. My men were sidhe, and that was also sterner stuff.

"Meredith, Meredith, come to me." He actually held his hand out to me, as if he would reach through the mirror and fetch me. Some of the sidhe could do just that. I didn't think Taranis was one of them.

Doyle stood, wrapping one hand around mine, but

standing feet apart, free hand loose at his side. I knew that stance. He was giving himself room to draw a weapon. It would almost have to be a gun because I had the hand he would have needed for the sword at his side.

Frost moved a little farther from the back of my chair, his hand still loosely on my shoulder. I didn't have to look at him to know that he was doing his own version of Doyle's preparations.

Galen stood up, which broke his contact with me. Taranis was suddenly edged with golden light. His eyes glowed with all the heat of green growing things. I started to rise from my chair. Rhys's hand pressed me down so that I couldn't move.

Doyle said, "Galen."

Galen went back to one knee, so he could touch my leg. The touch was enough. The glow faded, and the compulsion to stand faded. "This is a problem," I said.

Abe leaned against my other arm, causing his long striped hair to pool around the chair. He laughed, that warm masculine sound. "Merry, Merry, you need more men. It seems to be a theme with you."

I smiled, because he was too right.

"They would never arrive in time," Frost said.

I called out, "Biggs, Veducci, Shelby, Cortez, all of you."

Cortez had to stay with Nelson to keep her in her chair so she didn't go to the mirror, but the rest came to me.

"Meredith," Taranis said, "what are you doing?"

"Getting help," I said.

Doyle motioned the men to stand between us and

the mirror. They formed a wall of suits and bodies. It helped. What in Danu's name was the spell? I knew better than to invoke the name of the Goddess, I really did. But I had had a lifetime of saying it, like a human who says, "What, in the name of God?" You don't really expect God to answer, do you?

The room smelled of wild roses. A wind eased through the room as if someone had opened a window, though I knew no one had.

"Merry, cool it," Rhys said softly.

I knew what he meant. We had managed to keep some secrets from Taranis about just how active the Goddess was being for me. In faerie this was the beginning of full manifestation. If the Goddess—even a shadow of her—appeared in this room, Taranis would know. He would know that he needed to fear me. We weren't ready for that, not yet.

I prayed silently, "Goddess, please, save your power for later. Do not give our secret away to this man."

The smell of flowers grew stronger for a moment, but the wind began to die down. Then the smell began to fade like expensive perfume when the wearer leaves the room. I felt a tension go out of the men around me. The humans simply looked puzzled. "Your perfume is amazing, Princess," Biggs said. "What is it?"

"We'll talk about cosmetics later, Mr. Biggs," I said.

He looked embarrassed. "Of course. I am sorry. There is something about you people that just makes a poor lawyer forget himself." His words could be terribly true. I was hoping that no one in this room discovered just how true they could be.

"King of the Seelie Court, you insult me, and my court, and through me, my queen," I said.

"Meredith," his voice breathed through the room and caressed my skin, as if it had fingers.

Nelson whimpered.

"Stop it!" I yelled, and there was an echo of power to my voice. "If you do not cease trying to bespell me, I will have this mirror blanked, and there will be no more talks."

"They attacked a woman of my court. They must be given over to us for punishment."

"Give us proof of the crimes, Uncle."

"The word of a Seelie noble is proof enough," he said, and now his voice didn't sound seductive. It sounded angry.

"But the word of an Unseelie noble is worth nothing, is that it?" I asked.

"Our histories speak for themselves," he said.

I wished I could have afforded to have the lawyers move so that I could see Taranis, but I did not dare. With him blocked from my sight I could think. I could be angry.

"Then you call me a liar. Is that it, Uncle?"

"Not you, Meredith, never you."

"One of the men you accuse was with me when the Lady Caitrin claims he was raping her. He could not have been with her, and with me, at the same time. She lies, or she believes someone else's lie."

Doyle's hand tensed in mine. He was right. I'd said too much. Damnit, but these word games were hard. So many secrets to keep track of, and so hard to decide who knew what, and when to tell anyone anything.

"Meredith," he said, his voice pushing against me again, almost like a touch, "Meredith, come to me, to us."

Nelson made a sound like a soft scream. Cortez said, "I can't hold her!"

Shelby went to help him and I could suddenly see the mirror. I could see the tall, imposing figure. The sight was enough to add weight to his words, so it was like a push. "Meredith, come to me."

He held his hand out to me, and I knew I should take his hand, knew it.

The hands and bodies of my men pressed on my shoulders, arms, and legs, keeping me in my chair. I hadn't meant to, but I must have tried to rise. I don't think I would have gone to Taranis, but . . . but . . . It was good that I had hands to hold me down.

Nelson was screaming, "He's so beautiful, so beautiful! I have to go to him! I have to go to him!"

The woman's struggles sent Cortez and Shelby crashing to the floor with her.

"Security." Doyle's deep voice seemed to cut through the hysteria.

"What?" Biggs said, blinking too rapidly.

"Call security," Doyle said. "Send for help."

Biggs nodded, again too rapidly, but he walked to the telephone on his desk.

Taranis's voice came like something shining and hard, as if words could be stones thrown against your skin. "Mr. Biggs, look upon me."

Biggs hesitated, his hand hovering over the phone.

"Keep her in her seat," Doyle said, then he let me go to walk toward Biggs.

"He is a monster, Biggs," Taranis said. "Do not let him touch you."

Biggs turned wide-eyed and stared at Doyle. He backed away, hands up as if to ward off a blow. "Oh, my God," he whispered. Whatever he saw when he looked at my handsome captain was not what was there.

Veducci turned around from where he still stood in front of me. He took something from his pants pocket and threw it at the mirror. Dust and bits of herbs hit the surface, but they stuck to the glass as if it were water. The dry bits floated there, making small ripples on the supposedly solid surface. In that moment I knew two things: One, that Taranis could make the mirror a mode of travel between one place and another, an ability most had lost. Two, that he had truly meant "come to me." If I had gone to the mirror he could have pulled me through. Goddess help us.

Biggs seemed to wake from the spell, and grabbed the phone like he had a purpose.

"They are monsters, Meredith," Taranis said. "They cannot bear the touch of sunlight. How can anything that hides in the dark be ought but evil?"

I shook my head. "Your voice is only words now, Uncle. My men stand in sunlight, straight and proud."

The men in question looked at the king, except for Galen, who looked at me. It was a questioning look; was I better now? I nodded to him, shared with him a smile I'd been giving him since I was fourteen.

Taranis bellowed, "No, you will not bed the green-man, and bring life to the darkness. The Goddess has touched you, and we are the people of the Goddess."

I fought to keep my face blank, because that last comment could mean so many things. Did he already know that the chalice of the Goddess had come to me? Or had rumor planted something else in his head?

The scent of roses was back. Galen whispered, "I smell apple blossoms." Each of the men smelled the scent they had smelled when the Goddess had manifested for them. She was not just one goddess, but many. She was the face of all that was female. Not merely a rose, but all that grew upon the earth was in her scent.

Doyle came back toward us. "Is this wise, Meredith?"

"I don't know." But I stood, and they let their hands fall away from me. I stood in front of my uncle alone, with the men lined around me. The lawyers had moved back, frowning, puzzled, except for Veducci, who seemed to understand a great deal more than he should have.

"We are all people of the Goddess, Uncle," I said.

"The Unseelie are the dark god's children."

"There is no dark god among us," I said. "We are not Christians to people our underworld with terrors. We are children of the earth and sky. We are nature itself. There is no evil in us, only differences."

"They have filled your head with lies," he said.

"Truth is truth, whether in sunlight or darkest night. You cannot hide from the truth forever, Uncle."

"Where is the ambassador? He will search their bodies and find the horrors that the lady said were there."

There was a wind in the room now, a gentle breeze

that held that first warmth of spring. The scent of plants was mingling so that I could smell Galen's apple blossoms, Doyle's scent of autumn oak leaves and deep forest, and Rhys's sweet, cloying lily of the valley. Frost's was a taste like flavored ice, and Abe's was honeyed mead. The scents and tastes combined with the scent of wild roses.

"I smell flowers," Nelson said, her voice uncertain.

"What do you smell, Uncle?" I asked.

"I smell nothing but the corruption that stands behind you. Where is Ambassador Stevens?"

"He is being tended by a human wizard by now. They will cleanse him of the spell you placed upon him."

"More lies," he said, but there was something in his face that belied the strength of his protests.

"I have bedded these men. I know that their bodies hold no horrors."

"You are part human, Meredith. They have bewitched you."

The wind grew, and pushed at the surface of the mirror, with its bits of floating herbs, like wind on water. I watched the glass ripple. "What do you smell, Uncle?"

"I smell nothing but the stench of Unseelie magic." His voice was ugly with anger, and something else. I realized in that moment that Taranis was mad. I'd thought all his crimes had been arrogance, but looking into his face, my skin ran cold, even with the Goddess's touch. Taranis, King of the Seelie Court, was mad. It was there in his eyes, as if a curtain of sanity had lifted, and you couldn't miss it. There was something broken in his mind. Consort help us.

"You are not yourself, Your Majesty," Doyle said softly in his deep voice.

"You are the Dark, and I am the Light." Taranis raised his right hand, palm outward. I felt my guards move forward, toward me. They piled on top of me, pressed me to the floor, protecting me with their bodies. I felt heat, even through the flesh that protected me. I heard a noise, then Nelson was screaming and the lawyers were yelling. I spoke from the bottom of the pile with Galen pressed tightly against me. "What is it? What's happened?"

More male voices from the far door. Security had arrived, but what good were guns when someone could turn light itself into a weapon? Could you shoot through the mirror and hit anything on the other side? You could shoot out the mirror, but the bullet should stop at the glass. Taranis could hurt us. Could we hurt him?

Other voices seemed to be coming from in front of us, from the mirror. I tried to peer around Galen's arm, and the spill of Abe's long hair, but I was trapped in the dimness of their bodies, with the feel of more weight atop me, so that I was trapped and useless until the fight was over. I knew better than to order them off of me. If they thought it was safe, they'd move, and get me out of the room. Until that moment they were offering their lives to shield mine. Once I'd been relieved to know that. Now some of them were as precious to me as my own life. I had to know what was happening.

"Galen, what is happening?"

"I've got two layers of hair in front of me. I'm as blind as you are," he said.

Abe answered me. "Taranis's guard is trying to calm him."

"Why did Nelson scream?" I asked. My voice was squeezed a little from the weight of everyone atop me.

I heard Frost's voice yelling, "Get her out!"

I felt the movement before Galen grabbed my arm and pulled me to my feet. Abe had my other arm, and they were running for the far door. Running so fast they simply carried me between them.

Taranis screamed behind me, "Meredith, Meredith, no, they won't steal you from me!"

Light, golden-bright burning light, haloed behind us. The heat hit our backs first. I recognized Rhys's voice, yelling. I heard running behind us, but I knew that they would be too late. Unlike the movies, you can't outrun light. Not even the sidhe are that fast.

Chapter 5

ABE STUMBLED BESIDE ME, ALMOST JERKED ME down, but Galen swung me in his arms and sprinted for the door. He moved in a blur of speed that left the room in streamers of color. It was almost as if he didn't so much open the door and go through it but was moving so quickly that the door wasn't solid enough to stop us. I wasn't sure if the door opened or not, but we were on the other side of it. He turned me in his arms, so that he was carrying me like a child, or a bride on her wedding night. He moved down the hallway at a quick trot, away from the door and the sound of battle inside.

I could order Galen around more than most of the guard. I thought about ordering him to stop, but I wasn't certain what was happening. What if stopping was the wrong thing to do? What if the men I loved had given their lives to save me, and my stopping here would make that sacrifice worthless? It was one of those moments when I would have given almost anything not to be a princess. There were too many decisions, too many moments like this, where, lose or win, I would still lose.

He put me down, but kept my hand, as if he knew

I might go back. He'd pressed the button to call the elevator. I heard the machinery behind the doors whirring. I couldn't leave. I knew in that instant that when the doors opened, I wouldn't get on. I couldn't leave them. I couldn't leave them not knowing who was hurt, and how badly.

I stepped back, pulling on Galen's hand. He looked at me, his green eyes a little wide, his pulse still thudding against the side of his pale throat above the tie and collar the lawyers had made him wear. I shook my head.

"Merry, we have to go. My job is to keep you safe."

I just shook my head, and pulled on his hand. I tried to pull him back toward the doors that had closed behind us, or had not opened for us to go through. I still couldn't remember the door opening. The harder I thought about it, the less I seemed to remember of that one moment. It probably meant that Galen had, indeed, taken us through the door. Impossible, especially outside of faerie. Impossible, but it had happened, hadn't it?

The elevator doors opened. Galen stepped inside, but I kept his arm stretched out, because I did not step forward. "Merry, please," he said. "Please, you can't go back."

"I can't go forward either. If I am to be queen, then I have to stop running. To be ruler of a faerie court means I must be a warrior, too. I must be able to fight."

He tried to pull me inside. I put a hand on the wall to keep some leverage. "You are mortal," he said. "You could die."

"We could all die," I said. "The sidhe are no longer immortal. You know it and I know it."

He put a hand on the door that tried to close on him. "But we're harder to kill than a human. You injure like you're human, Merry. I can't allow you to go back inside that room."

I had a moment to understand that somehow this was a deciding moment. What kind of queen would I be? "*You* cannot allow? Galen, I must rule, or not rule. I cannot have it both ways." I pulled my hand free of his, and he didn't fight me.

He just looked at me, searched my face, as if he didn't know me. "You really are going back, and short of me throwing you over my shoulder, I can't stop you, can I?"

"No, you can't." I started walking back down the long hallway that we had just raced down.

Galen fell into step beside me. He unfastened the buttons of his jacket, and took out the gun he was wearing. He switched off the safety and chambered a round.

I reached behind my back to the nice little sideways holster, and took out my own gun. I'd replaced the Lady Smith that Doyle had taken off of me in faerie once before he was mine. It was the gun I was accustomed to, and a popular backup gun for a lot of police officers. Mostly male, strangely. The original push for the gun had turned off a lot of women. One of the colors the grip had come in had been pink. But in black or steeled blue it was still a good gun, and the one I was most used to. I didn't draw my gun as smoothly as Galen had, but it was a new holster, and a newish gun. It would take practice to be smooth. If Taranis was mad, I might get all the practice I needed.

Chapter 6

THE FAR SET OF ELEVATOR DOORS OPENED AND A SE-
curity guard stepped out. Emergency medical techs
rushed behind him with a wheeled gurney and medical bags. Two more EMTs with another gurney and
more equipment followed them. A second security
guard brought up the rear.

The EMTs hesitated for a second as the security
guard in the front pointed at the right door. The door
we'd come out of, of course. My pulse was in my
throat. Who was hurt, and how badly?

One of the EMTs, a woman, saw our guns. Without thinking, I pulled glamour around my hand so
that it looked as if I held a small clutch purse. The
woman frowned, shook her head, and followed her
partner.

Galen whispered, "Nice purse."

I glanced at his hand, and saw a small bouquet of
flowers. It looked real, even to me.

The security guard recognized us, or at least me.
"Princess, I can't let you go inside until we've secured
the area. Police are on the way."

"Do your job," I said. I hadn't argued with him. I
hadn't lied, but as soon as they went through the
door, I'd be right behind them. They'd called EMTs

and police. What in Danu's name had happened in there?

The doors hushed closed behind the gurney. Galen and I just started walking toward the doors. No discussion was necessary. I'd made up my mind, and he would follow my lead. There were moments when that was exactly what I needed from my men.

Galen opened the door, and used his body to shield me, just in case. If the fighting had still been ongoing, he'd have shoved me back. But I think we both believed that if the fighting was ongoing security would have had the EMTs wait for the police, not just let them inside.

Galen hesitated for a moment. I heard voices. Some panicked, some calm, all a little too loud. Abe's voice, saying, "Goddess, I wish I still drank."

A woman's voice. "We'll give you something for the pain."

I pushed at Galen's back, to let him know that I wanted to see. He took a breath deep enough that it shuddered through his body. Then he moved inside the room, and let me see what lay beyond.

One set of EMTs was clustered around Abe where he lay on his stomach nearest the door. They'd swept his long hair to one side, exposing scorch marks on his back. Taranis's hand of power had burned through suit jacket and shirt to the skin underneath.

One of the blue-suited security guards came toward us. "You need to wait outside until the police come, Princess Meredith."

Biggs, with his expensive suit singed on one sleeve, said, "Please, Princess, we can't guarantee your safety."

I looked at the big mirror. I heard Taranis's screams

in the distance, but he wasn't visible. He was screaming, "Let me go! I'm your king! Unhand me!"

The Seelie noble who stood front and center in the mirror was Hugh Belenus. He was, in fact, Sir Hugh, but didn't always insist on it like most of the Seelie Court. He was also one of the officers of Taranis's personal guard. Unlike the Unseelie Court, all the guards at Taranis's court were male. Even if you were a queen, you didn't get female guards. I had never realized before that Hugh resembled the king in one way. His long straight hair was the color of flames. Not sunset, like Taranis's, but the color of moving flame: red, yellow, and orange.

Frost and Rhys were standing in front of the mirror, talking with Hugh. Where was Doyle? He should have been with them. I had to walk farther into the room to see past the milling lawyers and security guards until I found the second set of EMTs with a second injured figure on a gurney. Doyle lay on the gurney, motionless. There was something wrong with his clothing. It was torn up, as if great claws had raked it. The world narrowed down, as if the edges of the room were collapsing, down, down, until all I could see clearly was him. In that moment, I didn't care about the mirror, or Hugh, or that Taranis had finally done something that he couldn't hide from the rest of the sidhe. There was just that still dark form on the gurney and nothing else.

Galen stayed with me, his free hand on my arm. I wasn't sure if he was guiding me, or holding me back. I stood beside the gurney, staring down at the tall muscled form of my Darkness. Doyle, who had fought a thousand battles before I was born. Doyle, who had seemed indestructible like his namesake. You cannot kill the dark, it is always with us.

His clothing wasn't torn; it was burned like Abe's. His black skin just didn't show the marks from a distance the way Abe's paler skin had, but there were shallow burns across his upper chest and one shoulder. And his face—one half of his face was bandaged from forehead to nearly chin. I knew that the fact that they'd tended his face first meant it was worse than his chest. There was a bag of clear liquid on top of his body. A flexible tube ran from it to his arm, where there was tape and a syringe.

I looked at the two techs. "Will he . . . ?"

"Unless shock sets in, it's not life-threatening," one of them said. Then they were pushing him toward the doors. "But we've got to get him to the burn unit."

"Burn unit," I repeated. I felt slow and stupid.

"We've got to go," the other tech said, and his voice was gentle, as if he knew I was in shock.

Rhys was beside me. "Merry, we need you at the mirror. Galen can go with them."

I shook my head.

Rhys grabbed me by the shoulders and turned me away from Doyle so I had to look into his face. "We need you to be our queen right now, not Doyle's lover. Can you do that, or are we on our own here?"

Anger was instant, anger that made my blood run hot. I started to say, "How dare you," but just then Taranis yelled, "How dare you touch your king!" I swallowed the words, but couldn't keep the anger off my face.

"Merry, I'm sorry. I'm more sorry than I can say, but we need you now."

My voice came tight, warm, but controlled, very controlled, "Call the house. Send one of the healers to the hospital, or maybe both the healers." I nodded, the anger beginning to fade under the thought that I didn't know how bad Doyle was hurt, or Abe. "Both," I said.

"I'll call them, I promise, but Frost needs you at the mirror."

I nodded. "I understand."

Rhys kissed me on the forehead. I blinked up at him. He got his cell phone out of his pocket. I told Galen, "Go with them to the hospital."

"My duty is you."

"Your duty is to go where your princess tells you to go. Now do it. Please, Galen, there's no time."

He hesitated for a breath, then he gave a nod that was almost a bow, and trotted after the rapidly moving gurney. I hadn't gotten to kiss Doyle good-bye. No, it wasn't good-bye. He was one of the sidhe. The greatest magicians and warriors that faerie had ever known. He would not die from burns, not even magical ones. I believed my own words in the front of my head, but the back of the mind is a cluttered, dark place that has nothing to do with logic and everything to do with fear.

I made myself start walking toward Frost's tall figure. One step at a time. I realized I had the gun still naked in my hand. The glamour hid it, but my concentration was bad. Did I want the Seelie to see the gun? Did I care? No. Should I care? Probably.

I moved my jacket aside to put the gun back in its holster. I had to stop walking to do it, but I put it away. One of the main reasons I did it was because if

Taranis managed to break free of his men and come back to the mirror, I didn't trust myself not to use the gun. That, I knew, would be bad. No matter how momentarily satisfying it might be, I was a princess, trying to be a queen, and that meant I couldn't indulge in fits of temper. They were too costly, as today's little disaster had proven. Damn Taranis, damn him, for not stepping down years ago.

I took a deep breath that shook around the edges. My stomach rolled with all the emotions I couldn't afford right now. I walked toward Frost and the mirror and Sir Hugh. I prayed to the Goddess that I wouldn't fall apart in front of the Seelie. Andais had temper tantrums that were infamous. Now Taranis had shown himself to be even more unstable. I walked to the mirror and prayed that I would be the ruler we needed right now. I prayed that I wouldn't fall apart or throw up. Nerves, just nerves. Please, Goddess, let Doyle be all right.

Once I said the prayer I truly meant, I felt calmer. Yes, I wanted to be a good queen. Yes, I wanted to show the Seelie that I wasn't as crazy as my aunt and uncle, but truly, none of it mattered to me as much as the man they'd just carted away on a gurney.

It wasn't the way a queen thought. It was the way a woman thought, and to be queen means you have to be queen first and everything else second. My father had taught me that. Taught me that before an assassin had killed him. I pushed the thought away, and went to stand by my Killing Frost.

I would be the queen that my father had raised me to be. I would not embarrass Doyle by being less than he'd told me I could be.

I stood straight, drawing myself up to every inch of height that I had. The three-inch heels helped, although standing beside Frost's tall figure, I couldn't help but seem delicate.

But I stood there and did my duty and it tasted like ashes in my mouth.

Chapter 7

SIR HUGH BELENUS GAVE A LOW BOW THAT SHOWED that his fire-colored hair had started the day in a complicated braid, but singed ribbons trailed from its remnants. When he stood up, I could see that the front of his tunic, all the way through two layers of undershirts, had been blasted apart to expose the pale golden skin underneath. The clothing was ruined, scorched, but his body seemed untouched.

"Sir Hugh stood in front of Taranis at the end," Frost said. "He took the brunt of the blow meant for Abeloec."

"What am I to say to that?" I asked, and my voice sounded completely normal. The very normality of it was almost shocking. A little voice in my own head thought, how can I sound so calm? Training? Shock?

"If Sir Hugh were not one of the elder sidhe, you could thank him for risking himself to save our warriors," Frost said.

I looked up at the tall man beside me. I stared all the way up to those gray eyes and found that they reflected a bare tree in a winter landscape, like a tiny snow globe caught in his eyes. Only his own magic or anxiety would fill his eyes with that image. Always before it had dizzied me to stare into Frost's eyes when they filled with that other place. Today, it seemed cool, calming. Today, he had the icy strength of winter in his eyes. A coldness that protected you, kept your emotions from eating you alive. I understood in that moment part of what had let Frost survive the queen's petty torments. He had embraced the coldness inside.

I touched his arm, and the world was a little steadier. There was something moving in the landscape of his eyes; something white, and horned. I had a glimpse of a white stag before Frost bent to kiss me. It was a chaste kiss, but that one gentle touch let me know that he understood what the calmness cost me. That kiss let me know that he understood what Doyle meant to me, and what he meant to me, and what he did not.

I turned back to the mirror with Frost's hand in mine.

Sir Hugh said, "I saw a vision in the sunlight, a white stag. It walked ghostlike just behind the two of you."

"How long has it been since you saw such a vision?" Frost asked.

Hugh blinked black eyes at me, but there were orange sparks and swirls in that blackness, like the ashes of a fire long banked. "A long time."

"You don't seem surprised at your vision, Sir Hugh," I said.

"There are swans in the lake near the Seelie mound. Swans with gold chains around their necks. They flew above us for the first time ever in this country, the night of your battle with the wild hunt."

Rhys's voice came casually from behind us. "Have

a care what you say, Hugh. We have lawyers present." Rhys came to stand on my other side, but made no move to take my other hand.

"Yes, our king has chosen a most regrettable moment to show this side of himself."

"Regrettable moment," I said, and didn't try to keep the sarcasm out of my voice. "Such mild words for what has just happened."

"I cannot afford anything but mild words, Princess," Hugh said.

"This insult to us cannot go unanswered," I said, voice still calm.

"If I were speaking to the Queen of Air and Darkness, I would worry about a war, or perhaps a personal challenge between monarchs. But I have heard that Princess Meredith NicEssus is a more temperate creature than her aunt, or even her uncle."

"A temperate creature?" I said.

"Temperate woman, then," Hugh said, and gave another low bow. "No insult was meant in my choice of words, Princess. I beg you not to take offense."

"I will do my best not to take offense, except where it is given," I said.

Hugh stood, and his handsome face, with its small neat beard and mustache, fought to not look worried. Hugh had been a god of fire once, and that was not a temperate creature. Many of the elemental deities seemed to take on the aspects of their elements. I had seen that intimately with Mistral, once a god of storms.

"And I," Hugh said, "will endeavor not to give offense."

Nelson's voice came from behind us. "How can

you be so calm? Didn't you see what just happened? They took your lovers out on stretchers." Her voice held an edge of hysteria that promised to get worse.

I heard soothing male voices, but didn't try and catch the words. As long as they kept her quiet and away from me, I no longer cared. There would be no charges brought against my men for the supposed attack on Lady Caitrin. Because if the Seelie played hardball, we could bury them with what Taranis had just done. And we had some of the top lawyers in the country as our witnesses. If Doyle and Abe hadn't gotten hurt, it would have been a lovely thing.

The far doors opened, and more EMTs came through. The police were here. I had no idea what had taken them so long to arrive. But maybe my sense of time had been affected. Shock can do that. It wouldn't even do me any good to look at a clock, because I hadn't looked at one before the event. For all I knew only minutes had passed. It may have just seemed longer.

"What are we to do about this incident, Sir Hugh?" I asked.

"There is no way to keep it quiet," he said. "Too many humans know. More will find out when your men reach the hospital. It will be the greatest scandal the Seelie Court has had in this country."

"Your king will deny that he did this," I said. "He will try and blame us somehow."

"He has not tried his rather human version of the truth since you helped release the wild magic, Princess Meredith."

"What does that mean exactly, Sir Hugh?" I asked.

"It means as much as I dare about my opinion of

my king. It means that when you released the wild magic it awakened some . . ." he seemed to search for a word. "Certain things. Things that do not take well to oathbreakers, or other things." He frowned as if even he wasn't happy with what he'd just said.

"Oathbreakers and liars fear the wild hunt," Frost said.

"I did not say that," Hugh said.

"I haven't heard this much verbal tap dancing from a Seelie noble in a long time," Rhys said.

Hugh smiled at him. "You haven't been at court in a long time."

"Did you know what Taranis was doing?" I asked.

"We had suspicions that the king was not himself."

"So polite," I said. "So mild."

"But accurate," Hugh said.

"What else has happened for you to be so cautious, firelord?" Rhys asked.

"I think that is a conversation for a more private audience, pale lord."

"I can't argue with that," Rhys said.

I was beginning to get the feeling that Rhys and Hugh knew each other better than I'd realized.

"What do we do about this day, and this moment?" I asked.

"I am but a humble lord of the sidhe," Hugh said. "I do not carry the blood of the royal line in my body."

"What does that mean?" I asked.

"It means that the humans aren't the only ones who have laws." Hugh stared at me with his black-and-orange eyes. He seemed to be trying to tell me something without saying it out loud.

"The Seelie would never go for it," Rhys said.

"Go for what?" I asked, looking from one to the other.

"The king lost his temper with one of the serving wenches," Hugh said. "A huge green dog appeared between him and the target of his anger."

"A Cu Sith," I said.

"Yes, a Cu Sith, after all these long years, a green dog of faerie is among us again, and protects those who need protecting. It would not allow the king to strike the serving girl. She seemed more terrified that he would blame her for the dog, but the king lost his anger in the face of the great dog."

I remembered the dog from the night of the wild hunt. The night when wild magic had been everywhere. Huge black dogs had appeared, and when some touched them, they had changed to other dogs. Dogs out of legend, and a Cu Sith had run out into the night toward the Seelie Court.

"I would be interested to see whose hand the Cu Sith would call master, or mistress," I said.

"If we invoke this law," Rhys said, "it will be civil war in your own court, Hugh."

"Perhaps it is time for a little civil disobedience," Hugh said.

"What law?" I asked.

Rhys turned to me. "If the monarch is unfit to rule, the nobles of the court can vote him, or her, incompetent. They can force him or her to step down. Andais abolished the rule in her court, but Taranis never bothered. He was too confident that his court loved him."

"So, you're saying, what?" I asked. "That Hugh

force a vote among the nobles and they choose a new king?" It had possibilities, depending on whom they chose.

"Not exactly, Merry," Rhys said

"Is she always this humble?" Hugh asked.

"Often," Rhys said.

"What?" I asked.

Frost said, "The Seelie nobles will never accept her."

"You don't know what has been happening here since she unlocked the magic. I think the vote may go in her favor."

"The vote go in my favor." I finally caught on. "Oh, no, you aren't serious."

"Yes, Princess Meredith, if you will agree to accept it, I will endeavor to make you our queen."

I just stared at him. I tried to gather my wits, my training at court, and all I could manage to say was, "How sure are you that this will work?"

"Sure enough to speak of it."

"That means very sure," Rhys said.

"I don't believe the Seelie will accept me as their queen, Hugh. But I know that before such a thing goes forward we must speak to our queen."

"Speak to Andais if you must, but whatever you are to the Unseelie, you have brought back the old magic to the outside of the hill. Inside we are still dead and dying, but our spies tell us that your faerie mound grows, lives. Even the mound of the sluagh is alive once more. King Sholto brags of your magic, Princess."

"King Sholto of the sluagh is a kind man."

Hugh laughed, an abrupt, surprised sound. "Kind.

The king of the sluagh? The nightmares of all faerie, and you call him kind."

"I find him so," I said.

Hugh nodded. "Kindness. It is not an emotion we have had in this court in years. I, for one, would like more of it."

"I understand that," Rhys said.

Hugh looked off to one side of the mirror, where we could not see. "I must go. Talk to your queen, but when the rest of the nobles know what Taranis did to Lady Caitrin, and that other nobles helped him, the vote will go against him."

"Did he get the lady to lie, or did he bespell her, too?" Rhys asked.

"He used his illusions to make three of our nobles appear as the three of you. But he made them monstrous, with projections and spines and . . ." Hugh shivered. "Her body was quite broken. She is even now still confined to her bed, even with our healers." He looked at me. "If you have need of healers for your men, but ask and it will be yours."

"We will ask if we need them," I said, and I fought the urge to say thank you because Hugh was old enough to be offended by it.

"What did the king hope to gain by such evil?" Frost asked.

"We aren't certain," Hugh said, "but we can prove that he did it, and lied about it, and that the nobles involved lied as well. It is an abuse of magic that has almost no precedent among us."

"And you can prove it?" Rhys asked.

"We can." He looked off to the side again. He turned back to us, but there was a look of concern on

his face. "I must go. Talk to your queen. Be ready."
He gestured, and we were looking at our own reflections.

"This smacks of court intrigue," Frost said.

I watched Rhys and myself both nod solemnly in the mirror. Neither of us looked very happy.

Veducci came up behind us. "You have been given amazing news, Princess Meredith. Why don't you look happier?"

I answered his reflection rather than turning around. "It has been my experience that court intrigue usually ends badly. The Seelie Court has treated me worse than the Unseelie Court all of my life. I do not believe that a few new magics will make me queen of a people who despise me. If by some miracle it happens as Sir Hugh has stated, then I will have two sets of assassins to deal with instead of one." As soon as I said it, I knew I shouldn't have. My only excuse was the total shock of what had just happened.

Rhys spoke quickly. "I assume the charges against me and my friends are dropped."

Veducci turned to him. "If what Sir Hugh has just said is true, then yes, but until the lady herself drops the charges, they don't go away."

"Even with what Hugh just said?" Frost asked.

"As you pointed out, court intrigue can get ugly. People lie."

"The sidhe do not lie," I said.

Veducci stared hard at me. "Have there been assassination attempts on your life other than the one that happened at the airport, where you were shot at?"

"She can't answer that without talking to Queen Andais," Rhys said. He put his arm across my shoulders. Frost did not give up my hand, so I stood pressed to both of them. I couldn't tell if Rhys's gesture was to reassure me or himself. It had been one of those days when we all needed a hug.

"You do realize that that *is* an answer?" Veducci asked.

"What kind of lawyer knows to carry just the right herbs in his pocket to disrupt such a spell?" I said.

"I don't know what you mean," he said with a smile.

"Liar." I whispered it, because I heard steps behind us.

Biggs and Shelby were there. Biggs's suit jacket was gone. His shirtsleeve was rolled back, and there was a bandage on his arm. "I think King Taranis's actions today put his accusations against my clients in serious doubt."

"We can't say yes to that without talking to some . . ." Shelby stopped, cleared his throat, and tried again, "We'll get back to you." He gathered his assistant and went for the door.

"The nice young woman who fixed up my arm says I have to ride with them to the hospital," Biggs said. "My assistant will take you to a room where you can rest and gather yourselves before you have to leave."

"Thank you, Mr. Biggs," I said. "I am sorry that the hospitality of faerie was not up to its usual standards."

He laughed. "That is the most polite way I have ever heard anyone apologize for such a fucking mess." He raised his injured arm a little. "It was hard on me, and on your men, but if your uncle, the king, had to choose a moment to have his meltdown, this wasn't a bad time for it. It certainly hurt his case and helped ours."

"I suppose that's one way of looking at it," I said.

Rhys hugged me, bumping his cheek against my hair. "Cheer up, sweets, we won."

"No, the Seelie came to the rescue and saved our asses," I said.

The female EMT came to touch Biggs's shoulder. "We're ready to go."

Nelson was strapped to a gurney and looked unconscious. Cortez was beside her, looking more annoyed than worried.

"Did Ms. Nelson get burned, too?" I asked.

Biggs opened his mouth to answer, but the med techs made him go with them. Veducci answered me. "She seems to be having an adverse reaction to the spell that the king put on you."

The look he gave me was entirely too knowledgeable. He knew magic. He wasn't a registered practitioner, but that didn't mean anything. A lot of humans who had psychic ability chose not to use it as a job.

"A look like that used to get a question," Rhys said.

"What question would that be?" Veducci asked.

"Which eye can you see me with?" Rhys said.

I tensed beside him, because I knew how this story always ended.

Veducci grinned. "The answer you're supposed to give is neither."

"The truth is both eyes," Frost said, and his voice was way too solemn for comfort.

Veducci's grin faded around the edges. "None of

you are trying to hide what you are. Everyone can see you."

"Cheer up, Veducci," Rhys said. "The days when we used to put your eye out for seeing the wee folk are long past. The sidhe never held with that. If you could see us, the biggest danger from the sidhe was abduction. We were always intrigued with the humans who could see faerie." Rhys's voice was light and teasing, but there was an edge of seriousness to it that made Veducci look wary.

Was I missing part of this conversation? Maybe. Did I care? A little. But I'd care more after I got to the hospital and checked on Doyle and Abe.

"You can all be mysterious later," I said. "I want to go check on Doyle and Abe now."

Veducci reached into his jacket pocket and held something out to me. "I thought you might want these."

They were Doyle's sunglasses. One side of them was melted, as if some hot giant hand had crushed them into melted wax. My stomach fell into my shoes, then back up to my throat. I thought for a second that I'd throw up, then my head thought I just might faint. I hadn't seen Doyle's face underneath the bandages. How bad was it?

"Do you need to sit down, Princess?" Veducci asked, and he was all solicitous. He actually moved to take my arm as if I wasn't already standing between two strong arms.

Frost moved so that the lawyer couldn't touch me. "We have her."

Veducci took a step back. "I see that." He gave a small bow and went back to the security guards who were talking to the police. A uniformed officer was waiting for us.

"I need to ask you a few questions," he said.

"Can you ask them on the way to the hospital? I need to check on my men."

He hesitated. "Do you need a ride to the hospital, Princess Meredith?"

I glanced at the clock behind the desk. We'd been driven here by Maeve Reed's driver in her limo. He'd planned on doing some errands for Ms. Reed, then coming back to pick us up in about three hours, or at least check on us. Surprisingly, it hadn't been three hours yet. "A ride would be lovely. Thank you, Officer," I said.

Chapter 8

DOYLE AND ABE HAD A ROOM TO THEMSELVES IN THE hospital, though when we hit the door with our nice escort of uniformed officers it was hard to tell who belonged in the room and who didn't. There was a crowd of my other guards and way more medical staff than needed to be here, and predominantly female. And why did the uniforms who drove us come inside? Apparently, the police were a little fuzzy on whether the attack on my guards was another attempt on my life. Better safe than sorry, they seemed to think. Seeing the number of men Rhys had ordered to meet us at the hospital, apparently he had thought the same thing.

Abe was on his stomach, trying to talk to all the pretty nurses. He was in pain, but he was still who and what he'd always been. He had once been the god Accasbel, the physical embodiment of the cup of intoxication. It could make you a queen. It could inspire poetry, bravery, or madness. So the legends said. He'd opened the first pub in Ireland, and was the original party boy. If he hadn't been wincing every so often, I might have said he was having a good time. Instead, he might just be putting on a brave face. Or he might be enjoying the attention. I still didn't understand Abe well enough to guess.

I had to weave my way through the crowd of my own lovely guards. On most days, I might have noticed them, but today they were just blocking my view of the one guard I wanted to see.

Some of them tried to speak to me, but when I answered no one, they finally seemed to understand. They parted like a curtain of flesh, and I could finally see the other bed.

Doyle lay terribly still. There was an I.V. hooked up to one arm, feeding him clear fluid. There was a small drip with knobs, which probably meant that some of the clear liquid was a painkiller. Burns hurt.

Hafwen stood tall and blond and beautiful beside his bed. She wore a dress that had been in style in the 1300s or earlier, a plain sheath that clung in all the right places, but was short enough at the ankles to give her room to move. When I'd met her she'd been in armor, a guard in my cousin Cel's service. He'd forced her to kill things for him and forbade her to use her amazing healing gifts because she refused his bed. True healers were rare among the sidhe now, and even the queen had been shocked at the waste of Hafwen's talents. She'd been one of the female guards who had left Cel's service to join me in exile. Queen Andais was also shocked, I think, at the number of female guards who chose exile over staying to serve Cel. I wasn't shocked. Cel had come out of his months of imprisonment crazier and more sadistic than when he'd gone in. He'd been put away for trying to kill me, among other things. His freedom had been the deciding factor of me going back into exile.

The queen admitted in private that she could not guarantee my safety around her son.

Hafwen and others had come west with tales of what Cel did to the first female guard he took to his bed. It was the stuff of serial killers. Except she was sidhe, and she would heal, she would survive. Survive to be his victim again, and again, and again.

At last count I had a dozen female "volunteers." A dozen in a month's time. There would be more, because Cel was insane, and the women had a choice now. Andais hadn't understood how so many of them could prefer exile to Cel's attentions, but then the queen had always overestimated his charms and underestimated his repulsiveness. Don't let me mislead you. Prince Cel was as handsome as most of the Unseelie sidhe, but pretty is as pretty does, and what he did was ugly.

I stood by Doyle's side, but he didn't know I was there. If I still had the wild magic of faerie at my command, I could have healed him in an instant. But the magic had spilled out into the autumn night and done wonders and miracles, and was still working them in faerie. However, we weren't in faerie. We were in Los Angeles in a building built of metal and man-made things. Some magics would not even work in such a place.

"Hafwen," I said, "why have you not tried to heal him?"

A doctor short enough that he had to look up at Hafwen but could look down at me said, "I cannot allow the use of magic on my patient."

I looked at him, gave him the full-on stare with the triple irises. Some humans, if they've never had to meet our eyes, are bothered by it. It can be a help in negotiations, or persuading. "Why can you not," I read his nameplate, "Dr. Sang?"

"Because it is magic that I do not understand, and if I do not understand a treatment I cannot authorize it."

"So if you understood you'd stop interfering," I said.

"I am not interfering, Princess Meredith, you are. This is a hospital, not a royal bedchamber. Your men are disrupting the operation of this hospital by their very presence."

I smiled at him, and felt my eyes stay cool and untouched by it. "My men have done nothing. It is your staff that is failing. I thought all the hospitals in the area had been briefed about what to do if one of us was brought in. Didn't they tell you what to wear, or carry, to help the staff function?"

"The fact that your men are using active glamour to bespell our nurses and female doctors is an insult," Dr. Sang said.

Galen spoke from the other side of the room. He was slumped down in one of two chairs. "I've told him over and over that we aren't doing anything. It isn't active glamour, but he won't believe me."

He looked tired, a tightness around his eyes and mouth that I hadn't noticed before. The sidhe don't age, really, but there are signs of wear. The way a diamond can be cut by the right kind of blade.

"I do not have time to explain to you, but I won't allow you to stand between my people and my healers," I said.

"She admits," he motioned at Hafwen, "that her

powers are not at full strength outside of faerie. She's not certain she can heal him. The more often his bandages are opened, especially with this many people here, the greater the chances that he'll get a secondary infection," Dr. Sang said.

"The sidhe do not get infections, Doctor," I said.

"Forgive me if I'm a little skeptical about that, Princess, but this man is my patient," Dr. Sang said. "I am responsible for him."

"No, Doctor, he is mine. He is my Darkness, my right hand. He would see himself as responsible for me, but I am trying to be his queen, which makes me responsible for all my people." I reached out to touch his hair, but drew back. I did not want to wake him if all we could offer was pain. For the healing we would disturb him, but simply because I could not bear to be so close and not touch him was not reason enough to wake him from the sleep that the drugs and shock had given him.

My hand ached to touch him, but I forced my hand into a fist at my side. Rhys's hand wrapped around my fist. I looked into his single triblue eye, his handsome face with the scars that had taken his other eye, only partially hidden by the white patch he'd worn today. I'd never known Rhys any other way. The face that rose above me when we made love, or looked up at me from the bed, was this face, scars and all. It was simply Rhys.

I touched his cheek. Would I love Doyle less if he was scarred? No, though it would be a loss for both of us. It would mean that the face I had grown to love would be forever changed. But damnit, he was sidhe. A simple burn shouldn't have damaged him like this.

As if Rhys read some of my thoughts, he said, "He will live."

I nodded. "But I want him healed."

"What about me?" Abe called from the other bed, and as so often, he sounded vaguely drunk. It was almost as if he'd spent so many years inebriated that he fell back into the behavior of it. A dry drunk, I think they called it, as if even without the drink and drugs, he wasn't entirely sober.

"I want you healed as well," I said. "Of course I do." But Abe knew where he stood in my affections, and he wasn't in my top five. He was okay with that. He, like many of the guards who had only been with us a few weeks, was just so happy to be having sex again that he hadn't had time to get his ego bruised by the competition.

"I really must insist, Princess, that you and all your men leave," Dr. Sang said.

The uniformed officer, Officer Brewer, said, "Sorry, Doctor, but more guards is okay with us."

"Are you saying that these men may be attacked inside the hospital itself?" he asked.

Officer Brewer looked at his partner, Officer Kent. Kent, the taller of the two, just shrugged. I think they'd been told to stay near me, but not what to tell civilians. We'd stopped counting as civilians, to an extent, when we were attacked. Now we were in a different category for the police. Potential victims, maybe.

"Dr. Sang," Frost said, "I am in command of the princess's guard until my captain tells me otherwise. My captain lies here." He motioned toward Doyle.

"You may be in charge of the guard, but you are

not in charge of this hospital." The doctor didn't even come up to Frost's collarbone. He had to tilt his head back at an extreme angle to look the taller man in the face, but he did it, and he gave him a look that clearly said that he wasn't backing down.

"We do not have time for this, Princess," Hafwen said.

I looked into her tricolored eyes: a ring of blue, silver, and an inner ring of lights as if light could be a color. "What do you mean?"

"We are outside faerie. That limits me as a healer. We stand in a building of metal and glass, a man-made structure. That also limits my powers. The longer the injury stays untended, the harder it will be for me to do anything for it."

I turned to Dr. Sang. "You heard her, Doctor. You need to let my healer do her job."

"I could remove him from the room," Frost said.

"I'm not sure we can allow that," Officer Brewer said, sounding uncertain.

"How would you remove him?" Officer Kent asked.

"Good question," Officer Brewer said. "We can't really condone violence against the doctors."

"We don't need violence," Rhys said. He nuzzled my ear, playing with my hair. That one small touch made me shiver a little.

I turned so I could see his face more clearly. "Wouldn't that be unethical, too?" I asked.

"Do you really want Doyle to look like me? I know he doesn't want to lose an eye. It plays hell with your depth perception." He smiled and tried to make it a joke, but there was a bitterness to it that no smile could hide.

I kissed the bow of his mouth. He had one of the most beautiful mouths of all the men. Pouting and full, it softened the boyish handsomeness of his face into something more sensual.

He pushed me away, toward the doctor. "The doctor doesn't understand, and we don't have time to talk it to death, Merry."

"Um," Officer Brewer said, "what are you planning to do, Princess Meredith? I mean. . . ." He looked at his partner. It was obvious that they felt out of their depth. Truthfully, I was surprised that there weren't more police here already. There were uniforms at the door, but no detectives, no higher echelon. It was almost as if the top brass was afraid of us right now. Not afraid of the danger. They were police; it was what they did. But afraid of the politics.

By now the rumors had spread. Goddess knew that King Taranis attacking Princess Meredith was juicy enough. But stories have a tendency to grow in the telling. Who knew what the police had been told by now? This case wasn't just a hot one, it was a potential career killer. Think about it—letting Princess Meredith get killed or having King Taranis injured on your watch. Either way, you were screwed.

"Doctor Sang," I said.

He turned to me, still frowning angrily. "I don't care how many policemen back you on this, there are too many people in this room for effective treatment."

I closed my eyes and let out a breath. Most humans have to do something to conjure magic. I spent most of my life shielding so I didn't perform magic by accident. Before my hands of power had come to me, just months ago, I spent time trying not to be distracted by passing spirits, small everyday wonders. Now all the practice keeping things out helped me keep things in, because my natural talents—or maybe my genetic heritage—had been kicked up a notch along with everything else.

Rhys said, "Stand back, boys."

The men moved back, and moved the two police officers with them. They gave the doctor and me a small circle of space. He glanced at them, eyes puzzled. "What's going on?"

I raised a hand to touch his face, but he grabbed my wrist to keep me from doing it. The problem for him was that I didn't need to touch him. Him touching me was just fine.

His eyes widened. A look of near terror transfixed his face. He wasn't looking at me, but somewhere deep inside himself. I was trying to be gentle, to use just enough and no more of the Seelie side of my nature. But fertility magic is sometimes an unpredictable thing, and I was nervous.

Dr. Sang whispered, "Oh my God."

"Goddess," I whispered, and leaned in toward him. I drew him away from the beds, away from Hafwen. I never touched him, only drew my arm away. His own grip on my wrist drew him with me.

I touched his face with my free hand. I hadn't thought about what lay on that hand. Inside faerie the queen's ring, as it had come to be called, was magical. In the human world, it was an ancient piece of metal, so old that the metal was soft. The ring was worn into an odd shape from centuries of being on the hand of one woman or another. Andais had admitted that she had taken it from the hand of a Seelie whom she had killed in a duel, a fertility goddess. I think Andais had taken the ring because she hoped it would aid the fertility of her own court, but she was a power of war and destruction. She was carrion crow and raven. The ring was not at its best with her.

She had given it to me to show her favor. To prove that she had indeed chosen her hated niece as a potential heir. But my power was not the battlefield and death.

I touched the man's face with that old metal, and it flared to life. For a second I thought it would tell me if he was fertile the way it could with the men of our court, but that wasn't what the ring wanted from Dr. Sang.

I saw what he loved. He loved his job. He loved being a doctor. It consumed him. I also saw a woman, delicate, with shoulder-length black hair shining in the sunlight from large windows that looked out on the street. She was surrounded by flowers. She may have worked there. She smiled at a customer, but it was all silent as if the sound didn't matter. I saw her face brighten, like the sky after rain when the sun breaks through, as she looked up and saw Dr. Sang come through the door. The ring knew that the woman loved him. I saw two yards that bordered each other here in Los Angeles. I saw younger versions of the two of them. They'd grown up together. They'd even dated in high school, but he loved medicine more than any woman.

"She loves you," I said.

His voice came strangled. "How are you doing that?"

"You see it, too, then," I said, voice soft.

"Yes," he whispered.

"Don't you want children, a family?"

I saw her, standing in the shop again. She was staring out at the passing tourists. She held a cup of tea with both hands. Two shadowy figures hovered around her, one boy, one girl.

"What is that?" he asked, voice so full of emotion that he sounded in pain.

"The children you would have with her."

"Are they real?" he whispered.

"They are, but they will only be flesh if you love her."

"I can't. . . ."

The phantom boy by her side turned and seemed to look directly at us. It was unnerving, even to me. The doctor trembled under my hand. "Stop it," he said. "Stop it."

I drew my hand away from him, but he still had his own hand on my wrist. "You must let me go," I said.

He looked at his hand as if he hadn't known that it was there. He released me. His eyes were almost panicked. He looked behind me at Doyle and said, "Get away from him!"

One of the female doctors said, "Dr. Sang, it's a miracle. He can use his eye again."

He went to join the other nurses and doctors hovering around Doyle's bed. He had to shine his own light in Doyle's now-opened eye. He shook his head. "This isn't possible."

"Will you allow me to do the impossible on Abe-loec now?" Hafwen asked with a small smile.

I'd have thought he would have argued, but he just nodded. Hafwen went to the other bed, and I got to do what I'd wanted to do from the moment I stepped into the room. I touched Doyle's hair. He looked up at me. His face was still blistered and raw, but the black eye that stared up at me was whole. He smiled until the corner of his mouth met the burns, then he stopped. He didn't wince, he simply stopped the smile. He was the Darkness. The dark doesn't flinch.

My eyes were hot, and my throat was so tight I couldn't breathe. I tried not to cry, because I knew that if I did I would lose control.

He laid his hand on mine where it lay on the bed railing. Just his hand on mine, and the first tears squeezed out.

Dr. Sang was beside us again. He said, "What you showed me was a trick to get me to let your healer work on him."

I found my voice, thick with tears. "It was no trick but a true seeing. She loves you. There will be two children, a boy first, then a girl. She is in her flower shop. If you call now, you may get her while she is still drinking tea."

He looked at me as if I had said something frightening. "I don't think a man can be both a good doctor and a good husband."

"That is for you to decide, but she will miss you."

"How can she miss me if I have never been hers?"

The nurses were very quiet listening to all of this. Goddess knew what hospital gossip would make of it.

"I did not see another face in her heart. If you are not hers, I am not certain she will ever marry."

"She should marry someone. She should be happy."

"She thinks you would make her happy."

"She's wrong," he said, but more like he was trying to convince himself.

"Perhaps, or perhaps you are the one who has been wrong."

He shook his head. He gathered himself to himself like other people would pull a warm blanket around their shoulders. I watched him rebuild his doctor persona. "I'll have one of the nurses re-dress the wounds. Can your healer do this to human wounds?"

"Sadly, our healing magic has always worked better on faerie flesh," I said.

"Not always," Rhys said, "but in the last few thousand years, yeah."

Dr. Sang shook his head again. "I would like to know how this healing works."

"Hafwen would be happy to try and explain it at a different time."

"I understand. You want to get your men home."

"Yes," I said. My tears had stopped under the doctor's questions. I realized that he wasn't the only one who had drawn himself to himself. In private I could fall apart, but not here in front of so many. Given the opportunity, the nurses and doctors could sell my emotional pain to the tabloids, and I didn't want that.

Dr. Sang went for the door, as if he needed to get away from us. He paused with the door partially open. "It wasn't a trick, or an illusion?"

"I swear to you that what we saw together was a true vision."

"Does that mean we'd live happily ever after?" he asked.

I shook my head. "It's not that kind of fairy tale. There will be children, and she does love you. Beyond that, I think you could love her, if you'd let yourself, but that may require work on your part. To love someone is to lose a certain amount of control over yourself and your life, and you don't like that. No one likes that," I added.

I smiled at him, as Doyle squeezed my hand and I squeezed back. "Some people are addicted to falling in love, Doctor. Some people love that rush of new emotions, and when that first rush of lust and fresh love is spent, they move on to the next, thinking the love wasn't real. What I felt in her, and potentially in you, is the love of years. Love that knows that that first rush of freshness isn't the real thing. It's the tip of the iceberg."

"You know what they say about icebergs, Princess Meredith?"

"No, what do they say?"

"Make sure the ship you're riding in isn't called *Titanic*."

Several of the nurses laughed, but I didn't. He'd made a joke because he was scared, truly scared. Something made him believe that he couldn't love both medicine and a woman. That he couldn't do justice to both. Maybe he couldn't, but then again. . . .

Rhys moved up beside me, beside us. He put his arm across my shoulders, not too tight. "Faint heart never won fair maiden," he said.

"What if I don't want to win the fair maiden?" Dr. Sang asked.

"Then you are a fool," Rhys said, with a smile to soften the words.

The two men stared at each other for a long moment. Some knowledge or understanding seemed to pass between them, because Dr. Sang nodded, almost as if Rhys had spoken again. He hadn't, I would have sworn to that, but sometimes silence speaks between one man and another much louder than any words. One of the greatest differences between men and women is that certain silence that women do not understand, and men cannot explain.

Dr. Sang went for the door. Before he and Rhys had had their moment of understanding, I would have bet even money on whether the good doctor would call the woman in the flower shop. But something about what Rhys had said had tipped the scales somehow. Now all I wondered was whether he'd call first or simply go to her.

Rhys hugged me and kissed the top of my head. I turned my face up so I could look at him. His smile was casual, almost teasing, but that one clear blue eye held something that was not casual in the least. I remembered a moment when the queen's ring had first come back to life on my hand. I had seen a ghostly baby before one of the female guards. Every man in the hallway had stared at her as if she were the most beautiful thing in the world. Every man except for four: Doyle, Frost, Mistral, and Rhys. Even Galen had stared at her. Later I'd had it explained that only true love would make you not gaze upon a woman that the ring had chosen. I had used the ring to see who among my guards would be the father of that almost-child, and given the female guard and the male guard to each other. It had worked. She had missed her period, and the tests were positive. It was the first pregnancy among the Unseelie since I was conceived. The ring, or something like it, had been the genesis for the Cinderella story. That moment when she stands upon the stairs and everyone stares at her. It was not mere beauty that captivated so, it was magic.

I truly loved Doyle, and Frost to a lesser extent. I couldn't imagine being without either of them. Mistral had been my consort in the moment when the ring had come back to life, so the magic had not worked on him. Instead, he was part of the working of the magic. But Rhys, he should have looked at that guard. But he had only looked at me, which meant that he loved me, and he knew that I did not love him.

The people of faerie are not supposed to be jealous or possessive of their lovers, but to love truly and not have it returned is a pain that has no cure.

I raised my face to him, inviting a kiss. His face lost all trace of humor. He was as solemn as the look in his eye. He kissed me, and I kissed him back. I let my body grow soft and clung to him as our lips found each other. I wanted him to know that I valued him. That I saw him. That I wanted him. I felt his body respond even through our clothes.

He drew back first, a little breathless, a hint of laughter to his voice. "Let's get our wounded home, and we can finish this."

I nodded, because what else could I do? What can you say to a man when you know you are breaking his heart? You can promise to stop doing what is tear-ing him apart, but I knew that I couldn't, wouldn't stop loving Doyle and Frost.

I was breaking Frost's heart a little, too, because he knew that Doyle had a bigger piece of my affections. If we had not been so intimate together, I might have been able to hide it from Frost, but he had taken to being with Doyle and me whenever we were intimate. There were too many men now to not share. But it was more than that. It was almost as if Frost feared what would happen if he left me alone with Doyle for even one more night.

What do you do when you know you are breaking someone's heart, but to do anything else would break your own? I promised Rhys sex with my kiss and my body. I meant it, but it wasn't lust that prompted the offer. I suppose in a way it was love, just not the kind of love a man wants from a woman.

Chapter 9

WE LEFT THE HOSPITAL TO FIND A BARRAGE OF RE-
porters. Someone had talked. We answered none of
the yelled questions, although they got plenty of pictures of Doyle in a wheelchair. The fact that he'd accepted it at all proved how hurt he still was. Abe, on
the other hand, had taken a wheelchair because he
was lazy and liked attention, though he had to sit to
one side to save his back. Hafwen had healed him,
but again not completely. We weren't in faerie, and
our powers weren't even close to their best.

The reporters knew what exit we were taking.
Someone inside the hospital would take home money
for either directing us to where the press waited or
telling them where we were coming out. Either way,
we were a moneymaking enterprise today.

Cameras blinded us. Hospital security had called
the police before we even got outside, so there were
other uniforms besides the two who still trailed us.
Officers Kent and Brewer hadn't liked me as much
since I had done magic on the doctor. They seemed
afraid of me. But they did their duty. They walked in
front and helped their fellow officers keep the crowd
back.

There was a moment when the reporters pressed

forward and the line collapsed toward us. Then my guards moved forward and the line steadied. Some of the men put their hand on the shoulder or back of the security guard or cop nearest them. I watched the humans stand a little straighter. It was as if by touch some of my guard could give courage and strength. I couldn't remember them ever being able to do that before, or was it just that the men who could do it had never been with me? What had I brought out of faerie with me into this modern world? Even I wasn't certain.

I watched them give courage with a touch, the way I could wake lust, and wondered if the touch would give them luck and courage for their day, or if it would fade like the lust I could inspire. When we had some privacy I'd ask.

There were too many of us for just one limo. There were two limos and two Hummers. One of each was black, the other white. I had time to wonder if someone had a sense of humor, or if it was an accident. I tried to help Doyle inside a limo, but Rhys moved me back so that Frost and Galen could help their captain inside. It seemed to take a long time. My vision was ruined with the flashing of cameras. Someone screamed over the mass of noise, "Darkness, why did King Taranis try to kill you?"

Rhys's hands tensed on my shoulders. Until that moment I, and probably he, had thought that some flunky had talked, but that one question said that whoever had talked to the press had known entirely too much. The only people who had seen what happened were security guards and lawyers, both professions that you were supposed to be able to trust. Someone had betrayed that trust.

We were finally inside the stretch limo. Abe was already lying on his stomach on the main seat. Doyle sat in one of the side seats, stiffly upright. I moved to sit with him, but he motioned me toward Abe. "Let him rest his head in your lap, Princess."

I frowned at him, wanting to ask why he was pushing me away. My expression must have asked for me, because he said, "Please, Princess."

I trusted Doyle. He had to have his reasons. I sat on the end of the big seat and eased Abe's head into my lap. He rested his cheek against my thigh, and I stroked the heavy weight of his hair. I'd never seen it braided before, like a Goth version of a candy cane, black, gray, and white. I guess they'd had to keep his hair away from the wound on his back somehow.

Frost sat on the seat opposite Doyle. Galen moved to take a seat, but Doyle said, "Take the second SUV. Rhys will take the first. We have too many guards who know only faerie. Be their modern eyes and ears, Galen."

Rhys patted him on the back. "Come on."

Galen gave me an unhappy look, but he did as he was told.

It was Frost who said, "We need Aisling in here."

"And Usna," Doyle said.

Frost nodded as if that made sense to him. It didn't to me, not yet. But then I hadn't had centuries of battle to get me past that shock and disorientation that seemed to follow like a fog.

The door shut, and we had a few minutes while

Rhys and Galen fetched the men they had asked for. "Why them?" I asked.

"Aisling was exiled from the Seelie because their sithen, their faerie mound, recognized him as the king in this new land, not Taranis," Doyle said. His voice sounded normal, not even a hint of tightness. Only his arm in its sling tied tightly to his chest and the bandage across his face showed what his voice should have held.

"So he needs to know that Hugh is trying to give away his kingdom," I said.

"No," Abe said from my lap. "It is not Aisling's kingdom now."

"But the sithen used to choose the ruler," I said.

"Yes," Abe said, "as the Lia Fail stone did once for the kings of Ireland. But the sithen can be a fickle thing. It liked Aisling more than two hundred years ago. He's not the same man who was exiled. Time has changed him. The Seelie mound may not want him now." Abe's voice sounded tired, trailing off around the edges.

I put my hand against his cheek. That one small touch made him smile.

"Usna's mother is still a favorite at the Seelie Court," Frost said, "and she still speaks to her son."

"So Usna might know if Hugh was part of a plot to get rid of Taranis," I said.

Frost nodded. Doyle said, "Yes."

I looked at both their faces, so distant and cold. It reminded me of the way they had been when they first came to me. Why were they being like this? I was royal, so I shouldn't show weakness by asking. But I was also in love with them, so while there was only

Abe to witness it, I asked, "Why are you both being so distant?"

They exchanged a look, and even through the bandages on Doyle's face I didn't like that look. It promised nothing that I would want.

"You are not with child, Meredith," Doyle said, voice still so controlled. "You are beginning to make it clear that you have chosen us. But if you are not pregnant then we are not your king. You must look at the other men with more favor."

"You get badly hurt and you go all crazy on me," I said.

Doyle tried to turn his head and look directly at me, but apparently that hurt too much, so he had to turn his whole body. "It is not crazy. It is sanity. You must not give your heart where your body does not go."

I shook my head. "Don't make decisions for me, Doyle. I am no longer a child. I choose who comes to my bed."

"We fear," Frost said, and he didn't look happy saying it, "that your caring for us is making it difficult for the other men."

"I'm sleeping with them. Considering that we've only been back a few weeks, I think I've given them plenty of attention."

Frost gave a small smile. "Sex is not all that a man craves, even after a thousand years of abstinence."

"I know that," I said, "but I only have so many hearts to give."

"And that," Doyle said, "is the problem. Frost told me how you behaved when I was injured. You cannot play favorites, Meredith, not yet." A look of pain crossed his face, but I didn't think it had anything to do with his injuries. "You know I feel the same, but you must be with child, Meredith. You must, or there will be no throne, no queenship."

Abe spoke, his hand resting on my leg beside his head. "Hugh didn't say Merry had to breed to be queen of the Seelie. He just offered her the throne."

I tried to remember exactly what Sir Hugh had said. "Abe's right," I said.

"Perhaps magic is worth more to them than babies," Frost said.

"Perhaps," Doyle said, "or perhaps Hugh plays some other game."

The limo door opened, and we all jumped, even Doyle and Abe. Abe allowed himself a small pain sound. Doyle was silent, only his face showing the pain for a moment. By the time Usna and Aisling had climbed into the car, it was back to its usual stoic expression.

The two new men found seats. Usna sat beside Frost, Aisling beside Doyle. Doyle said, "Tell them to drive."

Frost hit the intercom button. "Take us home, Fred."

Fred had been driving for Maeve Reed for thirty years. He'd grown gray and older, while she remained beautiful and untouched by the years. He said, "Do you want the cars to stay together, or do you want me to try to outrun the press?"

Frost looked at Doyle. Doyle looked at me. I had had more experience than any of them in being pursued by the press. I hit the intercom button above me, though I had to stretch for it. "Fred, don't try to outrun them. Today they'll hound us. Just get us home in one piece."

"Will do, Princess."

"Thanks, Fred."

Fred had been dealing with the "royalty" of Hollywood for decades. He seemed unimpressed with real royalty. But I guess when you've been driving the Golden Goddess of Hollywood around, what's a princess to that?

Chapter 10

USNA RELAXED HIS TALL, MUSCLED FRAME AGAINST the seat, as if we were on a pleasure drive. A sword hilt poked out of his long, loose hair, which fell around him in a riot of red, black, and white. The hair was patched, not striped like Abe's. Usna's eyes, though large and lustrous, were the plainest shade of gray that any of my guards could boast. But those shining gray eyes stared out through a veil of hair.

He'd had three reactions to his first time in the big city: One, he carried more weapons than he ever had in faerie; two, he seemed to hide behind his hair. He was always peering out of it, like a cat hiding in the grass until it springs on an unwary mouse. Three, he had joined Rhys in the weight room and added some bulk to that slender frame. The cat analogy came from the fact that he was spotted like a calico cat, and that his mother had been changed into the form of a cat when pregnant with Usna. She'd been pregnant by another Seelie sidhe's husband, and the scorned wife had decided that her outside should match her inside.

Usna had grown up, avenged his mother, and undone the spell, and his mother was living happily ever after in the Seelie Court. Usna had been exiled for some of the things he had done to avenge her. He'd thought it was a fair trade.

But it was Aisling, from his seat beside Doyle, who asked, "Not that I am complaining, Princess, but why are we in the main car? We all know that you have your favorites, and we are not among them." His comment about favorites echoed what Doyle and Frost had said earlier. But damnit, wasn't I entitled to have favorites?

I looked into Aisling's face, but could only truly see his eyes because he wore a veil wrapped around his head as some women did in Arabic countries. His eyes were spirals of colors that reached out from his pupil, not rings, but true spirals. The color of those spirals seemed to change, as if his eyes couldn't decide what color they wanted to be. He wore his long yellow hair in complicated braids at the back of his head so the veil could be securely tied.

Once, looking into Aisling's face had caused anyone, male or female, to fall instantly in lust with him. The legend said love, but Aisling had corrected me: It was lust unless he put effort into the magic; then it could be love. Once, even true love could have been broken by Aisling's touch. It had worked outside and inside faerie, once upon a time. We'd proven that he could still make someone who hated him fall madly in love, give up all her secrets, and betray every oath because of his kiss. It was why I had yet to bed Aisling— he and the other guards weren't sure if I was powerful enough to resist his spell.

His veil today was white, to match the old-fashioned clothes he wore. There hadn't been time to make new clothes for the newest guards, so they wore the tunics, pants, and boots that would have looked perfect in about fifteenth-century Europe, maybe a little later. Fashion moved slowly in faerie unless you were Queen Andais. She was fond of the latest and greatest designers, as long as they liked black.

Usna had borrowed jeans, a T-shirt, and a suit jacket from someone. Only the soft boots that peeked from the leg of the jeans were his own. But then a cat is less formal than a god.

"Talk to them, Meredith," Doyle said, and there was the tiniest bit of strain in his voice. The limo was a smooth ride, but when you have second-degree burns that started the day as third-degree burns, well, I guess there's no such thing as a truly smooth ride.

His comment had sounded too much like an order, but the strain in his voice made me answer. The strain and the fact that I loved him. Love makes you do all sorts of foolish things.

"Do you know who attacked us?" I asked.

"I know Taranis's handiwork when I see it," Aisling said.

"The other guards said Taranis went mad and attacked you all," Usna said. He drew his knees up tight, arms laced around them, so that his eyes were framed with his jeans and his hair. It was a frightened child's pose, and I wanted to ask if being among all this man-made metal was hard on him. Some of the lesser fey would eventually die locked inside metal. It made prison a potential death sentence for faerie folk. Lucky that most of us didn't break human law.

"What prompted the attack?" Aisling asked.

"I'm not sure," I said. "He just went crazy. I actually don't know what happened in the room, because

I was buried under a mound of bodyguards." I looked at Abe still lying in my lap, and glanced at Frost and Doyle. "What did happen?"

"The king attacked Doyle," Frost said.

"What neither will say," Abe said, "is that only Doyle throwing up his gun to deflect the spell saved him from being blinded. Taranis tried for his face, and he meant it to either kill or permanently maim. I haven't seen the old fart use his power that well in centuries."

"Aren't you older than he is?" I asked, peering down at him.

He smiled. "Older, yes, but in my heart I'm still a pup. Taranis let himself grow old inside. Most of us can't age the way a human can, but inside we can grow just as old. Just as unwilling to change with the times."

"The gun deflected Taranis's hand of power?" Usna asked.

"Yes," Doyle said, and he made a motion with his good hand. "Not all of it, obviously, but some."

"Guns are made out of all sorts of things that faerie magic doesn't like," I said.

"I'm not certain about the new polymer-frame guns," Doyle said. "The metal ones, yes, but since plastic doesn't seem to bother the lesser fey, I wouldn't swear that the new polymer guns would deflect anything."

"Why doesn't plastic bother the lesser fey?" Usna asked. "It's as man-made as metal, more so."

"Maybe it's not the man-made part, but the metal part that counts," Frost said.

"Until we know, I think only guns with more metal

than plastic should be used by the guards," Doyle said.

Everyone just nodded.

"When Doyle fell, the humans started screaming and running," Frost said. "Taranis used his hand of power on the room, but he seemed confused, as if he didn't know what to target."

"When he stopped firing, Galen and I were ordered to get the princess, you, out of the room, and we tried," Abe said. "That's when Taranis decided on me." He shivered a little, his hand tightening on my leg.

I leaned over and laid a kiss on his temple. "I'm sorry you got hurt, Abe."

"I was doing my job."

"Was Abeloec his target?" Aisling asked. "Or did he try for the princess and miss?"

"Frost?" Doyle said.

"I believe he hit what he was aiming at, but when Abeloec fell, Galen picked the princess up, and he moved in a way that I have not seen anyone move except the princess herself inside faerie," Frost said.

"Galen didn't open the door, did he?" I asked.

"No," Frost said.

"Galen carried you through the door?" Usna asked.

"I don't know. One minute we were in the room, the next we were in the hallway. I honestly don't remember what happened at the door."

"You blurred, then vanished at the door," Frost said. "In that first moment, Meredith, I wasn't certain whether Galen had gotten you out or another Seelie trick had stolen you away."

"Then what happened?" I asked.

"The king's own guard jumped him," Abe said.

"Truly?" Aisling asked.

Abe grinned. "Oh, yeah. It was a sweet moment."

"His most trusted nobles attacked the king?" Usna asked, as if he couldn't believe it.

Abe's grin widened, until it crinkled the edges of his face. "Sweet, isn't it?"

"Sweet," Usna agreed.

"Was the king so easily subdued?" Aisling asked.

"No," Frost said, "he used his hand of power three more times. The last time Hugh stepped in front of him, and used his own body to shield the room and the people inside it."

"Hugh the Firelord was able to take Taranis's power at point-blank range?" Aisling asked.

"Yes," Frost said.

"His shirt was scorched, but his skin seemed untouched," I said.

"And how did you see Hugh," Aisling asked, "if Galen had gotten you outside to safety?"

"She came back," Frost said, and his voice was not happy.

"I could not leave you to the Seelie's treachery," I said.

"I ordered Galen to take you to safety," Frost said.

"And I ordered him not to."

Frost glared at me and I glared back.

"You couldn't leave Doyle hurt, maybe dying," Usna said softly.

"Maybe, yes, but also if I am ever to rule, truly rule a court of faerie, I must be able to lead in battle. We aren't humans who keep their leaders in the back. The sidhe lead from the front."

"You are mortal, Merry," Doyle said. "That changes some rules."

"If I am too mortal to rule, then so be it, but I must rule, Doyle."

"Speaking of ruling," Abe said, "tell them what Hugh said about our princess being made queen of the Seelie Court."

"That can't be true," Usna said. He was staring at Abe and me.

"I swear it is true," Abe said.

"Has Hugh lost his senses?" Aisling asked. "No offense, Princess, but the Seelie will not allow an Unseelie noble who is part brownie and part human to sit on the golden throne. Not unless the court has changed a great deal in the two hundred years of my exile."

"What say you, Usna?" Doyle asked. "Are you as shocked as Aisling?"

"Tell me first if Hugh gave reasons for his change of heart."

"He spoke of swans with golden chains, and there is a green faerie dog in the Seelie Court once more," Frost said.

"My mother tells me the Cu Sith had stopped the king from beating a servant," Usna said.

"And you didn't share this with anyone?" Abe asked.

Usna shrugged. "It didn't seem that important."

"Apparently, some of the nobles have taken the dog's disfavor as a sign against Taranis," Doyle said.

"Also, he went buggers, mad as a March fucking hare," Abe said.

"Well, there *is* that," Doyle said.

Aisling looked at me. "They offered you the throne of the Seelie Court, truly?"

"Hugh said something about a vote among the nobles, and that if it went against Taranis, which he seemed confident it would, he would get them to vote me in as heir apparent."

"What did you say?" Aisling asked.

"I said we'd have to talk to our queen before I could answer their generous offer."

"Will she be pleased, or pissed?" Usna asked.

I thought it was a rhetorical question, but I said, "I don't know."

Doyle said, "I do not know."

Frost said, "I wish I knew."

We had a chance of being caught between a ruler of faerie who was crazy and a ruler of faerie who was simply cruel. I had found years ago that the difference between madness and cruelty doesn't matter much to a victim.

Chapter 11

DOYLE AND FROST PICKED USNA'S MIND FOR OTHER bits of unimportant news from his mother about the Seelie Court. There was a lot of it. Apparently Taranis had been acting erratically for some time. Aisling asked as we pulled into the gates of Maeve Reed's estate, "Why did you request me for this talk? Taranis forbade anyone to speak to me of the Seelie Court on pain of torture, so I have no intelligence to report."

"The Seelie sithen recognized you as king when we arrived in America," Doyle said. "You were exiled because of that."

"I am aware of what cost me my place at court," Aisling said.

"So the princess is in effect being offered your rightful throne," Doyle said.

Aisling's eyes went wide. Even through the veil his astonishment showed. Obviously he had not put two and two together and come up with that.

The door to the limo opened, and Fred held the door. We all stayed sitting while we waited for Aisling to digest this. "Close the door for a moment, Fred," I said.

The door closed.

"Just because the sithen recognized me more than two hundred years ago does not mean that I would still be its choice for king," Aisling said. "And it is not me to whom the nobles are making this offer."

"I wanted you to hear it first, Aisling," Doyle said. "I did not want you to think that we had forgotten what faerie itself offered you once."

Aisling looked at Doyle for a long moment. "That was a very decent thing for you to do, Doyle."

"You sound surprised," I said.

He looked at me. "Doyle has been the queen's Darkness for a very long time, Princess. I am beginning to realize that some of his finer emotions may have been buried under the queen's orders."

"That is the most polite way I've ever heard anyone say that we thought you were a heartless bastard, Doyle," Abe said.

Aisling's eyes crinkled at the edges. I think he was smiling. "I would not have put it quite that way."

Doyle smiled. "I think many of us will find that under the princess's care we are more ourselves than we have been in a very long time."

They all looked at me, and the weight of that look made me want to squirm. I fought it off and sat there trying to be the princess they thought I was. But there were moments, like now, when I felt that I could not possibly be everything they needed. No one could meet so many needs.

I got a whiff of a spring breeze and flowers. A voice that was not a voice, but more something that thrummed through my body, hummed along my skin and whispered, "We will be enough."

I knew it was the old idea that with God, or Goddess, on your side you could not lose. But there were moments when I was no longer certain that winning meant the same thing to me that it did to the Goddess.

Chapter 12

WE WERE MET BY A BOIL OF BODIES AT THE DOOR TO the big house. Dogs, faerie hounds, met us with barks, bays, yips, and noises that sounded like they were trying to talk. Since they were supernatural in origin I wouldn't have put it past them.

There were so many dogs trying to greet so many different masters at the door that we couldn't move forward. As dogs will, they were acting as if we had been gone days instead of only hours. My hounds were like greyhounds, but not quite. There were differences in the head, the ears, the line of body from shoulders to tail, but they had that muscled grace. In color they were white, a pure, shining white like my own skin, but with marks of red, again like my own hair. Minnie, short for Miniver, was white save for half her face and one large spot of red on her back. The face was very striking: red on one side, white on the other, as if someone had drawn a line neatly down her face. Mungo, my boy, was a little taller, a little heavier, and even whiter, with only one red ear to give him color.

Some of the larger hounds looked like Irish wolfhounds had, before they'd gotten mixed with anything less beefy. There were only a few of them among the greyhounds, but the few towered over everything else like mountains rising above a plain. Some had rough coats, some smooth, but all were a variation of red and white. Then you had the terriers that spilled around our ankles. They, too, were mostly white and red, except for a few who were black and brown. The old black and tan, brought back to existence by wild magic, was the breed that most of the modern terriers are descended from.

Rhys had the most terriers, but then he was a god of death, or had been. Our people see the land of the dead as an underground place, most of the time, so the fact that he had earth dogs was logical. He didn't seem to mind that he had none of the graceful hounds, or the huge war dogs. He knelt in the mass of barking, growling dogs, all so much smaller, and glowed with the joy that all of us showed. We had always been a people who honored our animals. They had been much missed.

There was one other exception to the color of the dogs—Doyle's hounds. They were not as tall as the wolfhounds, but meatier, black muscle over bone. They were the original shape the dogs had come to us in, black dogs, what the Christians called hellhounds. But they had nothing to do with the devil. They were the black dogs, the black of void and nothing from which comes life. Before there is light, there must be darkness.

Doyle tried to walk unaided but stumbled. Frost gave his strong arms to his friend. Strangely, there was no dog to greet Frost. He and only a few others had touched the black dogs, but they had not changed into some other hound for them.

None of us knew why, but I knew it bothered Frost. He feared, I think, that it was a sure sign that he was not enough to be truly sidhe. Once he had been the hoarfrost, Jack Frost, and now he was my Killing Frost, but there was always that insecurity that he was not born sidhe, but made.

Hovering above the sea of dogs were small winged fey: the demi-fey. To be wingless among them was a mark of great shame. All that had followed me into exile had been wingless until I brought new magic back to faerie. Penny and Royal, twins with dark hair and bright wings, waved at me.

I waved back. To be greeted like this by a cloud of demi-fey and our dogs was an honor I never thought I would have.

I offered to help Frost with Doyle, but Doyle refused. He wouldn't even look at me. His supposed "weakness" had cut him deeply. One of the big black dogs pushed at me and gave a soft growl. Mungo and Minnie both moved up, hackles beginning to rise. That was not a fight I wanted to see, so I backed off, calling them to my hands.

My hounds were capable of protecting me if they had to, but against the black dogs they looked fragile. I stroked their heads. Mungo leaned against my leg, and the weight was comforting. I wanted nothing more than a nap with my dogs on the floor by the bed, or at the door. Not all my men liked a furry audience, and sometimes neither did I. Regardless, we had one more task to do before we could rest.

We called my aunt, Andais, Queen of Air and Darkness, as soon as we got inside. I would have put Doyle and Abe to bed immediately, but Doyle had pointed out that if someone else told the queen before we did that I had been offered her rival's throne, she might view it as treason. She might view it as me jumping ship. Andais didn't take rejection, any type of rejection, well.

She was already fairly pissed that so many of her most devoted guards had dumped her for me. I didn't see it as dumping her for me. I saw it as them choosing a chance for sex after centuries of forced celibacy. For that, most men would have gone to any woman. It helped that I wasn't a sexual sadist and Auntie Andais was, but that, too, was a fact best not shared.

Doyle had insisted on being present for the call. He wanted her to see what Taranis had done. I think he thought the visual aid would cut through her usual fits of temper. She was more stable than Taranis, but there were moments when my aunt didn't seem entirely sane. Would she like this unexpected news or hate it? I honestly didn't know.

Doyle sat on the edge of my bed. I sat beside him. Rhys sat on my other side. He'd jokingly said, "You promised me sex, but I know you, you'll get distracted unless I stay by your side." It was a joke with some bite in it for Rhys and me. But Doyle said yes to his staying with us too quickly. It let me know that my Darkness was hurt worse than he'd let on.

Frost stood at the corner of the bed. It's easier to go for a weapon when you are standing.

Galen stood beside him. He'd insisted on being included in the call, and nothing anyone had said could dissuade him. In the end it had been easier to just give in. Galen's argument that we needed at least one more able-bodied guard on the call had some merit. But I think he, like me, wasn't sure what Andais would do with the news from the Seelie Court. He was afraid for me, and I was afraid for us all.

Abe lay on the far side of the bed. He hadn't wanted to be included, but hadn't argued with Doyle's order. I think Abe was afraid of Andais. Of course, so was I.

Rhys moved to the mirror. His hand was close to the glass, but not quite touching it. "Everybody ready?" he asked.

I nodded. Doyle said, "Yes."

"No," Abe said, "but my vote doesn't count, apparently."

Frost just said, "Do it."

Galen just watched the mirror with eyes that were a little too bright. It wasn't magic, it was nerves.

Rhys touched the mirror, using such a small piece of magic that I didn't even feel it. The mirror was cloudy for a moment, then the black bedroom of the queen appeared. But she was not there. Her huge black-draped bedspread was empty except for a pale male figure.

He lay on his stomach across the black fur and sheets. His skin wasn't just white, or even moonlight skin like mine, but so pale it had a translucent quality to it. It was what skin would have looked like if it could be formed of crystal. Except that this crystal was cut with long crimson slashes on arms and legs.

She'd left his back and buttocks untouched, which probably meant the cuts were for persuasion and not torture. Andais liked to go for the center of the body when she was causing pain for the sake of pain.

The blood shimmered in the lights, again with a jewel quality that I'd never seen in blood before. The man's hair spread to one side of his body, catching the light in small prism rainbows. He was so still that for a moment I thought there was some awful wound we could not see. Then I saw his chest rise and fall. He lived. He was hurt, but he lived.

I whispered his name, "Crystall."

He turned, slowly, obviously in pain. He laid his cheek against the fur underneath him, and stared at us with eyes that looked empty, as if there was no hope left. It hurt my heart to see that look in his eyes.

Crystall hadn't been a lover of mine, but he had fought with us in faerie. He had helped defend Galen when he might otherwise have died. The queen had decreed that all the guards who wished could follow me into exile and then too many of them had opted to come, so she had had to take back her generous offer. The men who had left were safe with me. The men who had not been in the first few groups that Sholto, Lord of That Which Passes Between, had brought to Los Angeles had been trapped in faerie with her. Trapped with a woman who didn't take rejection well, when they'd openly chosen another woman. I was seeing what the other woman, my aunt, thought about that.

I reached out toward the mirror, as if I could touch him, but it wasn't one of my powers. I could not do what Taranis had done so easily earlier today.

"Princess," Crystall whispered, and his voice was hoarse, roughened. I knew why his voice sounded like that. Screaming will do that. I knew because I had been at the queen's mercy more than once. The queen's mercy had become a saying among the Unseelie sidhe, as in, "I'd rather be at the queen's mercy than do that."

Andais had seen exile from faerie as worse than any torture she could devise. She did not understand why so many of her fey had chosen it. Just as she hadn't understood why my father, Essus, took me and our household into exile in the human world after Andais tried to drown me at six years of age. If I was mortal enough to die by drowning, then I wasn't sidhe enough to be allowed to live. Sort of the way you'd drown a puppy that your purebred bitch dropped after you realized it wasn't the mating of your dreams, but some mongrel that had gotten inside the fence.

Andais had been shocked when my father left faerie to raise me among the humans, and she had been equally shocked when, many years later, nearly her entire guard would have followed me into the Western lands. For her, to leave faerie was worse than death, and she couldn't understand why it wasn't a fate worse than death to everyone else. What she failed to understand was that the queen's mercy had become a fate even worse than exile.

I stared into Crystall's luminous, hopeless eyes, and my throat tightened around the tears that I knew I could not afford to shed. Andais had left us a present to look at, but she'd be watching, and she would see

tears as weakness. Crystall was her visual aid. Her
example to us, to me. I wasn't certain what the message was supposed to be, but in her mind there was
one. But, Goddess help me, other than her jealousy
and hatred of rejection I couldn't see any message
here.

"Oh, Crystall," I said. "I am sorry."

His voice had reminded me of the sound of chimes
in a gentle wind. Now it was a painful croak. "You
did not do this, Princess."

His eyes flickered toward what I knew was the
outer door, though I could not see that part of the
room. His face closed down, and for a moment where
there had been hopelessness there was rage. A rage
that he stuffed down, and hid behind eyes that
showed as neutral a face as he could find.

I prayed that Andais hadn't seen that moment of
rage. She'd try to beat it out of him if she had.

The queen swept into the room dressed in a loose,
flowing black robe. It left open a triangle of white
flesh, the flat perfection of her stomach and a trace of
her belly button. There was a thin cord tied across the
high, tight planes of her breasts that kept the front of
the outfit from spilling open completely. There were
long, wide sleeves that left most of her forearms bare.
She must have been called away on important business to have put on that much clothing with Crystall
still in her bed. He wasn't hurt enough for her to be
finished with him.

She'd tied her long black hair back in a loose tail of
hair. The ribbon she'd chosen was red. I'd never seen
her wear red before, not even a spot of it. The only

red the queen liked on her person was other people's blood.

I couldn't have explained it, but that red ribbon made my stomach clench tight, and my pulse speed. Andais slid onto the bed in front of Crystall, but close enough that she could stroke the untouched flesh of his back. She stroked him idly as you would a dog. He flinched at her first touch, then settled down and tried not to be there.

She looked at us with her tricolored eyes: charcoal, to the color of storm clouds, to a pale winter gray that was nearly white. Her eyes went so perfectly with the black hair and the pale skin. She was so made for Goth fashion, like Abe, except she was scarier than any Goth on the planet. Andais was serial-killer scary, and she was my father's sister, my queen, and there was nothing I could do about either.

"Aunt Andais," I said, "we have arrived from the hospital to tell you much news." We had already agreed that we needed to be clear from the beginning that we were telling her the news at the first opportunity.

"My queen," Doyle said, doing an awkward sitting bow as far as the bandages would allow.

"I have heard many rumors this day," she said, in a voice that some thought was a throaty, seductive sound, but that had always filled me with dread.

"Goddess knows what the rumors are," Rhys said as he moved back to stand by the bed, near me. "The truth is weird enough." He said it with a smile and his usual teasing lightness.

She gave him a flat look that was anything but

friendly. There would be no lightening her mood if that look was any indication. She turned those angry eyes back to Doyle.

"What could possibly injure the Dark itself?" Her voice was angry, and almost disinterested. She knew, somehow she already knew. Who the hell had talked?

"When the Light appears, the Darkness must leave," Doyle said, in his best flat, nothing voice.

She ran the bright redness of her lacquered nails down Crystall's back. She left red lines, though she didn't quite break the skin. Crystall turned his face away from the mirror and from her, afraid, I think, that he could not control his expression. "What light is bright enough to conquer the Darkness?" she asked.

"Taranis, King of Light and Illusion, is still potent in his hand of power," Doyle said, his voice even emptier than her own.

She dug fingernails into Crystall's back just below the shoulder blade, as if she meant to dig a handful of flesh out of his back. Blood began to show around her hand, like water filling a hole in the ground, slowly seeping upward.

"You seem preoccupied, Meredith. Whatever could be the matter?" Her voice was almost conversational, except for that edge of cruelty.

I decided to concentrate on the things that might distract her from tormenting the man in her bed. "Taranis attacked us through the mirror in the lawyer's office. He injured Doyle, and Abeloec. He was trying for me when Galen got me to safety."

"Oh, I doubt he meant to injure you, Meredith,

even in his madness. I suspect he was trying for Galen."

I blinked at her. The way she said it meant that she knew something that we did not. "Why would he target Galen?"

"Ask yourself first, niece, why he accused Galen, Abeloec, and Rhys of raping the Lady Caitrin." Her hand dug deeper into Crystall's flesh, causing tiny red lines to begin to trickle over his skin.

"I do not know, Aunt Andais," I said, and fought to keep my own voice even and empty. I was trying not to show either fear or anger, though right now, fear was by far the strongest emotion. She was pissed, and I didn't know why. If she knew about the offer of the Seelie throne to me, then she might be pissed at that, but if I blurted it out, she'd think I felt guilty and I didn't. She was always so difficult to deal with, like being in the middle of a minefield. You know you have to get to the edge, but how to do that without getting blown up, that was always the question.

"Oh, come, Meredith, think. Or are you so little Unseelie and so much Seelie that all you can think about is fertility?"

"I thought my fertility was supposed to be the thing I thought about most if I am to be your heir, Aunt Andais?"

She drew her fingers together, forcing a sound from Crystall. She'd made bloody scratches on his back like some evil flower carved into his flesh. She raised her pale hand so I could watch his blood drip down her fingers.

"Are you going to be my heir, Meredith, or is there another throne that calls to you more?"

There, she'd said enough that I could address it. "It is true that when Taranis was subdued by his nobles they offered me a chance at his throne."

"You told them yes." She hissed it at me, standing and striding toward the mirror.

"I did not. I told them we would have to discuss such news with our queen, with you, Aunt Andais, before I could say yes or no."

She was at the mirror now, blocking our view of the bed and Crystall. Her anger had awakened her power. Her skin was beginning to glow. Her eyes were filling with the light, but not the way that most of the sidhe's eyes glowed with power. She seemed to have light behind her eyes, as if someone had set a candle behind all that gray and black. For the rest of us, for the most part, the individual colors glowed, but not her. She was queen, and she had to be different.

"I heard you jumped at the chance, you ungrateful little bitch."

"You have been lied to then, Aunt Andais." I fought to keep my voice neutral.

"Yes, remind me that you are my bloodline, my last chance to have someone of my line to rule after me. If you would but get with child, Meredith. Goddess knows you're fucking everything in sight. Why are you not with child?"

"I do not know, Aunt, but I do know that we came directly here from the hospital. We came into the house and to this mirror. We came to call you and tell you all that has happened. I swear to you by the Darkness That Eats All Things that I did not tell the

Seelie I would sit upon their throne. I told them we would have to speak to our queen before we could answer them."

Her eyes had begun to dim. Her power was beginning to fold away. Something tight in my stomach eased a little. I had used an oath that no fey would have taken lightly. There were powers older even than faerie, and they waited in the dark to punish oath-breakers.

"You truly did not agree to sit on the golden throne and forsake our court?"

"I did not."

"I must believe you, niece of mine, but the Seelie Court is thick with knowledge that you will be the next queen of their court."

Doyle reached across his body and touched me with his good arm at the same time that Rhys touched my shoulder. I touched Doyle's thigh lightly and laid my hand on Rhys's hand. "What they say, or think, I cannot control, but I did not agree to it."

"Why not?" she asked.

"I have friends and allies among the Unseelie Court. To my knowledge I have no such thing at the Seelie Court."

"You must have powerful allies there, Meredith. They are voting Taranis unfit to rule even as we speak. They will then vote you queen. They would not do that unless you had been approached by the nobles of that court. You must have been courted by them before now. There must have been many secret meetings that I did not know of, and that none of our guards reported to me."

I was beginning to see where her anger was coming from, and I couldn't entirely blame her. "One of the reasons I said no, and made clear that I must speak with you first, was exactly that, Aunt Andais. I have not been approached in any way by the nobles. Taranis was almost unnaturally persistent in his desire to have me at one of their Yule celebrations, but other than that I have not had dealings with the Seelie Court. I swear this to you. That is why the offer makes me suspicious as to what they truly want of me."

"I know Hugh. He is a political animal. He would not have offered it to you unless he had a reason to do so. You swear to me that he has never before approached you about this?"

"I swear," I said.

"Darkness, tell me exactly what happened?"

"I fear, my queen, that I will be useless for this. To my deep shame, I was unconscious through most of it."

"You don't seem that injured."

"Hafwen healed me at the hospital or I would still be there."

"Abeloec," she said.

Abe stirred behind us on the bed. He'd tried very hard to go unnoticed. "Yes, my queen."

"Do you know why Taranis would target you?"

He sat up slowly, careful of his back, and ended by half kneeling almost on all fours behind us. "Once my power was necessary for the choosing of a queen, as Meabh's power was to the choosing of a king. I think Taranis heard rumors that my power was returned to me, in part. I think he feared that I would help turn Meredith into a true queen of faerie. If we had known that any noble was dreaming of offering her the throne, then the accusations against me would have made some sense. He wanted me away from the princess."

"Galen," she said, "why did he target you?"

Galen looked flustered for a moment. He shook his head. "I don't know."

"Come, Galen Greenknight, greenman, why?"

I had a thought. "He knows the prophesy that Cel got from the human psychic," I said.

"Yes, Meredith, because you and the greenman will bring life back to the courts. Taranis has made the same mistake my son did. He thinks that Galen is the greenman of the prophesy. Neither of them remember our history."

"The greenman means the god, the consort," I said.

Andais nodded. She turned those eyes to Rhys. "And you, why you? Have you figured it out yet?"

"He heard the rumor that I'm Cromm Cruach again. If I were truly back to my original strength then he would fear me."

"Rumor has it that you can bring death to a goblin with a touch again. Is that rumor true?"

"I have done it once," he said, "but whether it will work again, I do not know."

"The rumor might be enough for Taranis," she said. She seemed calmer. Which was good. She looked at Doyle. "I understand why he attacked you. If I were to try and kill the princess, I would kill you first, but he was wrong in not targeting our Killing Frost." She turned those calm eyes to the big man standing so silent beside the bed. "To kill Meredith and survive would require both your deaths, wouldn't it, Killing Frost?"

Frost licked his lips. He was right to be nervous. This was not a conversation that we wanted to be having with our queen. "That is true, my queen," he said.

"Did the Seelie Court make the same condition on you that I do? Do you need to be with child before you can sit their throne?"

"No, they offered the throne with no conditions except that the nobles of the Seelie Court vote Taranis out and me in."

"What do you think of that, Meredith?"

"I am flattered, but not stupid. I am wondering if the nobles are playing some game of their own choosing, and the offer to me is simply to buy them time to consolidate their own bid for the throne. A vote to put me on the throne would slow the process of choosing a new king, or queen, for the Seelie Court to a crawl."

Andais smiled. "Did Doyle reason it out for you?"

"No, my queen," Doyle said. "The princess is well aware of the Seelie Court's potential for treachery."

"Is it true that Taranis almost beat you to death as a child?"

"Yes," I said. In my head I added, as you tried to drown me. Out loud I kept my mouth shut.

Andais smiled as if she'd hit on the same memory

and it was a happy one for her. "Meredith, Meredith, you must learn to control your entire face. Your eyes betray how much you hate me."

I lowered my gaze, not sure what to say that wouldn't be a lie.

She laughed, and it was both a lovely sound and a sound that made me shiver, as if it were my own body lying on her bed unable to protect itself from what would come next. I wanted to save Crystall from her, but I couldn't figure out a way to do it. My trying and failing would just make her hurt him worse. She'd think it meant he was special to me, and it would amuse her all the more to slice him up.

"Now that I know that you have not been meeting with Hugh and the Seelie nobles in secret, I agree that they mean you treachery. Perhaps you will be their stalking horse to lure out all the would-be assassins. Or perhaps it is what you say, that they simply throw your name into the ring to slow the process while someone else consolidates their own power. I think the latter the more likely, but the offer is so completely unexpected that I have not had time to think clearly on it."

What she meant was that she'd been convinced that I'd betrayed her with the Seelie Court, so she'd been too angry to think clearly. I kept my reasoning to myself. I had my face enough under control that I could look back up at her. Or I hoped I did. How do you tell if your own face is neutral?

"The fact that Taranis knows of the prophesy that Cel got from the human prophet means that one of Cel's trusted people is spying for the king of the Seelie

Court." She tapped her chin with one bloody finger-nail. "But who?"

There was a sound from the mirror, almost the clanging of swords. I glanced at the clock. "We are expecting a call from Kurag, Goblin King," I said.

"You have call waiting on your mirror," she said.

I nodded.

"I've never heard of such a thing. Who did the spell?"

"I did," Rhys said. His face was still softly amused, but there was a wariness around his eyes.

"You will have to bespell my mirror as well."

"Gladly, my queen," he said, voice pleasantly neutral.

The clang of swords sounded again. "Perhaps you should come back to court and do that today."

"With apologies, Aunt Andais, Rhys is to bed me if we can get time between calls and emergencies."

"Would it upset you to see his pale flesh bleeding on my bed like Crystall's?"

There was no safe answer to that question. "I do not know what you want me to say, Aunt Andais."

"The truth would be nice."

I sighed. Doyle squeezed my hand. Rhys tensed beside me. It was then that Galen lost it. "What does it matter? Taranis attacked us today. He went so crazy that his own nobles jumped him and dragged him away. He's about to be voted out as king of the Seelie Court, and you want to spend time tormenting Merry about us!" He actually stepped close to the mirror and continued to yell at her. "Doyle almost died today. Merry could have died today, and then you'd never have a child of your blood on any throne. The Seelie nobles are up to something dangerous that involves our court, and you want to play these stupid, painful games. We need you to be our queen, not our tormentor. We need help here. Goddess save us, but we do."

We might have jumped him to keep him quiet, but I think we were all too stunned to do anything. The silence was heavy, broken only by Galen's too-fast breathing.

Andais stared at him as if he'd just appeared. It wasn't a friendly look, but it wasn't an unfriendly look either. "What help would you have of me, Greenknight?"

"Try to find out why Hugh offered the throne to Merry, really why."

"What reason did he give?" she asked in an amazingly calm voice.

"That there are swans with gold chains, and that a Cu Sith stopped the king from beating a servant. The Seelie think Merry is to blame or gets credit for the return of the magic."

"And does she?" Andais asked with that edge of cruelty beginning to creep back in.

"You know she does," Galen said, and there was no anger, just a sort of righteousness, as if it was just truth.

"Perhaps," Andais said. She turned her gaze to me. "I will try and find out if Hugh is being honest, or as treacherous as we think. You must have some magic over men that I do not see, Meredith. You have not even fucked Crystall, yet he seems strangely loyal to you. I will break him to my ways again, then I will choose another of the men who would have deserted me for you. Sidhe who would have rather followed you into exile than stay with me in faerie." She said the last almost in a thoughtful voice, as if she truly didn't understand it.

The truth was that it wasn't faerie they wanted to leave but her sadistic care, but that was a truth better kept to myself.

"If the Seelie offer is a genuine one, Meredith, you might consider taking it."

A thrill of fear ran through me. "Aunt Andais, I don't understand."

"Every man who prefers you to me makes me hate you a little more. Soon, my hatred for you may outweigh my desire for you to sit my throne. On the golden throne of the Seelie Court you would be safe from my anger."

I licked my suddenly dry lips. "I do nothing to anger you on purpose, my queen."

"And that is what is so maddening about you, Meredith. I know you do not do it on purpose. You simply are, and somehow by being yourself you part my nobles and my lovers from me. Your Seelie magic wins them away."

"I carry the hands of flesh and blood. Those are not Seelie hands of power, Aunt."

"Yes, and Cel's prophet said that if someone of flesh and blood sat the Unseelie throne he would die. He thought it meant your mortality, but it didn't." She looked at me, and there was something other than cruelty, though I wasn't sure what exactly. "Cel screams your name in the night, Meredith."

"He means my death if he can manage it."

She shook her head. "He has convinced himself that if he laid with you, you and he would have a child, and he would be king to your queen."

My mouth couldn't get any drier, but my heart rate could get faster. "I do not think that would work, Aunt Andais."

"Work, work—it is fucking, Meredith. The mechanics of it would work just grand."

I tried again, while Doyle and Rhys gripped me harder. Even Abe moved in at my back to put his face against my hair. Touching to comfort me.

"I suppose what I meant was that I do not think Cel and I would make a good ruling couple."

"Do not look so frightened, Meredith. I know that Cel would not make you pregnant, but he has convinced himself of it. I suppose I am warning you. He no longer wants you assassinated, but he would kill every lover you have, if he could."

"Is he"—I tried to think of a way to say it—"free to . . ."

"He is not imprisoned, but he is under guard at all times. I do not want my own guards to kill my only son to protect my heir." She shook her head. "Go, call the Goblin King back. I will try to find out if Hugh's offer of the golden throne is true or false." She was walking back to the bed as she spoke the last few sentences. "But first I will take out my anger and frustration at you on your Crystall. Know that every cut is a cut I would make on your lily-white skin if I didn't need your body whole." She crawled onto the bed and reached for Crystall. A knife had appeared in her hand, either by magic or it had been tucked into the sheets.

Frost got to the mirror first and cleared it with a touch. We were left staring at our own images. My eyes were a little too wide, my skin pale.

"Crap," Rhys said.

That about summed it up.

Chapter 13

THE MIRROR RANG AGAIN, A STRIDENT CLASH OF swords, as if blades had screamed down the sides of each other. It made me jump.

Rhys looked at Doyle and me. Doyle said, "Let Abe and me get out of sight. The fewer people in faerie who have this rumor the better, I think." He gave my hand a last squeeze. Then he tried to rise with his usual effortless movement, but paused in mid-motion. It wasn't a flinch so much as that he simply stopped trying to stand.

I put a hand on his back to steady him. Frost grabbed one of his arms, and it was probably more him than me that helped Doyle stand upright. Doyle tried to move away from Frost's arm but stumbled. Frost got a firmer grip on his friend. Doyle actually leaned a little on the other man, which meant he was in a lot of pain.

"You didn't take the pain medication that the hospital gave you, did you?" I asked.

The mirror clanged again, an even angrier sound than before, as if the next sound of swords would break one of the blades.

"The goblins are not known for their patience, Meredith," Doyle said in a tight voice. "You must answer the call." He started off, and didn't fight Frost from helping him, which meant he was very hurt indeed. More hurt than he'd let on. The thought of my Darkness being this injured made my stomach and chest tight, not just because I loved him, but because he was the greatest warrior I had. Frost might be as good in battle, but for strategy it was Doyle. I needed him, in so many ways.

It must have shown on my face because he said, "I have failed you."

"Taranis tried to burn your face off," Rhys said. "You failed no one."

The evil sound of swords filled the room again.

"Go," Rhys said. "I'll stay with her."

"You don't like goblins," Frost said.

Rhys shrugged. "I killed the one that took my eye. That's got to be good enough revenge. Besides, I won't let you and Merry down by being a big baby. Go, rest, take your meds."

"I'll take Doyle," Galen said.

We all looked at him. "If Merry can't have Doyle by her side for this call, then she needs Frost," he said.

Abe had managed to get off the bed on the other side. "I see that no one cares that I might need help."

"Do you need help?" Galen asked, as he moved to take Doyle from Frost. He actually held his other hand out to Abe.

Abe looked into his face for a breath, then shook his head, but stopped the movement as if it hurt. "I can walk, boy. The king's men jumped him before he could do his worst on my back." He moved toward the door slowly but surely.

Doyle let Galen help him out of sight of the mirror and toward the door. Frost came to stand with me and Rhys. Rhys reached toward the mirror, then hesitated. "I hate that you are going to be with these two tonight."

"We've had this discussion, Rhys. For every half-sidhe goblin whom we bring into his full power, our alliance with the goblins is lengthened by a month. We need their threat to keep us safe," I said.

The mirror made its ugly sound again. "The goblins do not wait with patience," Frost said.

"We need them, Rhys," I said.

"I know. I hate it, but I know," Rhys said. A look passed over his face too quickly for me to read. "One of these days I'd like you to be able to do things just because you want to do them, not because you're forced to do them."

I wasn't sure what to say to that.

Rhys reached out toward the mirror. The metallic shriek rose to a crescendo. I fought the urge to cover my ears. I couldn't afford to show weakness in dealing with the goblins. The two high courts of faerie would use weakness to their advantage. Goblin culture simply saw weakness as a reason to abuse you. You were either prey or predator to the goblins. I was working very hard not to be prey.

The mirror was suddenly a perfect window onto the goblin throne room. Their king was not there, though. Ash and Holly stood alone before the empty stone throne. It was Ash's hand on the glass when we saw them, his magic making the mirror sound like a battle.

He blinked solid green eyes into the mirror. There was no pupil, only a blind expanse of perfect grass green surrounded by a little white. His hair was yellow, cut short, because only the sidhe are allowed long hair on their men, but his skin was gold-kissed. Not sparkling with golden bits like Aisling's, but it was close. Both the twins had Seelie skin, sunlight skin. Moonlight skin like mine and Frost's was plentiful at both courts. That golden color, almost like a tan, was exclusively Seelie. The eyes were goblin except for the color. Holly strode to the mirror to stand by his brother. He was identical except that his eyes were the color of red holly berries, like his namesake. The red color with no pupil was not just goblin but Red Cap goblin.

Rhys moved back from the mirror to stand on the other side of me so that I was sandwiched between him and Frost.

"The bargain is over," Holly said, his handsome face contorted with rage. He was usually the one to lose his temper first.

"To keep us waiting like this is to make us lose respect in front of all," Ash said. He didn't sound much more reasonable than his brother, which was bad, since Ash was the voice of reason for the two of them.

"Queen Andais kept us overlong," Frost said.

Rhys just moved closer to me, as if the twins' anger alone could hurt me.

Their eyes flicked to him, then back to me. "Is this true, Princess?" Ash asked.

"The queen had much to show us," I said, and let my voice hold some of the upset I felt about Crystall and his fate in her bed.

"She's been entertaining the sidhe you left behind," Ash said.

Holly actually looked uneasy, his anger fading, which was unusual for him.

"Has the queen spoken to the two of you?" I asked.

They exchanged a look. Ash answered. "Apparently, the queen enjoyed watching us lick her blood off of your skin. We didn't think that any sidhe, even Unseelie sidhe, would be so goblin in their tastes."

Andais's blood had gotten on me in her most recent attempt to kill me. She'd been unhappy with me that day. Lately she'd been happier with me, so her murder attempts had stopped, and she was paying my legal bills.

"She offered you her bed?" Frost asked.

"We are not talking to you, Killing Frost," Holly said.

I put a hand on Frost's arm, letting him know that it was all right. "I must weigh the pride of all the men in my life," I said. "Frost is one of those men, and if tonight comes to pass as we have all planned, you will be, too. I know you feel that we insulted you by ignoring your call, but all of us have to wait upon the queen's wishes."

"We do not," Holly said.

"You turned her down?" I made it a question.

"We began the bargaining with what would be done and by whom," Ash said, "but she will not allow harm to come to her body. She only wishes to do harm to others."

"She actually tried to bargain that she would torture the two of you during sex?" I asked.

"Yes." Holly almost shouted it.

"She did not know that it was the gravest of insults to offer that to you," I said.

"But you knew," Ash said.

I nodded. "I visited the goblin court many times over my childhood. It was one of the few courts in faerie where my father felt that it was safe to bring me as a child."

"He would not have allowed you inside the Seelie Court," Ash said.

"No," I said.

"The goblins are not tamer than the sidhe," Holly said, his anger flaring again.

"No, but the goblins are honorable and do not break their rules," I said.

"Is it true that the queen tried to kill you when you were a child?" Ash asked.

I nodded again. "It is."

"So you were truly safer here with us than with your own kind," Ash said.

"With the goblins and with the sluagh."

Holly laughed, a harsh, unpleasant sound. "You were safer with us, and with the nightmares of faerie than with the pretty sidhe. I find that hard to believe."

"The sluagh, like the goblins, have laws and rules and they abide by them. My father knew your ways and taught those ways to me. It is why we are here speaking today."

"You have bargained most carefully, Princess," Ash said, and there was no lust when he said it, though it was sex we'd been bargaining over. No, there was respect in his face, in his eyes. I'd earned that respect.

"I am not surprised to see Frost, for lately he is half of your constant companions, but it is not usually Rhys who holds your other hand," Ash said.

"Where is the Darkness?" Holly asked.

"Yes, Princess, he has become like your shadow," Ash said. "But today you have only Frost and Rhys by your side. And it is well known that Rhys does not like goblin flesh," Ash said. He made that last comment sound suggestive.

Rhys tensed beside me, one hand going to my shoulder, but otherwise he held his temper.

Did they know that we had been attacked? If they did know, would they see it as an insult if we didn't tell them? The goblins were our allies, but not our friends.

"If the goblins are your allies," Ash said, "then should you have secrets from them?"

They knew. I made my decision. "Is the rumor mill traveling so fast in faerie?"

"There are those among the goblins who watch the human news. They saw the Darkness in a wheelchair coming out of a human hospital. We did not see it, so gave it no credit, but now he is missing from your side. My brother and I ask again, where is your Darkness?"

"He is healing."

"But injured," Ash said. He seemed a little eager at the news.

I fought not to lick my lips or show some other nervous habit. I spoke smoothly. "He is injured, yes."

"It must be grave for him to leave your side," Ash said.

"Darkness in a wheelchair like an invalid," Holly said. "I never thought I would see such a shameful thing."

"There is no shame in taking care of an injury among the sidhe," I said.

"A goblin so badly injured would either take his own life or others would take it for him," Holly said.

"Then glad I am that I am not goblin," I said, "for I injure all too easily." I'd mentioned my frailty on purpose. I hoped to turn their attention from Doyle and toward the sex we might be having tonight. Ash and Holly had never been with a human. They had never been with anyone who could be injured so easily, and death, true death, by accident, with no cold metal involved, was a novelty. Yes, Ash hoped to be king. Ash and Holly both hoped that I could bring them into their sidhe-sided magic as I had others. But it wasn't hunger for power that filled Holly's face with eagerness. It was hunger of a very different kind.

Ash's face remained thoughtful, not caught up in his brother's lust. Holly would be the one who might lose control and hurt me by accident, but it was Ash who would hurt me on purpose. He was just a little less goblin in his thoughts and a little more sidhe. If I could awaken true magic in him, he would be truly dangerous. Kurag, Goblin King, would do well to watch him. The goblins do not inherit their throne. They take it by force of arms, and they keep it the same way. The king is dead, long live the king.

"I will not be distracted, Princess," Ash said. "Not even by your white flesh."

"Am I so poor a prize then?" I asked, and lowered my eyes. The goblins liked their partners either bold as brass or demure. I wasn't capable of their level of boldness, so demure it was.

Ash gave an abrupt laugh. "You know exactly what you represent to us, Princess."

Holly stepped close to the mirror so that his handsome face filled more of the view. There was no distortion as with a camera. It was always as if the glass only separated one part of a room from another. He pressed his fingers against the glass. He looked at me, and there was something in his eyes beyond sex.

I shivered and looked away from him.

"I wish I could smell your fear through this glass," he said in a voice gone low and rough with need.

Frost moved closer to me. Rhys put his arm around my waist. I wanted the comfort, but we were dealing with goblins, and they would use it against us.

"We agreed to Darkness and one other watching our fucking," Ash said. "But he is injured, so I say we have no audience."

"No," I said, voice soft.

"Then all our negotiations must be redone," Ash said.

Frost started to say something, but I touched his arm. "You and Holly have the chance to bring magic, true magic, back to the goblins. You have a chance to be in the running for king of the Unseelie Court. You will not pass up such power because Doyle is too injured to watch us fuck. You will allow me to choose two other men to guard my safety, and to make certain we all have a care tonight."

"We do not take orders from the sidhe," Holly said.

"This is not an order. This is simply the truth." I looked at Ash, who was deeper into the room, farther from the mirror.

"We have given you our word, Princess," Holly said. "The goblins, unlike the sidhe, keep their word. We will do only what has been bargained for, nothing more. We will do nothing that you do not agree to."

"The guards will be there to see that in the midst of pleasure you do not get carried away, but they will also be there for another reason," I said.

"And what would that be?" Ash asked.

"To make certain that I do not lose myself to the moment."

"Lose yourself," Holly said. "What does that mean?"

"It means that we bargained that you would do nothing I did not agree to, or ask for. I fear that I may in the heat of the moment ask for things that my body cannot survive."

"What?" Holly asked, frowning.

"She's saying that she likes to be hurt, and she might ask for things that would damage her," Ash said.

"Lying sidhe," Holly said.

"I swear to you that I do not lie. I must have guards to keep me safe from myself."

Holly hit the mirror hard enough to make it shake on his end. It made me jump. "You are afraid of us," he said. "The sidhe do not crave that which they fear."

"I cannot speak for anyone but myself."

"Do you want me to hurt you?" Holly said.

I looked up then, gave him my gaze, full on, and let him see the truth. "Oh, yes."

Chapter 14

EVENTUALLY THE MIRROR WAS JUST A MIRROR AGAIN. The goblins would arrive tonight with a guard of Red Caps to make certain this was not sidhe treachery. With Doyle injured, I had to choose new guards to watch us, and frankly the ones I trusted most didn't want the duty.

Frost would have stood with Doyle, if ordered, but he didn't really enjoy seeing me with other men. He was okay with Doyle and himself being in the same room at the same time with me, but he didn't share with anyone else. Rhys was more open-minded about the sharing thing, but it would have been a type of torture to ask him to watch the goblins with me. Being a prisoner of the goblins had been what had cost him one eye.

"You meant that about wanting them to hurt you, didn't you?" Rhys asked.

"Yes," I said.

"Do you know how disturbing that is?"

I thought about it, then nodded. "You either get it, or you don't."

"I do not get it either," Frost said.

I kept quiet because Frost actually got it more than he thought he did. He didn't like causing me pain, but a little "tie me up, tie me down" worked just fine as foreplay for him. But since he didn't consider bondage the same thing as causing pain, I didn't argue with him.

"Doyle gets it," Rhys said.

I nodded.

"You enjoy normal sex, right?" Rhys asked.

"Normal is a judgment. The kind of sex I like is just the kind of sex I like, Rhys."

He took a deep breath and started over. "I don't mean to sound judgmental. What I mean is, do you have less . . . bondage sex with the rest of us because you think we won't do what you want? I guess I want to know that you really enjoy being with me."

I put my arms around him, but kept us far enough apart so I could gaze up into his face. "I love being with you, all of you. But sometimes I like something rougher. I wouldn't want to have the goblins' idea of sex every night, but the thought does excite me."

He shivered, and it wasn't from pleasure. No, it was definitely fear. "I know now, thanks to you, that only my ignorance of goblin culture cost me my eye. If I hadn't been just another arrogant sidhe, I'd have known that their culture allows even prisoners to negotiate sex. I could have forced them not to maim me. But I saw the sex as torture, and you can't bargain with torture."

"When a goblin tortures you, you'll know it."

He shuddered again.

I hugged him, trying to squeeze that haunted look from his face. "We need to decide who's going to guard my back tonight."

He hugged me tightly. "I'm so sorry, Merry, but I can't. I just can't do it."

I whispered into his hair, "I know, and it's all right."

"I will do it," Frost said.

I turned in Rhys's arms so I could see Frost. His face was at its arrogant best, coldly handsome. What I saw was that it wasn't his lack of enjoyment of what would be happening that would hamper his ability to guard me, but rather just how much he might secretly enjoy it. That would hamper him. He had a tendency to let his emotions cloud his judgment. Tonight would push too many of Frost's buttons for him to guard me well. If Doyle had been there to help force him through his emotional baggage, then maybe, but Doyle wouldn't be there tonight. Who could I ask to do this?

The mirror suddenly showed the queen's bedroom. We had put a spell on the mirror to keep anyone else from simply peeking in, but the queen had taken that badly. So she had ready access to the mirror. It meant we had no privacy, but it kept Andais's anger to a more manageable level.

It also meant that I'd started sleeping in some of the smaller rooms in the house. My excuse that sex exhausted us and we just fell asleep elsewhere was holding so far.

The queen was covered in blood from about mid-arm to her lower body. It was hard to tell with the black she was wearing, but the cloth seemed to be stuck to her body with the wetness of it. She held the blade in one hand, so covered in blood that I knew it must be slippery.

I didn't want to look at the bed, but I had to. I stayed in Rhys's arms and we both looked at the bed, in that slow-motion way you do when you both want to see and never want to see.

It had to be Crystall, but he was just a bloody form in the shape of a man. Only his shoulders and the width of his hips made me sure of the man part. He was still on his stomach, still where we'd last seen him. One arm lay half off the bed, the hand hanging in midair. The hand twitched involuntarily as if something she'd done to him had affected the nerves.

Tears simply spilled down my face. I couldn't stop them. Rhys pushed my face against his shoulder so I wouldn't have to see. For once, I let him. I'd seen what Andais wanted me to see, though I had no idea why she wanted me to see it. What she'd done to Crystall was usually reserved for traitors, enemies. People she meant to get information out of, or prisoners who were to be tortured for crimes. She had reduced him to a red ruin for what? *For what?* I wanted to scream it at her.

Rhys's arms tightened around me, as if he had read my intent.

"You lied about taking Rhys to your bed," she said at last.

"No," I said. "We just got off the mirror from the goblins." I wiped at my eyes and turned to face my queen. How I hated her.

"You seem a little pale and uncertain for sex, niece of mine." Her voice purred with pleasure at the effect she was having on me. Was that it, just a game to see how awful she could make me feel? Was Crystall so unimportant to her that he was just a body to use to hurt me?

"I will have Sholto fetch Rhys home. He can enchant my mirror as he enchanted yours, then he can join me, as he's always wanted to." She looked at Rhys then. She gave him the full look of those triple gray eyes. "You do still want me, don't you, Rhys?"

That was a dangerous question. Rhys spoke, carefully. "Who would not want to lie with your beauty? But you wanted Merry to be with child, and I must be here to do my duty by her, as you ordered me to do."

"And if I ordered you home?" she asked.

"You gave your oath that all the men who had come to my bed would be mine," I said. "You swore it."

"Except for Mistral. He I did not give to you to keep," she said.

"Except for Mistral," I said, voice soft and fighting to be even.

"Would it upset you more to see Rhys stretched across my bed like this?"

Again, a dangerous question. I thought of several things to say, then settled for the truth. "Yes."

"You cannot love them all, Meredith. No woman can love them all."

"True love, no, my queen, but love them, yes. I love them because they are my people. I was taught that you take care of those who are in your charge."

"My brother's words keep haunting me from your mouth." She flung her hand up, and I think not on purpose sent blood splattering across her side of the mirror. "Sir Hugh has contacted me. There is talk that Taranis will be forced to be a sacrifice to bring life back to his people. There is talk of regicide, Meredith. Talk that the Seelie Court has suffered under his reign of madness." There was something about the way she said that last that made my stomach clench.

Frost said, "He was quite mad this morning, my queen."

"Yes, Killing Frost, yes, you are still there. Still by her side. The Seelie want me to know that they mean no insult by offering you, Meredith, their throne."

"Is it done then?" Frost said.

"No, not quite, but you have perhaps a day and a night before Hugh's faction either loses or gains control of enough nobles to bring our princess to their throne. Hugh told me that I still had Cel to bring to my throne. That it wasn't as if Meredith were my first choice."

Did Hugh have any idea how much he had endangered me? Andais was not much more stable than Taranis. I had no idea how she would react to such talk from the Seelie Court.

"You look frightened, Meredith," she said.

"Shouldn't I be?"

"Why are you not thrilled at the possibility of being queen of the Seelie?"

"Because my heart lies with the Unseelie Court," I said finally.

She smiled then. "Does it, does it truly? Half my sithen is covered in white and pink and gold marble. There are flowers and vines everywhere. The Hallway of Immortality, which has stood as a place of torment for millennia, is covered in flowers. Galen's magic dissolved the cells, and I cannot make the sithen rebuild them. I have people tear up the flowers in the hallway, but they simply regrow overnight."

"I do not know what you want me to say, Aunt Andais."

"I thought the only revolution I had to worry about was one of arms and politics. You have shown me that there are other ways to lose power, Meredith. Your magic is possessing my sithen even with you in Los Angeles. The changes creep farther every day, like some kind of cancer." She laughed, but it held an edge of pain. "A cancer formed of flowers and pastel walls. If I let the Seelie have you, will my kingdom go back to what it was, or is it too late? Is that what the Seelie see, Meredith, that you will remake all of faerie in their image? You are destroying your heritage, Meredith. If I do not stop it, there will soon be no dark court left to save."

"It was not deliberate on my part, Aunt."

"If I give you to the Seelie, will it stop?"

I looked into those eyes. Eyes that held less sanity than they should have. "I don't know."

"What does the Goddess say?"

"I don't know."

"She speaks to you, Meredith. I know she does. But have a care. She is not some Christian deity to take care of you. She is the same power that made me."

"I know the Goddess has many faces," I said.

"Do you, Meredith, do you really?"

I just nodded.

"Enjoy Rhys while you can, because once you sit the Seelie throne, my guard revert to me. They guard only our noble line."

"I have not agreed. . . ."

She waved me to silence. "I no longer know how to save my people and our culture. I thought you were the solution, but though you may save faerie, you seem to be destroying the Unseelie way of life. Did the Goddess offer you a choice for how to bring life back to faerie?"

"Yes," I said softly.

"She offered you blood sacrifice or sex, didn't she?"

"Yes," I said. I couldn't keep the look of astonishment off my face.

"Don't look so shocked, Meredith. I was not always queen. Once no one ruled here who was not chosen by the Goddess. I chose death and blood to cement my tie to the land. I chose the Unseelie way. What did you choose, child of my brother?"

There was a look in her eyes that made me afraid to tell the truth, but I could not lie, not about this. "Life. I chose life."

"You chose the way of the Seelie."

"If there is a way to bring power that does not kill, why is it wrong to choose it?"

"Whose life did you spare?"

I licked suddenly dry lips. "Do not ask."

"Doyle?"

"No," I said.

"Then who!" She screamed it at me.

"Amatheon," I said.

"Amatheon. He is one of your newest lovers. He helped Cel torment you as a child. Why?"

"I don't understand, Aunt."

"Why?"

"Why what?" I asked.

"Why save him? Why not kill him to bring life back to the land? He was a willing sacrifice."

"Why kill him if I didn't have to?" I asked.

She shook her head sadly. "That is not an Unseelie answer, Meredith."

"My father, your brother, would have said the same thing."

"No, my brother was Unseelie."

"My father taught me that all in faerie from lowest to highest have value."

"No," she said.

"Yes," I said.

"I thought of you while I cut Crystall up, Meredith. The only hesitation I have about giving you to the Seelie is that, if I do, I cannot kill you without starting a war. I don't want to lose the option of torturing you to death, Meredith. I think once you are dead your magic will fade and the traitorous Goddess that comes to you will fade with it."

"Would you condemn all of faerie to death because it is not the faerie you wish it to be?" Frost asked, his face astonished.

"No and yes." With that the mirror went blank again. We were left staring at our own reflections. We all looked pale and shocked. Today no good news seemed to go unpunished.

Chapter 15

I WAS READY TO LIE DOWN AND GET SOME REST AND relaxation. It promised to be a long night. But I wasn't allowed to be alone. Not even just to sleep. Between Taranis's treachery and Queen Andais being able to see in the mirror at will, Rhys and Frost were just not willing to risk my being alone. I couldn't argue with them, so I didn't even try. I just started undressing so I could climb between the covers.

If it had been Doyle and Frost, they would both have stayed and we might have slept or we might have done something more active. But Rhys and Frost had never shared me, not even for sleep. There had been a moment of awkwardness as I undressed and they looked at each other.

It was Rhys who finally said, "I want sex with you before the goblins tonight, but I've seen that look on Frost's face before."

"What look?" Frost asked, but I didn't ask because I could see it, and I'd seen it before. Frost's need and uncertainty were plain in his eyes, in the lines of his mouth.

"I want sex," Rhys said, "but you need reassurance, and that takes longer to get."

"I do not know what you mean," Frost said in a

cold voice. His face was at its arrogant best again, that moment of uncertainty hidden behind years of courtly living.

Rhys smiled. "It's all right, Frost. I understand, really I do."

"There is nothing to understand," Frost said.

I slipped naked under the covers, almost too tired to care who won the conversation. I settled against the pillows and waited for one of them to climb into bed with me. I was so tired, so overwhelmed with all of the day's events, that it didn't seem to matter who slept next to me, as long as someone did.

"Doyle isn't just your captain, Frost. You've been each other's right hands for centuries. You're feeling the lack of him."

"We are all feeling the lack of him healthy at our sides," Frost said.

Rhys nodded. "Yes, but only you and Merry feel his loss this deeply."

"I do not understand you," Frost said.

"That's okay," Rhys said. He looked at me. The look asked me, did I understand? I thought I did.

"Come to bed, Frost. Sleep with me." I patted the bed.

"Doyle told me to take care of you until he is able."

I smiled at the face that was trying for blankness and failing around the edges. "Then come to bed and take care of me, Frost."

"You promised me sex, and I am going to hold you to it," Rhys said.

Frost hesitated by the bed. "We have never shared the princess."

"And we aren't going to now," Rhys said. "I'll

share sometimes with the newer men because Merry likes me better than she likes them." He smiled, and I returned the smile. Then his face sobered, and there was something far too serious in his face. "But I could not bear to share her with you and see how she feels about you. I know she loves you more, you and Doyle, but I do not wish the fact rubbed into my body like salt into a wound."

"Rhys," I said.

He shook his head, and pushed a hand toward me. "Don't try to save my ego. You'd have to lie to do it, and the sidhe don't lie."

It was Frost who said, "Rhys, I do not mean to cause you pain."

"You can't help being who you are, and she can't seem to help loving you. I tried to hate you for it, but I can't. If you get her pregnant, and I end up back with Andais, then I'll hate you, but until then, I'll try to share with some grace."

I wanted to say something to make it better, but what could I say? Rhys was right; any comforting words would have had to be lies.

"I do not slight you on purpose, my white knight," I said.

Rhys smiled. "We are both equally pale, my princess. We knew going into this that only one man can be king. Even I think that Doyle and Frost together make a good ruling pair for you. Too bad that even among the Darkness and the Killing Frost there will be a winner and a loser."

With that, Rhys left, closing the door behind us. I heard him speak to the dogs, who must have been waiting outside the door. We did not let the dogs in when we spoke to Andais because she had touched the black dogs and they had not transformed into special dogs for her. The magic had not known her, and she resented it. Frost feared that the lack of a dog meant he was not sidhe enough. Andais simply hated the fact that the returning power didn't seem to know her. She was queen, and all the power of her court should have been hers, but it didn't seem to be working that way.

I almost called to Rhys to let the dogs in but didn't, because it would be a reminder to Frost of what he lacked. The door closed softly, but firmly, and I was left looking up at the man who had stayed.

Frost took off his suit jacket, and the moment he did I could see all the weapons he was carrying. There were many guns and blades, but he was always armed for war. I counted four handguns and two blades in the front of the leather. There would be more, because there were always more weapons than met the eye with the Killing Frost.

"You smile. Why?" he asked softly. He began to undo the buckles that held the leather in place.

"I would ask what army you had planned to fight today with so many weapons, but I know what you feared."

He removed the weapons carefully and laid them across the bedside table. The armament on the wood was heavy with the potential for destruction.

"Where did you put your gun?" Frost asked.

"It's in the drawer of the bedside table."

"You took it off as soon as you entered this room, didn't you?"

"Yes," I said.

He went to the closet and hung the jacket on a hanger. He started unbuttoning his shirt with his back still to me. "I do not understand why you would do that."

"One, a gun is not truly comfortable. Two, if I had needed my gun in this bedroom, it would mean that all of you were dead. If that happened, Frost, one gun in my hands would not save me."

He turned with the shirt unbuttoned to his waist. He pulled it the rest of the way out of his pants. And tired as I was, seeing him tug the shirt out of his pants, watching him undo the last few buttons, made my pulse speed just a little.

His skin was a strip of whiteness against the lesser whiteness of the cloth. He slid the shirt over his shoulders, exposing his muscled strength in inches. He'd learned that sometimes letting me watch him slowly undress helped whet my appetite for him.

He hung his shirt on an empty hanger, even buttoning the collar so it would hang right and not wrinkle. But in doing so, he let me see the long line of his back and shoulders. He'd even swung all that silver hair over one shoulder so that the muscled smoothness of his back was an unobstructed show.

There were times when watching him hang up his clothes drove me nearly mad and had me making small eager noises before he was ready to come to bed. Today would not be one of those days. The view was lovely as always, but I was tired, and did not feel completely well. Part of it was grief and shock, but also the nagging knowledge that I was coming down with a cold or a virus. Frost had never had a cold. He had never had so much as the sniffles.

He turned to face me, his hands sliding around the top of his pants. He'd had to undo the belt earlier to take off the rig of weapons. I had to be more tired than I knew to have missed him unbuckling his belt.

He started with the button at the top of his pants, and I rolled over. I rolled so my face was buried in the pillow and I could not watch. He was too beautiful to be real. Too amazing to be mine.

I felt the bed move, and knew he was on the bed with me. "Merry, what is wrong? I thought you enjoyed watching me."

"I do," I said, still not looking at him. How did I explain that I was having one of those rare moments when my mortality seemed too real and his immortality too large a reminder.

"Am I not enough to please you without Doyle by my side?"

That made me turn and look at him. He was sitting on the edge of the bed, one leg bent at the knee toward me. His pants gapped where he'd undone the buttons but not the zipper, his belt framing the undone work. He was slumping a little so that the fine muscles and lines of his stomach bunched. I had a choice of looking down to his lap and what I knew was still covered by his pants, or up to the beauty of his chest and shoulders and that face. In a different mood I would have gone down, but sometimes a man needs you to pay attention to things above the waist before you move below.

I sat up, keeping the cover in front of my breasts, because with me nude sometimes Frost forgot to listen, and I wanted him to hear me.

He sat there with his hair pooling like silver fire

around his bare skin. He would not look at me, even though I knew he could feel the bed move as I inched close enough to touch his arm.

"Frost, I love you."

His gray eyes rose once, then went back to staring at his big hands where they lay in his lap. "Do you love me alone without Doyle's body beside me?"

My hand tightened on his arm while I tried to think what to say. This was certainly a conversation I hadn't expected to be having. I did love Frost, but I did not always love his moods. "I find you as desirable now as I did that first night."

He rewarded me with a small smile. "That was a very good night, but you avoided answering my question." He gave me the full force of his eyes then. "Which is answer enough." He started to get up, and I pressed my hand on his arm, not to force him, but to try to keep him where he was. He let me keep him sitting on the bed though he was stronger than I would ever be. There, that note of regret again.

I sighed, and tried to cut through his mood and mine to get to something better. "Is it because I turned away and did not watch you undress?"

He nodded.

"I don't feel well. I think I am coming down with a cold."

He looked at me uncomprehendingly.

"Remember that some of you thought that what happened inside faerie had made me immortal like the rest of you?"

He nodded again.

"If I'm coming down with a cold then it is not so. I am still mortal."

He put his hand over mine where it lay against his arm. "Why would that make you look away from me?"

"I love you, Frost, but loving you means that I will have to watch you stay young and handsome and perfect while I age. This body that you love will not remain. I will grow old and I will know death, and I will be forced to look at you every day and know that you do not understand. When I am very old, you will still take off your clothes and be as beautiful as you are now."

"You will always be our princess," he said, and his face showed that he was trying to understand.

I took my hand away and lay back on the bed, staring up at that impossibly lovely face. Tears burned at the back of my eyes and tightened my throat so that I could choke on regret. With everything that had happened today, all that had gone wrong, all the danger around us, I was ready to cry because the men I loved would always remain as beautiful as they were today but I would not. It wasn't death I feared, really, it was the slow decay. How had Maeve Reed's husband borne watching her remain while he grew old? How do love and sanity survive such a thing?

Frost leaned over me, and his shoulders were so broad that his hair fanned out around me like some shining tent, a waterfall caught in mid-motion to glitter in the dim light of my room. "You are young and you are beautiful this night. Why do you borrow such sorrows when they are far away, and I am right here?" He whispered the last words above my lips, and ended with a kiss.

I let him kiss me, but didn't kiss him back. Did he

not understand? Well, of course he didn't. How could he? Or . . . or. . . .

I pushed a hand against his chest and got enough space to look into his face. "Have you loved someone and watched her grow old?"

He sat back abruptly and would not look at me. I wrapped my hand around as much of his wrist as I could. It was too big for me to encircle it. "You have, haven't you?" I asked.

He would not look at me, but finally he nodded.

"Who, when?" I asked.

"I saw her through a pane of glass when I was not the Killing Frost but just Frost. I was just the hoarfrost made into something alive by the belief of the people and the magic of faerie." He looked at me, and there was uncertainty in that look. "You saw me in a vision once, what I began as."

I nodded. I remembered. "You came to her window as Jack Frost," I said.

"Yes."

"What was her name?"

"Rose. She had golden curls and eyes like a winter sky. She saw me at the window, saw me and tried to tell her mother that there was a face at the window."

"She had second sight," I said.

He nodded.

I almost let it go, but I couldn't. I just couldn't. "What happened?"

"She was always alone. The other children seemed to sense that she was different. She made the mistake of telling them the things she could see. They named her witch, and her mother with her. She had no father. From the talk among the other villagers she had never had a father. I heard them as I painted frost on their houses whispering that Rose was begotten by no man, but the devil. They were so poor, and I was just another part of the winter cold that hurt them the most. I wanted so to help her." He raised his big hands, as if he were seeing different hands, smaller and less powerful. "I needed to be more."

"Did you ask for help?" I asked.

He looked at me, startled. "Do you mean, did I ask the Goddess and consort to help me?"

I nodded.

He smiled and it lightened his face, made a joy shine through that he hid most of the time. "I did."

I smiled back at him. "And you were answered."

"Yes," he said, still smiling. "I went to sleep, and when I woke, I was taller, stronger. I found them fuel for their fire, all that long winter. I found them food." Then the joy fled from his face. "I took the food from the other villagers, and they accused her mother of stealing. Rose told them that her friend left it, her shining friend."

I took his hand in mine. "They accused her of witchcraft," I said softly.

"Yes, and theft. I tried to help, but I didn't understand what it was to be human, or even fey. I was so new, Merry, so new to being anything but ice and cold. I was a thought made into a being. I did not know how to be alive, or what it meant."

"You wanted to help," I said.

He nodded. "My help cost them everything. They were jailed and condemned to death. The first time I called cold to my hands, a cold so deep that it could shatter metal, was for Rose and her mother. I broke their bars and rescued them."

"But that's wonderful." Yet his hand convulsed around mine, and I knew the story didn't end there.

"Can you imagine what the villagers thought when they found the metal bars shattered and the two women gone? Can you imagine what they thought about Rose and her mother?"

"Nothing they hadn't already believed," I said softly.

"Perhaps, but I was a piece of winter. I could not build them a shelter. I could not keep them warm. I could do nothing but take them out into the dead of winter with every human within reach turned against them."

I sat up and tried to hold him, but he wouldn't let me. He turned away and finished his story. "They were dying because where I went, winter followed. I was still too much an elemental thing to understand my own magic. When all was lost, I prayed. The consort came to me and he asked me if I would give up all that I was to save them. I hadn't been alive very long, Merry, and I remembered what it had been like before. I didn't want to go back to that, but Rose lay so still in the snow, her hair fading into the whiteness, that I said yes. I would give up all that I was if it would save them. It seemed a suitable sacrifice, since my meddling, no matter how well intentioned, had brought about their misery."

He stopped talking for so long that I came to him and wrapped my arms around him from behind. This time he let me do it. He even leaned back against the pull of my body so that I cradled his upper body against my kneeling one.

I whispered, "What happened?"

"There was music in the snow, and Taranis, Lord of Light and Illusion, came riding on a horse made of moonlight. You have no idea how amazing a golden court could be when they rode out in those days, Merry. It wasn't just Taranis who could make a steed out of light or shadow or leaves. It was truly magical. He and his men lifted them out of the snow and began to ride away toward the faerie mound. I was content to lose her if it meant she lived. I waited to be blasted back to nothingness and I was content. I had saved them, and my existence for theirs seemed right. I won't say my life for theirs because I wasn't alive yet then, not as I am now."

I hugged him close, and he gave me more of his weight, so that I leaned back against the foot of the bed, and cradled him. I kept one hand on his chest so I could feel his words rumbling up through his body.

"She woke, held in the lap of one of the shining court. My little Rose woke. She cried out for her Jackie, for her Jackie Frost. I came to her as I had from that first moment. I came to her because I could do nothing else. She pushed herself from the arms of that shining lord of the sidhe and came to me. I was not as I am now, Merry. I was young and childlike. The Goddess gave me a body that could do more. But I was not one of the shining court. I was a lesser fey in every way. I suppose to human eyes I might have appeared as a boy of perhaps fourteen or younger. I looked a good match for my Rose."

He lay still in my arms.

"What happened to her mother?" I asked.

"She is still a cook at the golden court."

I kissed his forehead, then asked, "What happened to Rose?"

"We found shelter, and I used my magic to carry her far away from her village. People didn't travel then as they do now, and twenty miles was enough distance that we never saw any of the others again. She taught me how to be real, and I grew with her."

"What do you mean, you grew with her?"

"I looked like a boy of fourteen, as she was a girl of fifteen. As she grew, so did I. It was not sword and shield that I first learned with these arms, it was axe and any other work a strong back could do to help take care of his family."

"You had children," I whispered.

"No. I thought it was because I wasn't real enough. Now, since you remain without child I wonder if it is simply not my fate to have children."

"But you were a couple," I said.

"Yes, and a priest who was more friendly than Christian even married us. But we could not stay in any one village for long, because I did not age. I grew with my Rose until I am as you see me now. Then I stopped, but she did not. I watched her hair turn from yellow to white, her eyes fade from the blue of winter to the gray of snowy skies."

He looked up at me then, and there was fierceness in his face. "I watched her fade, but I loved her always. Because it was her love that made me real, Merry. Not faerie, not wild magic, but the magic of love. I thought I was giving up what life I had to save Rose, but the consort had asked if I would give up everything I was, and I did. I became what she needed me to be. When I realized that I would not age with her I wept, because I could not imagine being without her."

He came to his knees and put his hands on my arms, and stared down into my face. "I will love you always. When this red hair is white, I will still love you. When the smooth softness of youth is replaced by the delicate softness of age, I will still want to touch your skin. When your face is full of the lines of every smile you have ever smiled, of every surprise I have seen flash through your eyes, when every tear you have ever cried has left its mark upon your face, I will treasure you all the more, because I was there to see it all. I will share your life with you, Meredith, and I will love you until the last breath leaves your body or mine."

He leaned down and kissed me, and this time I kissed him back. This time I melted into his arms, his body, because I could do nothing else.

Chapter 16

WE ENDED WITH HIM ABOVE ME. HIS HAIR HAD COME unbound and fell around us like silver rain, if rain could be soft as silk and warm as your lover's body. Our skin glowed as if we'd swallowed the moon, and it was shining out of every inch of our skin. I knew my hair was a mass of red shining fire, because I could see the light of it from the edges of my eyes. His hair began to spark and shine as he moved above me, catching the light the way snow glitters in moonlight. I'd had other lovers who brought the sun to bed with them, but Frost was a winter's night with all that meant of beauty and harshness.

He was too tall, or I was too short, for him to lie down on top of me. It was neither enjoyable for me nor easy to breathe, so he held his upper body above me with the shining strength of pale, muscled arms. Gazing down the length of our bodies, watching him slide in and out of me, made me cry out, made me look away as if the sight of it was too wonderful and I had to find something else for my eyes to meet. What I met were his eyes. His eyes were gray like a winter's sky, but now with his power riding him they were more than just gray.

In the gray of his eyes was a glimpse of a snow-covered hill with a bare winter tree upon it. There was a moment of vertigo, as if I could have fallen into that landscape, into his eyes, and been some-where else. I closed my eyes then, because I was never certain where that hill was, or what tree it would be.

The rhythm of his body in and out of mine, the size of him gliding in and out of my body, was beginning to fill me up. The first faint glow of orgasm began to build.

"Merry, Merry, look at me." There was urgency in his voice, that rough urgency that said that he too was close.

I opened my eyes, and his were just above mine, wide, staring, demanding that I not look away. He moved one hand so that he gripped my hair near one cheek. "I want to watch your face," he said, his voice breathy and deep with effort.

There was snow in his eyes, falling on that lonely tree and the hillside beyond. Something moved in his eyes, a figure.

The rhythm of his body changed, grew more ur-gent, and it was too much. I could not watch his eyes while his body ran through mine. I tried to watch his body moving above mine, but his grip on my hair tightened, forcing my face to look up into his. His face was the face of my beloved, Frost. There was no vision in his eyes to distract me from the beauty of his face, the fierceness in his eyes.

I whispered, "Almost, almost, almost." Then one last thrust, and almost was now.

I screamed, and only his grip, gone almost cruel in my hair, kept my neck from bowing. He kept our faces staring into each other, tolerated no looking away. We stared at each other as our bodies rode the pleasure. His strength demanded that we share this, the most intimate of moments, with no flinching, no looking away, nothing to save us from the wildness in each other's eyes.

We fell into that wildness, that near-frantic fierceness. He cried out above me as I screamed my pleasure, then his body collapsed atop mine, and he lifted me in his arms, with his body still sheathed inside me. He knelt, pinning me to the headboard. I grabbed the wood to keep me where he seemed to want me. He had gone, but he was not spent. He proved that as he began to pound me against the wood, the bed shivering with the strength of it, the entire frame of the bed protesting the abuse.

I screamed for him, and fought to keep my hands on the wood to hold myself in place as he plunged inside me as deeply as he could. Deep enough from this angle that pleasure and pain rode each other, as Frost rode me.

I let go of the bed and ran my nails down his white skin. Where I bled him the glow of his skin split, but it wasn't blood that ran out. Blue glowing lines followed the lines of my nails and painted our skin. There was a moment when I saw a thorn vine around my forearm, and the head of a stag traced across his chest. His body shuddered against mine, inside mine as I painted his body with my pleasure and his pain.

He pressed me in his arms so that I saw the glow on his shoulder, and that sign of power I had seen before as the vine on my arm. I realized that the tattoo that had first appeared in faerie was the same image as in his eyes.

We stayed frozen a moment, pressed against the headboard. His heart beat so fast and so hard I felt it against the side of my face like a hand. He took us slowly to our sides so that we finally lay across the head of the bed on what pillows had not been knocked off.

"I had forgotten how magnificent you could be, Frost." The voice was not mine; it came from the mirror. Where a second before I could not have moved, fear made me sit up and grab for spilled sheets.

"Don't cover yourselves," Andais said from the mirror.

We drew the sheets over us.

"I said, do not cover yourselves, or have I ceased to be your queen?" There was an evil tone in her voice that made us push the sheets back. She'd seen the end of our lovemaking; no reason to be shy now, I supposed.

Frost kept himself pressed against me so that he was as hidden as he could manage. I found my voice first, and said, "My queen, what brings you to our mirror?"

"I thought I would see Rhys with you, or was that a lie when you said you'd be with him?"

"Rhys will have his turn, my queen."

She stared at Frost, as if I were not there. I looked at him, his body dewed with the sweat of his exertions, his hair a glorious tangle of silver, to decorate all that pale muscled strength. He was beautiful. Beautiful in a way that even among the sidhe not everyone could boast. Ironic that one who had not begun as sidhe would be among our most handsome men. But now that I knew that he had been shaped by love, not a desire for power, but selfless love, I understood. For love makes us all beautiful.

"The look on your face, Meredith, as you gaze upon him, what are you thinking?"

"Love, Aunt Andais, I am thinking of love."

She made a disgusted sound. "Know this, niece of mine. If the Killing Frost is not your king, I will have him back, and I will see if he is as good as he looks."

"He was your lover once, hundreds of years ago."

"I remember," she said, but not like it made her happy.

I didn't understand the look on her face, or the tone of her voice. I didn't truly understand why she had been so determined to catch me with Rhys—or, was she eager to catch me without him? Was she looking for an excuse to order Rhys back to faerie? If yes, then why? She had never treated him as one of her favorites, not in the memory of anyone I knew.

"I see fear in your eyes, my Killing Frost," she said.

My arms tightened around him. I couldn't help it. "Would you protect him from me, Meredith?"

"I would protect all my people from harm."

"But this one is special to you, isn't he?"

"Yes," I said, because anything else would be a lie.

"Frost, look at me." She ordered it.

He raised his eyes to her.

"Are you afraid of me, Frost?"

He swallowed hard enough that it sounded painful, and said in a voice gone rough, "Yes, my queen, I fear you."

"You love Meredith, don't you?"

He answered, "Yes, my queen."

"He loves you, niece, but he fears me. I think you will discover that fear is a more potent threat than love."

"I don't want to threaten him."

"One day you will. One day you will find that all the love in faerie is not enough to keep the man you love obedient. You will want fear on your side, and you are too soft to wield it."

"I am not frightening. I know that, Aunt Andais."

"I look at you and I see the future of my court and I despair."

"If love is the future of our court, Aunt Andais, then I am hopeful."

She looked once more at Frost, as if he was something to eat and she was starving. "I hate you, Meredith. I truly do."

I fought not to say what I was thinking, but she said, "Your face betrays you. Say what is in your mind, niece. I hate you, Meredith. What does that make you want to say to me?"

"I hate you, too."

Andais smiled like she meant it. The bed behind her had been stripped down to its bare essentials. Apparently Crystall's torture had produced too much blood even for her to sleep in. "I think I will have Mistral tonight, Meredith. I will do to that strong body what I did to Crystall earlier."

"I cannot stop you," I said.

"Not yet you can't." With that the mirror was blank again. I was left staring at my own startled reflection.

Frost did not look at the mirror. He just crawled off the bed and started getting dressed. He didn't even bother to clean up first. He just seemed to need to be dressed, and I guess I couldn't blame him.

He spoke without looking at me, all his concentration on getting his nakedness covered as quickly as possible. "I told you once that I would rather die than go back to her. I meant it, Meredith."

"I know you did," I said.

He started buckling on his weapons. "I still mean it."

I reached up to him. He took my hand, kissed it, and gave me the saddest smile I'd ever seen. "Frost, I. . . ."

"If you are going to be with Rhys before evening, I'd use another room. I would not want her as an audience again today."

"I'll do as you suggest."

"I'm going to check on Doyle." He had his clothes in place, and all his weapons. He was tall and handsome, and coldly beautiful. He was my Killing Frost, as arrogant and unreadable as when I'd first met him. But I carried with me the memory of his eyes wide and frantic as he plunged inside my body. I knew what lay inside that cool, controlled man, and I valued every glimpse of the real Frost. A glimpse of the man who had fallen in love with a peasant's daughter, and given up everything he ever knew to be with her.

He walked out of the room, tall and straight and, to most eyes, unmoved. But I knew why he left me there in the bed. He left because he was terrified that his queen would come back for a second peek.

Chapter 17

I TOOK FROST'S ADVICE, AND WENT TO ONE OF THE smaller guest rooms in Maeve Reed's huge guesthouse. She'd offered us the main house while she was away in Europe, where she'd fled because Taranis had tried to kill her twice with magic. Maybe soon we could tell her that Taranis was no longer a threat to her, or anyone, but I still had to get through today. I'd have liked to have found a place of our own by now, but with nearly twenty men to house and feed I couldn't afford it. I was still refusing to take aid from my aunt. I knew all too well how long and dangerous were the strings that she attached to all favors.

The adrenaline had worn off, and I was more tired than when I had started the day. I was coming down with something. Damnit.

I believed Frost would love me, but I wasn't sure how I would feel aging while they all remained young and fair. There were moments when I wasn't certain that I was a good enough person to be a good sport about that.

The room was dark. Blackout curtains had been added to the room's only window. The mirror over the dresser had been removed so that the wall was blank and peaceful. There would be no unexpected calls in here. It was one of the reasons I'd chosen the room. I needed rest, and I had had all I wanted of surprise mirror calls today.

Kitto had joined me, and he lay curled beside me under the smooth softness of clean cotton sheets. His dark curls rested on the curve of one of my shoulders, his breath warm on the mound of my breast. His arm lay over my stomach, his leg over my thigh, his other arm up where he could play idly with my hair. He was the only man in my guard shorter than I was, short enough that he could curl around me as I curled around the taller men. He was one of the first men to join me in exile. In the weeks that he'd been away from faerie, Doyle had forced him to use the gym. There was muscle under the white smoothness of his moonlight skin now. Muscle that had never been there before.

He was 4'11" with the face of an angel that had never quite gotten through puberty. But then goblins don't have to shave, and in that, his body had taken after that half of his heritage. I played with the soft curls of his hair, which had grown to touch the tops of his broadening shoulders. The hair was as soft as Galen's, as soft as my own.

My other hand was curled around his back. My fingers traced the smooth line of scaled skin that ran down his spine. The scales looked dark in dim light, but in brighter light his skin ran with rainbows. In the kissable mouth that rested against my breast were retractable fangs, connected to poison glands. His father had been a snake goblin. The fact that his father had raped his mother instead of eating her was unusual. Apparently snake goblins were a cold lot in every way. Passion did not move them, but something about Kitto's mother had wakened heat in his father's cold heart.

She had then abandoned her baby beside a goblin mound when she realized what he was. Goblins have been known to eat their own young, and sidhe flesh is highly prized. His own mother had put him out to be killed. Instead, he'd been taken in by a goblin female who had meant to raise him to a bigger size to eat him. But something about Kitto had moved her, too, and she had not had the heart to kill him. There was something in him that did indeed bring out the desire to care, to take care of, to protect. He had offered his life to save mine more than once, yet I still could not see him as my protector.

He raised huge almond-shaped eyes to me, a swimming pure blue the way Holly's and Ash's eyes were completely one color. Except Kitto's eyes were wonderful clear blue like a pale sapphire, or a morning sky.

"Who are you hiding from today, Merry?" he asked, voice gentle.

I smiled at him from my nest of pillows. "How do you know I'm hiding?"

"It's why you come here, to hide."

I traced the edge of his cheek. But for a few chance genes he would have been like Holly and Ash, tall and sidhe-beautiful with the extra strength and stamina of the goblins.

"I told you, I'm not feeling well."

He smiled, and propped himself up on one elbow so that he was looking slightly down at me. "That is true, but there is a sorrow to you that I would lift if you only tell me how."

"Just don't make me talk of politics. I need to rest if I am to do my duty tonight."

He traced his finger down the side of my face from temple to chin. It was a long, slow movement that made me close my eyes and catch my breath.

"Is that how you see the goblins you will bed tonight, as a duty?"

I opened my eyes. "It is not that they are goblins that makes them a duty."

He smiled, sliding his hand into my hair. "I know that. It is who they are, what they are, and you do not feel your best."

"They frighten me, Kitto."

His face was sober. "I fear them, too."

"Did they ever use you ill?"

"They have not much liking for male flesh. I have serviced them a time or two when they came to bed my master."

Kitto had survived in a culture more violent than any in faerie by doing what some people have to do in prison to survive. They choose someone powerful, or are chosen, and become their property. It was looked down upon, but strangely was honored as a profession. On one hand, goblins like Kitto were the victims of cruel humor; on the other hand, they were highly valued by their masters. Master was not a sexist term in goblin nomenclature. It could be male or female. It was simply the term for one who owned a slave.

"Serviced them?" I made it a question.

"I believe in pornography I would be what is termed a fluffer. They do everything together, do the brothers. I helped keep one ready while the other finished."

He said it as if it were the most normal thing in the world. There was no condemnation, no anger, nothing. It was the way of his world once. The only world he'd known until his king gave him to me. I tried very hard to give Kitto choices in his new life, but I had to be careful, because too many choices made him anxious. His entire world had literally changed. He had never seen electricity or a television. He was now living on the estate of one of Hollywood's leading actresses, though he'd never seen a single one of her movies. He was much more impressed that she had once been the goddess Conchenn—a secret that Hollywood did not know.

"I will be with you tonight, Merry. I will help you."

"I can't ask you. . . ."

He put his fingers against my lips. "You do not have to ask. None of your other men will know goblin culture as I do. I do not say that I could protect you from them, but I can keep you from falling into traps of custom."

I kissed his fingers and moved his hand away from my mouth so I could lay another kiss against the palm of his hand. I wanted to say, "I can't let you because they abused you," but he didn't see it that way. To tell him it was abuse when he didn't think it was seemed wrong. It was his culture, not mine. Who was I to throw stones after what I'd seen in Andais's bed today? Poor Crystall.

There was a soft knock on the door. I sighed, and snuggled deeper into the pillows. I did not want to deal with another crisis today. I had one all nice and scheduled for later tonight when the goblin twins arrived.

Kitto leaned over and whispered against my hair, "You are the princess. You can tell them to go away."

"I can't tell them to go away until I know what they want." I called out, "Who is it?"

"It's Rhys."

Kitto and I exchanged a look. He widened his eyes, his version of a shrug. He was right. It would have to be something important for Rhys to willingly see me in bed with a goblin, any goblin. He even liked Kitto, or at least had sat up late with him introducing him to marathon film noir movie sessions. He'd gone along with Galen when the two of them took Kitto shopping for modern clothes. But Rhys always left if it got physical with Kitto.

Whatever would bring Rhys willingly into this room had to be important. Important today meant bad. Shit. Out loud I said, "Come in."

Kitto started to move away from me as if he were going to leave, but I grabbed his arm and kept him propped on his elbow above me. "This is your room. You don't leave."

Kitto looked doubtful but he stayed where I wanted him. He was good that way. He followed orders beautifully, which was more than I could say for most of the other men.

Rhys walked in, closing the door quietly behind him. I studied his face, and he looked peaceful enough. "Doyle is a very stubborn man even for a sidhe."

"You're just figuring that out?" I asked.

Rhys grinned. "Fair enough. I knew it already."

"He still won't let Merry sit by his side?" Kitto asked. He looked perfectly at ease beside me now, as if he had never considered moving away.

Rhys moved farther into the room as he spoke. "He says, 'I am to protect her, not she me.' He further says that you need your rest for tonight, not to sit and worry over him."

"I would have cuddled him while we both slept," I said.

"His loss, our gain," Rhys said, grinning again. He took off his jacket.

"Our loss," Kitto said, a lilt of surprise in his voice.

Rhys paused, jacket in one hand. His shoulder holster was very stark against the pale blue of his shirt. Though the shoulder holster implied that it was just for guns, that wasn't true at all. All the men who had been with me for a few months had custom rigs made, I suspect by one of the leather workers inside faerie. No human could have made them so quickly and so perfectly. There were also intricate designs worked into the leather, and nearly ingenious ways to carry as many weapons as possible and still be able to slip modern jackets over them all.

Rhys stood there with a gun under one arm and a knife on the other. A second gun rode at his waist. There was also a short sword belted somehow across his back so that the hilt stuck a little out from behind his back on one side. He could grab it sort of like a gun worn at the small of the back.

"I touched you in the lawyer's office, and didn't feel all the weapons," I said. "There's a spell that affects sight and touch."

"If you didn't pick up on it, then it's as good as promised," Rhys replied.

"Why did I see the swords at Frost's and Doyle's backs?"

"The enchantment only works if you don't break the line of the clothing covering the holster. They keep insisting on huge swords that show around the edges of the jackets, so you see the swords. It also makes it more likely that people will notice their guns and other weapons. Once you draw attention to what amounts to an illusion, it begins to break down. You know that."

"But I didn't realize that that was what the leather rigs were, bespelled."

He shrugged.

"It must have cost a pretty penny."

"They were gifts," he said.

I gave him wide eyes. "Not this much magical work."

"You made yourself pretty popular among the lesser fey when you gave your little speech in the hallway, about how most of your friends were below stairs when you were a child, not among the sidhe."

"It's true," I said.

"Yes, but it also helped win them to you. That and you being part brownie."

"A lesser fey did the leatherwork?" I asked.

He nodded. "While the sidhe have lost most of their magic, the lesser fey have held on to more than we knew. I think they were afraid to point out to the sidhe that the lesser fey hadn't faded as much as the greater fey."

"Wise of them," I said.

Rhys was at the foot of the bed now. "Not that I don't like my nifty new leather rig, but are you delaying so you can think of a polite way to send me away, or is there a question you don't want to ask?"

"Actually, I am interested in the magic on the leather. We may need all the magical help we can get soon. But this is the first time you've willingly come into Kitto's room when I've been with him. We're wondering what's up."

He nodded and looked down, as if gathering his thoughts. "Unless you object, either of you, I'd like to join you for afternoon cuddling." He raised his face and displayed one of the most neutral expressions I'd ever seen from him. He usually hid his emotions behind a wry humor. Today he was serious. It wasn't like him.

"My opinion doesn't count," Kitto said, but he scooted down beside me, pulling the sheet up to cover most of himself.

Rhys put his jacket over one arm. "We've been over this, Kitto. You're sidhe now, which means you get to be as opinionated as the rest of us."

"Oh, please," I said. "Not as opinionated as all that. Kitto's sort of refreshingly undemanding."

Rhys smiled at me. "Are we that bad?"

"Sometimes," I said. "You're not as bad as some."

"Like Doyle," he said.

"Frost," said Kitto, then seemed shocked at his insult of the other man. He actually covered his face with the sheet, snuggling tightly against the side of my body. But there was a tension to him now that had nothing to do with sex. He was frightened.

Was he frightened of Rhys? He had tried to hurt, if

not kill, Kitto on at least one occasion when I first brought him to Los Angeles. Apparently, a few movies and shopping trips couldn't make up for earlier hostility. Sort of like parents trying to win over kids in a divorce. If you're mean, all the treats in the world don't make up for it later.

Rhys had been mean, and Kitto had been hiding that he was still afraid of the other man. I had missed it completely. I had thought we were as much a big happy family as we were going to get. How could I rule these people if I couldn't even keep peace and safety among my own lovers?

"I don't think Kitto's comfortable with you being here, Rhys," I said. I stroked Kitto's back under the covers. He snuggled harder against me as if afraid of what I would ask him. I didn't understand why "servicing" Holly and Ash didn't bother him, but Rhys did. Maybe it was a cultural thing that I didn't understand because I wasn't goblin enough. I would be their high queen, but I would never truly be goblin. They were our foot soldiers, our strong arm, and most likely to be cannon fodder. The Red Caps were our shock troops. But I was missing something, right this minute, about the goblin in my bed. He was truly sidhe by birth of his magic, but in his heart he was, and always would be, goblin, just as there was more human to me because I'd gone to human schools and had human friends. That more than genetics made me more human than I would have been, more American than I would have been in the way I thought. Sometimes I wondered if my father would have found another excuse to raise me outside of faerie if Andais hadn't tried to kill me. Father had felt that it was very important that I understand our new country.

"Kitto," Rhys said. "I know I was awful to you once, but I've tried to make up for it."

Kitto's voice came out muffled. "Did you do all of it just to make up?"

Rhys seemed to think about it. "At the beginning, but you're the only one who will watch more than two gangster movies in a row with me and actually enjoy them. The others tolerate it. Or were you just being polite?"

Kitto spoke, still under the covers. "I like James Cagney. He's short."

"Yeah, I like that about him, too," Rhys said.

"You are not small," Kitto said.

"For a sidhe I am."

Kitto pulled an edge of cover down so he could see the other man. I lay there unneeded. This was a guy moment that had strangely turned into a girl moment. I'd noticed with Kitto that the guy silence didn't quite work. He had an almost feminine need to talk, to express his thoughts and feelings, or they weren't real to him.

"Edward G. Robinson is short, too," Kitto said softly.

Rhys smiled. "Bogart wasn't all that tall either."

"Really? They make him look tall."

"Apple crates and camera angles," Rhys said.

Kitto didn't ask what he meant by apple crates, which meant that they'd already had a talk about shorter actors standing on things to look taller for the camera. It was also a cheap way to make your villain or hero look like he was strong enough to lift someone one-handed. Ah, B-movie magic.

Kitto came a little farther out of the covers. "What do you want, Rhys?"

"I want to apologize that I ever thought you were like Holly and Ash and the rest."

"I am not strong like they are," Kitto said.

Rhys shook his head. "You are kind and you crave kindness. That isn't a sin."

"You have explained this concept of sin, and if I understand it, then yes, Rhys, it is a sin to be weak among the goblins. A sin that most often ends in death."

Rhys sat on the corner of the bed. Kitto didn't flinch, which was a big improvement. "I heard that you're going to help Merry with the goblins tonight," said Rhys.

"Yes," Kitto said.

"We took another call from the goblins since Merry came in here."

Ah, here it comes, I thought.

Kitto sat up, drawing his knees tight in a hug, sliding the covers around him and a little off of me. "What has happened?"

"Kurag, Goblin King, was surprised that you would be willing to help with the brothers tonight. He said that Holly used you as a trollop when he couldn't find a female he liked."

"A lot of them used me when I was between masters." Kitto said it as if it were just ordinary.

"He said one of your masters was a favorite of the brothers, and that you helped with that, too." I knew Kurag hadn't used the word "helped." Goblins were blunt about sex, except for ones like Kitto, who had spent their lives having to be servile. Strangely, the weaker goblins were the ones who were best at diplomacy among their kind. When a misspoken word can get you killed or maimed, I guess you learn to mind your tongue. I know it had helped make me cautious.

"My last master enjoyed their company."

"What happened to your last master?" Rhys asked.

"She grew tired of me and set me free to find a new master." He touched my arm.

"You see Merry as your new master," Rhys said.

"Yes."

That was news to me. "Kitto," I said, and he looked at me. "Do you feel you have no choice when I ask you to do something?"

"What you ask of me is pleasant. You are the best master I have ever had."

It wasn't quite the answer I'd wanted. I looked at Rhys, trying to convey with my eyes "help me figure out how to ask this question."

Rhys answered it himself. "You aren't going to break a lifetime of habit with a few months of safety, Merry."

He was right, but I didn't like the fact that Kitto felt that he had little choice in his new life. "You are sidhe, Kitto," I said.

"But I am also goblin," he said, as if that settled it. Maybe it did.

"Why would you volunteer to be with Merry tonight with Ash and Holly?" Rhys asked.

"No one else here truly understands what they are capable of. I must be there to see that if harm happens it is not Merry that it happens to."

"You mean you'll take the abuse so she doesn't have to," Rhys said.

Kitto nodded.

I sat up and hugged him. "I don't want you to be hurt either."

He leaned into the hug. "And that is why I would take the hurt willingly. Besides, I am harder to hurt than you are."

"If you will allow me, I will join you and Merry this afternoon," Rhys said.

"Tonight, you mean," I said.

"No, I don't know if I'm that strong yet." He looked down, then up, but it was not me he looked at. "I don't know if I am as strong as my friend."

"Friend?" Kitto made it a question.

Rhys nodded.

"How can you say you are not as strong as me?" Kitto asked.

"I was the victim of the goblins who hurt me for a single night. Yet I have feared and hated all goblins for years. You have taught me that that was wrong. But I still don't know if I am strong enough to be in the room when Merry goes to the goblins tonight. I don't know if I can stand to be in the room and watch and guard her. You had years of . . . hurt, by the very goblins who will be here tonight. Yet you will give yourself to them to protect Merry. I say to you, Kitto, that that is a kind of bravery I do not have." His single beautiful eye shimmered in the dimness.

Kitto reached out and touched his arm. "You are brave. I have seen it."

Rhys shook his head and closed his eye. One lone

tear trailed down his face, shining more than any human tear would have in the twilight of the room.

Kitto touched that single tear with one fingertip. He offered the trembling drop to me, but I shook my head. He raised it to his lips, and Rhys watched him lick his tear off of his finger. Tears were not as precious as blood and other fluids, but they were still gifts. I knew that sometimes the goblins tortured simply to gather tears.

The sidhe would make you cry, but they didn't value the tears.

"Can I join you?" Rhys asked, and I knew it wasn't me he was asking.

Kitto gazed into his face and finally nodded yes.

Chapter 18

RHYS'S CLOTHES AND WEAPONS ENDED IN A HEAP BY the bed. Stripped, he was as amazing as ever. There were guards who had longer waists, or broader shoulders, but no one had the sculpted muscles in stomach, chest, arms, and legs that Rhys did. All of him was smooth and hard and strong.

The bed wouldn't have been big enough for me and two of most of the other men, but Kitto and Rhys both took up less room than most. There was room for the three of us.

I lay between the smooth, muscled weight of the two of them, and it felt so good. The sensation of it made me close my eyes and simply concentrate on the feel of their bodies against mine. I had needed this, to be comforted by people who cared for me, to be held, and not to have to worry. Had Doyle understood that I would have lain there tense, listening for his pain sounds, and not truly rested? Perhaps he had.

Only now, as Rhys and Kitto ran their hands over me, laid a kiss on first one shoulder, then the other, did I realize that it wasn't about sex today. It was about needing to be held, needing to be cared for. Was I so weak that I needed this, even when the man I said I loved was injured? Would I ever be truly content with the touch of just one man, no matter who it was?

I didn't love Doyle any less as I lay between the two men, but they gave me something he could not. They gave me uncomplicated touch. I did not love either of them in that way. I loved them, but . . . but their tears did not cut my heart. Their sorrows made me sorrow, but I did not bleed as they bled. Love makes you weak and strong. There had been that moment earlier today when I'd thought my Darkness was no more. It had been like losing a piece of myself. It had frozen me, made me lose focus. Dangerous, it was. But hadn't I done the same thing when Galen had nearly died by assassination in faerie? Yes, I had. I'd loved Galen since I was a child. A part of me would always love him. But it was the love of a child, and I was no longer a child.

"You're not paying attention," Rhys said.

I blinked up at him where he lay beside me. I must have looked surprised, because he laughed. "Your body was enjoying being touched, but your mind was a thousand miles from this bed." The humor died, leaving his face a little sad. "Has it happened already? Do Doyle and Frost get all of you now?"

It took me a moment to understand what he meant. "No, it's not that."

"She's thinking of politics and power," Kitto said from where his head lay on my hip and thigh.

Rhys looked at the other man. "In the middle of foreplay she's thinking about politics? Oh, that's even worse."

"She often touches me and thinks at the same time. It seems to clear her mind."

Rhys looked down at me from where he was propped up on his elbow. "Did all that touching simply clear your head?"

It was an insult to have not been paying attention. "I was enjoying it, Rhys, honestly. But my mind is racing a thousand miles an hour. I can't seem to make it still." I looked down my body to Kitto. "Do I truly use you simply to clear my mind?"

"I cannot be king for you, we all know that. I am content to have a place in your life, Merry. I wait upon you, and do tasks that most of your noble-born lords deem beneath them. I can be your lady-in-waiting, and no one else could do that for you."

"We have several sidhe women now," Rhys said. "If Merry wanted more ladies-in-waiting, she could have them."

"We do not trust them alone with our princess after only a few weeks out of Cel's service," Kitto said.

Rhys's face darkened. "No, we don't. Not yet."

"I love that no one can do these things for Merry but me," Kitto said.

I stroked his curls. "Really?" I asked.

He smiled at me and it filled his eyes with something more than just happiness. He had a place in my life. He belonged. It is not merely happiness we all seek. We seek some place where we belong. For the lucky few, we find it in childhood with our own families. But for most of us we spend our adult lives seeking that place or person or organization that makes us feel that we are important, that we matter, and that without us something would go undone and undoable. We all need to feel that we are irreplaceable.

"You do not touch anyone else but me to simply clear your head. You come to my room when you need to hide from the demands that the others put upon you. You come to me when you want to think. You touch me. I touch you. Sometimes there is sex, but often there is just the holding." He snuggled his cheek against my thigh. "No one has ever held me for comfort before. I find that I like it, very much."

I thought about everything he'd just said and couldn't argue with it.

"I thought you hid in Kitto's room because it was the only one without a mirror," Rhys said.

"That, too," I said.

"She does not just come to me in my room. She pets me when I am sitting under her desk. She has gone from seeing me always at her feet as a burden to counting on me being there to touch and be touched."

"Do the dogs ever crowd you under the desk?" Rhys asked.

"The dogs don't seem to stay under the desk when Kitto is there." I looked at him, my fingers playing in his hair. "Did you do something to the dogs?"

"My place is at your feet, Merry. They cannot have my place."

"They are dogs, Kitto, no matter how special and magical they may be. They are dogs. You are not."

He smiled, and it was a little sad around the edges. "But dogs fill many of the needs I fill for you. I have seen you stroking them, watched it calm you."

"Are you more jealous of the dogs than of the rest of us?" Rhys asked.

"Yes," Kitto said.

That made me sad, that he would see himself as so unimportant to me. "Kitto, you are important to me. Touching you is not like petting the dogs."

He moved his face so I could not see his eyes. He hid it by kissing my thigh, but he didn't want me to see his expression. "You are my princess."

I'd learned that the phrase "you are my princess" meant various things. That I was being stubborn, and I was wrong, but since he couldn't change my mind, he'd stop trying. It could also mean that he'd thought of something frightening and didn't want to share. Or that I'd done something to hurt his feelings, but he didn't feel that he had a right to complain.

So much in one small phrase.

"The goblins don't keep dogs. They never have," Rhys said.

I looked at him. "But faerie dogs are precious to all of faerie."

"The goblins used to eat them."

I looked at Kitto, who still wouldn't show his face. He kissed a little lower on my thigh, which meant Rhys was probably right.

"If any of the dogs turn up missing, I won't be happy."

"See," Kitto said. "They are important enough for you to threaten me over them."

"They are our pets and a gift of the Goddess and the wild magic."

"I know what they mean to all of you, but it is not me who you should caution. Holly and Ash will likely be too busy to worry over fresh meat, but they are bringing the Red Caps to guard them. The Red Caps will be wandering about while you have sex with the brothers. The Red Caps like their meat fresh and wriggling."

"Crap," Rhys said. "I knew that, but it's been so many years since I've had any dealings with the Red Caps, I forgot."

"They didn't help torture you?" I asked, before I could catch the thought.

"No. They remembered me before as Cromm Cruach, when I shed much blood for them to play in. They still feel that they owe me from back then."

"That must have been some bloodbath for them to feel they owe you anything after so many centuries," I said.

It was Rhys's turn to look away so I couldn't see his expression. "One of my names translated to red claw. It was a true name."

I understood that "true name" meant it was accurate in its description. I gazed at him, so pale and handsome beside me. His face was boyishly handsome with that full, kissable mouth. The scars were the only thing that made you see past the artifice of youth and humor. Without them to remind you that serious things had happened to this unaged man, you might mistake him for someone casual. Someone to be dismissed. He had certainly played that part for years at the court.

I traced the edge of the scarred area. Once he would have pulled away, but he knew now that, to me, the scars were just another texture on his body, just more things to touch and kiss.

He smiled down at me, and it made his face even more beautiful, in that way that a lover's face can suddenly shine down at you. Not with magic, but simply with pleasure in something you said or did.

"What?" I asked, voice soft.

"In all the long years since they took my eye, you are the only person who ever touched me like this."

I frowned up at him, and laid my hand against his face, the edge of the scar just another area under my hand. "Like what?"

He gave me a look, as if I knew exactly what.

"We are Unseelie. Things that others consider imperfections are marks of beauty among us," I said.

"Only if you are not sidhe," Rhys said. "To be truly scarred and sidhe is to be a living reminder that their perfect beauty could be forever marred. I am the ghost in the mirror, Merry. I remind them that we are only long-lived mortals, not truly immortal."

"Me, too," I said.

He smiled down at me again, pressing his face harder against my hand. "It's one of the reasons I always thought we'd make a good couple."

I frowned at him. "What?"

"Don't you remember, I took you on a date when you were sixteen."

"I remember." I let my hand fall back to the sheet. "I remember that you tried to persuade me to have sex with you, which would have gotten us both executed."

"I didn't actually try for intercourse. I just wanted to see which flavor of your family you took after."

I was frowning harder. "What does that mean?"

He smiled, gently this time. "Depending on how you responded to my overtures"—he waggled his eyebrows at the last word, and made me laugh—"I would decide whether to approach your father."

I had an inkling of where this was going. "You asked my father if you could be my fiancé?"

"I asked him to consider me."

"Neither you nor he ever told me that."

"It seemed clear from the beginning of all this that I wasn't a front-runner for your heart. You loved Galen more than me even when you were sixteen. Then your father gave you to Griffin, and if you had gotten pregnant, that would have been that."

My face clouded over at the mention of my ex-fiancé. He'd dumped me after years. Said I was too human, not sidhe enough for him. What he hadn't realized was that once he dumped me Andais would force him back into celibacy with the rest of the guard. He tried to join my little harem and I turned him down. The only reason he wanted to join was to have sex with someone, anyone. He didn't love me. I knew that.

What I hadn't expected was him selling some rather intimate photos of the two of us to the tabloids. I had loved him once. I wasn't certain he had ever loved me. He had sold the pictures and fled faerie. To my knowledge the long arm of faerie had never caught up with him. To my knowledge. I hadn't asked. I had loved him once. I did not want to know how he'd died, or be presented his head in a basket. Aunt Andais was capable of both, or worse.

Rhys touched my cheek, made me look up at him. "I shouldn't have mentioned his name."

"I'm sorry, but I hadn't thought about him in a while."

"Until I brought him up," Rhys said.

Kitto moved minutely on the other side of me. Until that moment he'd been so still I had almost forgotten that he was there. He was very good at that, but naked in a bed with me and Rhys, and still able to be nearly unnoticed . . . I was beginning to wonder if it was a sort of magic. If it was, then it wasn't sidhe. Snake goblins were used mostly for scouts, spying the lay of the land. Maybe they all possessed a natural talent for going unnoticed if they wished.

I looked at him, but didn't ask out loud if it was magic. Kitto would not believe it was magic even if it was. He saw himself as powerless, and that was that.

"Perhaps I should leave the two of you alone," he said.

"It's your room and your bed," Rhys said.

"Yes, but I will share it with my friend, even if I'm not included."

Rhys reached across me and patted the other man's shoulder. "That is a generous offer, Kitto, but I think there will be no sex this afternoon."

"What?" I asked.

He smiled down at me. "Your mind is full of all that has happened today, as a queen's mind should be. It makes for a good ruler, but bad sex."

I started to protest, but he cradled my chin in his hand. "It's okay, Merry. Maybe what we all need right now is to hold each other. Maybe it's about closeness."

"Rhys. . . ."

He moved so that he covered my mouth, lightly, with his hand. "It's all right, really."

I kissed the palm of his hand, then moved it away

from my mouth. "I understand now why not Galen. He's a political disaster. But you, you do politics just fine."

"Thanks for the compliment."

"So why?" I asked.

"Why did your father not choose me?" he asked.

I nodded.

Kitto slipped out of the bed. "This is sidhe business."

"Stay," Rhys said.

Kitto hesitated.

"Prince Essus told me that there was enough death in your life. He wanted you paired with someone whose magic was about life."

"Griffin's magic was beauty and sex."

"It complemented what your father hoped you would grow into magically." Rhys played with the edge of my hair. "He was right."

"If you were goblin," Kitto said, "beauty and sex would be useless. It would condemn you to be a slave to someone stronger and more able to fight. Your powers, Rhys, they would be valued above such soft things."

"Essus wanted something softer for his daughter," Rhys said.

"He would never have chosen Doyle, would he?" I asked.

"It would never have occurred to him that the queen's Darkness could ever be parted from her side. But no, I think if I was too harsh for his daughter to marry, then Doyle would have been out, too."

"I hadn't thought about who my father might have chosen for me among my guards."

"Hadn't you?" he asked.

"No."

Kitto had picked his jeans up off the floor where he'd let them fall. "I will leave you two to talk."

"Stay," Rhys said. "Help me understand why it's you Merry comes to when she wants to relax. I'm not her heart's desire. I'm not even the one who makes her heart beat fast by a feather's touch. I need to find a place in her life, too. Help teach me how to be something new."

"I will not teach you my place, for you will replace me."

"I will never be as undemanding of Merry as you are. I have neither the personality nor the patience. But teach me to be a little less pressure so that she might turn to me for something."

"Oh, Rhys," I said.

He shook his head, sending all that curly white hair sliding around his shoulders. "You like me. You've always liked me. You enjoy sex with me, but you do not burn for me. Strangely, you burn for colder things even than my powers."

"I am Unseelie sidhe."

"You are also Seelie sidhe."

"I am part that, yes, but I am also part human, and part brownie. But if you pushed me to name myself, what I am, I am Unseelie."

He smiled, a sad sort of smile. "I know that."

"Andais accused me of remaking the Unseelie Court into a mirror of the Seelie. I am not doing it on purpose."

"Remember what I said about you when you were

sixteen? That I wanted to see which side of your family you took after?" Rhys asked.

"Yes."

"I wanted you to take after the Seelie side of your family."

"My grandfather is an abusive bastard. My uncle is mad. My mother is a cold, envious social climber. Why would you want that in your life?"

"I don't mean their personalities, and I don't even mean the ones you referred to. Remember, I knew your ancestors before they were lost in the great wars in Europe. I knew some of the women of your mother's line. They were goddesses of fertility, love, lust. They were a warm lot, Merry, in that good, earthy way."

"So, what, you wondered if I had taken after my great-great-aunt?"

"Aunts," Rhys said, "and a great-grandmother or two. You reminded me of them. The hair, the eyes. I saw them in you."

"No one else did," I said.

"No one else was looking."

I rose and gave him a kiss. The kiss grew until I felt his body grow hard again, where all the talk had made it soft. He broke from my lips with a sound that was almost pain. "I can't keep being the gentleman if you keep kissing me like that."

"Then don't be the gentleman, be my lover."

Kitto finished fastening his jeans. "I will leave you to what the sidhe do best, other than magic. You are my friend, Rhys, I believe that, but you are not comfortable with me in the bed with you and the princess."

Rhys started to protest. It was my turn to put my fingers on his lips. "He's right."

He moved my hand. "I know. Damnit, I know. I thought if I could have sex with Kitto and you, I could guard you tonight with the goblins, but I can't."

"You have come a long way on the subject of goblins, Rhys. It's all right."

"Who will guard you tonight if Doyle is injured and my sensibilities are too delicate?"

"I don't know," I said, "and right this second I don't care. Make love to me, Rhys, now, just you. Be with me, help chase my thoughts to stillness." I rose and kissed him again and drew him down to me with arms and hands and eagerness.

I did not hear the door close quietly behind Kitto, but when next I opened my eyes, we were alone.

Chapter 19

RHYS MADE ME LIE ON MY STOMACH AND BEGAN TO breathe his way down my back. I would have said kiss, but it was too gentle for that. He caressed the skin with the barest touch of lips and breath. When he got low enough, he began to breathe and work those tiny, near-invisible hairs on the lower back, so that my body ran with goose bumps and involuntary shivers.

I raised my hips minutely from the bed in a silent invitation for him to do more.

He laughed that laugh of his that was masculine pleasure and his own amusement. But for once there was nothing of self-mockery in it. He laid a more solid kiss against the small of my back. I writhed for him, letting him know without words how wonderful it was.

He laid his weight on top of me, resting the hard, long length of himself between the cheeks of my ass. The feel of it made me cry out.

He wrapped his arms around me, forced me enough off the bed so he could cup my breasts in his hands. He held me tightly and firmly in the strength of his body.

"If I truly loved you," he whispered, "I would do

what Kitto has done. I would refuse to have intercourse with you. I would take myself out of the race for king. Kitto did it because he knows that neither court would ever let a half goblin sit as your king. They'd kill you both first."

He settled himself more firmly against me, pushing his hips just a little. It made me writhe as much as the weight of him would allow, but the seriousness in his voice didn't match what his body was doing.

Rhys continued to whisper against my hair. "I know you love Doyle and Frost. Hell, you even love Galen more than you love me, even now when you've both realized what a political liability he would be as king."

"Sometimes we have just oral sex now when we are together."

Rhys tensed above me, and not in a sexual way, but as if he was thinking. "Has he taken himself out of the race for king?"

"Not completely, but sometimes we don't do anything to make babies. We just pleasure each other."

"Interesting," he said, and it wasn't a seductive whisper this time.

I tried to rise, but he kept me pressed to the bed with a squeeze of his arms, a flex of his hips. I spoke, trapped underneath him. "Why is it interesting?"

"Galen has taken himself out of the running for king because he knows he isn't strong enough to help keep you alive. But he loves you, utterly loves you. He loves you enough to give you up if that's what's best for you. Gallant Galen."

I hadn't thought about it that way, but Rhys was

right. It was gallant and horribly brave. Galen still had a chance to be the father of my child, but the last few times we'd made love he had only used his chance for intercourse once. The rest had been amazingly fun, but nothing that would have made a baby.

Rhys wrapped those strong arms tight, so tight it was almost hard to breathe. He whispered against my ear, his breath hot. "If I truly loved you, I would take myself out of the running for king. I would help you get your heart's desire, which is Doyle and Frost. But I am too selfish, Merry. I cannot give you up without a fight."

I spoke in the voice that his grip allowed me, breathy. "It isn't a fight."

"Yes," he whispered fiercely. "Yes, it is. Not of strength of arms, maybe, but it is a battle. For some of us, the prize is to be king. But for most of us, Merry, we would want you as our prize even if there was no throne."

He shoved his body against mine hard and fierce until I cried out for him. Then he squeezed me even tighter until I thought I would have to ask him to stop so I could breathe. His voice was somewhere between a whisper and a hiss against my ear, so fierce, so full of emotion. "I want to win, Merry. I want you even if it breaks your heart. I am a selfish bastard, Merry. I won't give you up, not even to see you happy."

I lay underneath him and didn't know what to say.

He squeezed harder, and I finally had to protest, "Rhys, please. . . ."

He eased the grip of his arms just enough so that I could draw a good breath, but his fingers squeezed my breasts hard and firm. The harshness of it drew small noises from me.

"You like sex rougher than I do. Things that are simply pain to me make you shiver with pleasure." His grip on my breasts eased. "The goblins will do worse than that tonight to you, and you will enjoy it, won't you?"

"I've negotiated for pleasure tonight, Rhys."

He rubbed his face against my hair. "I could give you up to Doyle, or Frost, or Galen, if I had to. It would kill something in me, but I could do it. But I could not bare to lose you to Ash and Holly. I could not bear to have my Merry married to goblins, fucking goblins every night."

A sound escaped him that was almost a sob.

"Rhys," I said, "I. . . ."

"No, don't say it, whatever it is. Let me finish. I may never have the courage to say it all again."

I went still under him. I lay there with his body wrapped around me, and let him talk, if that was what he needed.

"I hate the thought of them with you tonight, Merry. I hate more that you are excited by the thought of them tying you up and fucking you. God, I hate that maybe most of all." His arms tightened around me once more. "See, I don't love you, not really. If I loved you, truly loved you, I'd want you to be happy. I'd want you to have the sex you enjoy, not just the sex I think you should have. But that's not what I want for you. I want you to be gentler than you are. I want you to want sex the way I make it. The way I like it. I hate that you want things that I think are pain and not pleasure. I hate knowing that though you enjoy sex with me, it's not everything you need, or want." He dug his fingers into my breasts again until I cried out again, and my body bucked under his.

He let go of me abruptly, pushing himself above my body so that his arms framed me on either side, but his hips were tighter against me.

"Because I hate the thought of the goblins with you tonight, because I want you with me more than I want you happy, because I am a selfish bastard, I'm going to fill your body with my seed, and I'm going to pray while I do it. I'm going to call power while I do it. I want you pregnant with my child, consort help me, but I do. Goddess help me, but I do. Not so we will all live. Not so Cel won't sit the throne, and divide us in civil war. No, nothing so noble, Merry. I want it, because I want you, even knowing you don't want me."

"I do want you," I said, and turned so I could look at him over my shoulder.

The look on his face was one that I would never forget. So fierce, so desperate, so wild, but not with sex or even lust or love. The look on his face was full of an awful loss. If I'd been sending him out to do battle with sword and shield, I wouldn't have let him go, because the look on his face was the look of a man who knew he wouldn't be coming back. The face of a man who knew he would lose this day, die this day. I would have held him back from the battle. I would have made him stay by my side, and kept him alive another day. But this was not a battlefield I could protect him from. It was my body and heart, and they had already chosen.

He shook his head. "No pity, Merry, at least save me that."

I turned away then, turned so he could not see the tears that shimmered in my eyes. It was the only way I could save him from my pity. I did love him, but not the way he needed me to love him. He was right, even our sexual appetites did not match.

He jerked my hips up off the bed. I tried to get up on all fours for him, but he forced my head down, so that my lower body was raised like an offering to him.

I felt the head of him pushing against me, but I was still too tight for the angle.

I said, "You'll need to use a finger to start. I'm too tight with no foreplay for this position."

He kept pushing at my body, harder, fiercer.

"You'll hurt yourself, Rhys," I said from where my face was almost buried against the pillows.

"I want it to hurt," he said. Then I felt him break the surface of me, find the barest part of himself inside me, and I stopped protesting. He forced himself inside me, fighting the tightness and the lack of wetness of my body. If I had been wired differently, it would have hurt. It wasn't that I couldn't be hurt, I could. Even intercourse for me could be done so it was only pain, but you had to work at it, you had to be bad at it. Bad in a way that Rhys was not.

I started screaming for him. My body orgasming simply from the feel of him forcing his way inside me. Not just one orgasm, but waves of them rolling over and over my body, making me writhe and push myself against the force and strength of him. The pleasure of it spilled out of my mouth in one ragged scream after another. I screamed, "Yes" and "God" and "Goddess" and finally at the end I screamed his name, over and over and over.

"Rhys, oh, god, Rhys!"

The dim room filled with the light of our bodies, glowing like twin moons of rising power. He made my skin run with light. He dug his hand into the shining garnet of my hair and jerked my throat backward as he rode me. The roughness of it made me scream again, but he let go of my hair as his body began to fight him for rhythm. His breathing changed and I knew he was close, close, and fighting to last that little bit longer, so that I would scream underneath him for just a little bit longer.

I was on all fours where his grip had moved me. My breasts hung down, slapping together from the fury of his sex. I screamed my pleasure. I filled the room with his name like a prayer to some angry god. Then his body made one last tremendous thrust so deep inside me that I knew it should have hurt, but there was too much pleasure for real pain.

His body shivered above me, thrusting again deep inside me. I felt him spill himself inside me in a hot wash of seed and power.

He'd said he would pray while he fucked me. He'd said he'd use his power to make me his. I should have been afraid, but I wasn't. I couldn't be afraid of Rhys.

I collapsed underneath him with his body still buried inside me. He lay on top of me, both of us too spent to move, our breathing a ragged sound, our hearts still in our throats. The glow of our bodies began to fade as our pulses slowed.

He finally rolled off, slowly. I lay where I was, too limp to move yet. He lay on his back, still breathing heavily. He spoke, in a voice still harsh from exertion. "The way you react to roughness urges a man on, Merry, even when I didn't think I'd like it."

"You were amazing," I whispered, my own voice a little rough from the screaming.

He smiled at me. "You really don't have any idea how good you are at this, do you?"

"I'm good, or so I'm told."

He shook his head. "No, Merry, no joke, you are amazing in bed, and on the floor, and on a sturdy table."

I laughed.

He smiled at me, and it was almost the old Rhys before he got so serious on me. Then that seriousness peeked out again. "I know that the goblins will have you tonight, and there is nothing I can do about it." His face went from serious to angry. "But when they shove themselves inside you tonight they'll be shoving my seed farther in."

"Rhys. . . ."

"No, it's all right. I know you're doing your duty as queen. We need the goblins as our allies, and this is the way to get the treaty lengthened. I know politically that it's a good idea, a great idea." He stared at me, and there was such pressure to that gaze that I had to fight to meet it. "But the idea of the two of them having you tonight—the way it's planned— excites you, doesn't it?"

I hesitated, then told the truth. "Yes."

"That is not Seelie Court. That is most definitely Unseelie Court. It's the part of you that I don't understand. It's the part that Doyle understands best, better even than Frost. He may be your Darkness, but he also holds your darkness as precious to him. I don't want your darkness, Merry. I want the light of you."

"You can't separate the light and the dark, Rhys. They're both a part of me."

He nodded. "I know, I know." He sat up and eased himself off the edge of the bed. "I'm going to go clean up."

"You were magnificent," I said.

"I'm already sore."

"I warned you, foreplay isn't just for my body's comfort."

"You did warn me." He gathered his clothes from the floor, but made no move to put them on.

"Enjoy your shower," I said.

"Want to join me?"

I smiled. "No, I need some actual sleep before tonight, I think."

"I tire you out?"

"Yes, but in a wonderful way." I curled on my side, pulling the sheet up.

Rhys went for the door. I heard him talking to someone outside. I heard him say, "Ask her yourself."

Kitto's voice came from the door. "May I come in?"

"Yes," I said.

He walked inside, the door closing behind him. He must have been sitting in the hallway the entire time. "Do you want to hold me while you sleep?" he asked.

I looked at his earnest face, so serious. He was always serious, our Kitto. "Yes," I said.

He smiled then, and it was a good smile. A smile

that we'd only discovered he had in the last little bit. He crawled under the sheet and slid his body against the back of mine. He spooned his nakedness against my body, and it was simply comforting. I would have turned down almost any other man at the door in that moment.

Kitto knew he would not be king, so the sex wasn't such a press to him. But more than that he valued the gentle cuddling almost more than the sex. After all, he'd had sex before, but I wasn't certain he'd ever truly been loved just for himself. I did love him. I loved them all, but Rhys was right, I didn't love them equally.

The constitution of our country says that all men are created equal, but it's a lie. I'll never be able to make a jump shot like Magic Johnson, or drive a car like Mario Andretti, or paint like Picasso. We are not created equal in talent. But the place where we are least equal is the heart. You can work at a talent, take lessons, but love, love either works or it doesn't. You love someone or you don't. You can't change it. You can't undo it.

I lay there drifting on the warm edge of sleep with the wonderful edge of good sex coating my body. Kitto's warmth and clinging shape held me as I drifted off. I felt safe, loved, and content. I wished Rhys would feel as good about this afternoon as I did, but I knew that that was a wish that wouldn't come true.

I was a faerie princess, but there were no faerie godmothers. There were only mothers and grand-mothers, and there was no magic wand to wave over a person's heart and make it all better. The fairy tales lied. Rhys knew that. I knew that. The man who was breathing at my back as he began to fall deeper to sleep knew that.

Fucking Brothers Grimm.

Chapter 20

WHILE MAEVE REED WAS OFF IN EUROPE STAYING OUT of Taranis's reach, she'd given us full use of her house. She said it was a small price to pay for us saving her life and helping her become pregnant before her human husband had died of cancer. So for once good deeds had been rewarded. We had a mansion on a huge plot of land in Holmby Hills, with a guesthouse, a pool house, and a smaller cottage near the gate for the caretaker-gardener.

I still slept in the master bedroom of the guesthouse, but there were now enough of us to fill the bedrooms of both houses. The men were having to double up in some of the bedrooms.

Kitto had gotten a room to himself because it was too small a room to share with anyone much above my, and Rhys's size. Which meant no one.

We'd planned on using the main house's dining room for the initial meeting with the goblins. It was a huge room that had begun life as a ballroom. So it was light and airy and full of marble. It looked like something out of a human fairy tale. The Seelie Court would have approved, but then Maeve was exiled from there, so maybe the ballroom/dining room was a piece of home for her.

Most of my bodyguards looked as at home here in the brightness as the glittering chandeliers above us. The guards whom Ash and Holly had brought didn't look at home at all.

The Red Caps towered over everyone else in the room. Seven feet of goblin was a lot of goblin. But that was short for a Red Cap. Most were closer to the twelve-foot mark. The average height was eight to ten feet. Their skins were shades of yellow, gray, and sickly green. I'd known that the goblins were bringing Red Caps as guards. Kurag, Goblin King, had felt that if he sent Ash and Holly without guards to us and something happened to them, it would be seen as a plot between him and me to rid himself of the brothers. Since the only way for him to step down as king and them to step up was for him to be dead at their hands, their deaths would be very convenient for him.

So why was he offering them to me to make them even more powerful? Because Kurag knew how his kingship would end, as all goblin kings ended. He wanted to ensure that his people were strong even after he died. He did not resent the brothers for their ambition. He just wanted to hold it off a little longer.

If the twins died by our hands, even by accident, without goblins around them, then it could be misconstrued. If the goblins thought that Kurag had had the brothers assassinated, his life was forfeit. All challenges were personal challenges. There were goblins who were assassins as a sideline, but they never took "jobs" where the victim was another goblin. They'd kill sidhe, or lesser folk, but never another goblin.

The only exception was if the goblin was one of the "kept," as Kitto had been. If you had a problem with one of them, their "masters" fought you. Because to be what Kitto was among them was an admission that he was not fighter enough to be part of the larger goblin culture.

I sat in a large chair that had been set up as a sort of temporary throne. The big table had been moved back against the wall, along with most of the chairs. Frost was at my back. Doyle was still closeted in his bedroom with the black dogs. Taranis had nearly killed my Darkness. If we'd been inside faerie proper, he might have been healed already. None of our magics were as strong here. It was one of the reasons that exile was so feared by most, because you were never as powerful outside of faerie.

"We have brought you inside so the human reporters cannot bandy it about in the press," Frost said in a voice as cold as his namesake. "But for the press I would not have allowed you inside our wards with such an army at your back."

I couldn't really argue with him, but I was strangely unworried. In fact, I felt better than I'd felt in hours.

"It is done, Frost," I said.

"Why are you not more worried about this?" he asked.

"I don't know," I said.

"If they were not goblins, I would say they had bespelled you," Rhys said.

Ash and Holly were impressed with all of the show, which set them apart from the other goblins and made them so much more sidhe.

"Greetings, Ash and Holly, goblin warriors. Greetings also to the Red Caps of the Goblin Court. Who leads here?"

"We do," Ash said, as he and his brother stepped up to stand before my chair. They were wearing the court clothes that they'd worn before, Ash in green to match his eyes, Holly in red to match his. The clothes were satin, and the height of fashion if the year happened to be between 1500 and 1600.

Their short yellow hair brushed their ears as they bowed. They'd started to let their hair grow, though it wasn't long enough to get them in trouble with the queen—it had to touch their collars for that.

"You've let your hair grow in the month since I saw you," I said.

They exchanged a glance, then Ash said, "We do it in anticipation of your magic bringing us into our sidhe-side powers."

"That's very confident of you," I said.

"We have every confidence in your powers, Princess," Ash said.

I looked at Holly. There was no confidence in his eyes, just eagerness. He got to bed me tonight; all else was just pretense. Holly would give me what the brothers truly felt. Ash was nearly as good at playing courtier as sidhe lord. I didn't trust either of them, but Ash could lie with his eyes and face; Holly couldn't. Good to know.

I looked past them to the Red Caps. I recognized some of them from the fight weeks before. They had stood by me, not the brothers, or Kurag their king. The Red Caps had obeyed me beyond what was required of them by treaty. I had not explored that strange obedience, so unlike the usual Red Cap attitude toward sidhe or female, because I wasn't sure how Kurag would take it. I did not want to be seen as trying to seduce, even politically, the most powerful warriors of the goblin race to my service.

Kurag desperately wanted out of the treaty with me. He feared that civil war was coming either within the Unseelie themselves or between both courts. He wanted no part of the coming battles, yet his treaty with me held him to me. I would not give him an excuse to pull out. We needed him too much. So I had not probed further into the Red Caps' motivations for their loyalty to me.

Now they stood before me, more of them than I'd ever seen in one place at one time. They were like a living wall of flesh and muscle. They all wore little round skullcaps. Most were covered in dry blood so that the wool was shades of brown and black. But about a third of them had blood running from their caps to trickle down their faces and stain the shoulders and chest of their clothes.

Once to be war leader among them you had to be able to make the blood on your cap stay fresh. The alternative was to kill a foe often enough to keep your hat red. This little cultural habit had made them some of the most bloodthirsty warriors in all of faerie.

I'd only met one Red Cap who could make his hat stay fresh and bright red: Jonty. He stood among them, in the front near the center. He was about ten feet tall, with gray skin and eyes the color of fresh blood. All the Red Caps had red eyes, but there are shades of red, and Jonty's were as bright as his cap.

When I'd met him his skin had reminded me of the gray of dust, but his skin didn't look dry or harsh now. He looked . . . like he'd had a good deep moisturizer used on all the skin I could see. Since goblins didn't go to spas, I didn't understand the change in his skin tone.

There were other changes as well. His hat bled in thick runlets of blood so that his entire upper body was soaked in it. The blood had trickled down his clothes, and dripped off the ends of his thick fingers as he stood there, making a delicate pattern of blood on the marble floor.

"Jonty, it is good to see you again." I meant it. He had saved us. He had forced the twins to join our fight. The Red Caps had followed him, not Ash and Holly.

"And you, Princess Meredith," he said in that voice that was so low it was like gravel rumbling.

"Should we have greeted the Killing Frost and Rhys?" Ash asked. "I am not completely clear on the rules of sidhe etiquette."

"You may greet them or not. I greet Jonty because he stood beside me in battle. I greet Jonty and his Red Caps because they helped me and mine. I greet the Red Caps as true allies."

"The goblins are your allies," Ash said.

"The goblins are my allies because Kurag cannot get out of our bargain. You would have let my men die that night in the dark."

"Are you going to go back on your bargain to bed us, Princess?" Ash asked.

"No, but seeing Jonty and his men reminds me, that is all." Actually, I was angry. Ash and Holly had been like all goblins, and most sidhe. It wasn't their fight, and they didn't want to die defending sidhe warriors who wouldn't have given a damn for them. I shouldn't blame them, but I did anyway.

Jonty had picked me up in his huge arms and run through the winter night toward the fight. Where he went, the other Red Caps had gone. Because the Red Caps went, the other goblins had to go. To avoid the fight would have branded them as weaker and more cowardly than the Red Caps. I'd known it was a point of pride, but Kitto had explained that it was more than that. It would have opened the other goblins to being challenged in single combat by the Red Caps who fought beside me. No goblin would have willingly invited such a challenge.

I knew what I owed Jonty and his men, but not why they had done it. Why had they risked everything for me? If I could have figured out a way to ask that wouldn't have insulted them, Ash and Holly, or even their king, I would have asked. But goblin culture was a maze that I did not have a map for yet. It had no room for asking why of a warrior. Why were you brave? Because I was a goblin. Why did you help me? Because no goblin turns from a good fight. Neither was completely true. But it was popularly true, and to say otherwise would bring into question Ash's and Holly's lack of enthusiasm.

Frost touched my shoulder, just a light touch. If Doyle had been there, he'd have touched me sooner. Frost didn't like why the goblins were here tonight. He didn't like me being with them, but he knew we needed them as allies.

Rhys spoke softly, "Merry."

I looked up at him, startled. "Did I miss something?"

"Yes." He motioned with his gaze at the twins.

I turned to them. "I am so sorry, but so much has happened today that I find worry overriding my duty."

"So the Darkness is still too injured to be by your side," Ash said.

"He will not be here tonight. I told you that earlier."

"Will Rhys and the Killing Frost be your guards tonight?" Holly asked.

"No."

Rhys couldn't do it. Frost I'd ordered not to. He could not hide his feelings well enough. I feared he would insult Holly with a look or a sound tonight. The middle of sex could be very like the middle of bloodlust in battle for a goblin. I didn't want to have Frost start a fight by accident.

"Amatheon and Adair will guard me." At the mention of their names, they stepped forward from the line of guards behind me. Amatheon was copper-haired, and Adair was crowned with a dark gold that had once been closer to just brown, before we'd had sex inside faerie and he had come back into some of his power. Amatheon had been a deity of agriculture. Adair was the oak grove, but also once a solar deity. I wasn't sure if he'd been solar, then downgraded to oak, or if he'd been both simultaneously. It was considered the height of rudeness to ask a fallen deity what their old powers once were. It was like rubbing their noses in their lost status.

"Is it true that fucking them is what turned Andais's garden of pain into the meadow it is now?" Holly asked.

"Yes," I said.

Rhys said, "I wish Doyle were here, I really do. I hate goblins, everyone knows that, so I don't trust my judgment with you."

"Rhys," I said, "what . . ."

"Is no one going to ask why they have brought every Red Cap the goblins have at their command?"

"I, too," Frost said, "do not wish Merry to do this. It colors my judgment as well."

"Well, I don't give a damn who she fucks as long as she eventually fucks me, so I'll say it. Why in the name of the consort do you have this many Red Caps with you?" Onilwyn stepped away from the rest of my guards.

Onilwyn was the most graceless sidhe I'd ever seen. There was something blocky about his muscular build. He was tall enough and he moved well, but he just wasn't made as smoothly as the rest. I was never sure why, and again, could not ask. It wasn't his roughness that made me not want to sleep with him. He was as handsome with his long green hair and lovely eyes as most of the sidhe. But if pretty is as pretty does, Onilwyn was ugly to me.

I'd managed not to sleep with him yet because I truly didn't like him. He had been one of Cel's friends who had tormented me when I was a child. I truly didn't wish to be tied to him by a child and marriage, so I'd refused him my bed. I'd given him permission to masturbate, which was more than the queen had allowed. He could entertain himself all he wanted. I just didn't want him entertaining me.

If I didn't get pregnant soon, he'd promised to complain to the queen. I had until the end of this month, because that was when I could bleed away my chances for a baby this cycle. The queen would force me into his bed. First, on the chance that I could get pregnant. Second, because she knew I didn't want to do it.

But sometimes it's the unpleasant person who will say what needs saying. I had not worried about how many Red Caps were in the room until Onilwyn spoke. That was wrong. I should have worried. There were enough of them that if they started a battle we might lose. Why hadn't it worried me?

My left hand pulsed so hard it brought a sound from me. My hand of blood liked the Red Caps. My power liked the Red Caps. Not good, or was it?

Ash and Holly exchanged a glance.

"The truth," I said. "Why did you bring every Red Cap the goblins can boast?"

"They insisted," Ash said.

"The Red Caps do not insist," Onilwyn said. "They obey."

Ash looked at the other man. "I would not expect a sidhe to know so much of us." He looked at me and gave a nod. "Except for the princess, who seems to make a study of all her peoples' cultures."

I nodded back. "I appreciate that you have noticed my efforts."

"I have noticed. It is one of the reasons I am here."

"I fought in the goblin-sidhe wars," Onilwyn said. "I saw the Red Caps ordered into battles that were sure death, but they never hesitated. I learned that they are oathed to never disobey the Goblin King."

"You are correct, greenman," Jonty said.

"They are also forbidden from competing for kingship," Onilwyn said.

"Also correct."

"Why are you all here?" Onilwyn asked.

I looked at Onilwyn. It wasn't like him to worry this much over my safety. Maybe he was worried about his own.

The Red Caps looked at Jonty. He looked at me.

"Why *are* you here, Jonty? Why did so many of your people come with you?"

"You I will answer," he said in that deep voice. He'd insulted everyone here. Ash and Holly, Onilwyn, everyone but me.

He came forward. Rhys and Frost moved a little in front of me. Some of the other guards moved out of their line behind us.

"No," I said. "He helped me save you all. Don't be ungrateful now."

"We're supposed to protect you, Merry. How can we allow that to approach you?" Rhys said.

I gave him an unfriendly glare. "He is not a 'that,' Rhys. He is a Red Cap. He is Jonty. He is a goblin. But he is not a 'that.' "

My anger seemed to surprise him. He gave a small bow and moved back. "As my lady wishes."

Normally, I would have tried to ease his hurt feelings, but tonight I had other things on my mind than juggling the emotional relationships in my life.

I stood up and the silk robe I was wearing brushed

the floor with a sound that was almost alive. The high-heeled sandals with their wraparound laces made a sharp sound on the marble.

High heels had been the only thing the twins had asked me to wear. The only request. I moved the robe so they got a flash of the four-inch heels, the laces that curved around my calf. I got a sound from Holly, low in his throat. Ash controlled himself better, but his face couldn't hold it all. They wanted my white flesh against their gold. They wanted to know sidhe flesh, and it wasn't all about power. They, like me, knew what it was to be the outsider. To be always different from those around you.

Jonty dropped to his knees in front of me. Kneeling, he looked me in the eyes. He made me aware of how small I was.

"Jonty," I said.

"Princess," he said.

I studied his face. Up close the change was even more startling. His skin was smoother, a softer gray. He smiled at me, and the teeth that I remembered as a mouthful of fangs were straighter, whiter, less frightening, more like a person's mouth than an animal's.

"What has happened to you, Jonty?" I asked.

"You happened to me, Princess."

"I don't understand."

"Your hand of blood happened to us all in that winter's night."

I frowned a little and tried to think of a way to ask my question. But how do you ask a question when you have no idea what to ask?

"I do not understand, Jonty."

"Your hand of blood has brought us back into our power."

"You have not come back into your full power," Holly said.

Jonty turned an evil look on him. "No, as the halfling says, no. But it is more power than we have known in centuries." He turned back to me, the anger fading from his eyes as he beheld me. There was a softness to his look that you didn't see in most goblins' eyes. Red Caps were known for their ferocity, not their kindness.

"Why have you all come, Jonty?"

"They want you to touch them as you touched us. They want you to bring them into their power, too."

"Why did you not ask me sooner?"

"Would you have done it?"

"You saved us, Jonty. I know that. But more than that, my job, my task as princess, is to bring power back to faerie. All faerie. That includes you and your men."

Jonty looked at the floor, and spoke as softly as his deep, deep voice would allow. "I knew you would not refuse us if we stood before you. I knew that your hand of blood called to us too strongly, if we were close to you, but I did not think you would simply say yes from a distance."

He looked up and his red eyes shimmered. Red Caps did not cry, ever.

A single tear slid from his eye. A tear the color of fresh blood. I did what I knew was custom among the goblins. Tears are precious, blood more precious yet. I touched my finger to his face and captured that single tear before it could mingle with and be lost in the blood that trailed down his face.

The tear trembled on my finger like a true tear, but it was red as blood. I raised it to my mouth, and drank his tear.

Chapter 21

THERE ARE MOMENTS WHEN THE WORLD HOLDS ITS breath. When the very air seems to pause, as if time itself has taken that last deep breath before. . . .

The taste of salt and sweet metal slid across my tongue. The liquid seemed to grow until, when it glided down my throat, it was like a drink of cool, clear water, if it could hold the salt of oceans and the taste of blood.

I saw the room in pieces, as if things were moving out of sync. A cloud of demi-fey flew into the room, though I knew they had been forbidden to come. Goblins thought them tasty. But the winged fey filled the room like a cloud of butterflies and moths, dragonflies and damselflies, and insects that had never appeared in nature. There seemed to be more of them than I knew had followed us into exile.

The air was alive with color from the fluttering of their wings, so many of them that they made a breeze that played in my hair and touched my face.

The dogs came next. Small terriers spilling around the feet of the goblins, as if the dogs did not care, and the goblins did not see them. The graceful step of the greyhounds next, picking their dainty way through the crowded room. They walked among the standing

Red Caps as if they were a forest to move through instead of people. Stranger yet, the Red Caps did not react to the dogs.

The dogs went to their masters. The terriers went to Rhys. Some of the hounds went to others of the guard. My two hounds came to me. Minnie with her face half red and half white as if someone had drawn a line down her face. Mungo with his one red ear and the rest of him white as a swan wing.

They had all been waiting . . . for us.

Frost's voice came from behind me. "Merry, what is this?"

It was Royal's voice, from where he hovered above me with his moth's wings, that answered. "It is the moment of creation, Killing Frost."

I stared up at the diminutive man. "I don't understand."

He smiled at me, but there was an eagerness to him that I did not trust. There was always something sensual, even sexual, about Royal. Since he was the size of a large Barbie doll, it was unsettling to say the least.

"We wait but for one piece more." This came from Penny, Royal's twin sister, who hovered beside him.

I didn't understand until the black hounds poured in like shadows with Darkness made flesh, whose eyes flashed red, green, and all the colors I'd seen in Doyle's eyes when his magic was upon him.

Doyle came through the door, leaning on the back of what looked like a black pony, a little bigger than the dogs. But a flash of those black eyes and I knew it was no pony. It pulled its lips back to flash teeth as sharp as any goblin's. It was a kelpie, though how it got here I had no idea. The kelpies had been hunted and destroyed in Europe before we ever came to this country.

Kelpies either lurked in water and drew their prey down like crocodiles or pretended to be ponies on land. Then when some unwary human got on, they galloped to the nearest water. They drowned their prey, or ate them as they drowned. Most of their victims were children. Children love ponies.

Frost and I both said "Doyle" together.

He managed a smile. His face was still bandaged, but he'd unbound his arm. He moved slowly, but he moved, with his hand on the back of the carnivorous pony.

"The dogs would not let me rest any longer," Doyle said.

I held my hand out to him.

Royal said, "No, Princess, that is not the point."

I looked up at him. "You said the last piece."

"He is the last piece, but you don't have to touch him. You have touched him enough for this moment to happen. You have touched them all enough to call us to you."

"I don't. . . ."

"Understand," he finished for me.

"No."

"You will," he said, and it was typical Royal, because he made it sound ominous.

Mungo nudged my hand. I stroked his head, and played with one silken ear. Minnie bumped my other hand as if jealous for my attention. I petted them both, feeling the warmth and solidness of them.

"There is no dog for me," Frost said. He had moved closer to me.

"What will be, will be," Royal said.

Then the demi-fey rose toward the high ceiling, sending light sparkling in rainbows from the crystal chandeliers. The light bounced and played off all of us. The goblins, even Ash and Holly, were still frozen out of time with us.

It was Jonty who blinked, and looked up at me. He, of all of them, who saw. His eyes went wide, then the world let out the breath it had been holding.

Chapter 22

THE WORLD EXPLODED, IF YOU COULD CALL LIGHT, color, music, and the perfume of flowers an explosion. I had no other word for what happened. It was like standing at ground zero on the first day that life walked on the planet, but it was also like standing in the most beautiful meadow in the world on a lovely spring day with the gentlest of breezes blowing. It was a perfect moment, and a moment of incredible violence, as if we were all gently torn apart and put together again in the blink of an eye.

Through it all, the dogs pressed close on either side. They anchored me, steadied me, kept me from breaking apart and flying into that moment. They kept me solid enough, sane enough, to survive.

I clung to their fur, the touch of them in my hand. And thought, *Frost has no dog to keep him here.*

I thought about screaming, then it was over. Only the sense of disorientation and the memory of pain and power, fading in the dance of light and magic, let me know that it hadn't been some sort of dream.

Doyle gazed at me across the back of his black dogs. He seemed to be healed, whole. He touched the kelpie, but did not lean on it. He stood straight and tall.

He reached up and pulled off the bandages to show that the burns were gone. I suppose if you're creating reality, a little healing isn't much.

Because reality had changed.

We were still in Maeve Reed's ballroom/dining room, but it wasn't the same room. It was huge, an acre of marble stretching in every direction. The far windows were a distant twinkling line.

There were demi-fey everywhere, as if too deep a breath would make you swallow one.

Ash and Holly swatted at them as if they were flies. I said, "If you harm them, I will not be happy."

The Red Caps did not swat at them. They did not threaten them. The huge men stood there and let the tiny things alight on them. They were covered in the fanning of butterfly wings, until you could barely see their flesh through the slow dance of color.

Jonty gazed up at me with those red eyes framed by the shining wings. The tiny hands clung to his bloody hat. They rolled in the blood, giggling, a sound like crystal chimes.

"You remake us, my queen," Jonty said.

I don't know what I would have said to that, but then Rhys's voice came. "Merry!"

That one word, that note of urgency was enough. I turned and knew that whatever I would see, I would not like it.

Rhys and Galen were kneeling beside Frost. He lay crumpled on his side, terribly still.

I remembered then what I'd thought. He had had nothing to hold on to while reality remade itself. He had been alone in the terror and beauty of it.

I ran to him with my dogs at my side, trippingly

close, but the magic was still here, still working, and I did not dare send the hounds away. The oldest magic that had ever belonged to the sidhe was in this room tonight. It was a magic that could be ridden, but never controlled, not completely. Creation is always a chancy thing, because you never know what it will be when all is said and done, or if it will be worth the price.

Chapter 23

VOICES FROM AROUND THE ROOM SAID THAT FROST was not the only one down. Holly and Ash had collapsed to the floor. The demi-fey closed on them now that they could not resist.

But the other men who had fallen had only other guards to touch them, to try and wake them. I touched the glittering fall of Frost's hair, drew it back from his face.

"What is wrong with him? With all of them?" I asked.

"I'm not sure," Rhys said, "but his pulse is fading."

I looked at him over Frost's still form. I knew my face showed the shock.

"They didn't have the dogs," Galen said. "They didn't have anything to hold on to when you created more faerie land."

Rhys nodded. His small sea of terriers sat unusually silent and solemn around his legs as he knelt.

I started to say "they are just dogs," but Mungo bumped my shoulder with his head. Minnie leaned against my side. I looked into her eyes and there was dog in there, yes, but there was more. They were dogs formed of wild magic. They were fey creatures, and that is not simply a dog.

I stroked her ear, so velvety. I whispered, "Help me. Help them. Help Frost."

Doyle strode farther into the room with the huge black dogs milling around him. One of the dogs broke from the pack and went to one of the other fallen. He sniffed the hair with a loud snuffling sound. Then he grew taller, bigger. The dog's fur ran in streamers of green, chasing the black away, and the fur growing a little longer, a little shaggier.

The dog was the size of a pony when it was solid green. A green like new grass, spring leaves. It turned huge yellow-green eyes to me.

"Cu Sith," Galen whispered.

I simply nodded.

The Cu Sith: "Hound of the sidhe" was the literal meaning of its name. Once every sidhe mound had had at least one as guard. One had been created, or reborn, on the night when the magic had returned in Illinois. Now we had a second, here and now.

It lowered its great head and sniffed at one of the fallen guards again. It licked him with a huge pink tongue. He gave a breath so big we heard it across the room. His body shuddered with the return of life, or the retreat of death.

The huge green dog moved from one to the other, and everywhere he touched, the men revived. He came to Onilwyn, still collapsed on his side. He sniffed him, then growled low and deep, like thunder contained in a rib cage. He did not lick Onilwyn back to life. The Cu Sith let him lie. Interesting that I wasn't the only one who didn't want to touch him.

The green dog came to the twins, sweeping the demifey ceilingward with its great head. But it sniffed them, and moved away, too. Not sidhe enough for the Cu.

Doyle's deep voice came, but there was an echo in it of the god. I looked at Doyle, and found his face distant, as if he saw something other than this room. Vision held him, or Deity, or both.

He spoke in a dialect I did not understand, and one of the black dogs moved forward. It went to the twins, and sniffed their hair. The black fur ran with a white that glowed and shimmered. The white fur was thicker, longer than the black, even longer and shaggier than the Cu Sith's green.

The dog was as large as the Cu Sith, maybe even a little larger. The fur wasn't so much long like a sled dog's as just unkempt. It turned eyes the size of saucers to me, huge and out of proportion to its doggie face. But then the look in its eyes wasn't exactly the look a dog gives you either. It was a look somewhere between a wild animal and a person. There was too much wisdom in those eyes.

Rhys said softly, "It's a Gally-trot."

"A ghost dog," I said. It was supposed to be a phantom that haunted lonely roads and scared travelers.

"Not exactly," he said. "Remember, some humans believe that all the fey are the spirits of the dead."

The Gally-trot leaned its huge white head over the twins, and licked them with a tongue that was as black as the fur it had started with.

Holly stirred, blinking bloodred eyes at the room. Ash made a sound that was almost pain as the Gallytrot licked him back to life.

I waited for the Cu Sith to come to Frost, or even the Gally-trot, but they didn't. The Cu Sith moved among my guards, receiving pets and strokes. It smiled in that way that dogs do, with its tongue out.

The twins seemed unsure what to make of the white dog's attention. It was Holly who reached up and touched it first. The dog bumped him so hard he almost fell over. It made Holly laugh, a pleased masculine sound. Ash touched the dog, too, and they communed with the huge beast.

The demi-fey were beginning to leave the Red Caps. The faces revealed were gentler, as if the clay of their bodies had been remade into something more sidhe, more human. Jonty's words came back to me, "You are remaking us."

I hadn't meant to.

But there were a lot of things I hadn't meant to do.

I stared down at Frost, and saw a gleam of blue at his neck. His tie had already been loosened by someone. I snapped off buttons in my haste to see, and found blue glowing on his skin.

Rhys and Galen put him on his back, and helped me tear his shirt open. There was a tattoo on his chest that glowed blue. It was a stag head with a crown in its antlers. It was a mark of kingship, but it was also a mark of the sacrificial king. The white stag was what he had made with his touch that night in the winter dark. The white stag is a thing to be hunted and to lead the hero to his destiny.

I stared at Rhys's face because he looked as horrified as I felt.

"What does it mean?" Galen asked.

"Once all new creation came with sacrifice," Doyle's voice intoned, but it wasn't his voice.

"No," I said. "No, I didn't agree to this."

"He did," the voice said. The look in Doyle's eyes was not him either.

"Why? Why him?"

"He is the stag."

"No!" I stood up, stumbling on the hem of my robe. I went toward the black dogs and this stranger in Doyle's body.

"Merry," Rhys said.

"No!" I screamed it again.

One of the black dogs growled at me. My power washed over me, burst across my skin. I glowed like I'd swallowed the moon. Shadows of crimson light fell around my face from my hair. I saw green and gold light, and knew my eyes glowed.

"Would you challenge me?" Doyle's mouth said, but it wasn't Doyle who I would challenge if I said yes.

"Merry, don't," Rhys said.

"Merry," Galen said. "Please, Frost wouldn't want this."

My hounds bumped my hand, and my thigh. I looked down at them, and they glowed. Minnie's red half of her face glowed like my hair, and her skin gave white light around my hand as I petted her. Our glows mingled. Mungo, with his red ear and white coat, looked as if he were carved of jewels.

The queen's ring pulsed on my hand. It, like so

many things, had more power inside faerie, and that was where we stood now.

I saw phantom puppies dancing around my hounds. I knew in that moment that Minnie was already pregnant. The first faerie hounds to be born in five hundred years, maybe more?

Minnie bumped my hip, made me look down at myself. Two small phantoms of my own, hovering around me. But I knew they were real. No wonder I'd been tired today. Twins, like my mother and her sister. Twins. And faint, like a thought that wasn't quite real, was a third. It wasn't real yet, just a promise of possibilities. It meant that the twins would not be all. There would be at least a third child for me with someone.

I realized as soon as I thought it that the ring had other powers. I wanted to know who the father was, and I could know here with the ring, inside faerie. I turned and looked at Doyle, and found the answer I most wanted. The ring pulsed, and the scent of roses rode the air.

I turned toward Frost. A child sat beside him, quiet, and too solemn. No, Goddess, no, not like this. Even the wonder of a child, of twins, could not make Frost's loss a fair trade. I did not know these phantom children yet. I had not held them. I did not know their smiles. I did not know how soft their hair was, or how sweet their skin smelled. They were not real yet. Frost was real. Frost was mine, and we had made a child.

"Goddess, please," I whispered.

Rhys moved through my edge of vision, and the

child reached up for him. It passed a phantom hand through his. He reacted to it, trying to see what had touched him. That wasn't right. I held two children inside me, not three. I was one father over the line.

But not for long, unless . . . I went to Frost. Galen caught me in his arms, and the ring pulsed hard enough to make me stagger. Four fathers for two babies. It made no sense. I hadn't had intercourse with Galen for more than a month, because we all agreed he'd make a bad king. He and Kitto had been the only ones who had let me indulge my penchant for oral sex to my heart's content. But you couldn't get pregnant from that.

The scent of roses was stronger. That usually meant a yes. Not possible, I thought.

"I am Goddess, and you are forgetting your history."

"What history are you forgetting?" Galen asked.

I looked up at him. "You heard that?"

He nodded.

"The story of Ceridwen."

He frowned at me. "I don't understand. . . ." Then comprehension slipped across his face. My Galen with his thoughts so easy to follow on his handsome face. "You mean. . . ."

I nodded.

He frowned. "I thought Ceridwen getting pregnant from eating a grain of wheat and Etain being born because someone swallowed her as a butterfly were both myths. You can't get pregnant from swallowing anything."

"You heard what She said."

He touched my stomach through the silk of the robe. A smile spread across his face. He glowed with joy, but I could not join him.

"Frost is a father, too," I said.

Galen's joy dimmed like a candle put behind dark glass. "Oh, Merry, I'm sorry."

I shook my head, and drew away from him. I went to kneel beside Frost. Rhys was on the other side of him. "Did I hear you right? Frost would have been your king?"

"One of them," I said. I didn't feel like explaining that Rhys had also, somehow, hit the jackpot. It was too confusing. Too overwhelming.

Rhys put his fingers against the side of Frost's neck. He pressed against his skin. His head dropped, so his hair was a curtain to hide his face. One shining tear fell onto Frost's chest.

The blue of the stag mark blinked brighter, as if the tear had made the magic flare more brightly. I touched the mark, and that made it brighter, too. I laid my hand on his chest. His skin was still warm. The mark of the stag flared into blue flame around my hand.

I prayed. "Please, Goddess, don't take him from me, not now. Let him know his child, please. If I have ever held your grace, bring him back to me."

The blue flames flared bright and brighter. They did not burn, but felt more like electricity, stinging and biting, but just short of pain. The glow was so bright I could no longer see his body. I could feel the smooth muscles of his chest, but I could not see anything but the blue of the flames.

I felt fur under my hand. Fur? Then I was not touching Frost. Something else was inside that blue glow. Something with fur and not man-shaped.

The shape stood, and moved high enough that I could not touch it. Doyle was behind me, folding me in his arms, picking me up off the ground. The blue fire died down, and a huge white stag stood in front of us. It looked at me with gray and silver eyes.

"Frost," I said, and reached out, but it ran. It ran for the far windows over the acre of marble. It ran as if the surface wasn't slick for hooves. It ran as if it weighed nothing. I thought it would crash into the glass, but French doors that had never been there before opened so that the great stag could run out into the new land beyond.

The doors closed behind him, but the doors did not go away. Apparently, the room was flexible still.

I turned in Doyle's arms so I could see his face. It was him looking out of his eyes now, not the consort. "Is Frost. . . ."

"He is the stag," Doyle said.

"But does that mean he's gone as our Frost?"

The look on his dark face was enough.

"He's gone," I said.

"He is not gone, but he is changed. Whether he will change back to the man we knew, only Deity knows."

He wasn't dead, exactly. But he was lost to me. Lost to us. He would not be a father to the child we had made. He would never be in my bed again.

What had I prayed? That he would come back to me. If I had worded it differently would he still have transformed into an animal? Had my words been the wrong ones?

"Do not blame yourself," Doyle said. "Where there is life of any kind there is always hope."

Hope. It was an important word. A good word. But in that moment, it didn't seem enough.

Chapter 24

"I DON'T CARE HOW MANY GALLY-TROTS YOUR MAGIC calls back," Ash said. "You swore you would lie with us, and you have not done so." He paced the room, hands pulling at his short blond hair as if he would pull it out.

Holly sat on the large white couch with the Gally-trot lying on its back in his lap, or in as much of his lap as it would fit, which meant it filled up a large portion of the large couch. Holly ruffled the dog's chest and stomach. Holly of the hot temper seemed more relaxed than I'd ever seen him.

"The sex was so she'd bring us into our powers. She's brought us power."

"Not sidhe-sided power," Ash said, coming to stand in front of his brother.

"I would rather be goblin," Holly said.

"I would rather be king of the sidhe," Ash said.

"The princess has told you that she is with child," Doyle said.

"You've come too late to the party," Rhys said.

"And whose fault is that?" Ash asked. He came to stand in front of me now. "If you had only bedded us a month ago, then we would have had our chance."

I stared up at him, too numb to react to his anger and disappointment. Someone had put a blanket around me. I huddled in it, cold. Colder than I knew how to cure. So funny, Frost was gone, and I mourned him by being cold.

There were diplomatic answers I could have given. There were many things I could have said, but I simply didn't care. I didn't care enough to mind my tongue.

I stared up at him. Galen slipped onto the couch beside me. He curled his arm around my shoulders. I snuggled in against him. I let him hold me. He had been standing with the others whom Doyle had called into the living room. Standing in case Ash's anger got the better of his sense. The goblin's anger had been so great that Doyle and Rhys were still standing. They wanted to be up and ready. In case this oh-so-reasonable brother lost his head.

Galen held me, closer now, but it wasn't for fear of Ash. I think he was afraid of what I might do. He was right to be afraid, because I was so unafraid. I felt nothing.

"Your king, Kurag, is happy with the new strength that has returned to the Red Caps," I said. "He is overjoyed at the Gally-trot. When your king is happy, warrior, you are supposed to be happy in his joy." My voice sounded cold but not empty. There was an edge of anger in my voice like a crimson thread in a field of white.

"If we were sidhe, but we are goblin, and kings are fragile things."

Galen moved a little forward beside me. I read his

mind, and knew the goblin did, too. He would shield me with his body. But it wasn't that kind of fight.

"Kurag is our ally. If he dies, the treaty between us dies with him."

"Yes," Ash said. "Yes, it does."

I laughed, and it was an unpleasant laugh. The kind of laugh you make because you can't cry yet.

The sound startled Ash. It made him take a step backward from me. No anger would have gotten such a reaction, but laughter, he didn't understand it.

"Think before you threaten, goblin. If Kurag dies, then we are honor bound to avenge him," I said.

"The Unseelie Court is forbidden to interfere directly in the line of succession of its subsidiary courts," Ash said.

"That is a bargain that the Queen of Air and Darkness made. I am not my aunt. I have made no such agreement to limit my powers."

"Your guards are great warriors, but they cannot prevail against the combined might of the goblins," Ash said.

"As I am not bound by my aunt's agreement, I am not bound by goblin rules."

Ash looked uncertain, as if he was thinking on what I had said but hadn't figured it out yet.

It was Holly who said it. "What will you do, Princess, send your Darkness to assassinate us?" He was still ruffling the huge dog, but his face was no longer simply happy. His red eyes stared at me with a weight and intelligence that I hadn't seen before in him. It was a look more often seen on his brother's face.

"He is no longer merely my Darkness. He will be king." But that had not been what I was thinking.

"That is another thing that makes no sense," Ash said. He pointed at Doyle. "How can he be king and father of your child, and he"—he pointed at Rhys—"and he?"—and at Galen last. "Unless you are having a litter, Princess Meredith, you can't have three fathers."

"Four," I said.

"Who. . . ." Then a look crossed his face and the first bit of caution.

"Killing Frost," Holly said.

"Yes," I said, and my voice was back to sounding empty. My chest actually hurt. I'd heard the phrase brokenhearted, but I hadn't actually felt it before. I'd come close, but never truly. My father's death had destroyed me. My fiancé's betrayal had crushed me. When I thought I'd lost Doyle a month ago in the battle, I had felt like my world would end. But until now, I had not truly been heartbroken.

"You can't have four fathers for two children," Ash insisted, but he had calmed a little. It was almost as if he saw my pain for the first time. I didn't think he cared that I was in pain, but it made him more cautious.

"You're too young to remember Clothra," Rhys said.

"I've heard the story, we've all heard the story, but that was just a story," Ash said.

"No," Rhys said, "it was not. She had a single child by all of her brothers. He was marked by each of them. The boy became high king. He was called Lugaid Riab nDerg, of the red stripes."

"I always thought the stripes referred to some kind of birthmark," Galen said.

Doyle's deep voice filled the room, and held an echo of godhead. "I saw that the princess will have two children. They will have three fathers each, as Clothra's son did."

"Don't try your sidhe magic on me," Ash said.

"It is not sidhe magic, it is god magic, and the same Deities serve and are served by all of feykind," Doyle said.

I was running slow, but I finally heard what he'd said enough to say, "Three fathers apiece? You, Rhys, Galen, Frost, and who?"

"Mistral and Sholto."

I stared at him.

"But that was a month ago," Galen said.

"A month ago," Doyle said, "and do you remember what we did when we arrived back in Los Angeles that night?"

Galen seemed to think about it, then he said, "Oh." He kissed me on the top of my head. "But I didn't even have intercourse with Merry. We'd all agreed I'd make a lousy king. Oral sex doesn't get you pregnant."

"Kiddies," Rhys said, "the raw magic of faerie was out that night. I was still Cromm Cruach, with the ability to heal and kill with a touch. Merry had given life to the dead gardens with Mistral and Abe. She had raised the wild hunt with Sholto. Wild magic was out that night. We were all touched by it. The rules are different when that kind of magic is out and about."

"You were the one who started the sex when we

got home, Rhys. Did you know this could happen?"
Galen asked.

"I was Cromm Cruach again, a god again. I
wanted to feel Merry under me while I was still. . . ."
Rhys put his hands out as if he couldn't quite put it
into words.

"I was just happy that everyone was alive," I said,
and my heart squeezed harder, as if it would truly
break. The first hot, hard tear crept out of my eye.

"He is not dead, Merry," Galen said. "Not really."

"He is a stag, and no matter how magical and wonderful that is, he is not my Frost. He cannot hold me.
He cannot talk to me. He is not. . . ."

I stood up, letting the blanket fall to the floor. "I
need some air." I started for the far hallway that
would lead farther into the house and eventually to
the backyard. Galen got up to follow me.

"No," I said. "No. Just no." I kept walking.

Doyle stopped me at the doorway. "I must finish
this talk with our goblin allies."

I nodded, fighting not to break down completely. I
couldn't afford to appear that weak in front of the
goblins. But I felt like I was suffocating. I had to get
somewhere where I could breathe. Somewhere where
I could break down.

I started down the corridor at a fast walk. My
hounds were suddenly beside me. I started to run and
they leaped with me. I needed air. I needed light. I
needed. . . .

I heard voices behind me, my guard, calling,
"Princess, you shouldn't be alone. . . ."

The hallway changed to a different hallway. I was

suddenly outside the dining room. Only the faerie sithen itself was capable of moving with my wish.

I stood there for a moment outside the big double doors, wondering what had we done to Maeve's house. Was the house now a sithen? Was the whole house now part of faerie? No answers, but just through these doors, and through the French doors that had never been there before, was outside, and air, and light, and I wanted it.

I opened the doors. I walked carefully on the marble in the heels that I'd worn to please the twins. I thought about taking off the shoes, but I wanted outside first. The dogs' nails clicked on the floor. The Red Caps stood when I entered.

They went down on one knee, even Jonty. "My queen," he said.

"Not queen yet, Jonty," I said.

He grinned up at me, and it was strangely unfinished without his pointy teeth and more frightening face. It didn't quite look like him until I saw his eyes. Jonty was still in there in those eyes.

"Once all rulers were chosen by the gods. It is the old way. The way such things are meant to be done."

I shook my head. I had never wanted less to be ruler of faerie. The cost, as I'd feared, was so terribly high. Too high.

"Your words are well meant, but my heart is heavy."

"The Killing Frost is not gone."

"He will not help me raise his child. That is gone, Jonty." I started across the vast floor toward the far doors. The windows were a line of brightness. I realized with a start that it had been night when we began this, and was still night outside the main house, but through the windows it was bright day. The sunlight had moved, shadows changing across the floor in the hour since it had appeared, but it ran on a different time than the outside world. It was as if the doors led into the heart of this new sithen. Was this our garden? Our heart of faerie?

Mungo bumped my hand. I stroked his solid head and looked into those eyes. Those eyes that were just a little too wise for a dog. Minnie rubbed against my other leg. They were telling me in the only way they could that I was right.

Rhys and Doyle said that the night we had conceived the babies inside me had been a night of wild magic, but this was wild magic, too. This was creation magic, and that was ancient magic. The most ancient magic imaginable.

The doors opened without my hand reaching out. The breeze was cool and warm at the same time. There was a scent of roses.

I stepped through the doors. They closed behind me and vanished. It didn't frighten me. I had wanted to be outside, and the hallways had changed for me. Inside the Unseelie sithen I could call doors. I didn't want a door right now. I wanted to be alone. The dogs were about as much company as I could stand. I wanted to grieve, and those closest to me were too torn between happiness and sorrow. Sorrow for Frost, but happiness at being kings. I could not bear the mingling of joy and sadness in them anymore. I would be joyful later. But for now, I needed to give myself over to other things. I stood in the center of a sun-drenched clearing with the dogs on either side of me. I raised my face to the heat of that sun and let go of my control. I gave myself over to my grief, with no hands to hold me and be happy. I held the grass-covered earth, the warmth of the dogs' fur, and finally wept.

Chapter 25

HANDS SLID OVER MY SHOULDERS. I STARTED, THEN turned to find Amatheon. His copper hair was haloed in the bright sunlight so that for an instant his face was lost to the brilliance. He seemed made for this new faerie of sunshine and warmth.

I let him hold me, tired from my weeping, exhausted in mind and body. I had had the greatest news of my life today, and some of the saddest. It was like being granted your favorite wish and then being told that the price would be your dearest love. It wasn't fair, and the moment I thought it, I knew that was a child's thought. I was not a child. Life was not fair, and that was just truth.

Amatheon raised my face to his with a gentle hand on my chin. He kissed me. The kiss was gentle, and I gave him gentle back. Then his hands on my back pressed me more tightly against him. His mouth became insistent on mine, asking me with tongue and lips to open for him.

I pushed against his chest so that I could see his face. "Amatheon, please, I have just lost Frost. I . . ."

He pressed his mouth to mine hard enough that I had a choice of opening my mouth for him or cutting my lips on his teeth. I pushed at him, harder.

The dogs gave a soft growl like music in unison.

I felt something around his mouth that shouldn't have been there, almost like a mustache and beard. The sunlight dazzled my eyes, and the sensation was gone.

He pressed me to the ground. I pushed at him again, and yelled, "Amatheon, no!"

Mungo rushed in and bit his arm. Amatheon cursed at him, but it wasn't the right voice.

I stared at the man above me. Sorrow was gone in a wash of fear. Whoever this was, it wasn't Amatheon.

He leaned over to force a kiss on me again. I raised my hands and tried to keep his face from mine. The moment the queen's ring touched his bare skin, the illusion vanished. The sunlight seemed to dim for a moment, then I was staring up at the face of Taranis, King of Light and Illusion.

I didn't waste time on surprise. I accepted what my eyes told me and acted. I said, "Door, bring me Doyle."

A door appeared beside us. Taranis looked shocked. "You want me. All women want me."

"No, I don't."

The door started to open. He raised a hand and sunlight hit the door like a bar of steel. I heard Doyle's voice, and others, yelling my name.

The dogs rushed him, and he rose to his knees, spilling golden light from his hands. It raised the hair on my body and forced another scream from me.

My eyes were dazzled by the light. I had a ruined glimpse of my hounds lying burned. Mungo was staggering to his feet to try again.

Taranis was on his feet, with my wrist in his hand. I fought to stay on the ground, to not go with him. Doyle and the others were just on the other side of the door. They would come. They would save me.

Taranis's fist came out of the light, and the world went dark.

Chapter 26

I CAME TO SLOWLY, PAINFULLY. THE SIDE OF MY FACE ached, and my head felt like someone was trying to beat their way out of my skull. The light was too bright. I had to close my eyes, shield them with my hand. I drew the silk sheet across my breasts. Silk?

The bed moved, and I knew someone was with me. "I have dimmed the lights for you, Meredith."

That voice, oh Goddess. I blinked my eyes open and wished I could believe it was a dream. Taranis was propped up on one elbow beside me. The white silk sheet rode low at his waist. The hair that traced his chest was a more solid red than the sunset color of his hair. A line of hair trailed lower, and I truly did not want him to prove that he was a natural redhead.

I held the sheets to my breasts like a virgin startled on her wedding night. I thought of a dozen things to say, but finally said, "Uncle Taranis, where are we?" There, I'd reminded him that I was his niece. I wasn't panicking out loud. He'd already proven he was crazy in the lawyer's office. He'd proved it again by knocking me unconscious and bringing me here. I was going to be calm, for as long as I could.

"Now, Meredith, don't call me 'Uncle.' It makes me feel old."

I stared up into that handsome face, trying to see some sanity that I could reason with. He smiled down at me, looking charming, and unworldly handsome, but there was no hint that what was happening was wrong, or strange. He acted as if nothing was wrong. That was more frightening than almost anything he could have done.

"All right, Taranis. Where are we?"

"My bedroom." He made a gesture, and I followed the line of his hand.

It was a room, but it was edged with flowering vines and trees espaliered to the wall, heavy with fruit. Jewels winked and glittered among the verdant plant life. It was almost too perfect to be real. The moment I thought it, I knew I was right. It was illusion. I did not try to break it. It did not matter that he used magic to make his room look lovely. He could keep his decorating tricks to himself. Though part of me wondered how I had been so sure so soon that it wasn't real.

"Why am I in your bedroom?"

He frowned then, just a little. "I want you to be my queen."

I licked my lips, but they stayed dry. Should I try reason? "I am heir to the Unseelie throne. I cannot be both your queen and queen of the Unseelie Court."

"You never have to go back to that awful place. You can stay here with us. You were always meant to be Seelie." He leaned in, as if to kiss me again.

I couldn't help it. I recoiled from him.

He stopped, frowning again. He looked like he was thinking and it hurt. He wasn't a stupid man. I think it was just another symptom of his madness. He knew, in some part of him, that he was in the wrong, but his madness wouldn't let him see it.

"Don't you find me handsome?"

I told the truth. "You are always handsome, Uncle."

"I told you Meredith, not Uncle."

"As you like. I find you handsome, Taranis."

"But you react as if I am ugly."

"Just because a man is handsome doesn't mean I want to kiss him."

"In the mirror, if your guards had not been with you, you would have come to me then."

"I remember."

"Then why do you recoil from me now?"

"I do not know." And that was the truth. Here, in the flesh, was the man who had nearly overwhelmed me numerous times from a distance with his compulsion magic. Now I was here alone, and he did nothing but frighten me.

"I am offering you everything your mother always wanted from me. I will make you queen of the Seelie Court. You will be in my bed and in my heart."

"I am not my mother. Her dreams are not mine."

"We will have a beautiful child." Again he tried to kiss me.

I sat up, and the world ran in streamers of color. Nausea made me gag. Gagging made the headache worse. I leaned off the side of the bed and was sick. Throwing up made my head feel as if it would explode. I cried with the pain of it.

Taranis came to the side of the bed. Through the ruin of my sight, I saw him hesitate. I saw the revulsion on his handsome face. It was too messy for him, too real. There would be no help from him.

I had all the symptoms of a concussion. I had to get to a human hospital, or a true healer. I needed help. I lay on the edge of the bed, my uninjured cheek resting on the silk sheet. I lay there waiting for my head to stop throbbing in time to my pulse, praying that the nausea would pass. Lying very still made it better, but I was hurt. I was hurt and I was mortal, and I wasn't sure Taranis would understand that.

He didn't touch me. He reached for a bell rope. He called servants. Fine with me. They might be sane.

I heard voices. He said, "Bring the healer."

A woman's voice. "What is wrong with the princess?"

There was the sound of a hand hitting flesh. He roared at her, "Do as you are told, wench!"

There were no more questions, but I doubted that any of the servants would ask again what had happened to me. They would know all too well.

I think I passed out again, because the next thing I knew was a cool hand on my face. I looked carefully, moving only my eyes to the woman's face. I should have known her name, but I could not think of it. She was golden of hair with eyes that were rings of blue and gray. There was a gentle air to her, as if by simply being closer to her I felt a little better.

"Do you know your name?"

I had to swallow past the bitterness of bile, but finally whispered, "I am Princess Meredith NicEssus, wielder of the hands of flesh and blood."

She smiled. "Yes, you are."

Taranis's voice came from behind her. "Heal her!"

"I must first ascertain how badly injured she is."

"The Unseelie guard went mad. He tried to kill her rather than see her go with me. They would rather have her dead than lose her."

The healer and I exchanged a look. The look was enough. She put a finger to her lips. I understood, or hoped I did. We wouldn't argue with the crazy man, not if we wanted to live. And I wanted to live. I carried our children. I would not die now.

Frost was gone, but there was a piece of him inside me, growing, alive. I would keep it that way. Goddess help me, please, help me escape in safety.

A male voice that was not Taranis's spoke from behind her, "Do you smell flowers?"

"Yes," the healer said, and she gave me another look that was too knowing for comfort. She motioned at the male voice and he stepped into view. He was tall and blond and handsome, and the epitome of Seelie sidhe breeding. Except that he didn't look arrogant; he looked nervous, maybe even a little afraid. Good. I needed him not to be stupid.

I whispered, "Goddess help me."

The scent of roses was stronger. A breeze played along my bare skin, made the sheets on my legs move with the touch of it.

The guard looked toward where the breeze was coming from. The healer looked at me. She smiled, even as her eyes looked too grave for comfort. She bore a look that you never want to see on a doctor's face.

"How hurt am I?" I spoke softly and carefully.

"There may be bleeding inside your head."

"Yes," I said.

"Your eyes are equal. That is a good sign."

She meant that if one of my pupils had been fixed, I would be dying. So that *was* good news.

She began to mix herbs from her leather bag. I didn't know what everything was, but I knew enough of herbal medicine to caution her.

"I carry twins."

She leaned close to me and asked, "How long?"

"A month, a little more."

"There are many things I cannot give you then."

"Can you not lay hands on me?"

"No healer in this court retains that power. Is it true that some in your court do?" She whispered the last into my ear, so close her breath moved my hair.

I whispered back, "True."

"Ah," she said, and leaned back. There was a smile on her face now, and a new sense of contentment that had not been there before. The scent of roses was stronger. I half expected the strong perfume to make the nausea worse, but instead, it eased.

"Thank you, mother," I whispered.

"Would you feel better if your mother was with you?" the healer asked.

"No, absolutely no."

She nodded. "I will do my best to see that your wishes are met."

Which probably translated to my mother being insistent. She had never had much use for me, but if I were suddenly going to be queen of the court she most coveted, then she would love me. She would love me with the same power that she had hated me with for years. She was nothing if not fickle, my mother. One of my names at the Seelie Court was

Besaba's Bane. Because my conception from one night of sex had condemned her to be at the Unseelie Court for years. It had been the marriage that had cemented the treaty between the courts. No one had dreamed that if neither court was breeding, a "mixed" marriage might be fertile.

The hatred and fear of the Seelie for the Unseelie showed in nothing so much as the fact that, with my birth, there had not been offers from the Seelie Court for more unions. They would rather die out as a people than mix with our unclean blood.

Looking into the healer's face, I wasn't certain that all the Seelie agreed with that decision. Or maybe it was the scent of roses growing stronger. All the flowers and vines of Taranis's room, and there had been no scent. It had looked pretty, but . . . it wasn't real. I knew in an instant of clarity that it was like much about the Seelie Court: illusion.

Illusion you could see and touch, but it was not true.

The healer stood and whispered to the guard. He took up a post beside me. Two servants came and began to clean the mess I'd made. Trust the Seelie Court to be more concerned for appearance than truth. They would clean up the mess even before I was healed, or before they were certain that I *could* be healed.

One of the servants had a fresh cut on her cheek and the beginnings of swelling. Her eyes were brown, and her face, though pretty, looked too human. Was she like me, someone of part-human parentage, or was she one of the mortals lured into faerie centuries ago? They got immortality, but if they ever left faerie, all their long years would catch up with them instantly. They were more trapped than any of us, for to leave faerie was true death to them.

She gave me a frightened look as she cleaned. When I did not look away, she held my gaze. There was a moment of great fear in her face. Fear for herself and, maybe, fear for me. Fear of Taranis. Someone had said that the Cu Sith had stopped him from striking a servant. Where was the Cu Sith now?

Something scratched at the door. I did not need to see the door to know that it was something large wanting inside.

Taranis's voice. "Chase that beast away from my door."

"King Taranis," the healer said, "Princess Meredith is beyond my ability to heal."

"Heal her!"

"Many of the herbs I would use would harm the children she carries."

"Did you say children?" he asked, and he sounded almost normal, almost sane.

"She carries twins." She had simply taken my word for it. I appreciated that.

"My twins," he said, and his voice was back to that arrogant crowing. He came back to the bed, sat on it, made me bounce. The headache and nausea roared back to life. I cried out as he scooped me up in his arms. The movement was agony.

I screamed, and the sound hurt me, too.

Taranis seemed frozen by my scream. He stared down at me, almost childlike in his lack of comprehension.

"Do you want your children to die?" the healer said from beside him.

"No," he said, still frowning and confused.

"She is mortal, my king. She is fragile. You must let us take her somewhere where they can heal her, or your children will die unborn."

"But they are my children," he said, and it was more question than fact.

She looked at me, then said, "Whatever the king says is truth."

"She bears my children," he said, and he still sounded a little unsure of himself.

"Whatever the king says is truth," she repeated.

He nodded, hugging me a little more gently. "Yes, my children. Lies, all lies. I was right. I just needed the right queen." He leaned down and laid the softest of kisses on my forehead.

The scratching at the door was louder. Taranis screamed, and stood with me in his arms. "Go away, foul dog!"

The movement was too abrupt and I threw up on him. He dropped me to the bed while I was still vomiting. The brown-eyed servant girl caught me, steadied me, so I did not fall from the bed to the floor. She held me while I threw up until there was nothing but bile and bitterness. Blackness tried to swallow the world again, but the pain was too great.

I lay in the maid's arms and moaned with the pain of it. Goddess and consort, help me!

The scent of roses came like a soothing wave. The nausea eased. The pain became a duller ache instead of a blinding thing.

The brown-eyed maid and the healer began to

clean me again. Most of it had gone onto the king, but not all.

"Let us help you clean up, my lord," the other maid said.

"Yes, yes, I must clean myself."

The brown-eyed maid looked up at the healer and the guard. The healer said, "Go with your fellow servant, help the king to bathe. Make certain he has a long, relaxing bath."

The maid's body tensed a little, then she said, "As the healer wishes, so shall it be."

The healer directed the blond guard to take me from the woman. He hesitated.

"You are a battle-hardened warrior. Does a little sickness make you flinch?"

He scowled at her. His eyes flared with a hint of blue fire before he said, "I will do what is needed." He took me from the maid. He took me gently enough, while the healer said, "Support her head most carefully."

"I have seen head wounds before," the guard said. He did his best to keep me still. When the far door to the bathroom closed behind the king and the maids, the guard stood just as carefully with me in his arms.

The healer went for the door, and he followed without a word. The scratching at the door held whining now, and when they opened the door the Cu Sith stood there like a green pony. It gave a soft woof when it saw us.

The healer whispered, "Hush."

The dog whined, but quietly. It came to the guard's side, so that its fur brushed my bare feet. The touch of it sent a thrill through my body. I waited for my head to hurt, but it didn't. I actually felt a tiny bit better.

We stood in a long marble corridor lined with gilt-edged mirrors. There were two lines of Seelie nobles in front of those mirrors. Each man and woman had at least one faerie dog at their side. Some were the elegant greyhounds like my own poor dogs. I prayed that Minnie would be all right. She had been so still.

Some of the dogs were the huge Irish wolfhounds, as they'd been before the breed had almost died out. These were nothing that had ever mixed with other breeds. They were giants, huge fierce things, some slick of fur, some rough. The looks in their eyes had nothing to do with sight and everything to do with battle. They were war dogs fierce enough that the Romans had feared them and collected them for the arena.

Two of the ladies, and one of the men, held small white-and-red dogs in their arms. All nobles love a good lapdog.

I didn't understand why they were there, but there was again something about the presence of the dogs that calmed me. It was as if a soft voice said, "It will be all right. Do not fear, we are with you."

I recognized Hugh of the fiery hair. "How badly hurt is she?" He had a brace of the huge Irish hounds. They were tall enough to look me in the eye with room to spare as I lay in the guard's arms.

"A concussion, and she is with child. A month gone with twins."

He looked startled. "We must get her away."

The healer nodded. "Yes, we must."

The nobles with their dogs closed behind us, so

that if Taranis had opened his door he would have seen a solid wall of sidhe nobles, and I would have been hidden from sight.

Did they truly mean to defy their king for me? We continued to hurry down the corridor as they spoke of treason.

A woman with hair that flowed in shades of blue and gray like sky or water spoke. It took me a moment to recognize her as Lady Elasaid. "The press secretary has already spoken to the human media."

"What did he say in answer to Queen Andais's accusations?"

"He said that we have offered the princess sanctuary after she was viciously attacked by her own guards."

"So they are telling the lies that Taranis told them," Hugh said.

Lady Elasaid nodded.

"Does the media know that he attacked us in the lawyer's office?" I asked.

They looked startled, as if they hadn't expected me to speak. I think that for them I was an object, and not quite real yet. They weren't joining my cause because they liked me or believed in me, they just believed in the magic and power I was helping bring back to faerie. I was simply the vessel for that power.

"Yes," Hugh said. "We made certain that it was leaked. They have pictures of your injured guards coming and going from the hospital."

We had come to a pair of huge white double doors. I had never seen this hallway. I had never before been honored with a trip to the king's bedroom. I hoped to never be so "honored" again.

Lady Elasaid came to my side. "Princess Meredith, I would give you my shawl to cover yourself, if you would like it." She held out a silken cloth in a brilliant green with gold designs. It matched my eyes. I looked at her, moving my eyes carefully so that nothing hurt. They had a plan. I didn't know what it was, but the shawl matching my eyes said that they had one. If even my clothes were being coordinated then they had a plan.

"It would be most welcome," I said, and again my voice was soft, because I feared what my head would feel like if I spoke too loudly.

I had been healed of worse injuries in vision, but this time the Goddess seemed content to make me feel better in inches rather than all at once.

Hugh spoke as Lady Elasaid and another noble lady helped me slip on the robe. For robe it was, not shawl. "With a little persuasion from some of us, the king demanded a press conference so that he could tell his side of the story. He wanted to override the monstrous lies that the Unseelie were telling. The conference was scheduled to speak about the earlier attack in Los Angeles. But they are still here, Princess. They are now waiting for the king to speak to them about the accusation that he has kidnapped you."

"He let press into the Seelie mound," I said.

"How could he allow the Unseelie to be more progressive than we? Andais had called a conference to demand your return. He would appear guilty if he did less."

I thought I understood now why Deity had healed me only in small bits, enough to function, but not enough to be well. I needed to look hurt for the press.

"Does he honestly believe what he said earlier, that he rescued me?"

"I fear so."

Lady Elasaid fastened a gold pin at the neck of the robe. "I would do your hair if there was time."

"We want her to look disheveled and injured," Hugh said.

I managed a smile at Lady Elasaid. "Thank you for the robe. I will be fine. Just get me to the press. I assume it's a live feed?"

Lady Elasaid frowned. "I do not understand."

"Yes," Hugh said. "It is live."

"Let us not linger here," the blond guard said.

"Only the king can see us here, and he no longer cares enough to use his mirrors for such things. We are safer here than in the next corridor," Hugh said.

"No one would dare spy on the king," a woman said.

So we stood in Taranis's own place of power, safe. Safe to plot behind his back. Safe from prying eyes, because they feared that he would see them, but his madness had made him blind.

I wondered who had first been bold enough to figure out that the king's own inner sanctum was the place to plot treason. Whoever it was would be someone to be careful of. If you plot the overthrow of one ruler, it makes the idea easier next time. Or so it seems.

"We wanted to see how sensible you were before we told you our plan," Lady Elasaid said.

Hugh said, "Head wounds can make a person unreliable, and this is too dangerous a game to have you privy to our secrets if you will blurt them out."

"May I speak freely here?" I asked.

"Yes," he said.

"Get me in front of the cameras and I'll play damsel in distress for you."

Hugh and several others smiled. "You do understand."

"I've been in front of the press my whole life. I understand their power."

"We made him swear a most solemn oath that he would not reveal himself to you until we were certain you would not spoil the plan if you knew him near."

I frowned at Hugh but it hurt, so I stopped. I said, "I don't understand."

There was movement near the far door, hidden by the crowd of people and dogs. The crowd moved to either side, revealing a huge black dog. Not as huge as some of the Irish hounds, but. . . . The black dog trotted toward me, his nails clicking on the marble.

I almost whispered his name but stopped in time. I held a hand out toward him. He laid his great furred head in my hand, then there was an instant of warm mist and prickling magic. Doyle stood before me, nude and perfect. He wore the only metal that seemed to have survived the transformation, the silver earrings that peeked from the fall of his ankle-length hair. Even the tie for his hair was gone.

He was unarmed and alone inside the Seelie mound. The danger he had exposed himself to made my stomach clench tightly. In that moment I feared for him more than for myself.

He took me in his arms, and I clung to him. Clung to the feel of his skin, the strength of him. I moved my head too quickly, and a wave of nausea blurred my vision. He seemed to sense it because he moved me to lie more prone in his arms. He knelt in the white-and-gold corridor, his darkness repeated in the mirrors as he held me.

There was a glitter on his cheeks, and I saw the Darkness cry for only the second time ever.

Chapter 27

I KNELT ON THE MARBLE IN DOYLE'S ARMS, MY HEAD resting on his chest. Just his touch seemed to ease some of my pain.

"How?" I asked.

He seemed to understand exactly what I wanted to know, as he often did. "This is not the first time I have come here in this guise. Many of the fey hounds began as black dogs. I am just one who has not chosen a master. I am quite the favorite among those who have not been blessed with a dog. They offer me choice tidbits and call me sweet names."

"He is skittish, and will not let them lay hands on him," Lady Elasaid said.

"He plays the dog to perfection," Hugh said.

Doyle looked up at them. "It is not play. It is a true form for me."

There was silence for a second, then Hugh asked, "Is the Darkness truly the father of one of your children?"

"Yes," I said. I held him as tightly as I could without moving my head too much. "It is too dangerous for you to be here. If you are discovered. . . ."

He kissed my forehead as gently as a feather's

touch. "I would brave much more than this for you, my princess."

My fingers dug into his arm and back. "I could not bear to lose you *and* Frost. I could not bear it."

"We have heard rumor of the Killing Frost, but we thought it only rumor," Hugh said.

"Is he truly dead?" Lady Elasaid asked.

"He is the white stag in truth," Doyle said.

Hugh knelt beside us, smiling. "He is not dead then, Princess. In three years, or seven, or a hundred and seven, he will return to his true self."

"What good is a hundred years to a mortal lover, Sir Hugh? His child will never know him while I still live."

Hugh's eyes flared as if someone had struck the embers of his power. There was a moment of fire in his eyes, like looking into two small fireplaces. He blinked and his eyes were only the colors of fire. "I have no words of comfort then, but the black dog's presence is one of the things we nobles have done to keep your aunt from starting true war with us. He will remain close to your side."

I grabbed Hugh's sleeve. "He is weaponless in this form. If discovered, can you protect him?"

"I am the captain of your guard, Merry. I protect you," Doyle said.

I leaned harder against the solidness of him, my hand on the other man's sleeve. "You are one half of a breeding royal pair. You are king to my queen. If you die, the chance of other children dies with you."

"She is right, Darkness," Hugh said. "It has been too long since there was life in the royal bloodline."

"I am not of the bloodline," Doyle said. His deep voice seemed to echo off the mirrors.

"We know the princess has made Maeve Reed, once the goddess Conchenn, with child by her human husband. We also hear rumors that one of your male guards has made a female guard pregnant," Hugh said.

"Truth," I said.

"If you could make one of us who is of the pure Seelie line pregnant, then all the king's support would fall away from him. I am sure of that," Hugh said.

Lady Elasaid knelt on the other side of us. "Most of his supporters are convinced that only the mongrels are breedable. They have decided that they would rather die as a race than pollute their blood. If you could prove them wrong on this, they would follow you."

"Some," Hugh said, "but not all. Some hate too deeply."

She nodded. "As you say, Hugh." There was something intriguing about the way she said it, the way she lowered her eyes.

"You want you and Hugh to be the experiment," I said.

She blinked at me. "Experiment?"

Hugh took her hand in his. "Yes, we would like very much to have a child of our own."

"When I am healed and safe, and my people are safe, then I would be happy to try a spell for you," I said.

Some tension went out of them, and they smiled at me, as if I'd told them that tomorrow was Yule and their most longed-for present was under the tree. I wanted to warn them that until the ring and the Goddess had told me they were breedable, I could guarantee nothing.

Doyle's arms tightened around me. He was right; now was not the time to undermine our allies' confidence in us. We needed them to get us out of here. I needed a hospital or a healer who could lay hands. And I never, ever wanted to go back to Taranis's bed.

I shivered, and fought to not move my head when I did it.

"Are you cold?" Doyle asked.

"Nothing that a blanket can help."

"I will slay him for you."

"No, no, you will live for me. Vengeance is cold comfort on a winter's night. I want you warm and alive beside me more than I want my honor avenged." I moved as carefully as I could until I could see his face. "As your princess, and future queen, I order you to forget vengeance for this. I am the injured party, not you. If I say it's not as important to me as the feel of you in my arms, you must honor that."

He stared down at me with those black eyes. His hair was a wild mass of thick blackness with the hint of silver rings peeking like stars from the blackness of his hair. He looked like the Doyle who came to my bedroom, not the braided and buttoned-up Doyle who guarded me. But the expression on his face was all about the guard, and something else. Something I hadn't expected to see, though I should have. There was a man's feelings for his love, who had been violated by another man. It was, dare I say, a very human emotion.

"Please, Doyle, please, let us tell the media what he

has done. Let us bring him down using the human law he sought to use against us."

"It has a certain poetic justice," Hugh said.

Doyle stared down at me for a breath, then gave one small nod. "As my queen wishes, so shall it be."

It felt as if the world took a breath, as if it had been waiting for him to say those words to me. I had no idea why those words now were so important, but I knew the sensation of reality changing. Those words, spoken here, had changed something large. Some event had stopped, or begun, because of this moment. I felt it, knew it, but not what it meant, or what the end would be.

"So mote it be," the healer said.

The other nobles echoed her. "So mote it be, so mote it be." Down the corridor, and just like that I understood. They had acknowledged me queen. Once you only needed so many nobles and the blessing of the gods to rule in faerie. Once, even longer ago, you had only needed the blessing. Now I had both.

"I would carry you to the ends of the earth and beyond," Doyle said, "but I must trust my most precious burden to others." He reached out as if he would touch the spreading bruise where Taranis had struck me, then he bent over and laid his mouth against mine. His hair slid over me like a warm cloak to help hide me.

He whispered, "More than life, more than honor, I love thee."

What do you say when a man whose entire existence had been his honor offers to give it up for you? You say the only thing you can. "More than any crown or throne or title, I love thee," I said. "More than any power in faerie, I love thee."

The scent of roses and deep forest was suddenly present, as if we'd stepped into a forest glade where wild roses had managed to grow.

"I smell flowers again," the blond guard said.

"The Goddess moves around this one," a woman said.

"Let us take her to the humans and see if they can do what we cannot," Lady Elasaid said. "Get her far away from here." She turned tricolored eyes shiny with unshed tears away as Hugh helped her stand.

Doyle stood up, carefully, holding me close, and trying not to move my head. He succeeded. I clung to him, not wanting him to let me go, even as I knew we had to separate.

Doyle and Hugh looked at each other. "Know that you carry the future of all of faerie in your arms, Sir Hugh."

"If I did not believe that, I would not be here now, Darkness."

Doyle lifted me away from his body, and Hugh's arms slid under me. My hands trailed over Doyle's bare flesh, so warm, so real, so . . . mine.

Hugh settled me as gently as he could in the curve of his arms, and the strength of his body. It wasn't his power as a warrior that I doubted, not really. It was simply that his arms were not the ones I wanted.

"I will be close by, my Merry," Doyle said.

"I know," I said.

Then he was the black dog again. He came to nudge my foot with the fur of his head. I touched him with my fingers, and the eyes were still Doyle's eyes.

"Let us go," Hugh said.

The rest formed a group around us. They closed in front as they opened the door, so that if there was an attack waiting, it would hit them first and not me. They were risking their lives, their honor, their future. They were immortal, which meant they had a lot of future to risk.

I prayed, "Mother, help them, keep them safe. Do not let them pay a hard price for what we are about to do."

The scent of roses was fresh, and so real that I thought I felt a petal brush my cheek. Then I felt another. I opened my eyes to find that it was raining rose petals.

There were gasps of joy and wonder from the nobles of the Seelie Court. The dogs capered and danced in the fall of petals. The petals looked very pink against the blackness of Doyle's fur.

Lady Elasaid said, "Once the queen of our court walked everywhere in a shower of flowers." Her voice was soft with wonder.

"Thank you, Goddess," Hugh said. Tears glittered on his face as he looked at me, tears that sparkled like water reflecting fire. He whispered, "Thank you, my queen."

He walked forward with me in his arms, tears of fire glittering on his face. We walked into the next room with pink rose petals floating down from nowhere like sweet rain.

Chapter 28

WE MOVED THROUGH ROOMS OF MARBLE AND GOLD. Rooms with cold pink walls with veins of silver and pillars of gold. Rooms of white marble with veins of pink and lavender and pillars of silver. Rooms of gold and silver marble with pillars of ivory. We moved always in a circle of falling petals, pink petals pale as dawn's first blush, dark as day's last salmon blaze, and a color deep enough to be purple. They fell around us, and I realized that the petals were the only living thing we passed. There was nothing organic in this place of marble and metal. It was a palace, but it was not a home for beings who had begun life as nature spirits. We were meant to be a people of warmth, life, and love, and there was none of that here.

I don't know what the other nobles would have done if we hadn't moved in the circle of that flowered blessing. They matched the rooms, dressed in stiff clothing of gold and silver and subdued color. They stared, openmouthed. Some began to follow us, like a parade that grows from sheer joy and wonder.

It was when I heard the first laugh that I realized that there was more to the nobles being won over than simply *seeing* the fall of petals. The *touch* of the flowers seemed to make them happy. They came to us with smiles, and voices of protest, of "Where is the king? What have you done?" When the voices died out, they simply followed us, smiling.

Hugh whispered, "I remembered loving Queen Roisin. I never realized that that love was partially glamour."

I almost told him that I wasn't doing this, but with that thought the scent of roses suddenly grew stronger. I'd learned that that usually meant either yes or don't. I guessed that I should not tell Hugh that I wasn't creating the flowers on purpose, and with that thought the scent of roses dimmed. I took it to mean that I'd done what she wished. I was content with that.

Doyle had had to drop back so that he was not right next to me. I understood that it was so no one would see and perhaps make a connection, but I had to fight both my feelings and the head injury not to look around for the big black dog. Hugh's huge shaggy hounds helped, both by partially blocking my view and by brushing me with their muzzles, touching my bare feet and hands. One was almost solid white, the other almost as solidly red with only small white markings. Every time they touched me, I felt a little better.

The petals rested on their great heads, then fell to the ground as they moved and snuffled at me. It was almost as if the dogs were more real to me than the nobles in their beautiful clothes. The dogs had been created from the magic that I had raised with Sholto. They had come from the same magic that had finally gotten me with child. The dogs had come from the same night and the same magic. A magic of making and remaking.

There were guards at the doors at the end of the room where we stopped. This room was formed of red and orange marble with veins of white and gold glittering through the stone. The pillars were silver with gold vines carved to look as if they bloomed with golden flowers.

As a child, I had thought the pillars one of the most lovely things in the world. Now I saw them for what they were, a stand-in for the real thing. The Unseelie Court, even without the new magic, had held the remnants of real roses. There had been a water garden in the inner courtyard with water lilies. Yes, it had also held a rock with chains fixed to it, so you could be tortured in a scenic setting, but there had been life in the court. It had been fading, but it hadn't faded completely when the Goddess began to move through me, through us.

In all the Seelie Court there was no life. Even the great tree in the main chamber was formed of metal. It was a thing of great artifice, amazing artistic achievement, but such things were for mortals. The immortal weren't supposed to be known only for their art. They were supposed to be known for the reality that the art was based upon. There was nothing real here.

The guards wore business suits. They looked more like secret service agents than Seelie nobles. Only their otherworldly beauty and eyes formed of rings of color showed them to be more than human.

Hugh held me a little closer. His hounds moved in

front of me. I realized that they were tall enough to partially block me from the sight of the guards.

Lady Elasaid moved to the front of the group. She spoke in a ringing voice. "Let us pass."

"The king's orders are clear, m'lady. No one else is allowed into the press conference without his express permission."

"Do you not see the blessing of the Goddess before you?"

"We are immuned to illusion by the king's own magic."

"Do you see the fall of petals?" she asked.

"We see the illusion of it, m'lady."

I could not see what she did, but she said, "Touch them."

"The king can make illusion touchable, too, m'lady Elasaid."

I realized that they had seen lies so long that they no longer recognized truth. All was doubt for them.

The blond guard had stepped a little in front of us, helping the dogs hide us from view. He turned to Hugh and whispered, "Shall I call?"

Hugh gave a small nod.

I expected the guard to take out a hand mirror or use the shiny surface of his blade, but he didn't. He reached into the leather pouch at his side and took out a very modern cell phone.

I must have looked surprised because he said, "We have reception near this room. It's why we put the press in here."

It was perfectly logical. He moved back, and others moved, gracefully, to help hide him from the view of the guards before the doors.

He spoke quietly, "We are outside the doors with the injured princess. The guards will not let us pass."

One of the guards near the door said, "Go back to your rooms. None of you have any business here."

The blond guard said, "Yes. Yes. No." He folded the phone shut, placed it back in his leather bag, and took his post at our side. He whispered to Hugh, so quietly that even I couldn't hear it.

The group of nobles and their hounds bunched up around me. If it came to an actual fight with swords and magic, they had left themselves no room to maneuver. Then I realized what they had done. They were shielding me. Shielding me with their tall, slender bodies. Shielding me with their immortal beauty. Me, who they had once despised, and they were risking all they were, all they had ever been, to keep me safe.

They were not my friends. Most did not know me. Some had made it clear when I was a child that they did not like me. They found me too human, too mixed of blood to be sidhe. What had Taranis done to them to make them so desperate that they would defy him like this for me?

There was a stirring in the front of the glittering throng around me, almost the way a field of flowers moves in a strong wind.

I heard the guard near the door, his voice rough enough to recognize among all the sweeter voices. "You are not allowed farther into our sithen, sir, by order of the king."

"Unless you want to fight us, we are coming through this door."

I knew the voice. It was Major Walters, head of the

special branch of the St. Louis Police Department that specialized in dealing with the fey. It had been an honorary title for years, until I came home. I didn't know how he'd gotten invited to a press conference, and I didn't care.

A second male voice came. "We have a federal warrant to bring the princess into protective custody." It was Special Agent Raymond Gillett, who had been the only federal agent who had kept in touch with me after the investigation of my father's death had gone cold. When I was younger I had thought he cared what happened to me. Lately I realized it was more about not leaving such a high-profile case unsolved. I was still angry with him, but in that moment, his familiar voice was a good sound.

"The princess is not here, Officers," said a second guard. "Please go back to the press area."

"The princess is here," Lady Elasaid said, "and in need of human medical attention."

You could feel the increased tension in the group of nobles, like a spring that had been wound once too often. To the human officers, they would be beautiful and unreadable, but I felt their energy rise like the first spark of heat from a match. The guards at the door would feel it, too.

The great black dog moved up on one side of Hugh. It didn't make me feel better. Weaponless against the might of sidhe guards, all he could do was die for me. I didn't want him to die for me. I wanted him to live for me.

"We have doctors with us," Major Walters said. "Let them look at the princess, and we'll go from there."

"The king has ordered that she not be given back to the brutes who injured her. She cannot go near the Unseelie again."

"Did he forbid her going near humans?" Agent Gillett asked.

There was a moment of silence while the murmur of power began to build among the sidhe around me. Slowly, almost imperceptibly, as if they were whispering their magic.

"The king said nothing about humans looking at her," a new guard voice said.

"We were told to keep her away from the press."

"Why would the princess need to be kept away from the press?" Agent Gillett asked. "She will tell them firsthand about being rescued from the evil Unseelie by your brave king."

"I do not know. . . ."

"Unless you think the princess will have a different story," Major Walters said.

"The king has given his oath that it is so," the talkative guard said.

"Then you have nothing to lose by letting our doctors look at her," Agent Gillett said.

The guard who had sounded agreeable said, "If the king is true to his word, then there is nothing to fear, Barri, Shanley. You do believe him, don't you?" There was the first real doubt plain in his voice, as if even among the king's most loyal the lies were becoming too heavy to bear.

"If she is truly here, then let her come forward," Shanley said. He sounded tired.

Hugh held me closer as the nobles parted like a glittering curtain. Only Hugh's hounds and the blond guard stayed in front of me. Doyle stayed to our side. I think that he, like me, was worried that the already suspicious guards would figure out who he was. They might let us go into the pressroom, but if they suspected that the Darkness was inside their sithen, they would go wild.

Finally, Hugh said, "Let them see."

Both the guard and the great dogs moved. Doyle moved a little behind Hugh so that he blended in with the other dogs, aside from his color. He was the only black one among them. To my eyes he stood out almost painfully, so black among all the Seelie color.

I must have looked even worse than I felt, because both the men were wide-eyed. They controlled it after that first glimpse, but I'd seen it. I even understood it. And it was as if that look let me feel again. I don't know if it was the magic, the fear for Doyle, or the fear that Taranis would find us. Or maybe the little screaming voice in my skull that had been growing louder. The voice that finally let me think the thought all the way through, to ask in my own head at least, "Did he rape me? Did he rape me after he beat me unconscious?" Was that what the great king of the Seelie considered seduction? Goddess, let him have been confused when he thought it possible that I carried his children.

It was like knowing that you were cut but only feeling pain after you saw the blood. I'd seen the "blood" on the faces of the police. I saw it in the way they moved toward me. The left side of my face ached and was swollen. I knew that it must have hurt before, but it was as if only now could I feel all of it.

The headache came back in a roar that closed my

eyes and brought a fresh wave of nausea. A voice said, "Princess Meredith, can you speak?"

I looked up into Agent Gillett's eyes. There was that old compassion there, that look that had made me trust him when I was a young woman. I looked into those eyes and knew it was real. I'd felt used by him recently, realizing that he'd kept in touch with me in hopes of solving my father's murder not for me, but for some purpose of his own. I had told him to stay away from me, but looking up into his face now, I understood what I'd seen in him when I was seventeen. For this moment, he cared, deeply.

Maybe he was remembering the first time he saw me, collapsed in grief, clutching my dead father's sword as if it were the last solid thing in the universe.

"Doctor," I whispered. "I need a doctor." I whispered because the last time I'd felt this sick, talking had hurt my head. But I also whispered because I knew it would make me seem more pitiful and if sympathy would get me in front of the press, I would play that card for all it was worth.

Agent Gillett's eyes hardened, and I saw again that purpose that had made me believe he would find my father's killer.

Tonight, that was all right. I carried my father's grandchildren inside me. But I had to get to safety. Strength of arms and magic are so often what the sidhe rely on, but they have never been weak. They do not understand the arsenal of the powerless. I understood, because I had lived in the land of the helpless most of my life.

I stopped fighting to be brave. I stopped fighting to feel better. I let myself feel how hurt I was, and how frightened. I let myself think the thoughts I'd been shoving back. I let them fill my eyes with tears.

The guards at the doors tried to move in front of us, but Major Walters used his officer voice. It echoed in the marble room and into the open door beyond. "You will move aside, now."

The talkative guard said, "Shanley, we have no healers who can cure this. Let the humans treat her." He had hair the flame color of autumn leaves just before they fall to the ground, and eyes of circles of green. He seemed young, though he had to be over seventy, because that was Galen's age, and he was the next youngest sidhe to me.

Shanley looked down at me. His eyes were two perfect circles of blue.

I lay in Hugh's arms and gazed up at him through tear-soaked eyes, and a swelling bruise that covered me from temple to chin.

Shanley spoke quietly, "What story will you tell the press, Princess Meredith?"

"The truth," I whispered.

A look of pain went through those inhumanly lovely eyes. "I cannot let you into that room." His words were his admission that he knew that my truth and Taranis's truth were not one and the same. He knew that his king had lied, and given oath on it. He knew, and yet he had made an oath to serve Taranis as a guard. He was caught between his vows and his king's treachery.

I might have pitied him, but I knew that Taranis would not be distracted forever in his bath. Not even with servant girls to abuse. We were inches away from the press and relative safety. But how to travel those last few inches?

Major Walters pulled his radio from a coat pocket and hit a button. "We need backup out here."

"If they come through, we will fight them," Shanley said.

"She is with child," the healer said. "She carries twins."

He looked suspiciously at her. "You lie."

"I have few powers left me, that is true, but I have enough magic left to sense such things. She is with child. I felt their heartbeats under my hand like the fluttering of birds."

"You don't get heartbeats this quickly," the guard said.

"She entered this sithen pregnant with twins. She was forced into the king's bed to be raped, pregnant with someone else's children."

"Do not say such things, Quinnie," he said.

"I am a healer," she said. "I must speak out at last. If it costs me all I am, all I have, I swear to you that the princess is at least a month gone with twins."

"You will take an oath on it?" he asked.

"I will swear any oath you wish me to take."

They stared at each other for a long moment. There was pounding on the door behind the guards and the sounds of struggle. The rest of the police and agents were trying to come in. The Seelie guards didn't want to injure the police in front of the press, with live cameras on them.

It sounded like the police didn't have the same compunction about the guards. The door shuddered under the weight of bodies hitting it.

The talkative guard went to stand by his captain. "Shanley, listen to her."

"The king took an oath, too," he said. "And nothing came to brand him an oathbreaker."

"He believes what he says," the healer said. "You know that. He believes, so he does not lie, but that does not make it true. We have all seen that in these last few weeks."

Shanley looked from his fellow guard to the healer, then finally to me. "Were the Unseelie raping you when our king saved you?"

"No," I said.

His eyes glittered, but not with magic. "Did he take you against your will?"

"Yes," I whispered.

A tear trailed from each of his beautiful eyes. He gave a small bow. "Command me."

I hoped I knew what he wanted me to do. I spoke as loud as I dared with my head pounding. "I, Princess Meredith NicEssus, wielder of the hands of flesh and blood, granddaughter of Uar the Cruel, command you to step aside and let us pass."

He bowed lower, and moved aside, still in that bow.

Major Walters spoke on his radio again. "We're coming through. Repeat, we're bringing the princess through. Clear the doors."

The sounds of fighting grew louder. The blue-eyed guard spoke into the air. "Stand down, men. The princess is leaving."

The fighting slowed, then there was no sound. The blue-eyed guard nodded at the other guards, and they opened the great doors.

Doyle moved up closer to me as Hugh carried me forward. For a moment I thought it was a magical attack of light, then I realized that it was lights for moving cameras and flashes for still ones. I closed my eyes against the blinding glare, and Hugh carried me through the doors.

Chapter 29

I WAS BLIND FROM THE LIGHTS. MY HEAD FELT LIKE IT was going to explode from the assault of it all. I wanted to scream at them to stop, but was afraid that would only make it all hurt worse.

I closed my eyes and tried to shield them with one hand. There was shadow against the light, and a woman's voice. "Princess Meredith, I'm Doctor Hardy. We're here to help you."

A man's voice. "Princess Meredith, we're going to put you in a neck brace. It's just a precaution."

There was a wheeled stretcher beside us suddenly, as if it had just sprung into being. The medical team started to swarm me. Dr. Hardy was shining a light in my eyes, trying to get me to follow it. I could follow it, but the other hands that I couldn't see, lifting me, starting to do things to me, panicked me.

I started to slap at them, to make small helpless sounds. I don't know what it was about what they were doing, but it was too much. I couldn't see who was touching me. I couldn't see what they were doing. I didn't understand what was happening. I could not bear it.

"Princess, Princess Meredith, can you hear me?" Dr. Hardy asked.

"Yes," I said in a voice that didn't sound like me at all.

"We need to get you to a hospital," Dr. Hardy said. "To transport you, there are things we need to do. Can you let us do those things?"

I wasn't so much crying as tears just seemed to be sliding down my face. "I need to know what you're doing. I need to see who's touching me."

She looked behind me at the barrage of media. The police had moved in to form a wall against them, but they would hear most of what we said. The doctor leaned very close to me. "Princess, were you raped?"

"Yes."

Major Walters bent close, too. "I am sorry, Princess, but I have to ask. Who did it?"

A sidhe guard by the door said, "The Unseelie did it, as they raped Lady Caitrin."

"Shut up!" Major Walters said. Then he turned back to me. "Is that true?"

"No," I said.

"Then who?"

"Taranis knocked me unconscious and I woke naked in his bed with him beside me."

"Liar!" the guard behind us said.

Shanley, who was in charge of these men, said, "She took an oath on it."

"So did our king."

"I cannot help that," he said.

"Taranis hurt me. He and no other. I swear it by the Darkness that Eats all Things."

"You are mad to make such an oath," a voice I didn't know said.

"Only if she lies." I think that was Sir Hugh. But

there was so much noise, so many voices. The press had begun to yell at us. They shouted their questions, their theories. We all ignored them.

Dr. Hardy began to speak quietly to me, to explain what was happening to me. She began to introduce me to her team. She would explain, and only then would they touch me. It began to help me lose that edge of hysteria.

Only when a voice sounded on the microphone that I still had not seen did I make them stop. The voice said, "We have told you what happened to the princess. The Unseelie guard who were supposed to protect her beat and raped her. Our king saved his niece from them and brought her to sanctuary here."

It was too much. No matter how I felt, I could not let them ship me to a hospital and leave that lie in the ears of the media.

"I need a microphone, please. I need to tell the truth," I said.

Dr. Hardy didn't like it, but Hugh and others backed me up, and they rolled me to the front of the room. They insisted that I keep the choking closeness of the neck brace on. I was already hooked up to an I.V. Apparently my blood pressure was low and my body was a little shocky.

The doctor stepped up to the microphone.

"I am Dr. Vanessa Hardy. The princess needs to get to a hospital, but she insists on talking to you. She is injured, and we need to get her to a hospital. This will be quick. I hope that is clear?"

Several of them said, "It is clear."

The press secretary was all pink and gold and sidhe

beauty. She didn't want to give up the mic. She'd heard enough from the doorway to worry her.

It was Agent Gillett who took it from her, and held it for me. You could feel the eagerness of the press like a sort of magic of their own.

A voice called, "Who hit you?"

"Taranis," I said.

There was a collective sigh of eagerness and an explosion of flashes. I closed my eyes against it.

"Did the Unseelie rape you?"

"No."

"Were you raped, Princess?"

"Taranis knocked me unconscious and kidnapped me, and I woke nude in his bed. He says we had sex. I will be taking a rape kit at the hospital. If it comes back positive for an unknown, then yes, my uncle raped me."

The police were holding the press secretary and some of the sidhe back by force. Some of the nobles and the dogs were helping them mind the crowd. I heard growls around me. The loudest was next to me. The great black head touched my hand. I raised fingers to stroke Doyle's fur. That one small touch was more comfort than anything else had been.

Dr. Hardy yelled above the chaos, "The princess has a concussion. I need to get her to X-ray or a CAT scan to see how serious it is. So we're leaving now."

I said, "No."

"Princess, you said you'd go quietly if you told the truth."

"No, it's not that. I can't have an X-ray. I'm pregnant." Agent Gillett was still holding the microphone close enough that the room had heard that. If we thought there had been chaos before, we'd been wrong.

The press were yelling, "Who's the father? Did your uncle make you pregnant?"

Dr. Hardy leaned close and whispered/shouted above the cacophony, "How far along are you?"

"Four to five weeks," I said.

"We will treat you and your baby like gold," she said.

I would have nodded, but the neck brace kept me from doing so. I finally said, "Yes."

She looked up at someone I couldn't see and said, "We need to get her to a hospital now."

We began to push our way toward the door. There were two main reasons we were having problems moving. One was the press. They all wanted one last image, one last question answered. The second was the Seelie guards and nobles who opposed Hugh. They wanted me to stay with them. They wanted me to recant.

Inhumanly beautiful faces kept hovering over me, saying things like, "How can you lie about our king? How can you accuse your own uncle of such a crime? Liar. Lying bitch," was the last one before the police got very serious about keeping the golden throng away from my face.

They tried to chase away the black dog, but I said, "No, he's mine."

No one questioned it. Dr. Hardy only said, "He doesn't go in the ambulance."

I didn't argue. Just Doyle beside me, in any form, was an improvement. Every brush of his fur against my hand was better.

There were so many people around the stretcher, so much light, that the only way I knew we were finally outside was the brush of night air against my face. It had been night when Taranis took me. Was it the same night, or the next night? How long had he had me?

I tried to ask what day it was, but no one heard me. The press had followed us outside the sithen. They trailed us with shouted questions and mobile lights.

The wheels of the gurney didn't like the grass. The bumps made my head ache more. I fought not to make small sounds of pain, and was able to do it until the medics closed around us so that I could no longer touch Doyle's fur. The moment I lost contact with him the pain was worse.

I spoke his name before I could stop myself. "Doyle," I said softly, a plea.

The huge black head shoved its way under the doctor's arm. It made her stumble. She tried to shove him away, saying, "Shoo."

"I need him, please."

She frowned at me, but she dropped back a step so the dog could be closer to me. Close enough that my hand could caress his fur on most of the bumpy ride. I'd never realized how uneven the grass around the mounds was until smoothness was what I needed. It had always seemed like such level ground until this moment.

One of the cameras peered over the shoulders of the medics. The light blinded me. The pain spiked hard and sharp, and nausea came with it.

"I'm going to be sick."

They had to stop the gurney, and help me lean over

the side of it. Between the tubes and board and neck brace, I couldn't have moved myself. I'd never rolled onto my side with this many hands helping me.

Dr. Hardy yelled while I threw up, "She has a concussion! Bright lights aren't good for her."

Being sick made the inside of my head explode, or that's what it felt like. My vision swam in ruins. A hand touched my forehead. A hand that was cool and solid and felt . . . like I should know it.

My vision cleared to find a man with a blond beard and mustache peering into my face. It was his hand on my forehead. A baseball cap was pulled low on his face. There was something about the blue eyes that looked vaguely familiar. Then while I still looked at this stranger's face, the eyes changed. One eye held three rings of blue: cornflower blue around the pupil, sky blue, then a circle of winter sky.

I whispered, "Rhys."

He smiled through the fake beard. He'd used glamour to hide his eyes and other things, but the beard was simply a good fake. He had always been the best of the men at undercover work when we were with the detective agency.

I was crying and not wanting to, because I was afraid it would hurt.

A voice came from behind him. "Remember our deal."

Rhys answered without turning around. "You'll get your exclusive televised interview as soon as she's well enough. I gave my word."

I must have looked confused because he said, "They let us come in as part of their crew for a promised interview, or two."

I reached for him with my free hand. He took it, and kissed my palm. The camera that had made me sick was back to recording, just at a slightly better distance.

"Is he one of your guys?" Dr. Hardy asked.

"Yes," I said.

"Great, but we need to keep moving."

"Sorry," Rhys said, and he put a hand on my shoulder as they moved me back to my back. My other hand searched again for the touch of fur and found it for a moment, then a hand found mine. I couldn't turn to see, and he seemed to understand, because Galen's face hovered over mine. He had a hat on, too, and he'd used glamour to make his green hair look brown and his skin look human. He let the glamour go while I watched, and it was smoother even than Rhys's. One moment a nice-looking human guy, the next Galen. Magic.

"Hey," he said, and his eyes filled with tears almost immediately.

"Hey," I said back. I had a thought for what might have happened if they'd been recognized earlier inside the mound, but it was a small thought. In that moment I was too happy to see them to worry about it. Or maybe I was just that sick?

Dr. Hardy said, "Any more Romeos going to come out of the woodwork?"

"I don't know," I said, which was the absolute truth.

"One more was inside with us," Galen said.

I couldn't think who else had glamour good enough to risk going inside before cameras and the Seelie. Some people's glamour actually didn't hold on camera, and the Seelie Court was ruled by the master of illusion. He was a bastard, but he would have seen through their disguises. My chest hurt with the thought of what might have happened. I clutched Galen's hand tighter, and wished I could move my head to look at Rhys.

Instead I was trapped staring at the night sky. It was a good sky, black and full of stars. It was the end of January, almost February. Shouldn't I be cold? The thought was enough to let me know that I wasn't nearly as aware of everything as I thought I was. Hadn't someone said I was going into shock? Or had I dreamed that?

We were at the ambulance. It was as if it had suddenly appeared to me. It wasn't magic, it was injury. I was losing little bits of time. That couldn't be good.

It was at the door of the ambulance that I found out who had had enough glamour to brave the press and the Seelie sidhe.

He had short blond hair, brown eyes, and a nondescript face, until he bent over me. He gave the illusion that the short hair grew into a long braid that I knew would sweep the ground. The brown eyes were three different colors of gold. The nondescript face was suddenly one of the most handsome in all the courts. Sholto, King of the Sluagh, kissed me ever so gently.

"The Darkness told me of his vision from the god. I am to be a father." He looked so pleased, all that arrogance softened.

"Yes." I said it softly. He was so pleased, so quietly happy. He had risked all to come and rescue me, even though I hadn't needed the rescue. But I barely knew

Sholto. I had been with him once. It was not that he was not lovely, but I would have traded much for it to be Frost leaning over me, speaking of our child.

"I don't know who you are, exactly, but the princess needs a hospital," Dr. Hardy said.

"I am a fool. Forgive me." Sholto touched my hair with such tenderness. Tenderness that we had not earned as a couple. I knew he meant it, but somehow it seemed wrong.

Then they lifted me and slid me inside the ambulance. The doctor stayed with me, and a male nurse. The rest went to a second ambulance or the driver's area of this one.

Galen called, "We'll follow you to the hospital."

I raised a hand, because I could not rise to see them off. The black dog looked down at me. He had jumped inside. The look in those black eyes was so not dog.

Dr. Hardy said, "No, absolutely not. Out dog, now."

The air was cool as if mist touched me, then it was Doyle in human form kneeling beside me. The nurse said, "What the hell?"

"I've seen your picture. You're Doyle," Dr. Hardy said.

"Yes," he said in his deep voice.

"If I tell you to leave?"

"I will not."

She sighed. "Give him a blanket, and tell them to get us out of here before more naked men show up."

Doyle draped the blanket around one shoulder and enough of him to make the humans comfortable. The other arm he kept out, so he could hold my hand.

"What would you have done if Hugh's plan had not worked?" I asked.

"We would have rescued you."

Not tried. Just, "we would have." Such arrogance. Such surety. It wasn't human. More than the magic, more than the otherworldly beauty, that was sidhe, and so not human. The arrogance wasn't pretense. Neither was the certainty. He was the Darkness. He had once been the god Nodons. He was Doyle.

He had moved so I could see him easily as the ambulance's wheels hit the road in a sound of gravel. I stared up into that dark, dark face. I looked into those black eyes. There were pinpoints of color in that darkness that were not reflections. He carried colors in the black depths of his eyes that were no colors in the ambulance.

Once he had used those colors to try to bespell me at my aunt's orders. A test to see how weak I might be, or how strong.

The colors were like multicolored fireflies, flitting and dancing in his eyes. "I can let you sleep until we reach the hospital," he said.

"No," I said. I closed my eyes against the pretty lights.

"You are in pain, Merry. Let me help you."

"I'm the doctor here," Hardy said, "and I say no magic on the injured until it's explained to me."

"I do not know if I can explain it," Doyle said.

"No," I said, eyes still closed. "I don't want to be unconscious, Doyle. The last time that happened I woke up in Taranis's bed."

His hand convulsed around mine, clutching at me

as if he were the one in need of comfort. It made me open my eyes. The colored lights were fading as I looked into them.

"I failed you, my princess, my love. We all failed you. We did not dream that the king could travel through sunlight. We thought that a lost art."

"He surprised us all," I said. Then I thought of something I wanted to know. "My dogs. He hurt them."

"They will live. Minnie will bear a scar for a time, but she will heal." He raised my fingers to his lips and kissed them. "The veterinarian we took her to said she is going to have puppies."

I stared at him. "The puppies weren't injured?"

He smiled. "They are fine."

For no reason I could think of, that one bit of news made me feel better. My hounds had defended me, and the king had tried to kill them. But he had failed. They would live, and they would have puppies. The first faerie hounds to be born in more than five centuries.

Taranis had tried to make me his queen, but I was already pregnant. I already had my kings. Taranis had failed in every way. If the rape kit came back positive, though positive seemed the wrong word, then I would see King Taranis, King of Light and Illusion, in jail for rape.

The press were going to eat him alive. Charged with the abduction, beating, and rape of his own niece. The Seelie Court had been the shining star of the human media. That was about to change.

It was the Unseelie Court's time to shine, even if it

was with a darkling light. We would be the good guys this time.

The Seelie had offered me their throne, but I knew better. Hugh and others might want me, but the golden throng would never accept me as queen. I carried babies whose fathers were Unseelie lords. I'd been the child of an Unseelie prince, and they had treated me as worse than nothing.

There would be no golden throne for me. No, if throne there be, then it would be the throne of night. Maybe the throne needed a new name? Throne of night sounded so sinister. Taranis sat on the Golden Throne of the Seelie Court. It sounded so much more cheerful. Shakespeare said that a rose by any other name would smell as sweet, but I didn't believe it. Golden throne, throne of night. Which throne would you rather sit on?

I'd survive tonight. I even knew I was trying to think of anything, everything, to keep from dwelling on what Taranis had done, and the fact that Frost wasn't going to be waiting for me at the hospital. I was finally pregnant, and I couldn't be happy about it. For political reasons the rape kit coming back positive would be good. It meant we owned Taranis. But for my own reasons, I hoped he'd lied. I hoped he hadn't had his way with me while I was unconscious. Had his way with me, nice euphemism. I hoped he hadn't raped me while I was unconscious. I hoped he hadn't raped me while I bled into my skull from the blow he had dealt me.

I started to cry, hopelessly, helplessly. Doyle bent over me, whispering my name and that he loved me.

I buried my hand in the warmth of his hair, drew him close so I could breathe in the scent of his skin. I buried myself in the feel and smell of his body, and wept.

I had won the race to sit on the throne of the Unseelie Court, and it was bitter ashes on my tongue.

Read on for an excerpt from

SWALLOWING DARKNESS

by

LAURELL K. HAMILTON

Available in hardcover from Ballantine Books

Chapter 4

DOYLE DIDN'T FLINCH, OR EVEN REACT. "IT IS A VERY small wound."

"But how did it happen?" Galen asked.

"I believe the glass is coated with some sort of man-made coating," Doyle said.

"So because it's man-made and not natural," I said, "it was able to cut you?"

"Normal glass would have still cut me."

"But it would have healed by now," I said, "without the man-made coating?"

"It is a small cut, so yes."

"But you were covering Merry's body when you were cut," Gran said, and her voice was flat, almost without accent. She could do that when she wished, though it didn't happen often.

"Yes," he said, and looked at her.

She swallowed hard. "I do nae have the magic resistance to be near my Merry right now, do I?"

"It is sidhe magic we will be fighting," he said.

She nodded, and a look of such sorrow came over her face. "I cannae be with ye, Merry. I cannae resist what they will make me do. It's one of the reasons I left their court. A brownie is a servant there, and when we are invisible to them, we are safe, but brownies were ne'er meant to dabble in court politics."

I reached out to her. "Gran, please."

Rhys stepped between us as she moved forward. "Not a good idea yet. We need to look at the spell first."

"I would say, I would ne'er hurt my girl, but if the Darkness . . . if Captain Doyle had not protected her, I would have cut her 'stead of his back."

"What could they have offered to Merry's cousin?" Galen asked.

"Mayhap the thing they offered me centuries ago," Gran said.

"What was that?" Galen asked.

"A chance to bed, and if left with child, marry one of their Seelie nobles. No one will touch Cair for fear that her . . . deformity will breed true. I was only half human and I worked in the court as a brownie, but I saw the Seelie and I wished to be a part of it. I was a fool, but it earned my girls a chance to be a part of that glittering mess. But Cair is always outside of it, because she looks too much like her ol' Gran."

"Gran," I said, "it's not—"

"No, child. I know what face I bear and I know that it takes a special sidhe to love it. I ne'er found that sidhe, but I was not part sidhe. I didnae have the blood of the court running in my veins. I was a brownie that got uppity, but Cair, she is one of them. It must be a thing of great pain to watch the others with their perfect faces get what she longs for."

"I know what it is like to be denied a place at court," Sholto said, "because you are not perfect enough to be bedded. The Unseelie sidhe run scared of my bed, for fear they will breed monsters."

Gran nodded and finally looked at him. "I am sorry that I said some of the things I said, Shadow Lord. I should know better 'en most what it is to be hated for bein' less than sidhe."

He nodded. "The queen called me Her Creature. Until Merry came to me, I thought I would be doomed to live out my life until I became simply, Creature, as Doyle is the Darkness." He smiled at me then with that intimate look that he hadn't quite earned yet. It was so odd to be pregnant after only one night with a man. But then, hadn't that been what happened with my father and mother? One night of sex and my mother had been trapped into a marriage that she did not want. Seven years of marriage before she was allowed to divorce him.

"Aye, the courts are cruel, though I had hoped the dark court a little less cruel."

"They accept more," Doyle said, "but even the Unseelie have their limits."

"They saw me as proof that the sidhe were failing as a people, because once they could bed anything and breed true," Sholto said.

"They saw my mortality as proof that they were dying," I said.

"And now the two they feared the most may be the saving of us all," Doyle said.

"Nicely ironic," Rhys said.

"I must go, Merry-girl."

"Let us test the spell and remove any lingering effects on you," Doyle said.

She gave him a look that wasn't entirely friendly. "Rhys and Galen can touch you. I do not need to," he said.

She gave a long breath, her thin shoulders going up and down. Then she looked at him with a softer, more thoughtful look. "Aye, ye should look at me, for the thought of you touching me was not a good one. I think the spell lingers in me mind, and it is not good to linger on such thoughts. They grow and fester in the mind and heart."

He nodded, still holding my hand in his. "They do."

"Test the spell, Rhys," she said, "then cure me of it. I must away, unless you can find a way for me to be proof against such sorceries."

"I'm sorry, Hettie."

She smiled at him, then turned a less happy face to me. "Sorry, I am that I will nae' be able to help ye through this pregnancy, or help tend the bairns for ye."

"Me, too," I said, and meant it. The thought of her leaving hurt my heart.

Rhys held the shining thread out. "I'd like your opinion on it, Doyle."

Doyle nodded, squeezed my hand, then walked around the bed to Rhys. Neither of them seemed to want to give Gran a clear way to touch me. Was it really that strong a spell or were they just being cautious?

If it was caution, I couldn't blame them, but I wanted to say good-bye to Gran. I wanted to touch her, especially if it was the last time I'd see her until after the babies were born. Just thinking that all the way through—when the babies were born—shocked me a little. We'd been trying to get me pregnant for so many months. So that the pursuit of the pregnancy had been all I'd thought about. That, and staying alive. I hadn't thought about what it would mean. I hadn't thought about babies, and children, and having them. It seemed a strange oversight.

"Your face, Merry-girl, so serious," Gran said.

I looked at her and remembered being very small, so small I could curl up into her lap and she seemed large. I remembered feeling utterly safe, as if nothing in the world could harm me. I had believed that. It must have been before I was six, before the Queen of Air and Darkness, Aunt Andais, had tried to drown me. That had been a moment that brought the reality of being mortal among the immortal home to me as a child. It was nicely ironic that the future of the Unseelie Court was in my body, my mortal body, that Andais had thought wasn't worth keeping alive. If I could be killed by drowning then I wasn't sidhe enough to live.

"I just realized I'm going to be a mother."

"Aye, you are."

"I hadn't thought about anything beyond getting pregnant."

She smiled at me. "It will be a few months before ye have to worry about mothering."

"Is it ever too soon to worry?" I asked.

Sholto had come to stand on the far side of the bed from Gran. Doyle and Rhys were looking at the thread. Doyle was actually sniffing near it, rather than using his hands. I'd seen him do that to magic before, as if he could trace it back to its owner like a hound on a scent.

Sholto took my hand in his, and I didn't pull away, but I saw Gran's face harden. Not good. I looked at him, and what I saw in his face reassured me. I'd expected him to look arrogant or angry, and have that directed at her. I'd expected that he took my hand to prove to Gran that she couldn't stop him from touching me. But his face was gentle, and he was gazing at me.

He gave me a smile as gentle as any I'd ever seen on his face. His triple yellow eyes with their individual lines of gold were soft, and he looked like a man in love. I was not in love with Sholto. I had only been alone with him twice, both times ended in violent interruptions, not of either of our doing. We didn't really know each other yet, but he looked at me as if I were the world, and it was a good, safe place.

It made me uncomfortable enough that I dropped my eyes so he would not see that my look did not match his. I could not show him love in my face, not yet. Love, for me, was made up of time and shared experience. Sholto and I had not had that yet. How strange to be with his child, and not to be in love with him.

Was this how my mother had felt? To be married, bedded, but not in love, then to suddenly find herself pregnant with the child of a stranger. For the first time, ever, I had some sympathy with my mother's emotional ambiguity toward me.

I had loved my father, Prince Essus, but perhaps he was a better father than he had been a husband. I realized in that moment that I truly knew nothing of how my father and mother had interacted. Had their tastes in bed been so different that they had no middle ground? I knew their politics were opposite poles.

I held Sholto's hand, and had one of those adult moments when you realize that your hatred for your parent may be, just may be, not completely justified.

It was not a comfortable feeling to think of my mother as the wronged party, instead of my father.

It made me look up at Sholto. His white blonde hair had begun to escape from the ponytail he'd worn to rescue me. He'd used glamour to make his hair look short, but the illusion might have been harmed if someone had become tangled in his nearly ankle-length hair. Strands of his hair trailed around a face as handsome as any in the courts. Only Frost had had a more masculine beauty. I pushed that thought away and tried to give Sholto his due. The tentacles had ripped his t-shirt apart. It clung like a lace of rags around his chest and stomach. Shreds of the cloth were still tucked into his jeans, held by its belt, and the heavier collar was still intact, so it, along with sleeves, kept it all in place, but the chest and stomach revealed were lovely. The skin pale and perfect. The tattoo that decorated him from just under the breast-bone to his belt looked like someone had drawn one of those undersea flowered anemones, done in shades of gold, ivory, and crystal, with edges of blue and pink; soft colors, like the sun caressing the edge of a seashell. One thicker tentacle had been drawn so that it curled up over the right side of his chest, so that it looked as if the tentacle had been frozen in mid-movement, so that the tip was close to the darker paleness of his nipple. I wasn't certain, but I was almost certain, that the tattoo changed. It was almost as if the tat literally was taken from what the tentacles were doing when he froze them into art.

I knew that the slender hips, and everything else that was held inside his jeans were lovely, and he knew what to do with them.

He raised my hand up, and his face wasn't soft now. It was thoughtful. "You look like you are weighing and measuring me, princess."

"As well she should be," Gran said.

Without looking at her, I said, "He spoke to me, not to you, Gran."

"So you would take his side over mine already?"

I did look at her then. I watched the anger in her eyes, and a covetousness that wasn't her, but might be my cousin. It was as if Cair had put her desire to possess into the spell, her jealousy given magical form. Subtle and nasty. Not unlike my cousin, come to think of it. Magic was often like that, colored by the personality of the maker.

"He is my lover, the father of my child, my future husband, my future king; I will do what all women do. I will go to his bed, and his arms, and we will be a couple. It is the way of the world."

A look of such hatred came over her face, and it was almost as if the expression were not hers. I clung tighter to Sholto's hand and had to fight the urge to wiggle a little further away in the bed from this woman, because though it was Gran, there was something in her that wasn't.

Galen moved up beside us. "The expression on your face, Gran, it didn't look much like you."

She looked at him, and her face softened, then that other looked out of her true-brown eyes for a moment. She looked down, as if she knew she couldn't hide it.

"And how do ye, feel, Galen, that you share her with so many?"

He smiled, and it was true happiness shining in his

face. "I've wanted to be Merry's husband since she was a teenager. Now I will be, and we'll have a child together." He shrugged, spread his hands. "It's so much more than I ever thought I'd have. How can I be anything but happy?"

"Do ye not wanne be king in yer own right?"

"No," he said.

She looked up then, and the other was in her eyes, sharp and pure and uncomprehending. "All of you want to be king."

"As her only king, I would be a disaster," Galen said simply, "I am not a general to lead armies or the strategist for politics. The others are better at all that than I am."

"You mean that." And the voice didn't sound very much like Gran at all.

I didn't fight the urge to wiggle closer to Sholto and Galen, and farther away from Gran and the stranger's eyes. Something was wrong with her; in her.

That strange voice said, "We could let her keep you, let her be queen of the Unseelie. You would be no threat to us."

"No threat to who?" Doyle asked. There was no sight of the thread now. I didn't know if they'd destroyed it, or just hidden it away. I'd been too caught up in Gran's strange state to notice. Not good that I hadn't noticed, but the world had narrowed down to the stranger in my grandmother's eyes.

"But you, Darkness, you are a threat." There was no accent now. It was simply well spoken words. Because it was Gran's throat saying it, the words still sounded vaguely like her, but a person's voice is made up of more than just their larynx, and mouth. There is a piece of yourself in your voice, and the words she spoke now, belonged in someone else's mouth.

She glanced across the bed at Sholto. "Shadowspawn and his sluagh are a threat." Shadowspawn was a nickname that even the queen rarely said to his face. A lesser fey, even my grandmother, would not have risked such an insult to the King of the Sluagh.

"What have they done to her?" I asked. My voice was soft, almost a whisper, as if I were afraid that if I spoke too loudly, it would tip the tension building in the room. Tip it over and spill it into something bloody and awful and irrevocable.

Gran turned to Doyle, hand spread wide. It was one of those moments that seemed frozen in time. It is the illusion that you have all the time in the world, when in fact, you have milliseconds, less, to react, to survive, to watch your life be destroyed.

He reacted in a blur of movement that I couldn't follow. He was simply a dark blur as the power burst from Gran's hand. A power that she had never possessed. White searing light burst and for a moment the room was illuminated in eye-searing brightness. I could see Doyle caught against that light, moving her arm, her body, away from the bed, away from me. I had an almost slow-motion view of the white light cutting across the front of his body.

There was a shuddering scream from near the window as the white light hit the giant tentacles still in the opening. The bed moved. It was Galen throwing himself on top of me, as a living shield. I had time to see Sholto leap over the bed, and go to join the fight, then all I could see was Galen's shirt. All I could feel was his body above mine, tensed for a blow.

Chapter 5

THERE WAS ONE TERRIBLE SCREAM, A SOUND OF SUCH desolation that I pushed at Galen, tried to move him away. I had to see. Doyle had been an immovable wall; Galen moved, but not away. His body was softer, less certain of itself, but I was just as trapped. I might have forced him to move if I'd been willing to hurt him badly enough, but I was unwilling to hurt more of the people I cared for.

Galen took a breath that broke into a sob. I heard Rhys's voice. "Goddess help us!"

I pushed harder at Galen's chest. "Move, move, damn it, let me see."

He turned back to me, pressing his face against my hair. "You don't want to see."

I'd been frightened before, now it was panic. I screamed at him. "Let me see, or I will hurt you!"

It was Rhys who said, "Let her see, Galen."

"No," he said.

"Galen, move, Merry isn't like you. She'll wan[t] see." The tone in his voice alone turned the pani[c] ice in my veins. I was suddenly calm, but it w[as] true calm, it was what happens when terror tu[rns] something that will let you function, for a time[.]

Galen moved slowly, reluctance in every mu[scle]

he crawled off the opposite side of the bed he'd
started on. He put himself close to the very thing he
hadn't wanted me to see.

I saw the nightflyer first, wrapped around Gran like
a shroud. One of the spines that they could carry inside their bodies had pierced her through. I saw the
spikes on the spine, and knew why the, he, for it was
he, had not taken the spine back out. It would cause
more damage going back, but it wasn't like a blade.
You couldn't cut it off so that the injured wasn't injured twice. It was a piece of the nightflyer's body.
Why not just take it back out and be done with it?

Gran's hand reached to empty air. She was still
alive. I sat up, tried to get up, and no one stopped me.
That was bad in and of itself. It meant there was
more. Sitting up I caught a glimpse of that more.

Doyle lay on the ground, eyes blinking up at the
ceiling. The front of his borrowed surgical scrubs was
blackened, peeled away to show the raw, burned flesh
underneath.

hys knelt beside him, holding his hand. Why
t he shouting for a doctor? We needed a doctor.
call button beside the bed.

fell, half crawled out of bed. When the IV
ore it out. A trickle of blood oozed down
if there was pain with it, I didn't feel it.
he floor between the two of them, and
I see Sholto on the far side of Doyle.
onto his side, his hair spilled across
ould not see if he were awake and
yond that. The remnants of the
the perfection of his chest now
red ruin. But whereas Doyle's in-

jury was on his stomach, the bolt of power had taken Sholto over the heart.

So much had gone wrong in so short a space of time that I couldn't take it all in. I knelt on the ground frozen in my indecision. A sound made me look at the woman who had raised me. If ever I truly had a mother, it was she. She stared at me with those brown eyes that had shown me all the kindness I had ever known. She and my father had raised me together. Now I stared up at her from my knees, the only way she would be taller than me as she had been when I was small.

The nightflyer unfurled its fleshy wings enough so I could see that the spine had taken her just under the heart. Maybe even gone through the bottom part of it. Brownies are a tough lot, but it was a terrible wound.

She stared at me, still alive, still trying to breathe past the dagger-like spine. I took her hand, and felt her grip that had always been so strong, frail, as if she could not hold my hand in hers, but she tried.

I turned to Doyle and took his hand in mine. He whispered, "I have failed you."

I shook my head. "Not yet." I said, "It's failure only if you die. Don't die."

Rhys went to Sholto and searched for a pulse while I held the hands of my mother and the man I loved and waited for them to die.

It was one of those moments when strange things come into your mind. All I could think of was what Quasimodo says as he gazes down at the archdeacon who raised him, dead on the pavement below, and the woman he loved hung and dead. "Oh! All that I have ever loved."

I threw my head back and screamed. In that moment, no baby, no crown, nothing, was worth the price in both my hands.

Doctors and nurses came. They fell upon the wounded and they tried to pry my hands out of Gran's and Doyle's, but I couldn't seem to let go. I was afraid to let go, as if, if I let go, the worst would happen. I knew it was stupid, but the feel of Doyle's fingers wrapped around mine, was everything to me. Gran's fragile grip was still warm, still alive. I was afraid to let go.

Then her hand spasmed against mine. I looked into her face, and the eyes were too wide, the breath not right. They eased her off the spine, forced the night-flyer back, and as the spike came out, her life spilled with it.

She collapsed toward me, but other arms caught her, tried to save her, pulled her hand away from mine. But I knew she was gone. There might be moments of breath and pulse, but it was not life. It was what the body does at the end sometimes, when the mind and soul are gone, but the body doesn't understand yet that death has come, and there is no more.

I turned to the other hand still in mine. Doyle gave a breath that shuddered. The doctors were pulling him away from me. Sticking needles in him, putting him on a gurney. I stood, trying to hold onto his fingers, his hand, but my doctor was there, pulling me backward. She was talking, something about me needing not to upset myself. Why do doctors say such impossible things? Don't get upset, stay off your leg for six weeks, lower your stress, cut back on your work hours. Don't get upset.

They pulled Doyle's fingers out of mine, and the fact that they could pull him away from me, said just how hurt he was. If he hadn't been hurt, nothing short of death would have moved him from me.

Nothing short of death.

I looked at Sholto on the floor. They had a crash cart. They were trying to restart his heart. Goddess help me. Goddess help us all.

The doctors were clustered around Gran. They were trying, but they had triaged the wounded. Doyle first, then Sholto, then Gran. It should have been comforting, and it was, that they took Doyle first. They thought they could save him.

Sholto's body jerked with the jolt of power they put through his body. I heard their words in snatches, but I saw the head shake. Not yet. They hit him again with more, because his body jerked harder. His body convulsed on the floor.

Galen tried to hold me, tears streaming down his face, as they put a sheet over Gran's body. The police in the room seemed unsure what to do with the night-flyer. How do you handcuff that many tentacles? What do you do when the room is charred, and the dead woman is the one everyone said, did it? What do you do when magic is real, and cold iron burns the flesh?

I saw the doctors shake their heads over Sholto. He was so terribly still. Consort help me, help me help them. Help me! Galen tried to press my face into his chest, to keep me from looking. I pushed him away, harder than I meant to, so he stumbled.

I went to Sholto. The doctors tried to keep me away, or talk to me, but Rhys kept them back. He shook his head, said something I couldn't seem to hear. I knelt by Sholto's body. Body. No. No.

The nightflyers that the police weren't trying to arrest, came to me, to their king. They huddled around him like black cloaks, if cloaks could have muscle and flesh, and pale unfinished faces.

A tentacle reached out to touch his body. I reached to the nightflyers on either side of me, as you'd reach for a hand of your fellow bereaved. The tentacles wrapped around my hands, squeezing, giving what reassurance they could. I screamed, but not wordless this time.

"Goddess, help me! Consort help me!" I was filled with such rage. Horrible burning rage, as if my heart would burst with it, my skin run in sweat with the heat of my anger. I would kill Cair. I would kill her for this. But tonight, now, this moment, I wanted our king to live.

I glanced into the face of the nightflyer beside me, the black eyes, the pale lipless mouth, the razor teeth. I watched a tear glide down that pale, flattened cheek. Their anger, their rage, their king, but . . . he was my king, too, and I was his queen, their queen.

I smelled roses. The Goddess was near. I prayed for guidance, and it wasn't a voice in my head. It wasn't a vision. It was knowledge. I simply knew what to do, and how to do it. I saw the spell all the way through, and knew if it were to work, there was no time to worry that at the end was potentially something horrible. Nothing that faerie could show me tonight would be as horrible as what I'd already seen. Night-

mares could not frighten me tonight, for I was past
fear. There was only purpose.

I reached out to Sholto. The nightflyers moved
their tentacles back so they only held my wrists as I
laid hands on their king's body. I had raised magic before, with sex and life, but that was not the only
magic that ran through my veins. I was Unseelie
sidhe, and there is power in death, as there is in life.
There is power in that which hurts, as well as that
which saves.

I had a moment of thinking of using this magic for
Doyle, but this magic was only for the sluagh. It
would not work for my Darkness.

The Goddess had given me choices along the way:
bring life back to faerie with life or death; sex or
blood. I had chosen life and sex, over death and
blood. In that moment, with Gran's blood on my
gown, I chose again.

I looked for Rhys, because I knew Galen would not
do what I needed, not in time. "Rhys, bring me
Gran's body."

Rhys had to argue with the doctors, and Galen
helped him win the argument. Rhys brought her body
to me. He laid her body on top of Sholto's, as if he
knew what I meant to do.

They say the dead do not bleed, but that's not true.
The recently dead bleed just fine. The brain dies, the
heart stops beating, but the blood still flows out, for
a time. Yes, for a time the dead do bleed.

Gran looked so small lying on top of Sholto. Her
blood flowed out and down his pale skin, over the
blackened burns the hand of power had made.

I felt Rhys and Galen at my back. I heard vaguely,

unimportantly, Galen arguing, but it didn't matter. Nothing mattered but the magic.

I put my hands with the bracelets of tentacles on top of Gran's thin chest. Tears bit at my eyes and I had to blink them away to keep my vision clear. My skin flared to life, moonlight glow. I called my power. I called all of it. If ever I were truly queen of faerie, princess of the blood, let it be this night, this moment. Give me all of it, Goddess, I ask this in your name.

My hair glowed so bright I could see the burning garnet of it from the corners of my eyes, see it flow down the front of my gown, like red fire. My eyes cast green and gold shadows. The nightflyers that touched me glowed white, and that glow slid around the circle of them, so that their flesh glowed like sidhe flesh, white and moonlight bright.

Sholto's body began to glow, as white and pure as our own. His hair ran with yellow and white light, like the first glow of dawn in a winter's sky. I heard his first breath, a rattling sound, the sound of death living in a gasp.

His eyes opened, wide and already full of yellow and gold fire. He stared up at me. "Merry," he whispered.

"My king," I said.

His gaze went to the nightflyers glowing around us. They burned as bright as any sidhe had ever burned. Sholto said, "My queen."

"On the life of my grandmother, I swear vengeance this night. I call kin slayer against Cair."

He put his hand over mine, and the glowing tentacles of the nightflyers flowed over his hand and mine, binding them together. "We hear you," the nightflyers said, almost with one voice.

"Merry," Galen yelled, "don't do this!"

But I understood something I had not before. When Sholto had called the wild hunt into being inside faerie, I had not been with him. I had already begun to run. I would not run tonight. We had called the power together with our bodies, and it was with our bodies that we would ride it.

"Get the humans out," I said, in a voice echoing with power, as if we knelt in a vast cavern instead of a small room.

Rhys didn't wait to ask questions: he forced Galen to help him. I heard Rhys say, "They will go mad if they see more. Help me get them out!"

I leaned into Sholto with our hands laced together by the nightflyers, glowing flesh on top of glowing flesh, so that when our lips touched, the flare of light was blinding even to me.

Out of that light, that pure Seelie light, the far wall with its broken window began to melt. Melt in the light, but it did not melt away. Out of the white, cool light, shapes formed. Shapes with tentacles and teeth, and more limbs then seemed necessary. But whereas the last time they had spilled out of darkness, and an unlight, now they poured of light and whiteness. Their skin was as white as any sidhe, but their forms were what the wild hunt of the sluagh was meant to be. They were formed to strike terror into the heart of any who saw them, and drive mad those who were weak.

Sholto, the nightflyers, and I, turned as one being toward the spill of shining nightmares. All I could see tonight was the glow of eyes, the alabaster shine of skin, the white, sharp, shine of teeth. They were a thing of terrible beauty, as hard and fine as marble brought to life, with a lace of tentacles and many legs, so that the eye tried to make of them one great shape. It was only with staring that you realized it was a mass of shapes, all different, all wondrously formed with muscles and strength enough to do their work.

The ceiling melted away and larger forms slid down toward us. The nightflyers released my hand enough for me to touch one of the tentacle's shapes. What had been a mass of shape, so confusing, so anti-dividual that even with power riding me, my mind could not make form of it. The magic protected me, or my mind might have broken, trying to see what dangled down from the ceiling. But the moment I touched that first shining form, it changed.

A horse flowed out of the mass of shapes. A great, white horse with eyes that glowed with red fire, and steam puffing from it's nostrils with every breath. Its great hooves struck green sparks from the floor.

Sholto sat with the small body in his arms. Gran looked so small, like a child in his arms. His arms, his chest, were covered in her blood as he held her out to me. There were other men in my life that would not have offered me the choice. They would already have decided what they would do, but Sholto seemed to understand that it had to be my decision.

I touched the neck of the horse, and it was real, and warm, and pulsing with life. I leaned against its shoulder, for it was too tall for me to mount without aid. It nuzzled my hair and I felt something in my hair. I reached a hand up and found leaves. Leaves and berries in my hair, woven in among the garnet glow of my hair.

Sholto looked at me, eyes a little wide, still holding the body of the woman I had loved above all other women. "Mistletoe," he whispered, "entwined in your hair."

I'd had it happen once before inside faerie, but never outside. I looked past the nightflyers, still glowing, and found Rhys and Galen, the only ones still in the room. Galen was shielding his eyes as the rest of us had done on that night that had brought power back to the sluagh. The night that Doyle had said, "Don't look, Merry, don't look." I had a moment to think of him, carried away from me. He was somewhere in this hospital, maybe fighting for his life. I started to lose my purpose, then I looked up at the writhing nightmares. I remembered that even a glimpse of what had boiled in the ceiling of the cavern had been madness. Tonight I could look into the center of that shining, writhing mass, and understand that it was raw magic. It was only a nightmare if that was what you thought it would be. Raw magic forms in the mind before it forms to the touch.

I stared into it, and knew until I finished this hunt there was no way to do anything else. It was like starting an avalanche, you have to ride it to its end. Only then could I embrace my Darkness once more. I prayed the Goddess would keep him safe for me until the magic freed me of its power.

Rhys gazed at it all with wonder in his face. He saw what I saw; beauty. But then he had been a god of bloodshed and war, and before that a deity of death. Galen, my sweet Galen, would never be anything so harsh. This was not a magic for the faint of heart. My heart wasn't faint; it felt as if my heart were missing. Whatever it was that allowed me to feel, was gone. I looked at Gran's body, and there was a roaring emptiness inside me. I felt nothing but vengeance as if vengeance could be its own emotion cut free of hate, or anger, or sorrow. Vengeance as if it were a force of its own, something almost alive.

Rhys walked to the circle of nightflyers gazing up into the writhing mass of white light and shifting shapes. He stopped at the glowing edge of the circle. He looked at me now. "Let me go with you."

It was Sholto who answered. "She has her huntsman for tonight."

Galen spoke, still staring at the floor. "Where is Merry going?" He still didn't understand. He was too young. The thought came to me; he was older than I by decades, but the Goddess whispered through my head, "I am older than all." I understood in this moment I was she, and that made me old enough.

"Take care of her, Galen," I said.

He glanced up at me and saw the horse with its flashing eyes and white skin. For a moment he wasn't afraid, he was simply amazed. He, like me, was too young to remember when the sidhe still had their shining horses. We had only had stories before this moment.

The circle of nightflyers parted and Rhys and Galen both reached upward, as if it were planned. The white shapes above us reached out toward them. Galen's reach was longer, so the horse that formed for him was as white and pure as mine. It turned flashing eyes that glowed golden to my red. There was no smoke from this one's nostrils, and the sparks from the hooves were as golden as its eyes. Only the size and the sense of strength let me know they were kin.

Rhys's hand brought a white horse, but it was like an illusion or a trick of the eye. One moment white and solid and very real; the next skeletal, like the proverbial steed of death.

Rhys spoke low and happily as he rubbed its nose. He spoke in Welsh, but a dialect I could barely follow. I could pick out that he was happy to see the horse, and that it had been too long.

Galen touched his horse as if he were certain it would vanish, but it didn't. It butted him gently in the shoulder, and made a high, happy whinny. Galen smiled, because you couldn't help but smile at that sound.

Sholto held the body out to Galen, and he took Gran gently in his arms. The smile was gone, and there was nothing but sorrow. I let him have the sorrow, let him grieve for me, because grief could wait, tonight there would be blood.

A shape from above touched Sholto's shoulder, as if it could not wait for him to touch it; like an over-eager lover. The moment it touched him, it formed into something white and shining, but it was not exactly a horse. It was as if the great white steed had mingled with a nightflyer, so that there were more legs than any horse would have, though one graceful head rose from strong shoulders. Its eyes were the empty black doll of the nightflyers that had begun to sing around us. Yes, sing, in high almost childlike voices, as if bats could sing as they flew above your head. I knew in that moment that my power had changed what this hunt would be. I was not sluagh, nor pure Unseelie, and though we would be terrible and we would bring vengeance, we would come on the songs of the nightflyers. We would come shining from the sky, and until the vengeance was done nothing could stand against us. The mistake last time had been not giving the hunt a purpose, but that mistake was not one for tonight. I knew who we hunted, and I had spoken her crime. Until she was hunted to ground, no power in faerie or mortal lands could withstand us.

Sholto lifted me up to sit me on the horse with its red glowing eyes. He mounted his own, many-legged steed. The nightflyers' song became a chant of words so ancient you felt more of the building fall away just at the sound of it. Reality tore around us, and I spoke the words, "We ride."

Sholto said, "We hunt."

I nodded, wrapping my fingers in the thick mane of the horse. "We fly," I said, and kicked my bare heels into her flanks. The horse leaped forward into the empty night beyond. I should have been afraid. I should have doubted that a horse without wings could fly, but I didn't. I knew she would fly. I knew what we were, and the wild hunt hunts from the air.

The mare's hooves did not so much strike the air, as simply run on it. Her hooves flared with green flame at each step, as if the empty air were a road that only she could see. Sholto rode at my side on his many-legged stallion. The nightflyers spilled around us, still shining, still singing. But it was what followed in our wake that would make the humans turn away and hide inside their houses. They would not know why, they would simply turn away. They would think our passing the cry of wild birds, or wind.

We rode in a shine of white and magic, and dark dreams flowed in our wake.

Chapter 6

THE MARE MOVED UNDER ME, HER FIERY HOOVES eating up the distance. The muscles in her back, the feel of her mane in my hands were real and solid, but the rest of it . . . the rest of it was dreamlike. I wasn't certain if the feeling of unreality was what it would have always been to ride with the hunt, or if it were shock of all that had happened, or if it were my mind's way of protecting me from sights that should have destroyed my mortal mind?

Sholto moved up beside me on his own pale horse. His hair flowed behind him like a shining cloak, all white with hints of yellow, as if bits of sunlight were held in his hair, as if that hot, yellow light could be ensnared in the pale beauty of his hair.

The February cold pressed around us, caressed my bare arms and feet, but my breath did not fog in the cold. My skin did not chill. It was as if the cold were a sensation, but it had no power over me. The smoke that flared from my mare's nostrils wasn't from the cold. I remembered tales of horses in the wild hunt with flaming eyes and hellfire spilling from their nose and mouth. We could have been riding true nightmares, black and full of fire and terror, but something about my magic had turned the hunt ever so slightly to something a little less automatically frightening.

If you saw black horses that breathed fire riding down on you, you'd be convinced of evil intent, but if you saw white horses spilling toward you, even with eyes that glowed, and a little green fire at the hooves, would you automatically assume evil, or would you pause, and marvel at the beauty? We rode the sky as if the Milky Way had brightened and turned into be-ings that could flow and travel the darkness.

I looked behind us and found that there were other horses, barebacked, rider-less, but they spilled like the foam of the sea at our backs. There were also hounds, white with red marks, like all faerie hounds, except that these hounds had glowing eyes, and they were bulkier than the slim hounds that had come to my hand only a few weeks ago. Those had looked more like greyhounds, but not these dogs. These were huge mastiffs except they were white and red and glowed against the darkness like some white ghost dotted with glowing red, like spilled blood across the purity of their coats.

The name for them came to me with a scent of roses and herbs. Hounds of the Blood; they were hounds of the blood. Bloodhounds were named not for their bloodthirstiness, but that once they were only owned by nobles; noble blood. But the hounds that rode at our backs, that began to spill around the legs of the horses, they were named blood for other reasons. They rode only for blood, and the gentleness of bloodhounds was not something that this pack would understand. That knowledge filled me with a fierce pleasure.

There were things behind the hounds and horses, shapes that writhed and boiled with bodies and limbs that were nothing you would ever see outside of the worst nightmare you can imagine. I stared into the abyss of things that I'd been told, not to look at, for fear that one glance would destroy my mind. But those shapes had been black and gray, and these shone like crystal and pearl and diamonds in a radiance that burned from within and just behind them. We trailed a shining cloud of light like the tail of a comet.

I had a moment to wonder if some telescope did pick us up, would that be what their human mind would make of us? Or would they see some falling star? Or would they see nothing? Glamour didn't always work around cameras and man-made technology. I said a prayer that we did not accidentally blast some poor astronomer's mind. I wished them well as they gazed at the night sky. I wished everyone well, save one person tonight. I realized I meant that. I wanted Cair dead for the death of our grandmother. The king's attack on me wasn't important to me anymore. I understood then that I was truly a part of the hunt. I was moved by the vengeance I had called down. We would hunt Cair for kin slaying, and then . . . then we would see.

It was strangely peaceful in this tunnel vision. No grief existed here. No doubts. No distractions. It was comforting in a sociopathic sort of way. And even that thought could not frighten me. I'd heard the term instrument of vengeance, but I had not truly understood what the phrase meant, until now.

Sholto reached out to me across the space between

our steeds. I hesitated then I reached for him, one hand still locked in the mane of my horse. The moment our fingers touched, I remembered myself, a little. I understood the true danger of riding with the hunt then, you could forget yourself. You could forget everything but righteous vengeance, and spend a lifetime listening for the words from some mortal, or immortal mouth. Oath breakers, kin slayers, traitors; so much to punish. It would be a simpler life than the one I was leading. To ride forever, to exist only to destroy, and have no other choices to make. Some saw the riders with the hunt as cursed, but I understood now that it wasn't how the riders saw themselves all those centuries ago. They'd stayed with the hunt because they wished to, because it felt better than going back.

Sholto's hand in mine reminded me that there were reasons not to let the hunt consume me. I thought of the babies I carried in my body for the first time since the ceiling and wall of the hospital had melted away. But it was a distant thought; I wasn't afraid. I wasn't afraid that I might die this night and the babies with me. Part of me felt untouchable and part of me felt like nothing, absolutely nothing mattered as much as vengeance. Nothing.

Sholto squeezed my hand, as the rhythms of our horses made our arms rise and fall between us. He looked at me with eyes gone to yellow and gold fire, but there was worry in his face, too. He was King of the Sluagh, the last wild hunt of faerie. He had been the huntsman before, perhaps with less magic at his back, but still, he knew the sweetness of vengeance.

He knew the simplicity of the hunt, and the almost seductive whisper of it.

His hand in mine, the look on his face brought me back from the edge. His touch kept me, me. Part of me resented it. Because with me the first whisper of grief returned. Gran, Frost, Doyle injured, my father. So much death, so much loss, and the chance for more to come. That was the true terror of love, that you could love with your whole heart, your whole soul, and lose both.

We began to spill toward the ground in a sweep of light that cast shadows on the ground below like the lights of some great magical plane. But we did not touch ground as they plane would have had to; we skimmed above the ground. We wove over treetops and across fields. Animals scattered before us. I felt the hounds flinch and try to give chase, but Sholto spoke one word and they stayed with us. We were not after rabbits tonight.

There was a flash of white and something much bigger than a rabbit dashed across the ground. The White Stag fled before us like all the other animals. I almost called his name, but if he has not even turned that great horned head, it would have broken my heart all over again. Then he was lost in the dark, as lost to me as Gran.

The faerie mounds came into view and we sped toward them. If there were guards out, they did not make themselves known. Did they not see us, or were they too frightened to draw attention to themselves?

The Seelie mound was before us. I had a moment to think, "How do we get inside?" But I had forgotten that a true hunt, with a true purpose, is barred by no door. We flowed toward the mound and the horses and hounds did not even slow. They knew that the way would open and it did. There was a moment when I felt the spell on the door and realized that someone inside had barred the way with their strongest spells. Had they thought that our court would attack tonight? Had they feared what the queen would do for her niece's rape? The thought was a distant one, as if I thought about someone else. I watched the spell spill away from the door in that spot just behind the eyes where visions happen. One moment the spell was golden and bright, the next it fell away like the petals of some great flower opening for us. The shining doors opened in a spill of warm, yellow light, and our white shine flowed into the gold of it, and we were in.